Devyn's Dilemma

Book Two of The Thousand Islands Gilded Age Series

by

SUSAN G MATHIS

HERITAGE BEACON

FICTION

DEVYN'S DILEMMA BY SUSAN G MATHIS
Heritage Beacon Fiction is an imprint of LPCBooks
a division of Iron Stream Media
100 Missionary Ridge, Birmingham, AL 35242

ISBN: 978-1-6452627-3-2
Copyright © 2020 by Susan G Mathis
Cover design by Hannah Linder
Cover model Karissa McIlrath
Interior design by Karthick Srinivasan

Available in print from your local bookstore, online, or from the publisher at:
ShopLPC.com

For more information on this book and the author visit: www.susangmathis.com

This is a work of fiction. Names, characters, and incidents are all products of the
author's imagination or are used for fictional purposes. Any mentioned brand names,
places, and trademarks remain the property of their respective owners, bear no
association with the author or the publisher, and are used for fictional purposes only.

All Scripture quotations, unless otherwise indicated, are taken from the Holy Bible,
King James Version.

Brought to you by the creative team at LPCBooks: Eddie Jones, Shonda Savage,
Denise Weimer, Steven Mathieson

Library of Congress Cataloging-in-Publication Data
Mathis, Susan.
Devyn's Dilemma/Susan G Mathis 1st ed.

Printed in the United States of America

PRAISE FOR *DEVYN'S DILEMMA*

Like a monarch emerging from her cocoon, Devyn McKenna spreads her wings in Mathis' latest Thousand Islands Gilded Age novel and learns how to fly with beauty and grace. Step into a castle on Dark Island, my friend, and savor this historical romance.

~**Melanie Dobson**
Award-winning author of *Catching the Wind* and
the *Legacy of Love* series

Spun with mystery, romance, and atmospheric history, *Devyn's Dilemma* captures readers' imaginations in a world divided by class yet brought together by the common bonds of humanity and love. A story *Downton Abbey* fans won't want to miss!

~**J'nell Ciesielski**
Author of *Among the Poppies* and *The Songbird and the Spy*

Devyn's Dilemma put me in mind of the old *Upstairs Downstairs* series on TV, but this is more of the downstairs, which is always more interesting. Romantic and satisfying, I think you'll love *Devyn's Dilemma*.

~**Ane Mulligan**
Amazon bestselling author of *Chapel Springs Revival*

Susan Mathis takes us to the Thousand Islands once more, this time to Dark Island, where The Towers castle stands. Reminiscent of *Downton Abbey*, the story reveals the lives and challenges of the servants who work for the millionaires of The Gilded Age. Hidden treasures and mysterious events add to the intrigue and love between a maid and a valet. Rich in detail, the fabulous setting carries the reader away to 1910 amid some of the most famous entrepreneurs the United States has ever known and makes you wish you were there.

~**Marilyn Turk**
Multi-published, award-winning author

Mathis weaves mystery, secrets, and false accusations into this Gilded Age tale of castles, their wealthy owners, and the heartfelt longings of those they employ. If you like *Downton Abbey*, you'll quickly find yourself lost in this story of love and intrigue set in America's Thousand Islands.

~**Davalynn Spencer**
Award-winning author of *An Improper Proposal*

Housemaid Devyn McKenna's life changes forever as she enters the employ of the kind Bourne family, in their castle-like lodge on Dark Island. Meeting handsome Brice McBride is just the beginning. A story of recovering from abuse and finding oneself, letting go of past lies and embracing truth for the future, *Devyn's Dilemma* is a delightful read that carries the reader into the world of Dark Island with author Mathis' vivid historical detail. You'll wish your visit there could last longer.

~**Kathleen Rouser**
Award-winning author of *Rumors and Promises*

Devyn's Dilemma is a history lesson you won't want to miss! With a passion for the Gilded Age and the heart of a writer, Susan Mathis brings another heartfelt story to life set during a fascinating slice of American history. Weaving countless hours of in-depth research and miles of solid foot travel in the breathtaking beauty of the Thousand Islands, Mathis melds historical fact with engaging and memorable characters—once again paying tribute to an era that uniquely shaped the country.

~**Jayme H. Mansfield**
Author of award-winning historical novels *Chasing the Butterfly* and *RUSH*

From character development to historical accuracy, *Devyn's Dilemma* is a delightful novel by Susan G Mathis. Her beautiful writing voice and obvious love for the rich heritage of the Thousand Islands shines through, enticing the reader to keep reading to a satisfying ending. Bravo, Ms. Mathis!

~Angela Breidenbach
Author
President of the Christian Authors Network

A romance, a mystery, and a wonderfully historic setting! Not only did Devyn and Brice's story warm my heart, it made me want to visit the Thousand Islands for myself. What a great combination of history and fiction.

~Anne Mateer
Author of *Wings of a Dream*

Devyn's Dilemma is an engaging, sweet romance with a fascinating setting in the Thousand Islands on the Saint Lawrence River. An unusual historical American family is portrayed through the eyes of its domestic staff, with the deep research we expect from Mathis.

~Susan Page Davis
Author of *Lady Anne's Quest* and *Maine Brides*

Congratulations to Susan G Mathis on another wonderful work of inspirational river fiction. Having studied the Bourne family for several years while working on our two Singer Castle books, we were delightfully surprised to see how Susan portrayed this loving and godly family in *Devyn's Dilemma*. I think the Bournes themselves would love this book! It is a great read for anyone who enjoys inspirational romance.

~Patty Mondore
Co-author of *Singer Castle* and *Singer Castle Revisited*
Co-producer of *Dark Island's Castle of Mysteries* DVD

Susan Mathis creates relatable fictional characters and masterfully sets them in a real place (Dark Island in the St. Lawrence River near Chippewa Bay, NY), living in a real home (the Towers, now Singer Castle) with a real family (that of Frederick and Emma Bourne), at a real time (1910). Mathis weaves in carefully researched events and cultural details of the era and the area to give breath and believability to persons and plot where all things work out together for good. *Devyn's Dilemma* is a tale you will be blessed to have read.

~**Judy Keeler**
Singer Castle historian
Co-author of *Meandering Among the Thousand Islands,*
Second Edition

Dedication

To my precious daughter, Janelle, who inspires me with her never-ending creativity and amazing mothering. Thank you for blessing me with your friendship and with four beautiful granddaughters, including Devyn McKenna, who inspired my character of the same name.

And to my loving husband, Dale, who patiently waits for me to get my hands off my computer and my mind out of the clouds, encourages me when I get inspired or need to work, and laughs with me when I get excited about some tidbit of history which I can add to my story. Thanks for journeying with me through this great adventure.

You are gifts from God.

ACKNOWLEDGMENTS

I hope you'll enjoy this second book in The Thousand Islands Gilded Age Series. What fun I've had writing this story, thanks to so many of you! I'm so grateful for all the special people who encourage and support me. I pray this story touches your heart.

Thanks to all my readers who share my passion and story with their friends and family, especially the Thousand Islands River Rats and those who enjoy the tales of the Thousand Islands stomping grounds. When I posted pictures on Facebook of the castle and island and asked you for your input, I got such creative and interesting responses that I implemented many of your ideas into the story. I'm thrilled you are a part of my journey, and I'm grateful for you spreading the word through your reviews, social media comments, and personal recommendations.

Thanks again to Judy Keeler, my Thousand Islands historical editor and president of the Alexandria Township Historical Society. Thanks for giving Dale and me personal tours of the castle and the island. There's nothing like experiencing the sights, sounds, and smells of the island and hearing its stories. Our time there helped me create vivid descriptions and tell a better story. Your invaluable edits, knowledge, and insight made everything historically accurate. And thanks to Patty and Robert Mondore for your input as well.

Thanks to Laurie Raker, Davalynn Spencer, and Barb Beyer, who so willingly and lovingly pored over the manuscript and gave me great suggestions and input to make the story even better. You are priceless.

Thanks to my many writer friends who have helped me hone my craft, encouraged me to keep on writing, supported me through my writing journey, and prayed for me. There are too many to mention here, but you know who you are.

Thanks for the support of my fellow authors in the Christian

Authors Network (CAN), the American Christian Fiction Writers Colorado Springs chapter (ACFW-CS), the Writers on the Rock group (WOTR), and, of course, my fellow authors at Lighthouse Publishing of the Carolinas.

Thanks to the stellar team at Lighthouse Publishing of the Carolinas, especially Denise Weimer, who is not only an incredible editor but has become a friend and made this book everything it can be. Without your faithful, hard work, this book wouldn't shine as brightly as it does.

And to God, from whom all good gifts come. Without You, there would never be a dream or the ability to fulfill that dream or even the opportunity to write *Devyn's Dilemma*—or any other book. Thank You!

CHAPTER 1

June 1910
Thousand Islands, New York

Devyn McKenna trembled as her brother, Falan, beckoned her into the skiff. She gazed at the choppy river, the dark clouds scuttling across the sky. Yes, she had to admit that the mighty St. Lawrence River was beautiful. But that same majestic water was also deadly—as she knew all too well.

She scowled and huffed as she shifted from one foot to the other. Why could she not work in Watertown or somewhere else far from the river? Why? She glared at Falan. This was *his* doing, just to spite her.

She turned her back on him before he could mock her angst as he always did. Before he could resurrect her pain. Her nerves prickled with memories she'd rather forget. Her burning eyes joined in the rebellion, threatening to spill tears.

She hated the river and what it had done to the ones she loved.

Falan scowled. "Come on, Devyn. We don't have all day. They're waitin' for ya, and there's a dinner party tonight."

She heaved a ragged moan and gathered her skirts to climb into the small, rocking boat. "I shan't be able to cross this divide too often."

He chuckled. "Y're such a baby. What happened before ain't got nothin' to do with today. I've lived on the island on and off near two years now, and I'm the better for it. You'll be, too, if ya grab hold of it instead a fearin' it."

Devyn had nothing left to say, at least to him. Instead, she sat down in the middle of the seat and held on for dear life. She had to remind herself to breathe, to swallow. As Falan shoved the boat off from the dock, every wobble and wave frightened her more. What if they capsized? She couldn't swim. She wouldn't survive. And this folly would be all for naught.

In sheer panic, Devyn began to stand up, but the rocking waves plunked her down on the hard bench. "Take me back. Take me back now! I cannot do this." Devyn's heart beat so fast that she feared it would leave her chest. She held her hand over it, but she broke into a sweat. A large knot filled her throat, threatening to choke her. "Take me back now!"

Falan gave her an annoying shake of his head and grunted. "Not on yer life. Or mine. I promised the Bournes, and Mama needs the money ta feed the young 'uns. Just stop yer hysterics, girl, or I'll slap it out of ya."

"I'm not a slave! Surely, I can find work inland. I can't live on an island. I beg you. Take me back."

Falan laughed at her. He actually threw back his head and laughed hard. Loudly and boisterously, mocking her.

Her eyes narrowed, and she dug her fingernails into her fists. "What kind of brother are you, that you have no compassion? You know my story. And you don't care?"

"I care. A bit." He quirked a brow and shook his head. "I put yer name forth fer Mama, *not* fer you. Ya gotta grow up sometime. Y're twenty years of age and need ta let go and move on. This can be yer ticket out of the hell ya caused."

Devyn shook her head in shame and defeat. She stared at the bottom of the skiff, hoping to make the growing nightmare go away. It only worsened her worry, so she looked up and tried to distract herself. She glanced at the shore and whispered, "Farewell, Chippewa Bay."

Falan ignored her and continued to row far beyond the shore. He passed one island and then another and another. Devyn sat silently, but her nerves screamed for safety. The seagulls swooped around them, one diving to catch a fish in its talons and then soaring above them. Why couldn't she be like them, free to go where she wanted to, to soar on the breeze instead of rocking in a skiff that could easily sink? She squeezed her eyes closed, but that only gave rise to visions of those memories that haunted her day and night.

She finally opened her eyes and beheld a majestic castle in the distance, a five-story stone mansion gleaming in the breaking sunshine, standing strong and solid on the small island before her. "Look at that castle. Who lives there?"

Falan smirked. He had become a little more muscular since he started working on the island for Mr. Reid, but he was still rather skinny for a construction laborer. His thin, inky hair and scant whiskers didn't help his scruffy appearance. Neither did his bony, hard-featured face, so much like their mother's.

But his dark, drooping eyes told a different tale. Ever since he'd been a wee thing, Falan's bold and brash actions had made him the local troublemaker. He'd given Mama fits daily. Years ago, he had gotten the lash from Papa, bless his departed soul, quite regularly.

At the memory of her father, anxiety welled up in her belly, but she shook it off. "Where is this prison you call a hunting lodge that you've chained me to? And when will we finally be out of this wretched boat?"

"It's not a prison, *princess*. It's the Bournes' grand summer home and hunting lodge called The Towers—that I helped ta build five years ago. Me and my old pal Oscar worked mighty hard on this place, and now I'm back workin' here again. This time, I expect a reward fer my troubles." He grinned, and his eyes flashed as they always did when he was into mischief. "And Dark Island isn't how it sounds. It's only called that 'cause there're so many dark evergreen trees on it. Ya may find many surprisin' things on the mysterious Dark Island. Stop frettin'. We'll be there presently."

Devyn rolled her eyes and looked down at her white knuckles. She tried to relax her hands as she sucked in a deep breath. "You never said the island was this far from the mainland. Am I to be stuck there all summer? The prospect is positively terrifying."

Ignoring her, Falan kept on rowing. As the skiff rocked toward the castle, Devyn's trepidation grew with each stroke of the oars. She nodded toward the massive edifice, its glass panes sparkling in the sunshine. "Please tell me that this monstrosity is not the Bournes' summer home you said was a hunting lodge. Tell me this is not where I'm to work. Really, Falan, how could you? You deceived me, just like you deceived Mama and Papa and the teachers and the preacher."

His dark eyes narrowed, and his brow creased until his forehead looked like several train tracks. "Stop it. Just stop the drama, Devyn. I'm tryin' ta help ya, whether ya realize it or not. I'm tryin' ta give ya a new start and get ya out of the fog you've been in for the past ten years. This can be yer ticket out!"

Scolded into silence, Devyn gazed at the castle as they drew nearer. She heaved a deep, ragged sigh. The tiny island would be her home for the next several months.

A mob of ducks swam close to the shore near a large boathouse. A meandering pathway rose to what most people would see as a beautiful stone castle that loomed large above the docks. A colorful Spanish red-tile roof and copper gutters, tarnished to a curious blue, crowned the edifice, and a round tower stood several stories tall, with a smaller tower barely visible in the rear of the castle. What must it be like inside?

Falan was well aware that she preferred to be behind the scenes, in a simpler and plainer realm than she'd ever find here. She liked to hide from the limelight. Formal and fancy goings-on turned her stomach. Finery and frippery repulsed her. And so did wealth—wealth she would never know.

Falan grunted as they pulled up to a long dock. "Mahlon, the butler, will meet ya and show ya around. With the dinner party tonight, I 'spect everyone's busy."

Devyn looked down at her clothes. "I cannot go in there. Not like this. What have you gotten me into, Falan?" Tears stung her eyes, but she blinked them back.

"Oh, please. You'll get a proper uniform soon enough. They all look like you do when they first come." He hopped out of the boat and tied it up. "Let's go. I have work ta do, and I'll not be reprimanded because of yer hysterics."

Reluctantly, Devyn took up her carpetbag with one hand and grabbed her brother's rough and calloused hand with the other. He hoisted her up and onto the dock and pointed to the bridle path. "Y're ta go up the path and through the front door. Just this once. Mr. Bourne insists that the house staff experience the grandeur of the castle the first time they come here. After that, y're always ta use the servants' hall door or pass through the tunnel. Always. See ya, kid."

With that, Falan sauntered off toward the north end of the island, leaving Devyn alone. She squared her shoulders, heaving her worn carpetbag up the bridle path until she reached the imposing wooden doors. Then she straightened her spine as she reached up for the ornate brass knocker. "I can do this! I … I must do this." She gave it three quick taps, biting her bottom lip as she waited.

With barely a creak or a groan, the heavy door opened. "Welcome, Miss McKenna. We've been expecting you." A dark-haired, middle-aged man dressed in impeccable livery greeted her.

She smoothed her hand over her threadbare dress.

Before she could respond, a handsome young man peeked out and opened the door wide. "Thank you, Mahlon. I'll attend to this."

"Very good, sir." The butler nodded, turned, and retreated into the castle without looking back.

Devyn blinked, assessing the younger man. Just who was this?

"Welcome." His enthusiastic greeting and kind expression, along with the bluest eyes she'd ever seen, warmed Devyn down to her toes. When he stepped out onto the stoop and stood straight and proper, he towered over her. His sandy blond hair appeared to be kissed by the sun as he smiled broadly and bent to retrieve her bag.

She fumbled for the handle. "I can carry it."

The man took it from her, shaking his head. "I'm Brice. Brice McBride, but Mr. Bourne calls me Mac." He shrugged sheepishly but still seemed proud of the nickname. "I have the privilege of getting you settled. You're Falan's wee sister, aye? Not so little and not so unbecoming as he reported. Shame on him." With that, Brice winked, sending a flame up Devyn's neck and straight to her cheeks.

"Thank you, Brice. Or should I call you Mac?"

"Call me either."

Devyn offered an apologetic smile. "Falan can be a jester."

"Aye, well, malarkey is one thing; deception is altogether another." A shadow passed through his azure eyes, darkening them as if a storm had descended.

She took one step into the entryway and stopped dead in her tracks. "And he deceived me about this being a hunting lodge. I had no idea it was so grand."

Brice laughed, his voice deep and comforting. "Aye, and I am to give you a tour. I was with the Bournes when they first viewed this place, and they reacted the same way as you. Mrs. Bourne was entirely overcome, though their primary home on Long Island, called Indian Neck Hall, is far grander." He allowed Devyn to take in the large stone fireplace, massive granite pillars, carved stone arches, and vaulted ceiling before continuing. "This is the Great Hall where we receive our guests. And look at these mirrors." He led her to the center of the room and pointed to the mirror over the fireplace.

"Oh my! It seems to go on forever." She snapped her head around to see a duplicate mirror on the opposite side of the room that created the illusion. "Amazing."

He grinned and motioned her on to what looked like a hall closet. "And over here is the wine vault. It holds an excellent collection."

"And suits of armor?" Devyn quirked a brow as she glanced at the armor standing at attention and then turned back to her tour guide.

"Aye, this room makes quite an impression for first-time guests, don't you think? The Bournes love to delight everyone who visits them." Brice set down Devyn's carpetbag and continued his tour of the lower level. He led her past the kitchen, gesturing toward it. "You'll see the kitchen soon enough. Everyone is reelin' just now preparing for a dinner party tonight, so we won't disturb them. But you'll be pleased to know it's a fully equipped, modern kitchen with indoor plumbing, a gigantic range, a dumbwaiter, and a servant call box."

She liked his slight brogue that was proof of his Irishness. He rubbed his clean-shaven chin, apparently debating with himself where to take her next. He was a head taller than her, his short hair neatly parted down the middle. His strong features made him appear rather aristocratic. But those eyes …

"This is the east wing where some of the servants reside, and the laundry is there too. You'll explore that another time." Brice touched her arm to turn her around, sending a shiver through her. He motioned her down the hall. "Are you cold? The castle can be chilly at times."

"I'm fine, thank you." She scurried past the kitchen and back into the Great Hall, where she hoped to catch her breath. His presence, his voice caused her heart to race.

Brice caught up with her. "Another fascinating detail about The Towers is that you'll find several secret passageways throughout the castle."

"I'm sorry, I just can't get over my shock. Falan told me none of this." Devyn rested her hand on her chest.

"Aye, well, let's finish touring the ground level, shall we?" Brice didn't wait for her to answer but led her once again back through the Great Hall to the other side of the fireplace. "Here's the library and billiard room, and over there …" He pointed to the left of a huge granite fireplace. "There's a hidden switch in the bookcase panel that opens a secret passageway so we servants can move from room to room without disturbing anyone."

Devyn grinned so wide that her lips felt dry and taut. She loved secrets and hidden places—and books. She loved to read and discover faraway places and marvelous stories. Maybe it wouldn't be so bad here, after all.

Brice turned back in the direction they had come, and Devyn followed him. In the Great Hall, he picked up her carpetbag and bid her to climb the wide granite staircase. She ran her hand over the smooth, cool wood of the pine balustrades with hand-carved newel posts.

"This is so beautiful. My brother said nary a word about its wonders."

"Figures. I imagine he'd rather speak blarney of more earthy things—and his wild dreams and crazy schemes."

Devyn furrowed her brow, considering the man before her. Why would such a fine gentleman know of Falan's vices? "You discern my brother's character well."

Brice nodded. "As you know, Falan helped build this place, so I've been acquainted with him for nearly five years now. Not to mention, the island is small and the company limited."

Exactly what she was afraid of.

~ ~ ~

Brice couldn't stop watching Devyn as she surveyed her surroundings. How could such a wee bonnie lass be related to the homely ruffian who was her brother?

Incredibly long eyelashes framed her large, sparkling blue eyes, and her full, pink lips were nothing like Falan's. Her thick, curly hair was the color of brown sugar, not black and scraggly like her brother's. Her tiny nose drew his eye to the one big dimple on her right cheek, both of which he'd love to touch, just once. Aye, she was thin and wispy like Falan, but this intriguing Devyn appeared gentle, almost fragile, like a young doe.

She ascended the stairs and turned toward him, gaze filled with wonder. What secrets did those sky-blue eyes hold?

At the top of the stairs, Devyn waited for him. He stuck his hand into a panel underneath a light fixture. "Under here is a hidden switch that will open another secret passageway." That would delight her for sure.

Her eyes widened as he pointed to the shadowy corridor that led to a spiral, stone staircase. "The passageways can be flummoxing, so we'll explore them later." He winked at her. Her manner of innocence, of curiosity, made him eager to show her more secrets of this grand castle.

Devyn peeked in and bit her pretty lip, but then she stepped back, both shuddering and smiling. "Who knows what might be behind those dark walls."

He took her elbow and led her into the wood-paneled living

room, and she gasped. She craned her neck at the huge moose, elk, and deer heads that overlooked the elegant room. "The men call this the Trophy Room, and for good reason." He chuckled as he gazed into her eyes. "Don't worry; they won't bite."

She giggled, relaxing from his jest, so he continued. "The ceilings are seventeen feet high, and see that painting up there? It's a portrait of King Charles II, who hid in the English castle that Sir Walter Scott talked about in his novel, *Woodstock*. That book inspired the architect, Mr. Flagg, to model The Towers after the castle in the story." He pointed to a portrait above the window alcoves. "There's a corridor running the length of the room from where the picture can be unhinged and opened so that one of us can view the guests to make sure their needs are met. I find it great fun."

Would she find it fun too? Observing such fine folk like a fly on the wall might suit her fancy as it did his.

Devyn nodded, smiling broadly. She turned to the hearth. "The fireplace is pink. How pretty! And what of these window seats?" She hurried over to the opposite wall that held three cozy alcoves. Taking a seat, she swept her hand along one of the plush, green velvet bench cushions. The delight on her face could not be denied. But then, she pulled back her hand as if touching a hot stove.

Blathers, but she is charming. He cleared his throat. "The pink marble was brought over from Italy and hand-hewn by Italian masons. The Pullman window seats are like ones in the luxury railroad cars. George Pullman also has an island and a grand castle called Castle Rest. It's just off Alexandria Bay."

She stood and smoothed the velvet cushion. "I've heard of it."

He smiled and motioned for her to walk toward the door. "Have you ever ridden on a train?"

"Never, but I'd like to. I'd rather ride in a train than in a nasty boat any day." Devyn crinkled up her nose.

Brice furrowed his brow. "You don't fancy boats?"

"I despise them. And the river." She bit her lip as if to hold back her emotions.

"Well then, this is quite a strange place for you to live and work. Why did you come?"

"I had to, for Mama. She needs the money for my three younger brothers." Devyn's eyes brimmed with tears, but she blinked them back into submission.

"Where is …" *No! Don't ask her.* "Ahem." He pointed to a door just off the Trophy Room. "There's a thoroughly modern water closet in there. And over here is the Round Room." He reached past her and cracked open the door to show her an office in the turret with several windows and a grand view of the river. "Mr. Bourne's summer office. He was the president of Singer Sewing Machine Company, you know." His voice smacked with pride, but he deserved to be proud of working for such a man.

"Naturally, Falan failed to mention that too." Devyn huffed.

Brice pulled her from her frustration by pointing to the antler chandelier above the office desk. "That is powered by gas and electricity, can you believe?"

"What a marvel!" She glanced out the window and turned back to him, cocking her head. Her brows furrowed with a question. "But this place, this castle, is a bit excessive for a hunting lodge, don't you think?"

He shook his head as his ears warmed. "It's the perfect retreat for the Bournes. And it is not your place to have such an opinion, miss."

"Yes. Well …" Devyn puffed a breath. "May I see my room and settle in, please?"

The atmosphere grew cold. She'd put up an invisible wall, a tall, rocky dam of protection against him.

Blathers! But the Bournes deserved respect from their employees. He reverted to a stiff, defensive posture, mirroring hers. "Certainly. This way." He silently led her up a couple flights of stairs to a large, dormitory-style room with five beds and large windows on three sides.

She entered, but he stayed planted in the doorframe. "There are four of you up here this summer. Nellie, Reagan, and Sofia came with us from the Bournes' residence on Long Island."

"Thank you for telling me." Devyn turned her back to him and started to unpack her carpetbag on the empty bed.

"I'll inform the head housekeeper, Mrs. VanLeer, that you're here, and someone will fetch you soon. You should probably change into that uniform." He pointed to a neatly folded pile of clothes, then cleared his throat, trying to soften his tone. "You'll find this to be an amazing place to work, Miss McKenna, if you'll but try to embrace it."

CHAPTER 2

Devyn changed into her uniform, donned her mobcap, and waited for Brice, or someone, to fetch her. She fingered the royal blue ribbon her father had given her for Christmas when she was just ten. "Royal blue for my pretty princess," Papa had said. It was her most treasured possession, the last gift she ever received from him.

She kissed it and set it on her pile of belongings as footsteps sounded on the stairs. *I'll apologize to Brice first thing for my rude behavior. Oh, why does people's disapproval vex me so?*

"Hello? Are you up here, Miss McKenna?" A young woman opened the door and popped into view. She smiled sweetly. "Ah, there you are."

It wasn't Brice, but Devyn forced a smile and walked up to her, extending her hand. "Yes, I'm Devyn McKenna, and you?"

"Reagan Kennedy. Pleased to meet you." A formal curtsy surprised Devyn.

Reagan appeared about her own age. She was a tall, thin beauty with fine features and gentle gray eyes. Her soft, upswept hair accentuated her tiny ears. Indeed, everything about her seemed to be soft.

"I'm Miss Marjorie's maid and have come to fetch you."

Devyn smiled. "Thank you. Do you know where I am to put my things?" She scanned the room. She had already peeked in the cupboards and found three that were used, presumably by Reagan and the other girls.

"You can take your pick of these two." Reagan pointed to two sets of cupboards nearest the empty bed where Devyn had laid her things.

She picked up her small pile of personal items. "Is it all right if I tuck them away now?"

"Yes, but hurry, please. You're needed in the dining room to help with tonight's dinner party." Reagan pursed her lips as she glanced at the door.

Devyn shoved her belongings in the chosen cupboard and nearly ran to join Reagan. "I won't be serving the table, will I? I fear I'd make a mess of things."

Reagan shook her head. "Oh no. There's the dining room staff for that. Our roommate, Nellie, is one of them. Brice often helps too. But sometimes you may be called upon to help with large parties from time to time. You'll likely be the Watch tonight."

Her brow creased as she considered the comment and descended the staircase. "'The Watch'?"

Reagan giggled, sounding more like a young girl than a lady's maid. "That's the person who secretly watches from the passageway and makes sure everyone has what they need."

"Oh, I see." Devyn grinned. Being the Watch sounded delightful. There she could serve but not be seen.

The two women journeyed down the rest of the stairs in silence. When they got to the Great Hall, a petite, middle-aged woman smiled at them. "Welcome, Miss McKenna, to The Towers. I anticipate that you will find your employ here a fine experience." She bustled up to her and put out her hand. "I'm Mrs. VanLeer, the head housekeeper. You will report to me."

Devyn curtsied and shook her hand, not sure which to do. "Thank you, Mrs. VanLeer. It's a pleasure to meet you."

Mrs. VanLeer tilted her head and chuckled. "I expect you'll still find it a pleasure by the end of the summer, dearie."

She nodded, not at all sure what that meant. Mrs. VanLeer examined her up and down until Devyn's face grew warmer with each passing moment. What could the missus be thinking?

"Oh, not to worry. I'm just taking stock of my new help. You seem like a fine and fit young woman, and it's a good thing too. Five stories can test your mettle, dear girl." Mrs. VanLeer motioned for Devyn to follow her toward the kitchen. But then they passed the kitchen and entered a small room that she reckoned was the missus' office. "Sit down, please."

Devyn sat stiff and still. She wished her brother or mother—or someone—would've told her more about the job and how to behave under such circumstances. She was just a small-town girl with no real skills, except caring for her younger siblings and sewing for a little pay.

"Your brother, Falan, gave us a glowing report of your skills and abilities. I presume you will even exceed them."

What skills? What lies did that brother of mine tell her? Devyn's heart raced at the thought.

Mrs. VanLeer wrote something in a small black book before continuing. "The island staff is small and must be versatile. Though you are hired as a housemaid, you'll do many other tasks, and you'll learn many new skills if you put your mind to it."

Devyn nodded as she fidgeted in her chair.

The housekeeper pressed her thin lips together, her chocolate brown eyes questioning. "I'd like you to speak, young lady. I want this to be a conversation."

Devyn swallowed. "Oh, I'm sorry. I'd be happy to serve in whatever capacity you deem best. I'm not the greatest cook, but I love to help people, and I like to learn new things."

A broad smile crossed Mrs. VanLeer's round face, and her dark eyes twinkled. "Now that's what I like to hear. Well, tonight you shall be the Watch for the dinner party. Tomorrow I will train you as a proper housemaid."

Devyn leaned forward. "Reagan said that I'd likely serve as the Watch, but what does that mean, exactly?"

Mrs. VanLeer stood, motioning her toward the door. "Come, and I'll show you."

The woman escorted her to the kitchen, where she briefly introduced Devyn to Cook, the three kitchen maids, and Sofia, her other roommate and maid to Mrs. Bourne. Without more than a quick "hello" and nod from them, they went through the servants' hall to a passageway that brought them to a circular stone staircase. She patted another door before turning to the stairs. "That door leads to the Great Hall." Then she started to climb the stairs. "This leads up to the living room on the first floor." Devyn followed. Once they were in the living room, they passed through it to another secret passageway near the powder room she had seen with Brice.

The missus reached into a fancy thermometer and wiggled a special release that popped open a door in a panel of the wall.

Devyn put her hands to her chest. "Goodness! How ever did the builder create such marvels? I think I shall forever be lost if I don't get my bearings soon. This is all so befuddling."

Mrs. VanLeer laughed with her eyes closed, holding her middle. "I know what you mean. But you'll learn. Now follow me."

They climbed the circular stairs. Mrs. VanLeer pointed down a foreboding, dimly lit hallway on their right. "This mezzanine level completely surrounds the living room, or the Trophy Room, as the men like to call it. We'll explore that later." She turned and led Devyn to a hallway on her left. "Here is where you'll keep watch through this screen." The missus stepped aside to reveal a grate through which Devyn could see the large, formal dining room complete with a magnificent marble fireplace. Its warm, walnut-paneled walls and fine, ornate furniture took her breath away.

"Oh, my goodness! How marvelous!"

Mrs. VanLeer chuckled. "I so enjoy the response from those who see this little secret for the first time. This is where you'll be stationed, silently watching the party for any needs that may come up. When you see someone who needs water or, well, anything, you quietly go down to the staff or to the butler's pantry and let them know."

Devyn curtsied. "That sounds lovely."

The housekeeper nodded. "Now I'll show you one more surprise, the butler's pantry, and the third set of stairs." She led her back down the stairs and into the hallway.

Here she reached under a light fixture. "There's a hook here that opens the passageway door. Use it only when others aren't around. After all, it's secret." Mrs. VanLeer's eyes twinkled like a little girl's who just stole a cookie from the cookie jar.

Devyn grinned. "Brice already showed me that but didn't take me in. I'm beginning to see now."

Mrs. VanLeer laughed softly. "I know that it's all rather confusing at first, but you'll learn your way around the castle soon enough."

A nervous giggle escaped her. "I do hope so."

Then the missus took her to the butler's pantry and down the winding wooden stairs. "We are now in the smaller tower you may have seen as you came to the castle." Soon they stood in a similar pantry just off the kitchen. "I expect that you're up for this challenge. You might be running up and down these stairs a dozen times tonight."

Devyn couldn't help but smile. "Oh, I will. My legs are sturdy, and my will is strong. Besides, it sounds like a splendid job."

Mrs. VanLeer patted her on the back. "That's what I like to hear. The girl who did this last summer got tuckered out more often than not and had quite a contrary disposition." She shook her head and scowled.

"I'll do my best, ma'am." Devyn curtsied, awaiting further instruction.

The housekeeper pulled out a small gold pocket watch and popped it open. "Dear me, I must go and attend to the missus for a few moments. Go back up and take a look in the dining room and butler's pantry, and then return to the Watch to familiarize yourself better with the view from there. I'll come back for you presently."

Devyn nodded as her superior left her in the small pantry. Excited to see the dining room up close, she ascended stairs that led through the butler's pantry to the dining room. Opening the door, she felt as if she were intruding on a king's court. The room was larger than her entire home, even larger than her small community church.

The furnishings were grander than she could see from the screen. She ran her hand over the smooth tabletop and then let her fingers dance across the ornate carvings of the wooden chairs. The intricately carved griffins—strange animals with the head and wings of an eagle and the body and tail of a lion—on the table legs made her both shiver and smile at the same time. The twinkling electric lights of the leaded, stained-glass chandelier over the table lit the entire room quite nicely.

Dramatic veins of white shot through the green marble fireplace. Over the fireplace, a huge mirror hung, making the room seem even larger and reflecting the chandelier's light with a warm sparkle. The heavy, ornate mantel held two large brass candelabras and a statue of a cowboy riding a bucking bronco. The plate on it read "*Bronco Buster* by Frederic Remington." The famous sculptor who summered on his nearby island?

To either side of the fireplace, doors opened into what appeared to be a breakfast room, sunny and warm with large windows overlooking the river on two sides. She glanced out the windows and couldn't help but grumble to herself. "I'd rather be in the dark or confined to the passageways than have to see this wicked river from every window."

Brice rounded the corner and shook his head. "The river isn't wicked. It's a jolly good wonder. I never tire of it." He stopped and looked out the window, smiling.

Following his gaze out to the main channel where a huge cargo ship passed by, she heaved a sigh. "I hate it. I'd rather be inland. Far inland and never have to see it."

Brice furrowed a brow. "You'll never rest easy here if you feel that way." He stepped closer to her, invading her space. "May I ask why you're not keen on the river?"

She narrowed her eyes and tightened her jaw. She slowly shook her head, warning him to not go there. Never go there.

"Sorry." He stepped back and raised his hands. "It's none of my business. What are you doing in here, anyway?"

Devyn recovered a measure of professionalism, whatever that might look like. "The missus sent me to get my bearings since I am to be the Watch tonight. I have yet to fully see the butler's pantry or what's beyond those." She pointed to three large doors beyond Brice.

"I'll show you both, but I fear you won't appreciate the latter."

He led her to one of the three doors, and she understood what he meant. On the other side lay a large terrace from which she could again see the mighty river on two sides.

Just then, another huge cargo ship passed by to the south and blasted its horn. Devyn jumped, and Brice touched her shoulder. "Fear not. The river is God's beautiful creation, Devyn. Like you."

She blinked, unsure of what she had just heard. *Me? God's beautiful creation? Never!* She glanced at him and scurried back to the safety of the dining room. Brice followed, and she addressed him over her shoulder. "I must see the butler's pantry and go back up to the Watch before the missus returns." She stopped and swallowed, clasping her hands. "And Brice, I am sorry for my defensiveness earlier … and just now. It's all been a wee bit … overwhelming."

Brice gently took her by the elbow and guided her toward the pantry, tottering her resolve to appear professional. "We all have our moments. Forgiven."

She sucked in a deep breath. "I appreciate that."

"Whatever troubles you about being here, I pray you will find the peace you need." He paused, his warm blue eyes homing in on hers. "There's an Irish saying I rather like. 'A light heart lives long.' I wish you a light heart, Miss McKenna."

"Th-thank you." She wasn't sure what else to say.

"This way." He opened the door and let her pass. As she did, the musky scent of his cologne tickled her nose and stole her breath.

~ ~ ~

The scent of lavender pleased Brice's senses as Devyn passed by him and entered the pantry.

He had been happy to find the bonnie lass exploring the dining room with the endearing wonder of a child as he happened upon the open door—and even more gratified by her apology.

But then there was her flummoxing reaction to the river views.

Such a curious combination of sweetness and something that seemed to border on bitterness. What would make this fair fawn so skittish, so resentful of the great St. Lawrence River? Had she had a near-drowning experience? Could she have toppled over from a boat and feared for her life?

His imagination ran wild with the possibilities, but as it did, his heart began to hurt for her. Surely something, or someone, had turned her against the river. Was it Falan? Could that scrappy lad have terrorized her somehow? Brice didn't doubt that he might have been the culprit. If he harassed her in any way during their tenure here, her brother would have to reckon with him.

Devyn's voice tore him from his thoughts. "This pantry is far grander than Mama's tiny kitchen—and far more luxuriously equipped." He followed her gaze as she surveyed the fully stocked room. Fine china, elegant stemware, and ornate chafing dishes filled the shelves. "That sink and those warming ovens are huge. And I've never seen the likes of those cut-glass cupboards!" She turned and pointed at an open box. "Is this the dumbwaiter?"

Brice nodded. "It is. You work it like this." He pulled a heavy rope, lowering the wooden box until it was out of sight. "Now it's down in the kitchen, and Cook can send up the hot food when it's time for dinner. Mahlon, the butler, or his staff, can set the food here in the warming ovens until it's ready to be served." He pointed to the two modern contraptions.

"I've never seen such wonders in all my life!" Her eyes twinkled like the stars.

"You've seen but a few of the marvels that are here. Maybe I'll run into you again so I can show you more of them." He allowed himself a teasing wink in her direction. "But now, off with you afore the missus tans your hide."

Brice smiled broadly as he waved her away.

~ ~ ~

Devyn giggled as she hurried back up the secret passageway stairs. She wouldn't mind running into Brice again either.

The rest of the afternoon and evening fairly flew by, and she enjoyed her task as the Watch. Brice served the table, so fine and handsome in his formal black tails. She watched the people around the table for any opportunity to alert him to one need or another, but her chances to assist seemed few and far between.

What was even more appealing to her, though, was the way

the entire Bourne family interacted with each other and with their guests. She hadn't officially met any of the Bournes yet, but it was obvious who was who.

Mr. Bourne was a commanding yet kind host, praying before the meal, smiling and laughing often, and always deferring to others as they talked. His gentle demeanor reminded her so much of her papa that her eyes brimmed over several times. Mrs. Bourne seemed equally kind, nothing like her stern and strict mother, who often scolded her children and interrupted others as they spoke.

The young woman at the table, whom she assumed was the one Reagan spoke about called Miss Marjorie, appeared to be about her own age. Like her parents, she laughed and smiled and seemed to be a most pleasant person.

Their guests were an older couple who chatted during the entire meal like two magpies, both of them drinking excessively and becoming louder and more boisterous as the evening progressed. Who were these people, and why were they the Bournes' friends?

Devyn shook off her musings and scanned the room. The guests' glasses were once again nearly empty, and it appeared that Brice hadn't noticed. She scurried down the stairs to alert him, but when she got to the dining room door, he was already refilling the glasses.

Another chance to serve … foiled.

She turned and trudged back up the hard, stone stairs as her angst grew. Couldn't she even meet the simple expectations of being the Watch? Would she even keep her job if she didn't prove she could be helpful?

CHAPTER 3

O nce the women retreated to the piazza and the men left to enjoy their after-dinner cigars and conversation on the terrace, Mrs. VanLeer appeared on the mezzanine. "You may take your leave now, Devyn, and get yourself settled before the others join you. Tomorrow you'll begin your housemaid duties at eight o'clock sharp. Have your breakfast with the others in the servants' hall, and I will meet you there."

Devyn curtsied, giving her an appreciative smile. "Yes, ma'am. Thank you for this opportunity."

The missus gave her a kind nod before retreating back down the stairs to the kitchen. Devyn followed and found everyone so busy cleaning up that no one even acknowledged her presence. Her chest tightening, she stood there uncertain of what to do until Reagan appeared, wiggling her finger.

"Come with me, please." Reagan smiled, and Devyn followed her up the stairs and through the now-empty dining room, into the Watch passage, and up a second flight of staff stairs. And they came out into a linen closet?

Devyn sighed, putting her hands on her hips and gazing back from whence they came. "I'm altogether lost, Reagan."

Reagan laughed, sounding like tiny bells. "You'll get acclimated. Just be patient. Come." She tweaked her chin toward the wooden staff stairway as they continued up to their fourth-floor dorm room.

"This is such a maze, I feel like a trapped mouse." Devyn began to unpin her mobcap.

Reagan giggled, chatting happily as she began undressing. "I know. I did too, at first. I'm glad to help you find your way, but I'm rarely done this early. Miss Marjorie has retired early this evening. Poor thing. She has a terrible headache."

Untying her apron, Devyn went to her bed and sat down. "I'm sorry to hear that. Maybe it was the ceaseless chatter of the dinner guests. Do you know who they were?"

Reagan shook her head. "No, but I think you're right. Miss Marjorie was quite fretful."

"Well, I'll pray for her speedy recovery."

"Thank you. She's a delightful young woman, and I'm blessed to serve her." Reagan slipped on her nightgown, and Devyn did the same. "You'll find the Bournes are a fine family and treat the staff kindly. This is my second summer here at The Towers, and I love it!"

Devyn scrunched up her nose. "If it weren't for the river, I think I'd love it too."

Reagan's soft features furrowed into tiny lines. "What's wrong with the river? It's a beautiful piece of the world."

She shook her head. "I hate it. Always have. Always will." She bit her lip and could feel herself tense up. Then her right eye began to twitch as Reagan stared at her, looking completely perplexed.

Thankfully, Reagan shrugged her shoulders and gathered her toiletries from a box under her bed. "Do you need the water closet before I take my bath?"

"Yes, please."

With a great deal of amazement, Devyn stepped down into the turret bathroom. It was like being in a fine hotel—not that she'd ever been in one. She giggled as she pulled the chain to flush the toilet and smiled as she cupped warm water from the heavy porcelain sink in her hands. When she finished, Reagan was waiting with towel in hand.

"A hot bath after a long day is simply scrumptious, don't you think?" Reagan's gentle gray eyes twinkled with delight. Without waiting for her to respond, Reagan grasped the doorknob and gave a nod. "Sleep well, my friend."

With that, Devyn was alone in the huge room. Friend? She'd called her *friend*. How could that be? She hadn't had a friend in nearly a decade.

And what of this place? Even the servants' quarters were unlike anything she'd ever seen. Hot water without hauling it to the tub as she always had done? A flushing commode? Electric lights? Her tiny home had neither running water nor electricity.

Brice was right; this castle had many, many marvels.

After straightening her things in the cupboard, she grabbed her precious ribbon and began tucking it under her pillow as she often did when she was lonely or afraid. But then she glanced at the mirror that covered nearly the entire closet door and took the ribbon with her to gaze at her reflection. Her home had nothing more than a tiny mirror hanging on the wall. It was barely bigger than her head, so seeing her entire form intrigued her.

She unpinned her thick, curly hair, combing her fingers through it and brushing back the stubborn locks that refused to comply before braiding it loosely for the night. She tied her ribbon on the end of her braid. Somehow it kept her father close.

She gazed at her reflection. Her ivory complexion appeared paler than usual, her eyes wide and lost-looking like those of a wee lass. After gazing at her slight figure through her threadbare nightgown, she shook her head. "What on earth are you doing here?"

Devyn blew out her frustration with a huff and climbed into bed. The newness of her surroundings must have kept her from noticing the details earlier. This one room was even larger than the dining room and ridiculously elegant for servants' quarters.

The pale-blue ceiling seemed to rise up to the sky, and the soft-yellow walls and electric candlestick lights made the room cozy and warm. Each bed and bedspread matched the wall's color, and the intricately woven rug in the middle of the floor brought beauty to the already lovely room. Windows on three sides were shrouded by darkness. At least at night, she wouldn't have to look at the river.

She sighed with contentment. Although a lowly maid, in a room like this, she felt special.

~ ~ ~

Blinking at the bright morning sunshine peeking through the windows, Devyn gulped in surprise. She must have fallen asleep before the others came up, even before Reagan returned from her bath, for she awakened to the rustle and quiet chatter of the girls dressing and making their beds.

Reagan caught her sleepy eyes and smiled. "Good morning, Devyn. Your first day here must have been exhausting. You slept the night away."

"Goodness! It must be all the newness." Devyn jumped out of bed, dressed, and hurried to catch up with the others while Reagan introduced her to Nellie and Sofia.

Nellie, the dining room maid, nodded a welcome and gave her hand a shake. The girl's too-tight uniform revealed her plump form, and her brown hair and dark features made Devyn think of the Italian family who lived in Chippewa Bay.

Sofia, Mrs. Bourne's lady's maid, reminded Devyn of her middle-aged aunt, Mildred. The woman's black hair and dark eyes were reminiscent of Falan's, but everything else about her seemed pinched and pursed.

The woman turned toward her, looking down her long, sharp nose, and said just one word that was somehow intimidating. "Hello." Then she turned toward the door, her heels tapping out a determined march.

Was that the epitome of proper professionalism?

Reagan shook Devyn from her assessments. "We'd better hurry. The call buttons will ring soon."

She followed her new friend down to the servants' hall, where she enjoyed a cheery breakfast of hot oatmeal with plenty of fresh cream and brown sugar. She listened to the happy banter of the others, who obviously knew each other well. Sofia never spoke but shot several confusing glances her way, and her heart pricked with loneliness. She was an outsider.

Soon Mrs. VanLeer sent her to give the library a thorough dusting. "Although we did a cursory cleaning in here, the room hasn't had a complete going-over since last summer. The previous housemaid fell sick on the way here, so there's much to do. Be sure to get behind all the books and in every corner. I fear there may be droppings left by the winter critters, not to mention bugs, spider webs, and more."

Devyn wrinkled her nose. "Yes, ma'am. My teacher always commended me for my thoroughness in my studies. I promise to apply myself just as carefully to my cleaning."

"Then I've hired well." The housekeeper peeked under a metal lampshade and ran her finger over the bulb, scrunching up her nose. "I trust there will be none of this dust left once you are finished. Be sure to wash the windows as well."

With that, she was gone, leaving Devyn to work in what she was sure would be her favorite room in the castle. While she appreciated the elegance of the dining room and living room, here were treasures beyond compare. Books. How she loved to read and escape to other worlds far more magical than her own.

She looked around the room, deciding where to start. The mantel and fireplace? The windows? The extravagant furnishings? No. It had to be the bookshelves. Her breath hitched at the thought of perusing such masterpieces.

She'd devoured every book she could beg or borrow from her teacher, the preacher, and old Mr. Jones, the local bookworm in her tiny village of Chippewa Bay. He had graciously allowed her to borrow and read anything she fancied, even *Robinson Crusoe* and other stories normally reserved for boys. Her mother always fussed at her for reading such nonsense, but her father had insisted that she could read anything she wanted to as long as it wasn't "vulgar or uncomely," as he had put it.

Then, when she was ten, everything had changed.

She blinked back tears as she remembered that terrible time in her life.

Shaking off her sadness, Devyn decided to start at the top of the shelves and work her way down. She climbed up on the stool the missus had left for her. Pushing a set of matching volumes aside to dust behind them, she understood why the missus told her to clean there. Animal droppings were everywhere.

"Yuck!" She exclaimed aloud, startling herself.

As she continued to clean, her heart clenched. For the past ten years, she had been forced to hide her love of books from her mother, reading only the Bible and an old hymnal while in her mother's presence. She had memorized many of the little biographies of the hymn writers and music composers and treasured her daily Bible reading. But she needed more, and while she hated sneaking around in order to read other books, the teasing from her brother and the berating from her mother made the nasty business imperative.

While she dusted the center bookshelf, one particular volume arrested her attention. She touched it gingerly, running her fingers over the spine until she could no longer resist. She grabbed the fine, linen-covered book and flipped through its pages. In the process, a small, folded piece of paper revealed itself.

Her eyes darted to and fro to make sure no one would see her carefully open the yellowed paper. She bit her lip as she read the faded script—no names, no date, no reference to anyone in particular—but the message mesmerized her.

My dearest,

Last evening left me breathless with the wonder of your touch. Could you be real or a vision of my imagination? I scarce can tell, even now as I write to you, for you are the most heavenly being I have ever known. Thank you for a night of ecstasy.

Forever yours.

Devyn's face flushed. Who would write of such intimate moments? She lifted the paper to her nose but discerned only a slight musky scent. Yet the handwriting was tight and bold, like a man's. She frowned. What sort of man would leave a letter like this for anyone to see? Surely, not a gentleman.

Suddenly, footsteps sounded from the Great Hall, and she hurriedly replaced the note and the book where she had found them. With her heart racing, she returned to her assigned task, sending dust flying through the sunlit air.

"Blathers!" Brice paused in the doorway, waving his hand in front of his face before succumbing to a sneeze.

"Bless you." Devyn giggled and slowed the frantic movements of her feather duster.

"It appears you take your work quite seriously." His voice held a humor in its deep abyss which quickly settled her heart back to its normal pace.

"I was just imagining all the fine tales that are held within these volumes. Oh, what stories they must tell!" She ran her fingertips along a row of books. "I just wish I could read them all." She couldn't help but close her eyes at the mere idea of it, squeezing them tight.

When she opened them just moments later, Brice was barely a foot from her face, studying her with those intensely crystal-blue eyes. Her heart sped up twice as fast as the note had caused it to. He put out his hand to help her down from the stool, and when she took it, butterflies alighted in her belly.

~ ~ ~

Brice couldn't resist a good Irish tease. "I would love to read *your* story from cover to cover. What might I discover?"

Devyn's eyes grew into those of a doe again, fearful and alert. She let go of his hand. Then she took a step away from him and bumped into the suit of armor tucked in the corner.

He caught her by the elbow, setting her aright and steadying her footing among the clatter of moving metal. He held back the belly laugh that threatened to bubble up. "Careful now. I won't bite, but that knight in his not-so-shining armor might not be so inclined to treat you quite as gently."

What was it about this woman that made him want to play with her skittishness and send her nervousness soaring? She was too innocently alluring.

He cleared his throat. "I came by because Mr. Bourne forgot the book he was reading."

She nodded, so he walked over and scooped up the volume from the side table, flipping it over to read the title and patting it gently. Devyn climbed the stool to return to her work. What was she hiding deep within that lovely exterior? Such a curious lass.

"Don't you love the smell of books?" As she looked to him for an answer, the little dimple on her right cheek appeared as she smiled, as it had the day before. Imagining tracing its contour, Brice tightened his hand.

"I do."

He had never met a woman who loved books, at least not as much as he did. But Devyn indeed appeared to treasure the tomes. Apparently, she could bury her nose in a book and get lost in its world in the shake of a lamb's tail, just as he could.

What would it be like to sit side by side in front of a blazing fire, talking about stories well into the evening? Wouldn't that be the most satisfying way to grow old with someone?

"Good morning. Mac. Miss." Mr. Bourne stepped into the room, sending Brice's heart flying. Had the man seen him staring at the lass? If so, he could be out on his ear!

Devyn spun on her heel, nearly losing her balance as she turned, looking as guilty as he felt. But Mr. Bourne seemed to notice none of it. He walked up to her, smiling, and nodded a greeting.

She tried to curtsy while still on the stool but started to teeter.

Mr. Bourne reached out and took her hand. "Careful, miss. You'll not break your pretty neck in my abode." He grinned and turned to Brice while helping her down. "There's a sturdier step stool in the kitchen, I believe. Fetch it for this young lady while we get acquainted, will you, dear chap?"

"Certainly, sir. Here's your book." He gave the volume to his master and tossed Devyn a quick wink before whisking around the corner.

That had been close.

~ ~ ~

Setting aside her duster, Devyn wiped her hands on her apron, then held them tightly in front of her.

Mr. Bourne strolled to a green wingback chair and sat down. "Welcome to The Towers. What's your name?"

"D–Devyn, sir." Her voice quivered, and her legs wobbled. She chewed her lip as he studied her, smiling all the while.

She studied him as well and perceived gentleness in his amber eyes. That plus his silvery, pleasant voice put her at ease, despite his aristocratic and regal appearance.

"Please. Sit." Mr. Bourne motioned for her to take a seat on the sofa near him.

Devyn sat.

"Tell me about yourself."

Who was she? A nobody. A nothing. "Well, sir, I'm just a small-town girl who wants to serve."

Mr. Bourne grinned, his mustache turning up. "And your family? I know your brother works for Reid but nothing more."

Devyn's heart raced like a wild pony. What could she say? "I come from a humble upbringing, and my mother and younger siblings live in Chippewa Bay. I was fortunate to go to school until I was ten and have studied on my own since then. I love books, sir, and I love to learn." She glanced at the bookshelves.

"That, my dear girl, is one of the strongest assets any person could have, and I respect that greatly. Do you see that little black journal?" Mr. Bourne pointed to a book on a small desk. "That is our borrowing ledger, and you may borrow any book here." He swept his hand in a wide arc. "Just record your name and the date you took it and the date you return it. I encourage reading for my family and staff alike."

Devyn nearly came off the sofa. "Really and truly? Oh, sir, thank you ever so much!" An unwelcome giggle left her lips, so she put her hand to her mouth, feeling her face flush.

"Never be ashamed of being excited about such things. I applaud you for your fervor." He leaned forward and took her hand, his eyes studying hers. "Pardon me, but I can't get over it. You remind me of someone. Someone once very dear to me. I loved her with all my heart. Her name was … Louisa." The man's eyes misted over, and his bottom lip quivered as he continued to hold her hand. His hand shook too.

She struggled for a response to this emotional revelation.

"I—I'm sorry for your loss, sir." She didn't know who Louisa was, but she sensed his pain, so much like her own.

Finally, Mr. Bourne let go of her hand and cleared his throat. He sat back in the chair and composed himself. "Did Mrs. VanLeer task you with giving this room a thorough cleaning?"

Devyn nodded and smiled. "Yes, sir."

Mr. Bourne's eyes twinkled as he stood. "Carry on, then. It was nice to meet you. I envision that you'll find Dark Island a life-changing adventure, my dear."

Devyn stood and curtsied low. "Thank you, kind sir."

Mr. Bourne nodded and quietly left the room. Devyn exhaled a shuddering breath and shook herself back to reality. Was the king of this castle really as kind as he appeared? Brice and Reagan believed so, and she had just experienced it. Could this summer prove life-changing?

"Here's the step stool, Miss McKenna." Brice walked into the room carrying a heavy wooden contraption. "It took me a while to locate it." He replaced the small stool with the stepping stool and motioned for her to climb it, taking her hand gently in his strong, manly one.

Lightning struck her chest, radiating heat up to her cheeks and sending her mind reeling. What was *that*?

"Are you all right? You're flushed." Brice gently pulled her back down off the stairs. "Perhaps you need a wee bit of a rest?"

Devyn straightened her apron and shook her head. "I'm fine, thank you. And please, call me Devyn." She scanned the room, putting her hand to her chest. "Mr. Bourne said we could borrow these books? This may be a summer to remember."

Brice smiled wide, his eyes turning to pools of crystal-blue anticipation. "I hope so, my bonnie lass. I do hope so."

His affectionate term, though spoken in a joking manner, ruffled her afresh. And why did she get the feeling that he referred to more than books?

CHAPTER 4

After lunch, Devyn surveyed her work in the library, pleased she had thoroughly dusted two entire sets of bookshelves from ceiling to floor. The debris, disgusting animal droppings, and filthy rags nearly filled a small bucket, but she wasn't sure how to dispose of the contents. She'd need another bucket before she was done. One more set of bookshelves and she'd be ready to work on the rest of the library.

Before she forgot, she chose a book to read. *Anne of Green Gables* by Lucy Maud Montgomery looked interesting. It was about an orphan girl, and she often felt like an orphan, even though she wasn't one. She signed her name to the ledger and set the book aside to take up to her room.

She scanned her surroundings and went over to the fireplace to grab the handle of the cinder bucket, mumbling to herself as she headed to the shelf. "This should work until I find where to dispose of the mess."

Then she glanced into the bucket. "AHHHHH!" She screamed, dropping it with a harsh bang on the hardwood floor. "Ewwwww!" She jumped back in horror. What was that dead, smelly thing? As the bucket lay on its side, only part of the deteriorating creature stuck out. A bird? A mouse? No.

"Devyn, are you all right? What's the matter? You're white as a ghost!" Brice ran into the room, eyes wide. He carried a pile of neatly folded clothes in his arms that he carefully laid down on a chair before hurrying to her side. "What's wrong?"

Devyn held her arms close to her body but thrust a finger toward the bucket. "What—what is that?"

Brice went over to inspect it, his eyes twinkling with amusement. "It's only a bat, dear Devyn. They tend to congregate on this island, and we often find them around, especially in the secret passageways, tunnels, and towers. They won't hurt you."

"A bat? I hate bats! They can bite you and spread disease. What's it doing in the castle?" Devyn's voice trembled, and her knees quaked.

Brice must have noticed, for he took her hand and led her to the sofa, bidding her to sit with him. "Compose yourself, my fearful fawn." He chuckled, but she took no offense at his laughter or the name. "Bats are actually our friends. They keep the bugs at bay. They eat mosquitos, flies, and the like. They won't eat you." He patted the back of her hand and then rubbed it round and round. His touch and the tender circular motion calmed her heart, mind, and body.

"What's going on in here?" Sofia's air of superiority seemed to fill the room, making Devyn sit up straight and hide her hand in the folds of her skirt. "What are you two doing? And what's this mess in the … ewwww! Another bat? Get rid of it at once, Mac." Imparting the nickname in a dictatorial tone, she folded her arms and glared at Brice with her dark, russet eyes and thin, pursed lips.

Brice held his ground, returning Sofia's glare. "I was tending to more important matters at the moment, thank you very much. And you are not my superior. I will dispose of the bat all in good time." He continued to stare her down until she faltered.

"Well, I never! This is improper behavior, Mr. McBride, and someone will hear of it." In a huff, Sofia turned on her toes and retreated into the Great Hall, her heels clicking loudly on the stone floor.

Brice rolled his eyes at the empty doorway. "Ach! Never ends with that one. Her shenanigans can put you on tenterhooks. Don't let them." He gave Devyn one soft pat before releasing her hand and rising. "Better?"

Devyn smiled sheepishly, raising her fingers to her flaming cheeks. "Sorry. I hope I haven't caused you any trouble."

He shot her his charming, crooked grin. "Not to worry, lass.

Sofia enjoys casting airs whenever she can. One day, I think she'll just float away with her haughtiness." Brice winked and turned to retrieve the bat and bucket. "And you needn't be embarrassed by your response to this rather foreign creature. Most females find them not to their liking."

Devyn giggled nervously as he picked up the bucket. She lifted the other one. "What shall I do with this?"

"Let me show you where the trash barrel is."

He led her outside and showed her where to dispose of the refuse just behind the kitchen. As they walked back to the library, he stopped to watch a ship pass the island. "These ships come from all over. I wonder where it's been and where it's going. Wouldn't it be interesting to know?"

Devyn took a quick glance at the ship, then headed back toward the castle. "I don't know about that rusty old boat, but I have to admit, I was wrong about The Towers. It *is* rather grand."

Brice's reply, barely a whisper, followed her inside. "You're a mystery, my dear Devyn."

~ ~ ~

Following Devyn back upstairs, Brice shook his head. If only he had the nerve to ask her what the real problem was. But he wasn't sure he could handle the answer if he did.

He hadn't slept well the night before. He just couldn't stop thinking about Devyn. Why would this charming lass be so utterly opposed to the river, so fearful, so timid? Worrisome nightmares had captured his dreams until he tossed and turned most of the night.

It wasn't the river but something much deeper and darker. Something more painful. And it wasn't just fear, but anger. Even if she'd had an accident on the river, she should simply fear it rather than be angry at it. He had to learn the truth, sooner rather than later. Maybe he could help alleviate her angst somehow.

"What are you doing with that pile of clothes?" Devyn questioned him as they entered the library.

As if shaken from sleep, Brice gasped. "Blathers! I'd better be about my duties. I was fetching Mr. Bourne's ironing and I, well, I got rather distracted." He gave her a quick bow, scooped up the pile of clothes, and nearly ran for the Great Hall.

Devyn giggled behind him.

~ ~ ~

Returning to her task, Devyn dusted the last bookshelf just as Mrs. VanLeer came to check in on her. The missus' amused gaze befuddled her. Had she missed something? Was she doing something wrong?

"I heard about the bat." The housekeeper's eyes fairly danced. "Fear not, dear girl. You'll get used to them." Mrs. VanLeer assessed her work, peeking behind a row of books, running her finger along the spines, checking for dust. "Spotless! Well done. Now that I have a moment, I'd like to show you this room's secret passageway. That way, you can slip in and out of this room whenever you are needed."

Mrs. VanLeer led her to the left side of the fireplace that Brice had pointed out the day before. It appeared to be just like the right side, but the missus pulled a penny out of her pocket and reached under the shelf. "Look here."

Devyn bent to see what she was doing. Under the mantel was some kind of circuit, and when the housekeeper put the penny to it, a piece of the wall creaked open.

Mrs. VanLeer grinned and pushed it closed. "Like magic. The coin completes an electric circuit." She pressed the penny firmly into Devyn's hand before continuing. "Keep this with you. But if you don't have the coin, you can still open it by pulling this ring and chain." She gave what looked like a regular switch a good yank, and the door popped open again.

"It looks like a light switch. How clever!" Devyn clapped her hands. "Where does the passageway lead?"

The missus shook her head. "Sorry, I don't have time to explore it with you now. But rather than me telling you, after you finish the last shelf, put the cleaning things away, and then you may investigate all you like until dinner. How does that sound?"

"Like a fairytale adventure." Devyn blushed when she realized how familiar her answer sounded. "Excuse me, ma'am. I spoke out of line."

Mrs. VanLeer patted her forearm. "No need. This place can seem like a fairy story, as you say. Carry on, then."

Devyn curtsied and returned to the shelf. So many mysteries in just one day. Who had written that love letter, and what lay behind the intriguing door?

Hopefully, a journey without bats.

A deep voice startled her. "She must be in here." Mr. Bourne.

She hadn't heard the footsteps in the Great Hall. Devyn began furiously dusting the shelf, hoping to appear the hardworking, faithful servant. Mr. Bourne swept into the room with his wife, and Devyn held her breath. Perhaps the master was looking for someone besides her.

"Greetings, miss. I'd like to introduce you to my wife." Mr. Bourne's commanding voice sounded neither angry nor unpleasant. He waited for Devyn to turn and look at them. When she did, both wore broad smiles. Mrs. Bourne was the same woman from dinner who'd been quite amiable to her guests. She could hope the missus would be kind like Mr. Bourne rather than contrary like Mama.

"This is Mrs. Bourne. She wanted to meet you after I shared about our conversation." Mr. Bourne tipped his head and touched her elbow.

Devyn curtsied low. "Pleased to meet you, ma'am." She lowered her gaze to the floor, but Mrs. Bourne came close and tenderly tipped her head up with a finger to her chin.

She looked at Devyn's face, her eyes lighting up, and then to her husband. "Yes, darling. They are the same. It's as if she were here with us again!" Mrs. Bourne's gentle voice was barely audible as her eyes misted over. So did her husband's. "Truly. I've never seen the like of it!"

Devyn's confusion sent a warm flush to her cheeks. What was it about her face that made the two of them sad and happy at the same time? She thought back to the conversation with the master of the castle. Could this have to do with Mr. Bourne's reference to a "Louisa"? If so, who was this Louisa, and why was Mrs. Bourne so overcome with emotion too?

The missus gave her a gentle pat on the shoulder, her singsong voice setting her at ease. "No need to worry, miss. You remind us of our daughter, Louisa. You have the same eyes and nose." The missus touched the tip of her nose, causing her to shiver. "And you even have a dimple on your right cheek as she did." Mrs. Bourne smiled so kindly that Devyn was tempted to run into her motherly arms.

Instead, she took a moment to assess the woman who seemed as kind as her husband. Mrs. Bourne's curly, graying hair was softly pulled up into a simple pompadour, giving her a rather regal appearance. And while her matronly figure betrayed her years and her motherhood, her clear, honey-brown eyes danced like those of a young girl. Even so, a shadow of sorrow shaded them. Louisa, Devyn supposed.

Mr. Bourne sighed. "Our sweet angel, Louisa, went to heaven when she was but five, and we miss her every day. But you … your face brings her back to us!"

Devyn blinked. She bit her lip, for she had no idea how to respond to his statement. Finally, she simply said, "I'm sorry for your loss. So very sorry."

Mrs. Bourne stepped back to join her husband. "It is nice to meet you, miss. We mustn't keep you from your work, but we hope you'll feel welcome in our home."

Mr. Bourne nodded. "And do remember to choose a book for your reading pleasure."

Devyn pointed to the novel. "I did. Thank you."

Mrs. Bourne picked it up, her eyes twinkling. "I love this story and the sequel, *Anne of Avonlea*. Be sure to read that when you're done. A girl your age will enjoy it even more." She set the book down and slipped her hand in the crook of her husband's arm.

"I will." Devyn curtsied as the master and mistress headed toward the Great Hall.

Mr. Bourne turned to his wife. "Shall we take a stroll along the

Indian Path, my dear?"

Mrs. Bourne agreed. "Yes. It's a lovely afternoon for a stroll."

After the front door closed, Devyn peeked out the library window to see them head partway down the bridle path and then make a right turn onto a dirt pathway that led into the woods. She couldn't hear them, but the master's head turned up in laughter that evidenced pleasant banter. *Oh to have such a sweet relationship one day and grow old with a kind man! Let it be, Lord. Please?*

With a contented sigh, she returned to the shelf and made quick work of it. Within an hour, she had completed her assigned task, put away her cleaning supplies, and turned to explore the secret passageway. She pulled out the penny, a little fearful that she might get a shock from this marvel of conduction. Peeking under the shelf, she found the two screws that would complete the tiny electrical circuit and slid the coin into place. At first, nothing happened. But then she adjusted it so that the penny touched both metal nobs. When she heard a click and a creak, the wall finally popped open.

The musty breeze that came from the opening quickly tempered her rush of excitement. Her heart began to beat wildly, not in a pleasant way, and her breathing picked up as well. She tried to calm down, but the more she tried, the more nervous she became. Indeed, she soon stepped away from the half-open door.

"Would you like some company? Miss Marjorie is out in her boat, so I have the time."

Devyn spun around to find Reagan awaiting her reply. She flushed with embarrassment but nodded furiously. Reagan's tiny laugh sounded like fine china clinking at a party.

Reagan stepped into the passageway, bidding her to follow. "I felt the same as you when I first came here. Secret passageways can be daunting, even for the strong of heart. I nearly fainted dead away when they sent me through them alone for the first time."

The confession calmed Devyn, but she remained planted in the library. "Thank you for understanding. Now ... where does this go?"

Reagan returned to her and slipped her arm into the crook of Devyn's. "Let's explore it together, shall we?"

She grabbed her book, and for the next hour or so, they explored all the passageways, up and down stone steps, through dimly lit corridors, and up and down more circular steps. On one landing, Devyn stopped and looked back at the narrow climb. "How does one carry things down these stairways?"

Reagan's girlish voice reverberated off the stone walls. "Very carefully, but with practice, you'll get used to it. And when the family's away, we can use the regular stairs and hallways."

The eerie gas lighting made the passageways a little creepy, and a plethora of electrical wires liberally laced the otherwise bare walls. Everything was cold stone, and Devyn rubbed her arms more than once. She wasn't sure if the chill originated from the temperature or the spooky ambience.

During their tour, Reagan shared a wealth of information. "There are twenty-eight rooms and even a dungeon, which I'll show you in a minute. It was designed by the famous architect, Ernest Flagg."

When they got to the dungeon, Devyn stopped, her jaw dropping open. "It's just a round, empty room with iron bars on it. Do the Bournes use it?"

Reagan laughed. "Oh no. It's here just for the fun of it. Mr. Flagg modeled it after a castle in England with a dungeon that was used regularly."

At one point, they came to the steps leading to the Watch passageway. They peeked into the dining room as Devyn had done while keeping watch, and then they took the mezzanine level passageway and peered into the Trophy Room through the round portrait. Slowly, the maze was becoming more familiar and a little less scary.

Finally, they climbed the stairs until they came to the highest room in the castle. Reagan smiled. "This room was officially named the Map Room, but Miss Marjorie has claimed it this summer for her abode. She calls it the Rapunzel Room."

Both of them giggled at the reference to the fairytale, but it seemed to fit since it was five stories up. Reagan put her hand to the doorknob. "Since Miss Marjorie is out on her boat, I can show you her room." She opened the door to a soft-green room with several large, multi-paned windows from which one could see the river on three sides. Again. The bed, dresser, and vanity fit around the windows, and a cozy fireplace was tucked in one corner.

Reagan closed the door, took Devyn's hand, and grinned. "It's only down from here, and I've yet to count the steps to the bottom. Shall we?"

Devyn grinned back, nodding in agreement. "Let's do."

Though she was around twenty years old, Reagan's face looked like a little girl's at Christmas. "Ready? Set. Go!"

Off they went, counting each step until they got to the very bottom. Breathless, they huffed and puffed until they recovered from the exertion.

Finally, Devyn asked, "Well? What did you count?"

Reagan gulped and grinned. "Eighty steps from the top floor to the bottom." She stomped her foot on the very last step.

Devyn laughed. "Me too! What's next?"

With such a friend, the island's secrets could turn into pleasant surprises.

CHAPTER 5

Early Sunday morning, Devyn woke to a fierce summer storm. She loved the morning rain falling in such heavy sheets. She took a full-lung whiff as she hurried to shut the windows nearest her.

"My, but you're chipper on this stormy morning, Devyn." Reagan glanced at her, tilting her head as she finished making her bed.

"I love summer storms and the refreshing rain. I just wish we didn't have to close the windows. Before long the room will smell rather stuffy, don't you think?" Devyn glanced at the already made beds as she tucked her royal blue ribbon safely into her drawer. As usual, Nellie was at her post early, ready to serve the Bournes their breakfast. "Where's Sofia?"

Reagan slipped on her apron. "Mr. and Mrs. Bourne are going to the Sunday services on the mainland this morning, so Sofia went to tend the missus early."

Devyn glanced out the window and brushed a stray curl off her face. "On such a blustery day?"

Reagan tilted her head. "The Bournes are faithful Christians, and the steamer is safe."

They headed down the stairs for breakfast, chatting like old friends, and Devyn had to ask. "I have yet to see the tunnel. Is it as spooky as the secret passageways?"

"No. The tunnel is lit and dry, but sometimes bats hide in it. Oh, but yesterday was fun, don't you think?" Reagan's eyes sparkled like jewels.

At the memory, Devyn knew her eyes mirrored her friend's. "Yes!

Thank you for joining me in the passageway exploration. I don't believe I could have done it alone." With her sheepish confession, she shrugged her shoulders.

"It's always more fun to share adventures." Reagan smiled as they entered the servants' hall and dished up their steamy oatmeal. "I believe a hot cup of tea is in order today. Want one?"

Sofia looked up from her meal and nodded. "I'll have a cup, please."

She expects us to wait on her just because she's older? Isn't she a mere servant too? Devyn shook off her irritation and took two cups to the table, one for her and one for Sofia. Reagan carried her own.

Devyn returned to the stove and brought the bowls of oatmeal to the table as Mrs. VanLeer swept into the room, nodding a greeting. "Mr. and Mrs. Bourne are off to Chippewa this morning." She shook her head, clicking her tongue. "They'll catch their death in this blustery weather." She gave a great sigh. "Since they will be away most of the morning, Devyn, I'd like you to give the entrance hall a thorough going-over. I noticed some dust and fingerprints yesterday, and we can't have either."

Devyn swallowed a sticky lump of oats and dabbed her lips with a napkin. "Yes, ma'am."

"I expect Miss Marjorie will sleep in on this dreary day. I certainly would." The missus nodded to Reagan, then addressed the staff. "We'll have our Sunday Vespers at five o'clock." After that, she left as quickly as she had appeared.

Devyn quirked a brow at Reagan. "Vespers?"

Reagan nodded, setting down her spoon and wiping her mouth. "The Bournes are a family of faith, and they encourage ours as well. Every Sunday, we have a time of worship and prayer. It's called Vespers, and the time together is simply lovely." Her face assumed a gentle quality.

"That's kind of them." Devyn took another bite as Brice came in the room, scooped a full bowl of oatmeal, and sat across from her and the others.

"Well, they're off, and though I know the boat is sound, I do wish they'd have stayed here today." Sprinkling a mound of raisins and brown sugar into his bowl, Brice's eyes turned clouded like the skies outside. "I admire their commitment to their faith, but that wind is blowing something fierce."

Cook tapped her wooden spoon on the table. "Enough chatter. Eat!"

Brice glanced at Cook. A crooked smile appeared, and he winked at Devyn. "And how are you ladies faring on this blustery day?"

Reagan cocked her head toward Devyn and addressed Brice. "Fit as a fiddle and glad it's the Sabbath. Say, did you know that Devyn here loves summer storms?"

"Truly? So do I. Storms are crackin' jolly, I say. Everything feels clean and new afterward. I don't even mind the thunder and lightning or the rolling waves, except when I'm in a boat. I still don't feel comfortable with that." Brice took a sip of his tea, and then his brows furrowed. "But you hate the river. How do you reckon the two?"

Without allowing Devyn time to respond, Reagan nodded. "That is perplexing. Why do you dislike the river so much, Devyn?"

Sofia turned up her long nose with an accusing air of disdain. "Yes, why would anyone not love this beautiful piece of paradise?"

Devyn's cheerfulness faded. Her face flamed, and she shrugged off the inquiries. "It's not important. I must find Mrs. VanLeer and be about my work." She scurried to the sink, washed her bowl and cup, and fled from the inquisitors.

Why did they want to know her private affairs? It was none of their business!

~ ~ ~

Something inside Brice began to ache as Devyn evaded their questions. Why did she hold onto her secrets so tightly, so fearfully? That concerned him more and more each time the river entered their conversations.

Once again, the lass reminded him of a fragile fawn, afraid that a predator would attack at any moment. Their innocent inquiries were perceived as deadly arrows that could pierce her through. Oh how he wanted to alleviate her pain and protect her from whatever it was! He wanted to help, but how?

Asking about her fears in public had certainly not proven helpful. He scolded himself at his error and scolded the girls when they murmured among themselves about Devyn's rapid exit. "Let her be. All of you. It was wrong of us to prod her." Rising, he glared at the other staring servants, who quickly turned to the business of eating their breakfast.

He followed Devyn out of the servants' hall, through the kitchen, and out into the hallway. There she was leaning against the wall and swiping tears away with her shirtsleeve, eyes squeezed shut. What did the poor lass think of him starting such a conversation? What an idiot he was! Why had he opened his big mouth and brought her shame?

Brice brushed her shoulder with the tips of his fingers, trying not to frighten her. The moment he touched her, fire radiated up his arm and into his cheeks. When she looked at him, he shook his head. "Ach! I'm so sorry. I didn't mean to pry. Didn't mean to cause you pain. I never want to."

Devyn stared at him, her stormy eyes matching the day. Apparently, matching her mood. But hurt also flowed from them, and she turned to wipe away evidence of her tears. She straightened her back and lifted her chin. Up went her wall, ready to protect her. "Thank you. Do you know where the missus might be?"

"In the Great Hall, I 'spect, surveying the work to be done. She's a faithful, hardworking soul." He heaped a boatload of gentleness into his words, hoping to reconnect somehow.

But she'd have none of it. Without a word, she nodded and hurried away.

~ ~ ~

"Ready?" A few minutes after her encounter with Brice, Mrs. VanLeer met Devyn in the Great Hall. "I'd like you to concentrate on the staircase today."

"Yes, ma'am." Devyn ducked her chin as she took the bucket of cleaning supplies the housekeeper handed her.

Mrs. VanLeer studied Devyn as if weighing her mood. "We don't often work hard on the Sabbath, but I don't know when else we'll have the chance to get this clean. When you're finished, you're free until Vespers."

"I'm happy to be working on this dreary day. Thank you, Mrs. VanLeer. I'll do my best." Devyn smiled and ran her hand over the warm, smooth wood. "It's such a beautifully carved staircase." She swirled the cleaning cloth over the ornate end post. It had a polished wooden ball on the top and an intricately designed flower in a square piece of wood just below it.

"It is beautiful, to be sure. Why don't you start at the top and work your way down? And dust the light."

"Yes, ma'am."

Devyn grabbed the pail and a broom and climbed the four flights of stairs. She began dusting and rubbing the rich pine balustrades, newel posts, and bottom rail. As she polished inside and out, voices murmured below her, but she couldn't make out the words.

Leaning over the handrail, Devyn looked down the curving flights of stairs to the suit of armor in the Great Hall. Her social situation felt similar, as if she were spiraling down to foreboding dangers. Could she save herself, or would she fall to her demise when the people here found out her secrets?

"Don't be so opinionated, Sofia. It's not at all becoming." Reagan's voice came from below, taut with irritation.

"I saw her. She was flirting with Mac at breakfast. I think she pretended to be upset about the conversation so that he would follow her, just as she did with the bat. So she could catch him with her wily ways. This is not the proper conduct for a mere housemaid here or anywhere. She is quite unqualified for a position in the Bourne household, of that I am sure!"

Sofia was talking about *her*!

Devyn recoiled, pressing her back against the wall. Footsteps followed the closing of a door, but she couldn't tell what floor they came from.

At least Reagan was defending her. But that Sofia! How dare

that nasty old maid falsely accuse her?

After a few moments of silence passed, Devyn returned to her task. She couldn't hide forever. But she gritted her teeth until her jaw began to ache. Her knuckles were as white as the cleaning cloth in her hand. Honestly, she *was* unqualified and didn't know how to properly conduct herself in such a place. But what was she to do?

"Oh. It's *you*." Sofia appeared on the landing below her and shot her a victorious smirk, head held high as she ascended and swished past Devyn. "Excuse me."

Devyn glared at her, wishing she had the courage to give her a thorough tongue-lashing. But Sofia was her elder and personal maid to the lady of the castle. She didn't know what Sofia might do if she crossed her, so she chose to ignore her instead. She turned her back and dusted the floorboards without a word.

"Hmmm ..." Sofia's footsteps tapped judgment above Devyn into the room nearest the stairs.

She didn't hear the door close, and she refused to look up to chance finding the woman ruling over her. Finally, the door clicked, and she blew out a ragged breath.

She continued polishing the banisters and sorting out her muddled thoughts, but her frustration grew at the mix of false accusations and accurate assessment.

"What's that woman's problem?" Her taut voice startled her, and she slapped a hand over her mouth. She glanced around to make sure no one had heard her, and only then did she relax again.

Truth was, she feared the haughty old maid and the trouble she might cause. Who knew what power she might wield? Better to avoid her wrath altogether than tangle with a viper.

A level and a half down, she came to the point where she might be able to dust the massive light fixture suspended from the ceiling. But how could she reach it safely? The ornate chandelier hung between the staircases, several stories high. She looked down to the bottom floor and gasped. It was twenty feet or more to the Great Hall! Still, the missus had specifically bid her to dust this fixture, so she gathered her courage to do just that.

After wiping the sweat from her brow, Devyn held onto the

railing with one hand and leaned over it as far as she could. She was able to reach the near side of the glass-and-brass fixture, but how could she get to the far side of it to clean it safely? She decided to use the end of the broomstick and cover it with her cloth. That might work.

Bracing herself as she stretched over the rail, she held the heavy broom with both hands and was doing a splendid job when the broom began to teeter precariously. If she dropped it, the thing might damage the fine artwork on the wall or the suit of armor below!

She'd leaned over as far as she dared in an attempt to steady the broom when she lost her footing and began to fall.

Suddenly, strong hands grabbed her and pulled her back to safety. She held on to the broom and turned to thank the person, but no words came.

Brice.

He took hold of the broom and grinned, those piercing blue eyes bidding her peace. Without thinking, she threw her arms around him, relief flooding her mind and gratitude flooding her soul.

"What is going on here? Devyn? Mac?" From the floor below, Mrs. VanLeer glared up at her and then at Brice.

Devyn flung her arms to her sides, pasting her lips together.

Brice stepped back and plunged his hands into his pockets. "Pardon, missus. Devyn lost her balance and needed steadying. An innocent happenstance, I do assure you. We wouldn't want an accident on your watch, would we?"

The missus' brows furrowed into deep lines, and she folded her arms over her ample chest, assessing the situation. She shook her head. "Leave the chandelier be, Devyn. I'll have one of the stronger and taller staff attend to it from now on. Be about your work, then."

Mrs. VanLeer turned on her heel and disappeared. When she was gone, Devyn gazed into Brice's amused face. He pressed his mouth into a straight line, but his eyes danced with mirth, and his lips curled upward in a losing battle. Then he burst into laughter.

"Sorry. I shouldn't laugh, but did you see her face?" He pointed to where she had stood. "What did she think we were doing?" Brice continued to chuckle as he swept a hand over his mouth, the grin remaining.

Devyn failed to see the amusement, although he did seem more handsome than ever with his dancing blue eyes. She feigned anger. "What's so humorous, sir? I could have fallen to my death. But thank you. Thank you for saving me." She curtsied to him and looked at his polished wingtips.

With a gentle fingertip, Brice tipped her face up to look at his. "No need to curtsy to a fellow servant, my bonnie lass. I'm jolly glad I was here to help." For a moment, she wasn't sure he wouldn't up and kiss her right then and there.

Devyn stepped back, pinned herself against the banister, and sensed her defenses implode. At his tenderness, her eyes threatened to overflow, but she blinked the moisture back. How was it that this man's Irish charm could tear down her security wall faster than anyone or anything?

"Thanks again." She cleared her throat, pasting on a quivering smile. "I do believe you're my knight in shining armor today."

Brice smiled and glanced over the banister at the armor below. He stood so close to her that she could smell his woodsy scent just like her father's.

"I'm keen you think so, but it was nothing." Brice gently turned her toward him. "Best be about your work afore the missus returns."

Devyn tried to take the broom from his hand, but he held it fast.

"Oh no, you don't. You return to the safety of the steps, and I'll tend to this."

For the next few minutes, Brice dusted the massive light, and Devyn polished the banister. They worked side by side in comfortable silence, and Brice's occasional glances revealed that he enjoyed their nearness too.

He finished and assessed his work, leaning on the cloth-covered broom. "Isn't this staircase grand? All this granite alongside the warm, polished pine make for quite an entrance to the upstairs rooms, don't you think?"

She nodded.

Brice seemed to notice something, climbed to the nearest

landing, and retrieved a scrap of paper. "Say, is this yours?" He descended to Devyn's level and held out a folded note.

"No, and it wasn't there earlier. I'd have seen it." She reached for it. "May I?"

He handed her the paper. "What does it say?"

Devyn opened it, scanned the note, and folded it back, shoving it into her apron pocket. Heat rose up her neck and onto her cheeks. "Nothing important, I'm sure."

"Nothing?" Brice questioned her with his brows furrowed. "Your blush and the expression on your face as you read it tell me otherwise."

"I'm just not sure the writer would want me to share it." Devyn turned to finish her work. "Thank you for your assistance, sir." She didn't want to hurt him, but she needed him to respect her wish for the contents to be private.

"All right. I'll see you at Vespers. Until then, stay safe, my bonnie lass." He didn't wait for her to answer but turned and ascended the stairs almost silently.

Once she heard the door close above her, she sat on the step and pulled out the note.

Dear M,
I must meet with you immediately. I have some scandalous news to share.
Yours always, S

It had to be Sofia's note, but to whom? *M*? Mrs. Bourne? Or *M* for Mac?

Had Falan shared her secret with Sofia? Did she know? Devyn's throat nearly closed up with the lump that kept on growing at the thought. Surely, her brother wouldn't be so cruel, so heartless.

Maybe he would.

CHAPTER 6

The previous day's rainstorm had cooled the air to a pleasant temperature, but Monday was a busy workday. Devyn scurried from bedroom to bedroom, pulling off the bed sheets for washing. After depositing everything in the laundry, she returned to make beds and tidy the rooms. It was nearly noon before she finished.

She cut through the butler's pantry and descended the passageway staircase to the kitchen below, nearly bumping into Brice halfway down.

"Aye, there you are, my bonnie lass. I've been looking all over for you. Before lunch, I am to help you take a pot of soup to the Reid workers and show you the north boathouse. Since the footmen have the day off, it seems the missus thinks my newest job is as a tour guide." He flashed his charming, crooked grin and turned to descend the stairs. "Follow me, please." He chuckled as he feigned a tour-guide tone.

Devyn followed. "I'm sorry I'm a burden. All this extra work for you."

Brice stopped short and turned to her. "Blathers! I enjoy showing you around. Really, I do. Mr. Bourne is out on his boat again and is so self-sufficient these days, I barely have anything to do. Besides, I enjoy your company."

His gaze nearly made her dizzy. She exhaled and smiled as they descended the stairs.

Once in the kitchen, Cook gave Devyn a large basket of rolls and bid Brice to carry the heavy cast iron pot of soup. "My staff are busy with baking and laundry, so I'm obliged the missus lent me the two of you. Now skedaddle."

Devyn curtsied, and Brice led the way to the underground tunnel. Once inside, she relaxed when she observed the wide paved walkway, high plastered walls, and sufficient lighting. The night before, she had dreamed of a dark, dirty, cobwebby, skeleton-riddled passageway. "This is a rather pleasant tunnel, far different than I had imagined."

He chuckled, a deep baritone laugh that sounded like music. "Yes, Mr. Bourne does everything with excellence. Since I am to be your official tour guide and your scallywag of a brother told you nothing, may I give you a bit of the Bourne family story?"

"I'd like that. Please do." Devyn shifted her breadbasket to her other hip as she stepped closer to Brice and intently listened as she followed.

"Mr. Bourne was the president of Singer Manufacturing Company and a major part of its international success. He's a brilliant businessman and involved in several other businesses too—a bank, cement business, motor parkway, and railroad, to name a few." Brice stopped and turned to her. "But what's best about this man is that he's kind, generous, and godly."

Devyn blinked. "I sensed that when I met him. Those are rare qualities in one so accomplished."

He nodded. "Aye, and he's a self-made success. His father was a struggling preacher, but providence smiled on him when he met Alfred Clark, son of the co-owner of Singer, after Mr. Bourne sang in the Mendelssohn Glee Club with Clark's son. Then he found his pot of gold." Brice glanced at the ceiling. "I love how God works everything out for His purposes, don't you?"

She nodded even though she wasn't so sure and took a step forward. "We'd better get this food to the men." And hopefully not run into her scoundrel of a brother.

Brice transferred the cast iron pot to his other hand. "Aye. You're right. I tend to lose myself when I talk of Mr. Bourne's grand achievements."

For the rest of the journey, they trod in silence, and Devyn pondered Brice's words. Did God truly work things out for His purposes? Then why had He let such tragedy happen to her? No!

Brice must be mistaken, and he also thought a little too highly of his employer. While he seemed a good man, he was still just a man.

As the tunnel opened up into the bright sunshine, Brice set the heavy pot on the pavement and stretched his hands. His eyes widened as he caught sight of her. "Are you all right? You look ghostly." He touched her arm gently. "Steady, girl."

Devyn shook her head. "I'm fine. I was just daydreaming."

"Looks like you had more of a nightmare to me."

She shrugged her shoulders and straightened her spine. "I'm fine. Stop fussing over me. Let's get this food to the boys before it's cold."

~ ~ ~

Brice picked up the pot and led the way into the boathouse, frustration itching his neck, an itch he couldn't scratch away.

Blathers! Why did she always do that? They would just begin to step into a deeper conversation, and she'd erect a brick wall between them. Why? He'd like to smash it to smithereens and be done with it.

He glanced her way and noticed the beautiful glints of auburn in her hair, her soft cheeks, her trembling lips, that adorable dimple on her right cheek. Though he'd like to touch her hair, to feel her soft skin, to playfully poke that dimple, he wanted to stop her trembling most of all. But to do that, he'd have to scale that infernal wall. And even if he did, she might impale him if he got too close to her pain.

Brice shot up a prayer for this sweet, hurting woman, a lovely lass he hoped might one day open her heart to him.

As they entered the building, he resumed his tour. "Mr. Bourne has tasked the Reid Company to add an extra forty feet to this north boathouse. That way, it will hold the Bournes' hundred-and-eleven-foot steam yacht, the *Sioux*. When complete, there will be living quarters for up to nine servants, the power plant, and beams under water with screw jacks to raise the yacht up and get it out of the water for safe winter storage. There will even be a chimney installed for the smokestack of the steamer to let out its exhaust.

Pretty ingenious, don't you think?"

"You're a man of many details, sir. I had no idea." Devyn gifted him with a smile.

His heart danced a jig in response. "Aye, well, let's deliver this food, shall we? Then we can resume our tour with empty arms."

Brice bid her to follow him up to a partially finished second floor, which he informed her would include several bedrooms, work and storage rooms, a servants' hall, and more. They left the food with the attendant and returned to the bottom floor, the main part of the boathouse.

At the end of a long hallway, he showed Devyn the expanded boat slip that would house the Bournes' steamer. "That hole in the roof is where the chimney will be. In the future, the steamer can be lit without smoke filling the slip. Brilliant, aye?"

She grinned. "Aye."

He pointed over the water to a door built into the ground with a pipe sticking out. "Over there is a smokehouse." Brice touched Devyn's back and with a gentle push led her to a door on her left. "And this is the powerhouse that gives everything on the island the light, heat, and hot water we use."

Devyn peeked into a large, noisy room filled with gigantic machinery and scores of knobs and levers and instruments. He chuckled at her wide-eyed amazement.

She giggled but took a half step back. "Oh my! What a marvel! Is it safe in here?"

Brice nodded and led her into the room, showing her around and giving her lots of details, just as a tour guide should. He enjoyed the role, especially with her. The men working on the equipment cast narrow-eyed glances at her but said nothing. How many women visited such a manly abode? Very few, if the workers' faces disclosed the truth.

Upon exiting the powerhouse room, Brice spotted Mr. Labrese. "If you'll excuse me for a minute, I need to speak with the head boatman." He jerked his chin toward Labrese, who stood at the end of the dock.

"Certainly. I'll just wait here and enjoy my surroundings." Devyn smiled as she took a step closer to the rock wall of the boathouse slip.

~ ~ ~

Devyn smiled at Brice's animated discussion with the boatman. She glanced out at the river beyond them, wrinkling her nose at the fishy scent of her watery enemy. She folded her arms around her middle and rubbed them, not sure why she was chilled. Footsteps behind her drew her attention.

"You. What are ya doing here, sister? This is no place for a girl." Falan's rancid breath was but inches from her right ear. He'd been chewing tobacco again.

Devyn stepped away from him and bumped her shoulder on the damp boathouse wall. Hard. She rubbed it. "I was delivering your lunch, if you must know." She rolled her eyes at the brown-toothed smirk on Falan's face.

"It ain't safe here, ya know. My crew can be mighty crude." Falan glanced over his shoulder and grinned.

If they were friends of his, she didn't doubt they'd be a rough bunch. Devyn followed his gaze to the doorway where five other men just as scruffy as her brother stood. "I can imagine. But Brice is my guide and my chaperone." She motioned to him in the distance. Just then, he had his back to her. She shivered, wishing he would turn and notice her predicament.

Falan's voice grew raspy and menacing. "You'd better be behavin' yerself up at that fancy castle, little sister. Ya lose yer job, and you'll be sorry. And you'll stay away from that goody-two-shoes Mick if ya know what's good for ya!" He shot a look at Brice, narrowed his eyes, and gritted his stained teeth before turning back to her with a scraggly brow raised. "Now, ya wanna meet some real men? I can introduce ya to some."

"No. No, I don't!" Devyn wilted under his meanness, just as she always did. She tried to step away from him, but an ice sled blocked her way.

As if he fed on her fear, Falan fairly growled to his friends, "Hey, fellers. Come here and meet my baby sister." He bid them to join him with a crook of his finger.

The roughly dressed workers sauntered over, blocking Devyn's route of escape. The men touched her hand. Her cheek. Her hair. Leering faces bent close. Falsely crooning voices said, "Oooh, she's a pretty thing" and "What soft skin ya have, princess." She tried slapping their hands away and ducking out of their reach to no avail. They closed around her like a suffocating wave while Falan merely chuckled and crossed his arms in front of his chest.

Devyn's heart raced so fast she feared she'd faint. Her palms broke out in a sweat, and tears popped out of her eyes. "Brice!"

As soon as Devyn screamed, the men, including her brother, disappeared through the doorway, pushing and shoving each other as they went.

Brice whipped around and ran to her side. "What happened?" He grabbed her trembling hands, rubbing the backs of them with his thumbs. "Did those men harass you?"

Devyn swallowed hard. "Falan."

"What did he do to you? The sleeveen will receive my vitriol for this." His gaze darted to the door with narrowed eyes and a full-blown scowl on his face. He touched her arm and called out to Labrese. "Thanks for your advice. Talk to you later."

The boatman waved and returned to his work.

Brice took her hand and slipped it through his bent arm, patting it furiously. His gaze darted to and fro, a scowl on his face. "Let's get out of here. This is no place for a lady. And be assured, I'll report this matter at once."

Devyn shook her head, sniffling back her fears. "No. Please don't. I'm all right. Just had a fright, 'tis all." If Falan got fired, without a doubt, she'd somehow receive his wrath and probably more.

"Aye, well the eejit better stay clear of you—and me!" His face turned nearly scarlet, and his voice quivered with anger.

She tried to calm him. "I'm all right. I'm just glad he's down here and not at the castle."

When plump, warm raindrops fell on their faces, Brice glanced up at the darkening sky. "Let's go back through the tunnel." But as he turned toward the hallway where Falan and his friends had fled, she hesitated. Brice gave her hand a squeeze. "You're safe with me, Devyn. They'll not harm you as long as I have breath in my body. Do you want to talk about it?"

Devyn shook her head and then laid it on his strong bicep. Just for a second. She was safe.

She looked up at him, and he nodded, but a pained expression masked his handsome features. "I'm here if you do. He'll not treat you badly on my watch. Ever. I'm sorry I wasn't there for you."

"But you were. At least, when I needed it most."

He gave her a slight smile, and they began their trek back toward the castle. When the tunnel took a sharp turn to the right, a huge black cat came pouncing out of the shadows with an alarming *meow*. Both of them jumped, but Brice quickly relaxed and grinned, addressing the animal.

"TomTom, you fool cat. What are you doing in here? Staying dry and chasing critters, I 'spect."

Devyn blinked as he bent down and petted the monstrous black feline that must weigh well over twenty pounds. "He's the biggest cat I've ever seen!"

Brice chuckled. "He's well fed, I'll give you that. Catches every critter on the island. I've only ever seen one small muskrat my entire time here, and that was in the storage room where the cat's not allowed. So TomTom's fine work gives you one less thing to worry your pretty head about."

Warmth enveloped her like a gentle breeze. She'd never had someone—especially a handsome man—seem to care for her as Brice did. Except her father. And with that thought returned the demons, tormenting her again. Her stomach churned, and she swallowed the bile that threatened to embarrass her.

The wall. Where was her wall?

Devyn wrung her hands and looked toward the castle. "I need to get back to my duties. The laundry must be done by now."

Brice straightened and assessed her with his head tilted to one side. "But ... why? The missus tasked me to show you around. I've not finished my tour."

"Surely, she didn't expect us to be gone this long. People might talk. I *must* go."

Brice grabbed her hand. "Devyn, please. Wait. Whatever is the matter?"

"I need to get back, sir. Please." By now, she was nearly undone, and she could hear it in the squeaky tremble of her voice. She sounded like a frightened child, and she felt like one too.

Brice threw up his hands in defeat. "All right. But let me walk you back. There are bats in the tunnels, especially during a rain, though they are usually asleep during the day."

"Bats? I hate bats!" She grabbed his arm and pulled him in the direction of the castle.

"Slow down, my wee fawn, or we'll both end up in a tumble. Then they *will* talk!" With a wink, Brice pulled her to a normal gait.

Devyn asked what she'd contemplated for days. "Why ... why do you call me 'fawn'?"

Brice stared at her intently, searching her face. "When I was but a wee laddie back in Ireland, I happened upon a newly born fawn in the blackberry brambles just behind my cottage. I watched that timid, trembling creature find her footing and, in time, grow into a strong doe. She was the most beautiful thing I'd ever seen, but by springtime, the doe had run off with a handsome buck, off to claim her future."

Confused, Devyn furrowed her brow.

Brice sighed, shrugging his shoulders. "You just, well, remind me of that marvelous creature."

"But I'm not fragile. I try to be strong. Always."

His gentle hand on her cheek warmed her skin, and a cocoon of butterflies seemed to burst within her. If only she could stop time, right here and now, forever. "I know you try, but you don't always have to try so hard." He let out a ragged breath.

"Oh, but I do." Devyn took a step back and tried to cool her cheeks with the palms of her hands. Her gaze drifted to the wall, and she stopped short. She pointed to a small spot near the floor where a piece of the plaster had fallen off. "Look. What is that?"

They both drew closer and crouched. Writing? A little blurred but still readable. Brice read it aloud. "In the tea garden."

"What do you make of that?" She bit her lip, perplexed but curious.

"I have no idea. The tea garden is off the Indian Path, down toward the west side of the island." He pointed to the western wall and then shrugged his shoulders as they stood up again. "It's a mystery to me. Strange things can happen on an island, especially one named Dark Island. Maybe someone buried treasure and is informing his accomplice? Maybe someone is meeting a sweetheart there?" He grinned at the notion.

But she wasn't amused. "Do *you* meet special someones while here on the island?"

Brice scowled as if she had socked him in the gut. "What are you insinuating, Devyn? Why would you say such a thing?"

Wishing she could take back the stinging suggestion, she stepped back. In her heart, she knew he'd never do something improper. Would he? He'd been so friendly to her. More friendly than anyone had ever been. Then they'd uncovered not one mysterious message together, but two. Could he have anything to do with those? "I … nothing. I only supposed, well, after the note you found on the staircase yesterday …"

He surveyed her face, apparently not remembering. "What note?" Then it seemed to dawn on him. "Oh, the sheet of paper you so quickly shoved in your pocket? What does that have to do with me?"

Slowly, she pulled it out of her pocket and handed it to him. When Brice read it, he laughed. "And you think 'M' is me? Not on your life, dear girl. Sofia tries to entangle everyone in her scheming webs, but she and I barely have a working relationship, despite the fact that she serves Mrs. Bourne and I serve Mr. Bourne. Besides, there are several *M's* on the island, especially on Reid's crew. But she's up to no good, I'll give you that."

CHAPTER 7

The next day, as Devyn washed her breakfast plate, Mrs. VanLeer bid her to follow her. "Mr. Bourne is off on a fishing trip today, so it's a good day to do a thorough cleaning of his office."

Devyn wiped her hands on a towel and turned. "Yes, ma'am. But where is it? I haven't been there since Brice toured me around the first day I was here."

"Of course." Mrs. VanLeer pointed to the secret passageway. "The Round Room is this way." She led her up the stairs to the second floor. The office was just off the south corner of the living room. The missus paused in the doorway, smiling, cocking her head, and resting her chin on her right hand. "These turret rooms are so charming. This office, the two round bathrooms, and even the dungeon."

"I never imagined such things would be in a home." Devyn chewed her lip, fearing impertinence.

The missus blinked and chuckled, then stepped out of the way to let Devyn go inside. "Sorry, but I do tend to get carried away with this magical place." Her grin gave away a slight embarrassment, but just as quickly, she returned to her professional demeanor. She went over to one of the windows and looked out. "What a spectacular view of the St. Lawrence, don't you think?"

Devyn nodded, but she didn't look out the window.

"Be sure to clean everything in here. It's perplexing how, after all our efforts when we opened the castle, the dust and spiders seem to constantly return." Mrs. VanLeer huffed as she pushed back the heavy tan drapes, sending dust flying. She pointed to the ceiling. "See all those cobwebs?"

The windows had a plethora of spider webs on them, and several spiders were alive and working. Devyn shuddered.

The missus touched her arm. "Don't worry. None are poisonous."

Devyn stifled a moan. "Thank you." Then she glanced at the desk. "Dare I move the papers?"

"Yes, but put everything back exactly as it was. Mr. Bourne is meticulous about his office. And when you dust the antler chandelier, please be gentle. It's designed to be powered with both gas and electricity, and we don't want to damage it."

Devyn gazed at the interesting light fixture with both admiration and trepidation. "Of course. It's magnificent, and I'll be careful. I won't get a shock, will I?"

Mrs. VanLeer shook her head. "No. It's switched off and safe. The windows need cleaning too. Any questions?"

"No, ma'am." Devyn smiled and curtsied, ready to get to work. "Thank you for this opportunity to work here. It's a grand castle, to be sure."

Mrs. VanLeer quirked a brow and smiled. "And I had the distinct impression that you were none too happy to be here. Well, carry on, then." She turned on her heel and left the room, leaving the door slightly ajar.

Devyn reflected on the missus' comment. Yes, she had been frank about her dislike of the river and working on Dark Island. Had Brice shared her thoughts with others? If so, he would get an earful, to be sure. But she had to admit that the castle was growing on her, and the river wasn't quite as distasteful as she had thought. She walked over to the window and, for once, tried to admire the view without her sieve of bitterness marring it.

Sparkling sunshine dancing on the tiny waves.

Birds swooping and soaring on the breeze.

Boats traveling along the main channel of the mighty river.

And beyond, the many tiny islands dotting it.

It all made a rather pretty picture.

She closed her eyes and whispered a prayer. "If you can, Lord, take my pain, my hatred, my fear, and wash them away with the current below." Could He do that?

Shaking herself from her melancholy, Devyn glanced around the circular room. It wasn't huge, maybe twelve feet in diameter. The walls were the same heavy granite that covered the outside of the castle, roughly grouted but somehow fitting for a gentleman's office. The room had two desks, two typewriters, and a huge safe.

She tentatively went up to the safe and ran her fingers over the gold letters on the door, *F. G. Bourne*, and above it *Herring-Hall Marvin Safe Co.* in smaller letters. Devyn's heart skipped a beat. The safe was … open? Why? What should she do? Someone might accuse her of opening it, and then what?

Withdrawing her hand, she stepped back and turned away. She bit her lip as she glanced over her shoulder at the small, dark cavity before picking up her cleaning cloth and avoiding the predicament altogether. She would decide what to do about the safe later.

Where to start her cleaning? Spiders. They had to go first. She took her broom and covered it with a cloth, using it as a weapon to chase away every eight-legged intruder. She stomped on those that fell to the floor and scurried away from one that was intent on getting into her hair. Dangling from a fine web, the spider seemed to dance in midair, chasing her like a miniature bully. She swatted at the creature, squealed once, and finally triumphed over it, squashing it until it was pulverized into nothing.

Once the spiders and their webs were eradicated, she turned to the dusting. A large wooden letter holder stood about three feet high on a second desk, which she decided belonged to Mr. Bourne's assistant or secretary, whomever that was. She counted the cubbyholes—one hundred—and dusted every one of them as well as the top and sides, careful to replace the dozens of papers in each used cubby.

She hummed a tune as she worked and turned to the desk and the clutter on it, careful to replace each item exactly. Would Mr. Bourne really notice if an item was an inch or two off, especially if it wasn't his desk? Shrugging her shoulders, she glanced over at the safe again. How could someone so meticulous leave it unlatched?

Suddenly, Brice walked into the room and stopped mid-step. "Oh, I didn't know you were here. Top of the morning to you, my bonnie lass! 'Tis a crackin' day, aye?" His face flushed and his ears turned pink as he glanced around the stone-walled room. He whistled when his gaze fell on the desk she had cleaned. "Thank you. I had intended to get rid of those spiders myself but haven't had the chance. And my desk is immaculate. Right fine job you're doing, Devyn. Mr. Bourne will be pleased as a peach pie, he will."

Devyn wiped her furrowed brow, gesturing toward the desk. "So that's your desk? Are you his secretary too?"

Brice laughed that deep baritone laugh she enjoyed so much. "His assistant, thank you. I do a bit of everything. Since Mr. Bourne retired from the Singer Sewing Machine Company, I'm not only his valet but also an apprentice businessman of sorts. He says he sees promise in me, and I aim to meet his expectations by learning the business and all he will show me."

"What a wonderful opportunity for you, Brice." But so far beyond her lowly station.

He grinned, shrugging his shoulders. "Aye. I do whatever he needs and relish the variety of work, from doing books to putting on his cufflinks. I want to be like him one day—a wealthy, successful businessman and a fine, upstanding Christian gentleman." His eyes took on a misty sheen.

"I have no doubt you will be." And his noble sentiments brought her attention back to the safe. Should she alert Brice to it being opened? But what if he accused her of opening it?

Brice followed the direction of her gaze, and she sucked in a worried breath, biting her lip. Her heart raced.

He harrumphed and opened the vault wide. "Blathers! I did leave it open. I meant to close it last night after Mr. Bourne had me fetch some papers."

At his declaration of responsibility, Devyn whooshed out the breath she held, came up behind him, and peeked inside. Piles of papers and stacks of money. And what appeared to be a golden cup and a trophy of some sort.

"What's that stack of white cloth?" Devyn asked, pointing.

Brice touched the fine material reverently. "Christening gowns from his four children who died as wee mites." He glanced out the window. "If I recall correctly, Frederick was eight, Louisa was five, Helen was just two, and Kenneth was seven. I think he still mourns them."

Devyn put her hand to her chest. "How tragic! Mr. and Mrs. Bourne spoke of Louisa, but … are you all right?"

Brice blinked, appearing to be lost in his own thoughts. "I worried all night about this safe being open. Couldn't recall if I failed to shut and lock it. I nearly got up to check on it but fell back to sleep. I'm just glad we didn't have a pirate invasion during the wee hours." He glanced at her and grinned, relief apparent in his sparkling eyes. Riffling through the papers, he retrieved one and read it, mumbling to himself. Then he closed the safe's door, pulled the lock arm down, and spun the combination wheel several times. "I'm just glad Mr. Bourne didn't find it open."

"Indeed." Stepping back, she murmured the single word in a low tone.

He snapped a glance at her, his eyes narrowed before they grew large with alarm. "You won't tell, will you? About the safe, I mean."

Devyn raised her right hand. "Never. I shall never be the one to share personal information. I'm not that kind of girl." She paused as her previous concerns came to mind. "But may I ask you something, please?"

"Anything, lass." Brice blew out a breath and relaxed.

"Did you tell Mrs. VanLeer that I didn't want to be here and that I hated the river?"

Brice's forehead wrinkled. "Nae. I wouldn't do that. But I have been talking to the Father about it." He looked to the floor, his face twisting. "It pains me to see you hurting so, Devyn."

Devyn's eyes brimmed with tears at the tender compassion of this handsome man. Her "thank you" came out as little more than a whisper.

Brice took her hand in his large one and squeezed it. "I'm sorry, but I must get this letter in the mailbag before the postal boat comes. But know this, I will never betray your trust."

The lump in her throat forbade her to comment, so she simply nodded. He seemed to understand and bid her farewell before exiting the room.

After composing herself, Devyn returned to dusting both chairs and typewriters, running her fingers over Brice's keys, knowing he had touched them many times. The memory of his kind words and admission of praying for her touched her deeply. If only God would give her such a man to be her husband one day. But no! She would never deserve such a fine person after she'd ...

She stomped her foot. Hard. She would not go down that path. She had work to do! She wiped down the windowsills and decided to finish Mr. Bourne's desk before fetching some vinegar water to clean the windows.

The surface held a stack of papers and a book as well as an inkwell and a fine pen. She carefully began to dust, whispering a prayer of thanks for Brice's visit and their conversation. But the open journal drew her attention, and she couldn't help but read the entry.

> *I regret that I deeply offended Frederic Remington, a great artist and my neighbor, when I built The Towers. He painted a picture of it but told others that the castle spoiled the neighborhood. Since his fine Ingleneuk Island is so close to my Dark Island and just across the shipping channel, had I known that he cherished the quiet of his secluded fortress of rest so passionately, I would have gone to him and beseeched his forgiveness and friendship before he died last year. Forgive me, Lord, as I heard about this too late to help. I mourn that the construction of my castle disrupted his personal retreat from the world and ...*

"What are you doing, miss?" Mrs. Bourne stood in the doorway, arms folded, scowling at her. She tilted her head and pursed her lips.

Devyn shrank back, ashamed that she'd fallen to the temptation of reading someone else's journal, especially after she had vowed not to betray Brice. Instead, she'd betrayed Mr. Bourne!

"I ... I am so, so sorry." Devyn stared at her shoes. For the longest time, she stood in silence, knowing that the missus still stared at her, angry, disappointed, or worse. Would she be punished?

Dismissed? Her stomach churned until bile filled her mouth.

The door gently clicked closed.

Mrs. Bourne came near and touched her shoulder. "Look at me, please."

Devyn glanced at Mrs. Bourne's eyes—sad, disappointed, but not angry.

"Temptation and enticements allure us at every turn, dear girl, but we must master them." The missus gently took her by the arm and bid her to sit in Brice's chair as she sat in her husband's. Mrs. Bourne regarded the journal entry Devyn had read.

"My husband is a wise but tender man, and he spends much of his office time discussing his cares and concerns with the Almighty." She tapped the journal with her finger. "He would not mind that you read this, but it was not yours to read."

"I know, Mrs. Bourne, and I am truly sorry. I should never have looked at it while I was dusting." Devyn's voice cracked at her confession.

Mrs. Bourne smiled. "I imagine it must have been difficult to dust the journal and the desk without reading it. You're forgiven. Just don't go looking for temptation from now on."

At Mrs. Bourne's kindness, Devyn choked back a sob, and a tear slid down her cheek. She swiped it away with her sleeve and bit her lip.

Mrs. Bourne rolled her husband's desk chair up to her and cleared her throat. She took Devyn's hand and patted it. "There, there. Let's move forward. But I must ask you, have you seen anything else I should know about?"

Devyn gazed into her kind, motherly face. "Yes."

Mrs. Bourne's expression held only gentleness, and it gave her the courage to go on.

"When I was dusting the library, I came across a love letter of sorts. I wasn't snooping, really I wasn't. But when I dusted a book, it opened to the letter."

Mrs. Bourne touched her cheek. "Are you all right? You're as white as a sheet." She wrapped Devyn in a hug, tight against her ample bosom, and stroked her hair. Suddenly, she pulled away.

"Wait! Was it quite old and unsigned?"

Devyn nodded. "Yes."

"Oh my! If it's what I think it is, I've been searching for that for ever so long. I've looked for it at Indian Neck Hall and, well, just everywhere." Mrs. Bourne's face grew decades younger in a single moment, and her eyes danced with delight. Like a young schoolgirl, she grabbed Devyn's hands and pulled her toward the door. "Show me where it is, please, my dear girl!"

Devyn giggled at her excitement. "Surely. I'd be glad to."

Together, the two descended the stairs, Mrs. Bourne fairly dragging her along. When they got to the library, Devyn searched for the book.

"Hmmm … they all look so similar." She riffled through dozens of books as she tried to remember which volume the letter was in.

"Don't worry. If it's here, we'll find it." Mrs. Bourne stared at the shelf expectantly.

Devyn continued to search, opening several books to find only bound pages until she came to a pale, linen-covered volume that appeared to have something inside. "Here it is!" She carefully withdrew the paper and handed it to the missus.

Mrs. Bourne grinned so widely that her smile lines nearly covered her cheeks. She opened it and scanned the fragile page. "This is it! Thank you ever so much. It was the first letter Mr. Bourne wrote to me after we were married." Apparently realizing what Devyn had read, the missus turned a deep shade of scarlet and held the letter to her breast. She glanced at Devyn and shrugged her shoulders. "I pray that you have such a loving husband one day, miss."

Now it was Devyn's turn to blush. She curtsied. "Thank you, ma'am. I appreciate your well wishes … and your forgiveness."

Mrs. Bourne nodded and waved a matronly hand. "Off with you, or Mrs. VanLeer might wonder where you are."

Returning to the Round Room, Devyn found Mrs. VanLeer waiting, eyes flashing as they took her in. "Where have you been, Devyn? I had expected to find you at your duties."

"I'm sorry, missus, but Mrs. Bourne asked me to fetch her something."

A shadow of shame instantly passed across the missus' countenance. "Excuse me. Of course, Mrs. Bourne takes precedence. Always." She cleared her throat and surveyed the room.

Devyn stepped toward her. "I still have the windows to clean, but as soon as I fetch the vinegar water, I'll have it done in a jiffy."

"You've done a fine job of it." Mrs. VanLeer waved her arm. "Carry on. And excuse my outburst, please. I'm having one of my headaches again."

"I'm sorry. I'll pray for you as I work." Devyn interlaced her fingers as she spoke.

The missus rubbed the back of her neck. "Thank you. We'll talk again at lunch."

Devyn smiled and curtsied again, wishing she could hug the woman. As she fetched the cleaning solution and then washed the windows, she reflected on these two ladies who had extended her mercy. Her mother had never given her such a gift, ever. And her brother certainly lacked the skill.

How was it that these two fine women of stature found it so easy to exhibit grace? Oh how she wished she could be like them— caring, kind, but skilled in their own right. To be a true Christian woman who cared about her fellow man. She thanked God for the graciousness and forgiveness she had received and prayed that, one day, her wish might come true.

And while she was at it, she added one more wish to her list. For a loving husband, just as Mrs. Bourne had said. She swallowed hard and blinked. What if that man was Brice?

CHAPTER 8

During the staff supper, Mahlon, the butler, announced that three of the Bourne children would be visiting. "The family received a wire notifying us that Howard, May, and Marian will be coming up from Cooperstown in their touring car. They should be here tomorrow, and Labrese will be ready to pick them up in the launch."

Devyn searched the faces of her new acquaintances to see what they thought about the news. All of them smiled. Well, Sofia sort of smiled. After Mahlon gave them some general instructions about the visit and warned them about how busy they would be and how they all needed to be flexible, he whisked Mrs. VanLeer away for a private discussion.

Devyn turned to Reagan. "Tell me about each of them, please. I want to be well-informed."

Sofia rolled her eyes in a manner that Devyn couldn't fail to notice. She chose to ignore it.

Reagan swallowed and wiped her mouth. "Howard is the baby, the youngest of the four sons. He's eighteen, but he escorts his sisters on all their road trips."

Brice nodded. "I like Howard—a lot. He's a jolly good, car-driving, ever-moving lad who loves to travel, race boats, and enjoy life to the fullest."

Sofia scowled before adding her two cents. "Howard may be the baby,"—she glared at Reagan—"but he's very mature. To be tasked with chaperoning his older sisters says a lot about his potential."

Brice and Reagan snickered, glancing away from Sofia as Nellie excused herself. "I'm off, then. See you upstairs, ladies."

Sofia slapped her hands on the table and stood. "Well! I'm done here too." She gathered her plate and cup, leaving in a huff.

Brice and Reagan both sheepishly grinned and shrugged their shoulders. Reagan chuckled. "For some reason, Howard has always been Sofia's favorite."

Devyn set down her fork. "And the girls? What about them?"

Reagan smiled. "Oh yes. The girls are May and Marian. May is twenty-nine, and Marian's twenty-eight."

"And?" Devyn waved her hand in a circular motion, smiling and bidding her to elaborate.

Brice laughed. "Patience, lass." He glanced at Reagan, who cocked her head for him to continue. "May is the belle of the ball, so to speak. A Mr. Ralph Straussburger, who graduated from the Naval Academy, has been courting her, so we'll likely see a wedding celebration next year."

Reagan continued the family description. "Marian loves her dogs, especially Russian wolfhounds. She's content with a quiet, simple life, except for when she shows the dogs."

Brice lifted a finger to add another fact. "And their sister, Florence, is twenty-four, but she's married, with child, and has an adorable wee lad, Anson. She's a real beauty and a serious and avid reader. You remind me of her, Devyn."

Her face flamed. She glanced at Reagan, who grinned. Devyn quickly took a mouthful of beans and chewed ever so slowly, buying a chance to think. She kept her eyes on her plate, grateful Reagan was the only other person left at the table by then. How should she respond to that comment? Did he really think that highly of her? Surely not. But she had to answer somehow, so she barely whispered, "Thank you," and darted her hand up to tuck a stray curl behind her ear.

As was the case for the rest of the staff, the remainder of the evening and all the next morning found Devyn scurrying around the castle preparing it for the arrival of the Bourne children. She changed the bedding and tidied the second-floor bedrooms, and when she went up to Marjorie's room, she was surprised to see an extra bed in there. Which girl would share the room with her youngest sister?

As she made the two beds, she pondered what it would be like to have sisters—or any siblings who were close and enjoyed being together. She only had brothers who seemed to dislike her just as much as her mother did. Maybe more. Falan surely did. She swallowed a lump and turned her thoughts to the Bourne sisters.

She had only met the vivacious Marjorie a few times, but her interactions with her had always been pleasant. Although Reagan told her the youngest Bourne daughter was just twenty years old, the same age as herself, she seemed so much older. Marjorie had her own speedboat and was always out on the river, even during the day, driving her boat. Fast. She was quite the modern woman.

Just as Devyn put the final touches on the room, voices drifted up the stairwell.

She recognized Marjorie's gregarious laugh. "Oh, May! It's so good to see you again. And how is your charming Mr. Straussburger? You do make such a lovely couple. Do I hear wedding bells?"

"He's just enchanting, Hooley, and his business is going gangbusters. I anticipate that we will marry next year."

Hooley? Why was May calling Marjorie "Hooley"?

Devyn heard the sisters coming up the wooden stairs from the third floor, so she whisked out the door, down the passageway stairs, and through a secret door on the second floor. She wiped her brow. When did the three of them get here? She hadn't detected a boat nearing the island or been told they had arrived. Pleased she'd completed her tasks, she wove through the dining room and down the pantry stairs to the kitchen.

Mrs. VanLeer startled her as she opened the door. "There you are. Everything spit-spot upstairs? They are here already." She gestured to the kitchen staff, scurrying around like a whirlwind. "I'm just glad we're almost ready. Mrs. Bourne expects a rather formal luncheon for her children on their first day here."

Devyn nodded. "The rooms are ready. But please, missus, might I ask a question?"

The missus quirked a brow and nodded. "Of course."

"Miss May called Miss Marjorie 'Hooley.' Why is that?"

Mrs. VanLeer chuckled. "Well, now, I don't rightly know. That's just been her nickname since she was a wee thing." She shrugged. "Now for the luncheon, I need you to be the Watch. But afterward, the missus has requested that you help Reagan with the lady's maid duties for the girls while they are here."

Devyn sucked in a breath. "Me? But … I don't know anything about such work."

Mrs. VanLeer waved away her concerns. "Don't worry. Reagan will show you, and the girls are quite used to the casual and simple. On their excursion here and during their time in Cooperstown, they didn't even have one lady's maid attend them. Can you imagine?" The missus gave an expressive roll of her eyes. "It will be good training for you, Devyn. Now gather some lunch and take it up to the Watch. The family will be at the table quite soon, I suspect."

Devyn curtsied and gathered a lunch of bread, cheese, and a small chunk of ham. She poured some water into a tin cup and took her meal up to the Watch, happy to have a few moments to eat it in the quiet.

Soon Mr. and Mrs. Bourne entered the dining room arm in arm, dressed as if they were attending a formal dinner. A woman's laughter sounded in the hallway, so she strained to see who it was.

"Daddy! Mother! It's so good to see you. Did you get my letters?"

Mr. and Mrs. Bourne each took a turn kissing their daughter on the cheek and wrapping her in a hug. "Yes, dearest Marian, we did. It sounded like you had a lovely time in Cooperstown."

Marian's penetrating voice was loud and strong, so Devyn could hear her clearly. "The guesthouse we stayed in was quite lovely, though I dearly missed seeing Mrs. Clark, God rest her departed soul."

Mrs. Bourne patted her hand as she led her daughter to the table. "Come, child, and sit. The others should be here soon. Tell me more. Is everyone well? Is the town as enchanting as ever?"

Marian took a sip of her water before answering. "Yes, Cooperstown is beautiful, and Otsego Lake is still just as pristine."

Mr. Bourne sat back in his chair. "I do miss Alfred. Mr. Clark was such a good friend. If it weren't for him taking a chance on me as a young man, I'd never have become the president of Singer Sewing Machine Company. I'd never have supervised the completion of the Dakota apartment building. I'd never have become a millionaire, and we wouldn't have this fine hunting lodge."

Mrs. Bourne giggled. "So true. But this is so much more than a simple hunting lodge, dearest husband. I love this place more and more every year."

Mr. Bourne reached over and kissed her soundly in front of Marian and all the staff. He said something, but Devyn couldn't hear him. What intimacies had he shared?

She sighed at the tender scene. She'd never seen her parents kiss, never seen anyone kiss before, for that matter. What might that be like? What a sheltered world she came from!

Marjorie's voice pulled Devyn from her thoughts as she swept into the dining room, her elbow linked through that of another young lady, with a young man following close behind. Marjorie nearly squealed with excitement. "Mother. Daddy. They're all here!"

Giggles and a hearty laugh accompanied the siblings to the table. After a round of affectionate hugs and kisses from their parents, they all drew up chairs as the staff began to serve them.

Mr. Bourne turned to the other daughter. "May, how do you fair, dear girl?"

May's back was to Devyn, but her dark hair danced as she spoke. Thankfully, her voice carried clearly. "I'm fair as rain, Daddy, but guess what? We're actually here to celebrate you! We read in the papers about a girl out in Washington, a Sonora Dodd, who arranged for several churches to celebrate the first Father's Day with sermons touting the praises of fatherhood."

The young man sitting at the end of the table—who had to be Howard—joined in. "Yes, the article said she wanted to honor her father because he was a single parent of six children and because, last year, the local government had established several Mother's Day celebrations, but Sonora and her siblings had no mother to celebrate."

May finished, "So we want to have our own special Father's Day celebration for you."

Marjorie chimed in. "Isn't that just the loveliest idea, Mother?"

Mrs. Bourne beamed, clasping her hands to her chest. "Indeed, it is! And I say *hurrah* to a grand celebration."

All four children clapped heartily as Mr. Bourne stood and bowed until he almost landed his chin in his plate. "Thank you, dear family. I am honored to be your daddy!"

Devyn laughed aloud and quickly covered her mouth, hoping they hadn't heard her. But, of course, there was far too much merriment around the table for them to hear her high up in her perch.

She continued to watch for any needs, but Mahlon and Nellie and Brice seemed to have everything well in hand. They served the soup and then the main course of fish with potatoes and vegetables.

"What is this sauce, Mother?" Marian smacked her lips as she savored the orange condiment.

"It's called Thousand Islands Dressing, my dear. Isn't it yummy?"

Howard took a hearty mouthful and nodded. "It's quite good. Where did it come from?"

Mr. Bourne answered. "It's a great story, really. Remember George Boldt, who built Boldt Castle on Heart Island near Alexandria Bay?"

Howard nodded. "Of course, Daddy. It nearly rivals The Towers. Nearly."

The entire group chuckled, and Mr. Bourne continued. "Yes, well, as you know, he used to manage the prestigious Waldorf-Astoria Hotel in New York City. His friend and the maître d'hôtel, an Oscar Tschirky, accompanied Mr. Boldt to the castle several times. Once, while on the Boldt's yacht, Oscar found out the crew had left the salad dressing behind, so he concocted this one. Boldt liked it so well that he named it Thousand Islands Dressing and began serving it in all his hotels, or so it is said, anyway. Since then, it's become quite popular."

Marjorie smiled. "What's in it? I cannot tell."

"I don't know." Mrs. Bourne turned to Mahlon. "Do you know,

sir?"

"I'm sorry, missus, I don't." Mahlon motioned for Brice, apparently to go and find out. Brice left the room, and Devyn debated if she should go too, so she ran down the stairs and nearly bumped into him.

"Steady, lass. You'll be breaking someone's nose with your hurriedness."

Devyn giggled. "Sorry. I wasn't sure if I should assist with the matter. I don't seem to be much help as the Watch since you all have things so well in hand."

Brice grinned. "I believe you were sent to be the Watch so you could learn about the personalities of the Bourne children more than to watch the water glasses."

"Oh." Devyn tucked a stray hair behind her ear.

"Come with me." Brice wiggled his finger, and she followed him to find Cook. "Excuse me, Cook. The missus would like to know how the Thousand Islands Dressing is made."

Cook furrowed her brow and wiped her hands on her apron. "It's easy enough. Mayonnaise is mixed with a few tablespoons of sweet pickle relish, ketchup, cider vinegar, and a finely chopped egg. Then we add a few teaspoons of minced onion, sugar, salt, and pepper. The secret is to make it the day before so the flavors mix well."

He bowed slightly. "Thank you, Cook."

The plump older woman clucked her tongue as she turned back to the stove. "Don't know what they want that recipe fer. None of 'em cook."

Devyn and Brice laughed at her comment. Brice waved her back up the steps. "Enjoy the show, my bonnie lass. I just hope I can remember the recipe."

"You will. You have a keen mind, Brice." She smiled as he winked before leaving the room.

As she climbed the stairs back to the Watch, her pulse quickened at the sound of one of the women crying. Mrs. Bourne.

"... I still can't think about Cooperstown without remembering that terrible July when our firstborn died there. Poor, sweet

Frederick. He was not yet nine."

"But in those short years he was with us, did he not bring us much love and joy, my sweet?" Mr. Bourne took out his handkerchief and wiped his wife's tears, while their children looked on.

May nodded and turned toward Marian. "We remember him, Daddy. He was a good boy."

Marian agreed. "And we remember little Louisa and Helen too."

Sadness crept over the room so deep Devyn could feel it all the way up into the passageway. She prayed for the Bourne family, that God would heal their hearts … and heal her heart too.

Howard stood and clapped his hands. "All right, family. Let's turn to brighter thoughts, shall we? Sisters, we have a party to plan!"

As if the sun came out and pushed away the storm that passed through the dining room, Howard turned the mood to celebration, just like that. How ever did he do it? Maybe Brice was right about this young man being the life of the party. But was Sofia correct in her assessment of him too? He was quite handsome with his sandy brown hair and steely blue eyes. She could see them when he turned toward her, and they danced when he spoke.

Mrs. Bourne laughed softly. "Leave it to my Howard to chase away the gloom. I do love you, son."

"Thanks, Mother. We're so glad to be home. How about taking a nice, long boat ride?"

Marjorie clasped her hands together. "You know I'm always up for a spin on the river. We can take out the *Moike*, and I'll drive. Or do you want to join us, Daddy?"

"No, no. Your mother and I have had quite the excitement for now. We'll rest while you young people go and play. That way we can fully enjoy your company this evening."

Marjorie smiled, addressing her siblings. "I'm going to enter the local boat races with the *Moike* this summer. My speedboat is proving to be one of the fastest on the river, and I intend to beat all the men. Prepare for the ride of your lives, dear siblings."

May laughed. "Our little sister's such a tomboy. Next, you'll be fishing with the men."

"What would be wrong with that? I love fishing." Marjorie feigned offense but took her sister's arm as they left the room.

The family continued to banter, but Devyn couldn't hear what they were saying from where she stood. What would it be like to be a part of such a loving family? She had no idea, but she'd like to find out.

CHAPTER 9

After the luncheon, Devyn was sent to Miss Marjorie's room. She opened the door, gulping a bit of air following her exertion. "My, but this is quite a climb."

Reagan turned to her and glanced into the passageway. "Yes, five stories up."

Devyn wrapped her arms around her waist, scrunching up her face. "Oh, Reagan. I don't know if I can be a lady's maid. There's so much to learn. I'm a mere housemaid and a novice at that."

Reagan laid down her sewing and hurried to her, grasping her hands. "Stop worrying! I'm here to train you. I'll take care of Miss May along with Miss Marjorie, especially since they'll both be in this room. You'll have only Miss Marian to attend to, so no fretting." She shook a finger at her playfully. "She's ever so easygoing and doesn't worry a whit about proper social frivolities, especially here on the island. None of them do, really."

"I'm glad of that. Where do we start?"

Reagan grinned, her eyes twinkling. "At the beginning, of course."

Devyn joined her in a giggle, her tension lessening at her friend's confidence.

"Let's see." Reagan put her finger to her cheek and glanced around the room. She lifted her chin, her tone teacherly. "A lady's maid is a private servant to her mistress. In a typical day, we may bring up tea before breakfast, put the room in order, and lay out her necessities for walking, riding, or driving—two of which don't apply on an island, of course."

Devyn smiled. That she could do easily enough.

Reagan opened the chifforobe door to reveal a rainbow array of clothing. She closed the door and went to the dresser where she opened an exquisite jewelry box.

"They're beautiful." Devyn put her hand to her chest at the sight of the twinkling treasures.

Reagan nodded and continued. "A lady's maid will also care for her mistress' jewels, assist her in changing for tea, put her evening ensemble in order, assist her in dressing for dinner, and help her in undressing. Finally, a lady's maid keeps her lady's wardrobe in repair and washes the lace and fine linens." She paused to catch her breath. "Oh, and she also packs and unpacks for the mistress when traveling."

Devyn's heart sped up, and nervous perspiration tickled her skin. "It seems rather daunting."

Reagan shrugged her shoulders. "It sounds that way, but you don't do all of it every day. Basically, every day you assist her with arranging her hair, dressing, caring for her clothes, and running errands. She may even have you write letters as she dictates them. You *can* write, correct?"

Devyn bit her lip. She knew Reagan would never intentionally offend her, but it seemed that way. "Of course. After my schooling, I continued learning on my own. My teacher said I had the finest penmanship he had ever seen."

"Good. Miss Marian loves to write letters to her many friends, and I think she's even a part of a few chain letters. They're all the rage, you know. But she especially likes to correspond with her sister, Florence." Reagan gave her a knowing grin.

At the mention of Florence, Devyn's cheeks warmed. She put her hands to them.

Reagan's eyes grew wide with concern. "Did I say something wrong?"

Devyn gulped. "No. Nothing."

"Brice seems quite smitten with you, don't you think? For Florence to remind him of you, well, that's quite a compliment. I've never seen him care for someone before."

Devyn shivered at Reagan's assessment, whether out of pleasure or not, she couldn't tell. She had to change the conversation, and fast. "Tell me more about my duties, please."

Reagan shrugged and opened Miss Marjorie's chifforobe. "Just remember that you have to be flexible here on the island, for the staff is limited. Sometimes you'll serve tea or accompany Miss Marian to town or on a boat ride to the bay. But since they are only going to be here a week or two, it shouldn't be too complicated."

Devyn shook her head. "I expect there won't be many boat rides. I fear I may hinder the fun."

Reagan raised her brows as she questioned her. "Why? The Bournes have a fantastic collection of yachts and speedboats. Mr. Bourne even has an electric gondola! I consider it a magical adventure every time I'm invited along."

"I fear I'd consider it a curse, but no matter. I will serve in the capacity I am given." Devyn wrung her hands. "So to whom do I answer?"

Her friend tilted her pretty head. "Well, that's a bit tricky. You'll answer to Miss Marian while she's here, but technically, your superior is still Mrs. VanLeer. But because Sofia serves as the senior lady's maid, she is above you in station and will try and boss you around. Don't let her."

Devyn let out a very unladylike grunt and rolled her eyes. "That woman is always giving herself airs."

Reagan laughed lightly. "So true. She's a bitter old maid who was jilted at the altar, or so I've been told. She likes to make people's lives miserable like her own. No matter. The reality is that you'll be an in-between maid, answering to Miss Marian when she needs you and Mrs. VanLeer when she doesn't."

"But I know nothing about high society dress and hairstyles. Whatever shall I do?"

Reagan gave her a scolding glance. "You are worrying too much. I'll be happy to do Miss Marian's hair, and you can watch and learn. As for the dress, I'll give you a primer right now."

"Oh, that would be wonderful, thank you." Anything she could do to better prepare herself would be welcome.

Folding her hands at her waist, Reagan nodded. "The Gibson

Girl S-shaped figure may still be fashionable, but the Bourne women tend to be on the cutting edge of freedom. Back on Long Island, they may look the part with their upswept hair, floor-length skirts, high-collared blouses, and small waists. But they seldom wear corsets anymore, especially here on the island."

"So what am I to do? If you do her hair, and her dress is more relaxed, I fear I may be idle quite often."

Devyn's nerves calmed again at the sound of Reagan's laugh.

"It's like a dance, really. You simply adjust to her needs, that's all."

Reagan went to the closet and proceeded to show her each of the different styles of clothing. "Normally, society women are expected to change their outfits three or four times a day, so they often divide their day into what they need to wear. In the morning, they don coordinated blouses and skirts for making or receiving social calls. In the early afternoon, they often change into tea dresses. Then they may change again for a more formal dinner and sometimes again for after-dinner activities. But on the island, things are different, and they may even wear tea dresses the entire day. Marian will let you know. Follow her lead."

Devyn smiled as she gazed at the beautiful pastel rainbow of dresses and then touched an elaborately trimmed blue gown. "Do they wear these fine things on their boat rides? Do they know how to swim?"

Reagan nodded as she fingered through Marjorie's wardrobe. "They all like to swim. There's a private swimming beach on the far side of the island, and it's quite fun to see the siblings play in the water together." She pulled out a navy-blue dress. "Here's her bathing costume." She even showed Devyn a hat that matched the blouse-bloomer outfit.

"It's lovely. My best dress isn't this fine!" Devyn touched the soft fabric. "Oh, it looks like there's a tear here." She pointed to the hem of the blouse.

"Oh, thank you. You have sharp eyes. I'll fix that today." Reagan gave her a sheepish glance.

Devyn smiled wide. "I did quite a bit of mending and sewing

in Chippewa Bay, even for pay. But there weren't enough jobs, and that's why I came here to work."

Reagan took the blouse from her and set it on the bed. "I presume that you'll enjoy your time here. I'm sure glad you've come."

"Thank you, Reagan. I'm happy to know you."

After a moment of silence, Reagan turned back to the closet and continued. "The Bourne women have only the best. After all, they live in Oakdale on the famous Long Island and frequent New York City high society affairs. Here it is much different, and I think they rather enjoy the reprieve from it all." She closed the closet door and turned to Devyn. "Before the missus tasks you with another job, let's go and unpack Miss Marian's trunk and see what she brought."

She followed Reagan's lead as they descended to the guest room where Miss Marian was staying and began unpacking her trunks. Reagan sorted through her things, placing them in piles on the bed. "As I suspected, Miss Marian has brought her veiled silk hats and straw bonnets. And here are some silken undergarments." She showed Devyn the items as she pulled them from the trunk. "These cotton stockings are for day, and the embroidered silk stockings are for the evening."

Devyn nodded, trying to file the information in her mind.

Reagan reached deep into the trunk. "And look, she even brought her bustle, which she likely wore in Cooperstown. But you probably won't see her in much of this unless she's invited to the Frontenac Hotel or another one of the fine Thousand Islands resorts for a party. If they do attend a formal affair, don't worry, I'll guide you."

Devyn grinned. "You read my mind. Should we even unpack all this if they'll only be here a short while?"

Reagan nodded firmly. "Yes. As a lady's maid, that's our task. We must be ready in a moment's notice for whatever is needed. At their residence on Long Island, the ladies have much more—lingerie, morning gowns, afternoon gowns, walking dresses, cycling outfits, costumes for traveling in a train or in a motor car, and elegant gowns for weddings, the theater, or holidays."

"Really? No wonder they need a personal maid. How ever did

she do it while in Cooperstown?"

"Oh, the sisters help one another. The Bourne women are quite independent. But the fancy hotels also have a lady's maid on hand to help when they need it."

Devyn contemplated such a life. "Amazing. You must work very hard when they are at their family estate."

"At Indian Neck Hall? Oh, not nearly as hard as most lady's maids. The Bourne women are fashionable but not overbearing or demanding. They aren't haughty or high-minded either. We are quite blessed to be in their employ."

Devyn stepped over to the bed filled with Marian's things, fingering the silks and satins. "It sounds like they exercise the virtues of the love chapter in Corinthians."

Reagan furrowed her brows, and then her face lit up. "You're right. I never thought of that, but they *are* a family of faith."

Once Miss Marian's things were unpacked, Mrs. VanLeer sent word for Devyn to report to her in the Great Hall. There the housekeeper pointed out the small, closet-like room just off the Great Hall. "I'm sorry to drag you away from the delights of Miss Marian's wardrobe, but I need to send you back to dusting. Start with the wine vault, and be sure to wipe every bottle. Last night's wine bottle was so dusty the butler sneezed."

Devyn curtsied, disgruntled to be pulled away from Reagan's tutelage and Marian's lovely things to clean a closet. "Yes, Mrs. VanLeer."

After the missus left, Devyn shook off her disappointment, gathered the cleaning supplies, and hurried to the wine vault. She climbed the three stone steps and opened its heavy wooden door. Just inside and to the left was a set of empty shelves. The arched stone ceiling and granite floor made it cool and comfortable, and the other walls contained hundreds of terra-cotta cubbyholes just the right size for holding wine bottles. The holes were nearly three-quarters full, and she wiped her forehead at the thought of dusting so many.

She wiped bottle after bottle, hole after hole. Now and then, she found a dead bug or stray web spinner, but she was pleased to find so few. The different labels on the bottles were interesting, some in languages she didn't know, and she considered where they all came from and how costly they might be.

As she rounded the corner to dust the final wall, she detected voices in the Great Hall. She listened, recognizing Sofia's gravelly tones.

"The local help has little skill and even less etiquette to carry out her tasks." Sofia huffed and then sighed so loud that Devyn could hear her in the wine vault. Who was she talking to?

"If anyone can teach a cow to fly, it would be you. Maybe take her under your wing and show her a thing or two?" Was that Mr. Howard? The Bourne's son? Would the old maid speak to the young master so?

"She'll not rest under my wing. Shall we catch some fresh air, sir? I would relish a stroll while your mother naps."

"Yes, I was just heading outside myself. You can catch me up on all the island gossip."

The door closed, and Devyn peeked out to find the Great Hall empty. What kind of relationship might be going on between those two? Had Sofia been talking about her? She sucked in her bottom lip, gnawing on it and the possibilities as she returned to work.

Halfway down one of the rows, she began dusting a cubby and found an old, rolled-up newsprint with something inside. She pulled it out and carefully unrolled it, the paper crinkling in her hands.

She scanned the front page. "1905?" Just then, a key fell out and clattered onto the stone floor, making her jump. A chill ran down her spine as she glanced out to the Great Hall to make sure no one had heard. Seeing no one, she read the note. "Fourth rock on the right."

Once again, she had intruded on someone's secret.

With a delicate touch, Devyn rolled up the newsprint with the note and key inside it and returned it to its place. But she studied where she had found it—three rows from the left and twelve holes up from the bottom. What could the note mean, why was it there, and who had written it?

As she continued to dust, the front door opened, then closed, with Sofia's grumbling following closely behind. Devyn couldn't hear what she said, but …

"Yes, well, you'd better go, Sofia." Brice? His voice sounded stilted, irritated.

Sofia grumbled again. "We shall see about this, young man. You may be male, but I am still your elder, sir."

Devyn hid behind the vault door. Next came the prim and proper *clip, clip, clip* of Sofia's steps and then the more masculine *clomp, clomp, clomp* of Brice's shoes, ascending the stairs and fading beyond her hearing.

She released her breath. Peace again. And here she had thought dusting in the wine cellar would prove less exciting than learning how to dress Miss Marian! It seemed nothing about The Towers was boring.

A few minutes later, the empty vault shelf opened, and Brice emerged through a secret door. Devyn jumped and lost hold of the heavy wine bottle she was dusting. It tumbled to the floor, crashing, breaking, and splashing dark red wine on her uniform and all over the wine vault that she had just cleaned. "Brice! How dare you sneak up on me like that! What kind of a hooligan are you, anyway?"

Brice blinked, appearing quite perplexed. But then his face turned hard, and his eyes narrowed to a stormy blue. His brow furrowed into a wavy line. "Excuse me! I had no idea you were in here. Mr. Bourne sent me for a bottle of wine, so I came through the passageway like I always do. And I'm no hooligan, miss!" He huffed and clamped his lips closed, working his jaw furiously.

"You should've warned me you were approaching, sir. Now look at this mess!" Devyn held her ground, too angry, embarrassed, and scared to do much else. What must that wine cost? Would it be taken out of her pay? Would she be dismissed? Because of him?

"You seem to think you're above your station, speaking to me like this. How dare you? You must never forget your place. You are but a housemaid, one of the lower in this house, to be sure." He slapped his hand to his chest, scowling at her. "I, on the other hand?

I am valet to the great master of this house."

Stunned into silence, Devyn sniffed as he grabbed a bottle of wine and hurried out of the vault and into the secret passageway, slamming the door behind him.

How dare he leave me with this mess and not even apologize!

Devyn peeked into the Great Hall, relieved that no one had caught the interchange or her breaking a bottle of Mr. Bourne's fine wine. She gathered the pieces of glass, cutting herself twice. She sucked her bleeding fingers as she hurried to fetch a bucket of water. First, she dipped her fingers into the cool water to soothe them, and then she washed the wine from her uniform hem. At least today she wore the dark gray one. She returned to the vault and removed every trace of the accident by wiping the spills off the floor, the cubbyholes, and the bottles—again.

The nerve of him! How could Brice be so nice one minute, converse with the likes of Sofia the next, and then cast such derogatory remarks at her? Her seething anger turned to painful hurt when she thought about how he had put her in her place so condescendingly. She had actually begun to think him an ally, a friend, maybe more. But no! He must be a scoundrel—just like her brother.

CHAPTER 10

Two days without speaking to him. Two nights with little sleep. Devyn succumbed to regret, worry, and sadness as she tidied the breakfast room. Sun shone through the windows, making the French provincial breakfast table, chairs, and buffet nearly sparkle. But the eyes of the large moose head over the buffet seemed to judge her.

Though relieved that no one had questioned her about the wine, the broken glass, or her cut fingers, she still felt guilty for not reporting the accident. But what seemed worse was living with regret over how she had spoken to Brice and how the quarrel had seemed to create a cavern so deep between them that she feared their growing affection for one another might never be the same.

Just when she had begun to care.

During those two days of silence, she'd seen him here and there. But his cool demeanor and the icy glances he cast her froze her heart. Yes, he'd tried to talk to her once, but they'd been interrupted. And this morning? He'd even sidestepped her in the hallway as if she had the pox.

No words. No friendliness. Nothing.

Why had she raised her voice at him? Accused him? Yes, she was wrong. She knew it, but what could she do?

She'd repented for her part over and over again, stroking her treasured blue ribbon, hoping it might comfort her trembling heart. But she wasn't the only one in the wrong. Brice had snapped at her too. Why was he so prideful?

She'd lain in bed last night begging God to give them the opportunity to right the situation. But when would they have the chance to do that?

As Devyn returned the clean silverware to the buffet drawer, the door squeaked open behind her. Brice entered quietly, leaving the door slightly ajar. "Devyn. May I speak with you, please?"

An apple-sized lump filled her throat, so she simply nodded, wringing her hands.

Brice's shoulders sagged as he gazed at the floor. "I've been an eejit. I am so sorry for the uncharitable words I spoke to you in the wine vault. I had no right. I fear my Irish temper has gotten the best of me far too often these days, and I am deeply ashamed." He looked up at her, and his pain-stricken, misty-blue eyes hurt her heart.

She swallowed. "I, too, am so dreadfully sorry for accusing you and yelling at you in such a manner. I have barely slept for the sorrow of it. I wish my nerves didn't control me so. Forgive me." Devyn's heart raced as she curtsied, holding her hand to her chest.

Brice took a step toward her, his crooked grin spreading like the rising sun. "I do. And you'll forgive me?"

She returned a timid smile. "Yes. Of course."

"Shall we start afresh?" Brice cocked his head and put out his hand as if wanting her to shake it. "I am Brice. Plain old Irish-tempered, fallen creature of God, Brice."

She took his hand, giggling. But before she could speak, he grasped her hand with both of his and stroked it so tenderly, so gently, that an entire cocoon of butterflies burst in her belly and flamed her cheeks. He gazed into her eyes, holding them fast with a dizzying reality.

He cared.

Clearing his throat, Brice let go of her hand and stepped back, breaking the spell. "The missus said you had a few hours off today, and so do I. If you have no other plans, may I show you a special haunt?"

"A haunt?" Sounded eerie. She bit her bottom lip. What did he have in mind?

Brice chuckled, deep and warm. "Beg pardon. Poor word choice for my fearful fawn. I'd like to show you the Grand Tower. You haven't been up there yet, have you?"

She shook her head. "No. The opportunity hasn't been afforded me."

Brice glanced around the room and opened the door wide. "It looks like you're finished in here, so allow me to show you a marvel." With a wave of his hand, he bid her to exit the breakfast room.

Devyn silently thanked the good Lord for bridging the divide between them. After two torturous days, she could bear it no more. God had answered her prayers!

Once they entered the corridor that led to the observatory tower, Devyn stopped at one of the dozen windows that lit both sides of the long hallway. "I wondered what it was like in here. 'Tis rather pleasant." She gazed out the window. "And it has a beautiful view of the gardens."

"I agree, although in the heat of the summer the passageway can get rather warm and stuffy when all these windows are closed." Brice led her to the end of the corridor and opened a wooden door leading to a large, square room with multi-paned windows on all four sides. "Up here." He pointed to a set of stairs, and they climbed up another level to find a nearly identical room, but with a table full of papers and charts, three chairs, and a tubular-shaped instrument.

She hurried over to it and touched it. "Is this a telescope? I've only read of such an instrument."

Brice nodded. "It is, and 'tis a beauty."

She assessed the wooden tripod and long, white-and-black scope as Brice ran his hands along a wooden leg. "It's a rare Preis-Fernrohr telescope with fine Zeiss optical glass. Its sixty-eight-millimeter refractor made by the famous Emil Busch from Germany gave us a crackin' view of Halley's Comet last month."

"You? You saw it?"

Brice stood a little straighter. "I did indeed."

She had read about the comet in the paper, and her pastor had prayed for safety at church that weekend, but otherwise, there had been little fuss about the celestial event in Chippewa Bay.

Devyn giggled. "A crotchety old neighbor of ours, Mr. Flannery, said a French astronomer claimed the comet would snuff out all life on planet Earth. The eccentric man had even bought a leather gas mask and an anti-comet umbrella. And then he told everyone in our village about the impending danger and promptly went into seclusion." She shrugged her shoulders. "I thought the fuss all rather silly."

Brice chuckled. "Aye, and in hindsight, it was. We came to the island early this year just to enjoy a view of the comet from here in the tower. Mr. Bourne loves all things new and modern, so he bought this telescope and these charts. I learned how to calculate when the comet would be over us, and we spent nearly six hours up here gazing at its majesty." He led her over to the table filled with charts of the stars, handwritten notes, and a small pillbox. Brice tapped the box. "He also bought some anti-comet pills, just in case. But we didn't use them."

"Mr. Flannery did, as well as quite a few others in Chippewa Bay."

"Tens of thousands did. Can you believe how the press spread panic around the globe?"

Devyn bit her lip at the memory. "I read that poisonous cyanogen gas would kill us all, but I didn't believe it. And besides, I couldn't afford the pills or anything even if it did."

"The worst was how so many unscrupulous people got rich through the scams they concocted, preying on the innocent. Thankfully, the comet caused no harm." He paused as his mouth turned up on one side. "Did you know that England's King Edward VII died while the comet was passing by? It was quite a day."

"As I recall, that day was rather un-amazing for me. What did the comet look like?"

"Oh, Devyn, never before had I understood so clearly the Scripture that says, 'The heavens declare the glory of God.' The comet's tail was a beauty, especially out here where no lights hid its luster. The head of it was as white as the clouds, and hundreds of thousands of tiny particles danced like fairy dust across the sky." He laid his hand on the scope. "This telescope is the best on the market and was well worth the money. The Bournes even had a celebration when it was over—with champagne and a rather fine meal. I wish you had been here."

She couldn't imagine all of that happening in this small room. "Was everyone up here?"

"No, just Mr. and Mrs. Bourne, Miss Marjorie, and me. I had been trained how to use the telescope, so I served as the resident scientist." Brice grinned and puffed his chest so wide she supposed he might pop some of his vest buttons. "Just one of the many hats I'm privileged to wear for this fine family."

"You are blessed indeed, sir." Devyn assessed this handsome man before her. "Will you stay in service forever?"

"Working for a man such as Mr. Bourne tempts me to stay in service. But truthfully, I dream of one day being just like him—a faithful, honest, successful, and kindhearted businessman. He wasn't born into wealth. He earned his fortune by taking the Singer Manufacturing Company to its international success. He has also wisely diversified his holdings into the Long Island Motor Parkway, the Long Island Railroad, the Bank of Manhattan, the Knickerbocker Safe Deposit, and others. He's become one of the wealthiest men in the world."

"He is a good man, Brice. I understand why you esteem him so."

"To be like him would be a dream come true, and to be able to serve my fellow man with charitable giving like he does would be the icing on the cake." Brice heaved a huge sigh, his eyes dewy.

"I hope you will. But how are you not overcome with apprehension to work for such a man?"

"Oh, no need, my bonnie lass. He casts no airs and deeply cares for his fellow man, whether rich or poor. He gives much to charity and makes no pretense of being better than others. I dare say there is no man like him."

Devyn chewed on her lip as she pondered his words. The faraway look in Brice's eyes reminded her of how her father looked while worshiping on Sunday morning. More and more, Brice evoked memories of Papa, and each instance hurt and healed her at the same time.

~ ~ ~

"May I ask you something?" Devyn bit her lip, her eyes imploring him.

Brice quirked a brow. "Certainly."

"In the wine vault, I came across an old newsprint with a note and a key rolled up inside it. Do you know what it could mean?"

He shook his head. "I've never come across it. What did the note say?"

Devyn furrowed her brow. "Something about a rock and where it was."

"Shall we investigate? I'm utterly curious." Brice grinned, and they left the tower to find the note.

Brice felt like a dozen fish flopped in his gut. Such an interesting woman he'd never met. Innocent but intelligent. Full of astonishment and curiosity. Sparkling blue eyes that danced when she learned something new.

But most of all, a heart that was humble and forgiving.

As they entered the tunnel, Brice bumped into her. "Excuse me. I'm a clumsy lout these days."

She smiled, her soft, full lips turning up and causing her dimple to appear.

"I bet that dimple of yours was a kiss from an angel."

"What a sweet thing to say. My mother always called it a defect." A shadow passed over her face.

"Defect? Bah! It makes you even more beautiful than you would be otherwise."

Her smile vanished as she wrapped her arms around her middle. Then she chewed on her lip.

How did that prick her pain? Befuddled, he gently pressed her forward. "Let's find that note, shall we?"

They walked along in silence, but his mind whirled. Until he had met this woman, he'd almost always been in control of his feelings. Now everything seemed topsy-turvy, and he disliked that feeling greatly. His dreams fixated on her, and during the day, he found himself taking circuitous ways about the castle, hoping to bump into her. But when he did, his mouth ran wild, his temper too often flared, and he said things he would never, ever say—until now.

Entering the vault, the ugly scene from earlier that week played in his head. Why had he demeaned her so? He'd been mulling that over ever since. He respected Devyn for overcoming her fears and navigating her way on this island. But he'd been irritated by Sofia and then so embarrassed by his egregious behavior that he'd remained tongue-tied until today. He hated his stubborn pride, his volatile temper, his arrogant words.

In truth, he was no better than she, now or then. An orphan. A poor Irish nobody who'd been plucked from obscurity and given the honor of such a high role as valet to the likes of Mr. Bourne.

Who was he to judge and intimidate her? He would never forget his unkindness. Yet she had forgiven him. The question was, could he forgive himself?

He shook himself from his negativity as Devyn searched for the secret key and clue. Then he caught a whiff of her womanly scent that captured his thoughts of what might be if he weren't such a clod. Could he ever be worthy of such a lass?

"Here it is!" Devyn had found the newsprint, key, and note. She handed the paper to him to read for himself.

He took it in and glanced at her, as perplexed as she looked. "'Fourth rock on the right.' I've never seen this, nor do I know what it means. The handwriting isn't familiar either. But let's try to solve the mystery together, shall we? There's a rock wall at the beach. Maybe it's there."

Devyn nodded. "Maybe. I do so love mysteries, and we've discovered two in recent days. The writing on the tunnel wall, and now this."

He shrugged as he returned the note and key to the cubbyhole. "This island holds many. Shall we explore a bit?" He presented his elbow, and she slipped her hand into it.

Her warm touch sent a shock through his body as he scanned the Great Hall to make sure no one saw them exit the tiny room together. It mightn't be seen as proper. Not yet.

Since no one was around, they exited through the front door. Brice closed it quietly. After stepping off the stoop, Devyn stopped and took in the view. "I believe I'm beginning to enjoy being here. It's rather peaceful, and the people are kind. Well, most of the people." Her confession surprised him, and by the tone of her voice, it surprised her too.

He cast her a sideways glance as they approached the shore. "Aye, well, there will always be the prickly sort wherever you go. You mustn't let them goad you."

She tweaked her chin toward the small island in the distance. "What island is that? Do you know?"

"Chimney Island. In Canada. The French had a stronghold there during the French and Indian War, but Mr. Bourne had the chimney repaired and is planning to sell the island. Mr. Bourne owns another Canadian island—that one." He pointed to a tiny plot of land sticking out of the river about a half mile away. "It's Corn Island, where we grow our summer produce."

"I'd heard of it but didn't know where it was."

"When Mr. Bourne began building this castle, he purchased yet another piece of Canadian soil on the mainland and brought two thousand loads of topsoil here to fill the castle grounds and gardens. I didn't see the island before but hear it was quite rocky."

"That was clever of him. It wouldn't be such a beautiful island otherwise."

As they walked along the shore, Devyn leaned into his arm, so he continued to share with her. "The *New York Times* reported that moving the Canadian soil to Dark Island was 'probably the first and greatest actual annexation of Canada ever achieved by the United States.'" He glanced at her, trying not to smile.

"It was?" Her eyes widened as her eyebrows raised.

"They were jesting, of course. But the paper continues to report Mr. Bourne's many accomplishments quite often." He lifted his chin and grinned. A tinge of pride leaked into his statement, but pride in one's employer was a good thing, wasn't it? He could only ever devote his skills and loyalty to someone who commanded his respect. Someone like Mr. Bourne.

"But of course." Her cheeks turned bright red, likely from missing the tongue-in-cheek manner of the news story. He'd have to be more careful not to embarrass her.

He gazed north, redirecting the conversation. "I love that we get to enjoy a Canadian sunrise and an American sunset. A piece of our hearts left in two countries."

"I never thought of it that way. I think I've always taken Canada's close proximity for granted. I suppose not all Americans get to experience such intimacy with another country." She sucked in a breath. "Excuse me, sir. I misspoke."

"Of what? I heard nothing inappropriate." He brushed off her faux pas.

Nevertheless, she changed the topic. "Tell me more of Indian Neck Hall I so often hear about. Please?"

"You'd be amazed at it, my bonnie lass. Indian Neck Hall makes this place appear to be but a small lodge indeed. Ernest Flagg, the same architect who built this fine castle, designed the Bournes' main home on Great South Bay in Oakdale, New York. Georgian style. In 1897, it was said to have been the largest estate on all of Long Island. The residence has more than one hundred rooms!"

"Goodness! I still get lost in The Towers. I'd never find my way around a place like that."

"You'd learn, and it isn't quite as confusing as the castle. Mr. Bourne didn't build such a place for show. He built it in time for their twenty-fifth wedding anniversary. I wish you could see it."

Devyn shook her head. "I'm just an unimportant Chippewa girl who will likely never leave northern New York, let alone ever see something like that. But I would sincerely like to have such a grand adventure."

He turned to face her, to make her understand. "Oh, but you must never think of yourself as unimportant. God made a unique and fascinating person when He made you."

Her eyes filled with tears, but the sweetest smile he'd ever seen graced her face. A comfortable silence hung in the air as they watched fish jump and flocks of gulls swoop and soar on the breeze. Then they continued to meander along a path until they came upon the small beach.

"Is this the swimming beach? I'm told the family enjoys it. Do you swim?" She picked up a clamshell and examined it.

He nodded. "Occasionally, but I'm not a strong swimmer."

She scrunched up her face, looking like she'd seen a ghost. "I do not swim at all." She'd scarcely gotten her statement out when a giant ship passing by blew its horn, causing her to jump and let out a squeak. "We rarely heard such sounds in the bay. I fear I'll never get used to the ships' noise."

"I daresay you will. As a young boy, I grew up near the docks of Belfast and heard the ships' blasts day and night. Eventually, your ear learns to block out such sounds."

He scanned the rock wall around the beach. "There are no rocks here that could hold any treasure. Not against the river's current. The note must refer to some other place."

"True. We'll just have to look elsewhere."

He stuck his forefinger in the air. "Wait here. There's one other place nearby, but it's rather muddy. I'd hate for you to soil your dress."

She nodded. "All right. I'll just enjoy the fresh air and find some shells."

"Back in a jiffy." He waved at her as he rounded a large boulder and carefully descended a bank to a favorite fishing spot on the shore where several rocks might hold the treasure.

What a turn of the tides the day had brought. From fretting to joy. And forgiveness caused it all. "Thanks, Lord, for Your mercy to us both."

He checked the area where he'd thought the fourth rock might be, but it obviously wasn't the right place either. Where could it be?

As he rounded the boulder to return to Devyn on the beach, a man's voice carried on the breeze. He peeked from behind the rock. Devyn held several shells in her hands, her eyes wide. And was that Falan with his back to Brice?

"My, but ain't you the spittin' image of a bedraggled fraidy-cat. What're ya searchin' fer?"

Devyn stepped back and shoved the shells in her pocket. "I had some time off and took the liberty to enjoy a beautiful day. What are you doing here?"

Falan smirked. "Watchin' *Cinderella* make a fool of herself with that too-good Mick!" He grabbed her wrist, pinning her between the water's edge and himself. "I'm warning ya. Stay away from him."

Brice jumped out in full view of them both. "Get your hands off her, you scrappy rogue!"

Devyn slipped to the right, away from her brother's grasp. But instead of joining Brice, she darted back toward the castle.

So much for an enjoyable day looking for treasure. Instead, her brother faced him with the narrowed eyes of a rabid weasel.

CHAPTER 11

The next afternoon, Sunday, Devyn followed Reagan into the piazza, carrying a silver tray of tea, tiny sandwiches, dainty cakes, and other delights for the Bourne children.

"I can't get the third mouse into the trap. This is so exasperating!"

Upon hearing Marian's strange, emphatic comment, Devyn furrowed a questioning brow at her friend.

Reagan laughed. "Oh, that's the Three Blind Mice game. Surely, you've seen it since it was created in Watertown. Over a hundred thousand were sold in New York City department stores, and the advertisement for it said it was so addicting that husbands often came home to wives playing it and their dinner uncooked."

Devyn giggled as she shook her head and whispered, "I've only ever heard of it. Never seen it."

They set their trays down and arranged the tea service. Reagan poured the steaming brew into fine china teacups. Devyn took a cup to Marian first, peeking over her shoulder to see what the fuss was about. The flowery scent from Marian's upswept hair wafted in the air, her pale pink teagown the same color as the roses growing in the castle's garden.

"Have you ever played this game?" Marian glanced up at Devyn while furiously twisting and turning the open, round box with three marble-like wooden balls in it.

"No, miss." Devyn watched as Marian tried to maneuver one ball through an opening and toward the center. Two balls circled the center, but one popped out.

"Well, you simply must try it sometime." The lilt in Marian's voice told her that despite her aggravation, she enjoyed the game.

"You have to get these three mice through the maze and into the trap at the center without touching them. It's not as easy as it looks."

"It looks like fun." Devyn curtsied and then scurried to the tea table to get another cup and take it to May, who sat on a white wicker chaise with a Sears catalog opened on her lap.

May took the cup and stirred her tea aimlessly. "I must confess I dream about my Mr. Straussburger far too often these days—and nights." As if leaving another world, May blinked and looked at Devyn as if she'd seen a ghost. "Sorry, I thought you were Marian." A soft blush colored her cheeks as she smiled.

"Would you care for a plate of refreshments?" Devyn bit her bottom lip, trying not to grin at May's words.

May nodded before returning her gaze to the catalog. "A little of everything would be lovely." She traced her finger down the unmentionables page.

Her brother, Howard, scoffed. "You two should get hitched and be done with it."

May stuck her tongue out at her brother and took a sip of tea.

Devyn hurried to retrieve a plate, restraining a giggle at the interchange. What would it be like to sit around and dream of a man she loved? A picture of Brice filled her thoughts, but she pushed it back. Yes, her heart was growing quite fond of him, but surely a life of service together would not include lying on a chaise with a catalog and choosing her unmentionables.

Reagan grinned. "Are you thinking of Brice? Your face betrays you, my friend."

Devyn huffed and feigned offense. "Hush. We must serve the tea." But her cheeks indeed burned as hot as the teacup in her hands. She hurried to Marjorie and set the cup and saucer on a table next to her.

"Thank you, and I'd like just sandwiches and nuts, please. Sweets don't appeal to me right now." Marjorie glanced up from her book. "Do you like to read? Your name is Devyn, correct?"

"Yes, miss. And I do dearly love to read, thank you." At Marjorie's acknowledgment, she made bold to peek at the volume in the young lady's lap.

Marjorie held up her book and showed Devyn the cover. "This is *Woodstock* or …" She flipped to the title page. "*Woodstock* or *The Cavalier*. A tale of the year sixteen hundred and fifty-one by the author of *Waverly, Tale of the Crusades*." Marjorie closed the book and smiled at her. "Sir Walter Scott wrote this story about King Charles II hiding from Sir Oliver Cromwell. Did you know our architect, Ernest Flagg, was reading this when Daddy requested he build a hunting lodge? This very book was the inspiration for The Towers, and I hear the castle in the story was much like ours—or rather, ours is like it. I've read it twice and still find it quite mysterious and intriguing. There's another copy in the library. You should read it."

"I will, miss. Thank you." She'd check it out right after she read *Anne of Avonlea*. Oh to have so many fine choices in reading material all the time! Maybe the book would shed some light on the mysterious castle and the notes she kept finding. She filled Marjorie's plate and turned to give it to her.

Devyn cleared her throat. "May I ask a question?"

Marjorie set her book on her lap. "Of course."

She pointed to a round dial on the ceiling. "What's that dial?"

"Oh, it's connected to the weather vane on the highest point of the roof. With it, we can see the direction of the wind anytime we want, which is good to know before we take our boating adventures."

"How clever that is! Thank you for telling me."

Howard addressed Brice as he entered the room. "Whatever happened to your face, Mac? Looks like you've been in a brawl."

Devyn held back a gasp. His right eye was nearly swollen shut, and an ugly black-and-blue bruise surrounded it.

"Had a mishap with an exposed root of the old oak tree on the Indian Path yesterday." Brice shrugged his shoulders, shot a glance at Devyn, and then directed his one good eye toward Howard. "Guess I'm a rather clumsy lout." Two scratches on his left cheek revealed more than he admitted. And a white bandage wrapped his right hand.

Falan? Had they had an altercation after she'd fled the beach?

Surely, a tree root hadn't caused this. But why was Brice lying? Why cover up for Falan?

Devyn's heart began to race as she tried to reason it out. She had to talk to Brice alone.

Brice handed Howard an envelope. "Your father sent this for you to look over."

Howard took the envelope and laid it on the table. "First things first. Play King's Castle with me, will you, Mac? These sisters of mine are caught up in their own little womanly worlds at the moment." Howard flashed a grin toward the girls and patted the table before opening a game box.

Mac pulled up a wicker chair to join him at a small square table. "Your father doesn't need me at the moment, so I'm happy to serve, sir."

"Sir, nothing. You're older than me and one of my closest friends. Who are you trying to impress?" Howard turned toward the tea table and evaluated Reagan and then Devyn. "Ah. Taken a fancy to her, eh?"

Devyn pretended not to hear but glanced at Reagan, who stared out the window to the pouring rain. Thank goodness, she'd been oblivious to Howard's comment. She turned to Devyn and spoke quietly. "Isn't the scent of rain lovely? I can smell it, even with the windows closed and these fresh flowers right here." She leaned over the sill to sniff cut lilacs in a huge vase.

"Yes. It's a good day for staying inside. Will the family spend all afternoon here?" She cut her gaze to the siblings.

"Sometimes. More often than not, they observe the Sabbath with quiet repose. No swimming, boating, or other exertions. Just loving family time."

Devyn pursed her lips before commenting. "My family spent very little time together, and when we did, we usually argued."

Reagan touched her forearm. "That is sad, to be sure." She scanned the room, everyone relaxing in the peace of the day. "I like observing a quiet Sunday rest. I didn't understand the value of the Sabbath until I came to work for the Bournes. But I've discovered that having a day that's different from all the others is a gift from

God, even if I'm serving."

A gift from God? The Sabbath? Apparently, God had been the first to observe it in such a way. Even He rested on the seventh day. "But we're still working. That's not a Sabbath rest for us."

"Haven't you noticed how Mrs. VanLeer gives us much less work, and the family rarely asks us for much more than helping with the necessities? Why, we even get Sunday afternoons off now and then."

"So how is the game played?" Brice's question broke into her conversation with Reagan, and Devyn smiled at his interested tone. He must like to play games.

Howard handed Brice a pawn. "It's simple, really. Players flick the spinner and move according to the spin's number. But if you land on the feather end of the arrow, you immediately move to the arrow's tip. Some of these moves are beneficial, but others may take you farther away from the inner ring and the finish space. First one to finish wins. You go first, Mac, since you're my elder."

While Devyn enjoyed the friendly banter between servant and master, she still stopped short when the Bournes called Brice *Mac*. Reagan excused herself to attend to other things, so Devyn had full charge of the tea and watched to be sure everyone's needs were met. Should she ask Brice if he'd like something?

"Really, Mac. What happened to you?" Howard spun and moved his pawn.

"It's as I said. I'm fine."

Howard surveyed Brice from head to toe, but before he could ask further questions, Devyn hurried up to them. "Would you care for anything? Sir? Brice?"

The young master pointed to his teacup. "I'll have some more. And a few of those little cakes. They're not but a bite apiece, so I can't seem to get enough of them."

"Of course, sir." Devyn curtsied and glanced at Brice.

He cleared his throat and shook his head, brows furrowed. "Thank you. No. I'm fine."

She took Howard's cup and plate and returned with the tea and a full selection of cakes just as Brice's pawn landed on a feather and slid the opposite direction of the finish line.

"You're heading the wrong way, man!" Howard laughed. Then he looked at Devyn. "And what do you think of the game?"

Devyn blinked, unsure of what to say. "It appears to be quite enjoyable, sir."

Howard laughed again. "Only if you head in the correct direction, right, Mac?"

Brice scrunched up his face in mock offense. "Right, Master Bourne."

Howard slid out of his chair. "Say, I need to visit the … well, I'll be back shortly. Would you please play the game in my place for a few minutes, miss? The old man will show you how." Without letting her respond, Howard tweaked May's hair as he jogged out the room.

Devyn glanced at the girls before casting Brice a wide-eyed look.

Brice patted Howard's chair. "It's all right. He rarely sits still for long. It's your turn. Just spin and move."

Devyn perched on Howard's chair and did as Brice suggested, whispering to him, "What happened to you? Really. Was it Falan?"

Brice nodded, scanning the room with a darting glance. "I'll tell you later. Just play the game, please."

Brice took his turn. Devyn followed, but Marjorie emptied her teacup. Devyn motioned toward the young lady with her head. "Take your turn, Brice, while I attend to Miss Marjorie."

She went to Marjorie, retrieved the cup, and returned to her with a full cup of tea.

"Thank you, Devyn."

Devyn curtsied before returning to Brice and the game.

After a few more turns, Devyn was way ahead. Howard came back and scanned the board. "Well, I see you're beating the pants off the old man. Good for you! Do you want to finish or shall I?"

Devyn glanced at Brice and shook her head. "I should attend to my duties, sir."

Howard studied them, and a strange expression appeared on his face. "Hmmm … I see. Well, carry on, then."

Devyn tried to guess what Howard was thinking but didn't

know him well enough. Instead, she approached his three sisters to make sure they had all they needed. Marjorie was deep into her book and waved her off. Marian had pulled her chair next to May's chaise, and the two were twittering about the latest underclothes. Both wanted their tea warmed, so Devyn took the pot to them. Thankfully, one of the kitchen maids had brought a fresh pot minutes before.

"And how's my family this rainy afternoon?"

Mr. Bourne sauntered into the room with Mrs. Bourne on his arm. He guided her up to the men playing their game. Brice rose, but Mr. Bourne gently slapped him on the shoulder and bid him to sit. "Finish the game, Mac. It's fine."

The couple strolled to each of their girls and gave them a pat, a gentle tweak to the hair, a loving touch. The longing ache to be a part of such a family settled deep in Devyn's heart.

Mrs. Bourne gestured to Devyn, snapping her out of her daydream. "We'll have tea over here at the puzzle table, dear. I think Mr. Bourne and I will work on the lighthouse for a spell."

"Right away, ma'am."

Devyn brought tea and samples of the food. She curtsied, preparing to leave, but Howard slapped the table, shaking the board game and knocking the pawns around.

"I won!"

Brice ran a hand over his chin, scanned the game, and shook Howard's hand. "Congratulations, Mr. Howard, on a game well played."

"You should thank your friend. She moved my pawn along quite well, I think." The young man grinned at Devyn.

Her face creasing into a gentle smile, Mrs. Bourne surveyed Devyn and Brice. "Why don't the two of you take your leave and rest until Vespers? We'd like a little family time with these young people of ours."

"Yes, ma'am." Devyn turned wide eyes on Brice. Here was her Sunday reprieve only minutes after she had bemoaned the lack of one. And her chance to find out what had happened with Falan.

Brice bowed toward her, his battered face revealing none of his emotion. "Shall we?" He swept his hand toward the door.

~ ~ ~

Brice sighed as he followed Devyn out the piazza door, closing it behind him. How much should he reveal of the altercation between her brother and himself? He'd struggled with that question nearly all night, wishing he didn't have evidence of the fight on his person.

Devyn pointed like a schoolmarm sending a bully to the woodshed. "To the tower, if you please." It wasn't a request.

He bid her to lead, and soon they were in the lower level of the tower, an empty and little used space. Good choice.

"First, are you all right?" Tears filled Devyn's eyes, her long lashes catching one and splashing it onto her cheek. She swiped it away.

"I'm fine." He laid his hand on his chest, minimizing his true feelings. "I'm fine. Really. It looks worse than it is."

She puffed out a breath, her shoulders relaxing. The tension in the air seemed to dissipate. "What happened? Tell me all. Please."

"After you ran off, I lost my Irish temper again and whooped Falan good. He got in a few blows, as you can see, but I let that scrappy sleeveen know that if he ever touched you again, he'd pay a much higher price."

"But why did you lie and say you tripped on a tree root?" She tilted her head, a stray curl falling over her forehead. "And you didn't report him?"

"Well, that became a bit complicated when he threatened to report you and have you dismissed. He claimed some 'scandal' you committed back in Chippewa Bay would ruin you for good."

Devyn bit her lip until he feared for the sight of blood.

He took her hand in his. "I don't believe him, but you know how convincing he can be, and I feared for your job. Feared I'd never see you again. I could not bear to never see you again, Devyn."

A long, deep silence ensued as Devyn seemed to take in what he'd said. Her face twisted as though with tormenting thoughts, but what were they?

"Say something." *Please, trust me with your secret.*

Devyn pulled her hand from his and turned her back to him, her head hung low, her shoulders drooping like an old lady's. She swiped at her cheeks.

He gently turned her to face him. "Please. Are you angry with me? I need to know what you think."

She just stared at the wide, polished boards beneath her feet.

"Look, I'm sorry I hit your brother. Sorry I lost my temper. Sorry I am not the gentleman you think I am. But when I saw him treat you so roughly and threaten you, I could bear it no longer." He balled his fist, shifting his weight from side to side. "Truly, I felt guilty that I had neglected to deal with the boathouse incident when he and his ruffians accosted you, so when he harassed you again, I'd had enough. I'm sorry. I know he's your brother. Your flesh and blood. I had no right."

Devyn licked her lip and furrowed her brow, shaking her head. "You misunderstand. I don't blame you for fighting him. I am honored. Humbled. Ashamed."

"Ashamed? Of what?"

"I did cause scandal to my family. A terrible, life-altering scandal. It is as he said, and I should not have this place of service. If the Bournes knew the truth, I'd be out on my ear. Maybe worse."

He tried to take in her words but could not. What kind of scandal could this gentle fawn have ever committed that would have caused such shame to her family? That had caused her brother to hate her to the point of threatening to expose her? And what kind of family did she come from, anyway?

"I see. Well, the Bible says, 'The truth shall make you free,' and we must believe it. Living a lie will imprison you worse than that dungeon up there." He pointed above them. "Can you tell me and be free? I'll not judge you."

Devyn looked into his eyes until he grew desperately uncomfortable. She seemed to be sizing him up. Finally, she whispered her answer. "I cannot. I'm sorry."

CHAPTER 12

After returning *Anne of Green Gables* to the library, Devyn signed out *Anne of Avonlea*, anxious to devour its story as she had the former book. She had often identified with Anne's loneliness, coming to an island so isolated and not knowing anyone. She also wished she'd had a Matthew and Marilla to love her.

And what would it be like to attend a ball as the Bournes would this very evening? What would it be like to wear a fine gown with puffed sleeves? With a sigh, she picked up the book, taking it with her to breakfast.

The mouth-watering aroma of sausage and eggs made her stomach growl. As Devyn greeted the employees gathered in the dining hall, Sofia nodded curtly, staring at her with narrowed eyes. "When do you have time to read, bookworm?" She looked down her nose at the novel and back up to Devyn with questioning scrutiny. "You mustn't have enough work around here. Perhaps I shall see you find more to do."

Devyn pretended not to hear. She served her plate and took a seat, while Brice and Reagan cast Sofia a look of disdain.

Reagan greeted Devyn with a smile. "We have an exciting day ahead of us. It's ever so fun to see the Bournes in their finest attire. An evening of dinner and dancing at the Crossmon House. Imagine." She aimed a rapturous glance at the tin ceiling before looking back at her. "Are you ready to dress Miss Marian in her best this afternoon?"

Devyn shifted in her seat, turning away from Sofia's gaze, and swallowed a bite of breakfast before speaking. "I … I think so. I'm finding I rather enjoy helping her dress, though dressing her for a ball is a bit scary. And I'm not sure about coiffing her hair properly."

"After I dress May and Marjorie, let's meet in Marian's room and make a party of it. I'll prepare everything and assist you as needed. It'll be fun for the sisters and for us."

Sofia huffed loudly and rose from the table.

Devyn ignored her. "Thank you, Reagan. That sets my mind at ease." And her stomach too. She'd fretted half the night. She took a bite of the sausage as she sensed Brice's eyes on her.

"I'm sure you do splendidly with your lady's maid duties, Devyn. You have an artistic eye and a keen mind."

"Thank you, sir." She glanced his way, unsure if it was the comment or the spicy sausage she ate that caused a flash of heat to climb up to her cheeks. She took another bite of egg to avoid more talk. She hated when conversations centered on her. She had to change the topic. Fast. She turned back to Reagan.

"The missus has me cleaning the Great Hall first thing, but I will be ready to help you after lunch. Is that all right?"

"Oh yes! The siblings are taking a boat ride this morning, so I'll have time to set everything aright." Lifting her coffee for a dainty sip, Reagan examined Brice with narrowed eyes. "Your bruise is nearly gone. You heal quickly. Good for you."

Devyn snapped her head toward him, but she had no need to fear, for he only gave a sheepish nod.

After finishing her breakfast, Devyn took her book to her room before gathering the cleaning supplies.

Entering the Great Hall, she reviewed what she'd need to do—dust, mop, and wash the many panes of glass. The summer sun shone through the large windows, showing the need for them to be cleaned. She brushed away a touch of shame that she hadn't seen to them before now. Was this place growing on her? She smiled to realize it was.

The first thing she needed to do was rid the room of the pesky web spinners. How so many spiders snuck in and made this grand castle their home both irritated and intrigued her. After several weeks of often eradicating the nuisances, she'd found mastery over them and had no remorse … or fear … when killing them. She took her broom and swept every web from the arches, the corners, the candlestick light fixtures, the hearth, and even off the suits of armor. Truly?

Feeling a bit like a knight who slew her dragons, she hummed a hymn as she thoroughly dusted the intricate wooden chairs, polished table, and infinity mirrors.

After she mopped the floor, she hurried to the kitchen to retrieve the vinegar water for the windows. Upon returning, she found muddy footprints all over the floor and Sofia standing on the first landing of the staircase. "Dear me. I must have tracked in some dirt." She smirked and continued to climb the stairs without apology.

Devyn shook her head and remopped the floor. "Childish. Why would she be so childish?"

"Who's childish?" Brice stood in the doorway of the wine vault.

"Sofia. She tracked mud over my clean floor and smirked about it."

"She's a pill, I'll give you that. But hold her shenanigans at bay." He let out a slow whistle. "I must say, you've become quite adept at overpowering the onslaught of spiders around here. I'm rather proud of you."

"Thank you. I'm quite pleased to have victory over my fear of them." She giggled at her admission.

Brice continued to stand in the doorway, respecting that a newly mopped, wet floor came between them. "Tonight will be special, seeing everyone in their finest, don't you think? I only wish I could see you decked out in such finery. I know you'd remind the lot of them of Florence."

"Yes, well, I don't believe I'm anything as beautiful as Miss Florence, though I've only seen her in photographs."

"You are. Believe me. You are." Brice winked at her, but then his face turned a deep red, and he angled toward the vault. "I must choose a bottle to chill. The Bournes like to enjoy a glass before they leave for evening events."

Uncertain how to respond to Brice's unexpected and lavish affirmation, Devyn glanced out the window. What? What was Falan doing with Nellie? She watched in horror as her brother grabbed Nellie's shoulders and planted a firm and furious kiss on her lips! "Brice! Come quickly."

But Brice was gone, disappeared through the secret passageway.

~ ~ ~

Devyn should report that scallywag brother of hers! Poor Nellie had been shaking like a leaf when Devyn had run to the girl's side. Falan had disappeared into the trees and was nowhere to be seen. That scoundrel! Nellie said she was unhurt and insisted that she didn't want to report him, though she refused to say why.

What had Falan said to her to keep Nellie from speaking the truth? Like Brice, he had the maid tongue-tied, enslaved to secrecy. Why?

Devyn hung her head when she realized that she, too, was in their company, for she feared to report him as well, worried that she'd be incriminated with him since she was his sister. And she didn't want to lose the job she'd begun to love, the people she'd grown to care about, and the island life that somehow inspired her to a brighter future.

With a sigh, she completed her morning task and headed to the servants' hall. Since the others had eaten earlier, she enjoyed an unusually quiet lunch, lost in her thoughts. Afterward, she climbed the stairs to Marian's room, both excited and anxious about preparing the miss for her special evening.

Marian was a fine woman, kind and gracious, and Devyn had to admit she rather enjoyed the position of lady's maid, even if it was only for a short while. To her surprise, she was quite good at it, and the things she didn't know she was learning fast.

Upon opening Miss Marian's door, she found Reagan placing several hairbrushes, combs, hair ornaments, and appliances on the vanity table. Three comfy chairs encircled the vanity, awaiting the ladies. "The sisters should return anytime now. I'm sure they'll want a bath, and then we'll partially dress them and do their hair before we don their gowns. After they're ready, Howard will join them, and at seven, they will take the boat to the Chippewa Bay dock, where a carriage will be waiting to take them to Alex Bay. The missus has asked me to go with them since they've all decided to stay at Crossmon House for the evening."

Devyn grinned. "I'm glad it's you, not me!"

"Oh, I think you'd enjoy it immensely, my friend. I've only been to the Crossmon House once, last year, but it's lovely, and the atmosphere at such parties is just thrilling. Gaiety and glamour seep through the entire place, and even though I stay in the ladies' chamber, I can still hear the music from the ballroom. When the evening concludes, our beautiful Bournes return satisfied, albeit quite exhausted." Reagan paused for a moment, biting the tip of her finger and tilting her head as she surveyed the vanity. "Yes. I think we're ready."

Devyn wasn't so sure. "Can you please talk me through it? At least until they return."

Reagan took her hand and pulled her near. "Exactly what I was thinking. Well now, I think we'll create the Colonial on May and Marian, so I'll do May first, and you can see how it's done. Then you can copy my work on Marian. How's that sound?"

"I'm sorry, but what's the Colonial?"

"Oh, it's the latest evening style for hair and all the rage." She motioned with her fingers on her own head. "The hair is loosely drawn back from the face, coiled low on the head with curls artistically falling over her shoulder. It's really quite lovely."

Devyn touched her hair, gazing in the mirror. How would such an elaborate style look on her? "It *sounds* lovely, but can I accomplish such a feat?"

Reagan pursed her lips. "You're such a worry wart. Brice is right. You have an artistic gift and will do just fine. Since you began learning the ways of a lady's maid, you've picked up the trade much faster than I ever did."

"Thank you. I'll do my best. But what about Marjorie?"

Reagan giggled. "She's an independent sort and likes her hair different than her sisters. Another very modish style is with the hair arranged rather high on the head and decorated with a bunch of curls on one side. Curls are the keynote of hair fashion this summer, you know. Or she may want one of these jeweled metal bandeaux …" She pointed to two bands, one with silver sequins and one gold band with interlacing rings. "She'll tell us what she wants. Though plumes and aigrettes are also used, here in the islands, it's not as elaborate as in the city."

"It all sounds quite elaborate to me."

"Oh, for holidays and high-society affairs, it can be quite daunting." Reagan shrugged her shoulders and lifted her tiny eyebrows. "But it's such fun nevertheless." A satisfied smile caused her to look prettier than ever.

"I'm so glad you're my mentor and friend, Reagan. I can't imagine learning all this from another, especially from the likes of Sofia." She wrinkled her nose at the thought.

"Happy to be of assistance." Reagan bowed low in mock servitude. "You're an easy pupil, to be sure."

Just then, the three sisters burst through the door chatting happily, windblown and ready for baths. Reagan followed May and Marjorie to their parents' bath while Devyn drew a bath for Marian. While her mistress bathed, Devyn studied the hair things.

Soon Reagan, May, and Marjorie joined Marian and Devyn for their hair styling. Reagan created a perfect Colonial on May, and Devyn copied her, crafting a flawless hairstyle for Marian.

Marian turned to her and took her hand. "Why, you're a master of hairdressing, I do believe. Well done!"

She curtsied, relieved and proud. "Thank you, Miss Marian. Truly."

Marjorie chose the gold-ring bandeau, and Reagan created a lovely but simple style that suited the young woman perfectly. After the girls donned their gowns, jewelry, and cloaks, Reagan and Devyn carried their smaller cases downstairs, having already packed the overnight trunk and had it sent to the boathouse.

In the Great Hall, Howard and Brice waited for the women, gazing up the stairs in admiration. "My sisters should be on the cover of a magazine. Surely." Howard bowed low, and Brice followed. "Splendid!"

The three Bourne women glowed at the compliment, cheeks rosy, smiles wide, and eyes sparkling. Reagan also smiled, and Devyn realized she must also be glowing like her mistresses. She'd accomplished another new task and had done it well!

"My children. Can there be three more beautiful women and a handsome young man on these islands this evening? I daresay not!" Mr. Bourne sauntered out of the library with Mrs. Bourne close behind.

"I agree, Mr. Bourne. They are resplendent. I pray you have a lovely evening, children. Say hello to all our friends and give them my regrets. I fear my rheumatism is acting up again."

"It won't be the same without you, Mother and Daddy." Marian kissed her parents on the cheek, and her siblings followed suit.

"The night is warm, but it may be chilly crossing the channel. Keep your cloaks on, children." Mr. Bourne's eyes sparkled with pride. "Off with you, and enjoy every moment."

Brice took the cases from Reagan and Devyn, whispering as he grasped the handle. "I'll be back in a jiffy. Care for an evening stroll?"

Devyn nodded, excitement stirring her blood. As the party departed, she was left alone in the Great Hall with Mr. and Mrs. Bourne. "I'm sorry to hear of your troubles, ma'am. May I get you anything?"

"A cup of hot tea? That would be lovely." Mrs. Bourne rubbed her hands together, eyes betraying her pain.

Mr. Bourne raised a hand. "I'll have a cup too. And if Cook has something sweet, bring two. We'll be in the library."

"Right away." Devyn curtsied and hurried to the kitchen. One of the kitchen maids quickly made a pot of tea, set two teacups on the silver tray, and added a plate of shortbread cookies. Devyn entered the library with tray in hand.

"I hear you've become quite a professional lady's maid, miss." Mrs. Bourne took a teacup from Devyn.

She smiled in an attempt to cover her surprise.

"Do you not believe it? My daughters and Reagan do not lie."

"Oh no, ma'am. I just know I have much to learn." Her voice

and her hands shook as she spoke. She feared she'd offended the missus.

"I wasn't scolding, dear. I was trying to encourage you. Please sit."

Devyn sat on the edge of a nearby chair. The couple grinned at one another, and Mr. Bourne winked. "I daresay, you're the spitting image of our Louisa. The way you looked when you were nervous just then, well, it touches my heart."

"But doesn't she also remind you of Florence? Florence has the same mannerisms as her dear departed sister, so that makes sense." Mrs. Bourne's voice caught, and her eyes brimmed over with tears. "Honestly, dear, you remind me of both of them."

What was she to say to that? "I hope my presence pleases you and not offends."

As if the couple planned it, both spoke at the same time. "It pleases us."

A gentle silence filled the room as the mantle clock ticked away the time. Devyn wasn't sure if she should stay, leave, speak, or remain quiet. In the distance, the front door opened and closed, and Brice came into the library and bowed. "May I serve you, sir?"

Mr. Bourne shook his head. "No, no. Mrs. Bourne and I will read a while before we retire. You're dismissed for the evening. And you, too, miss."

Devyn glanced at Brice, hoping her excitement about being with him—which rivaled that of the siblings going to a ball—wasn't obvious to the Bournes.

CHAPTER 13

Devyn touched her cheek for the hundredth time, remembering the tender kiss Brice had planted on it over a week ago during their stroll on the Indian Path after the Bournes had left for the ball. Her heart skipped a beat as it always did when she thought of that kiss. Yes, it had only been on her cheek, but it was given with greater love than she'd had in more than a decade.

Embracing the tenderness of the memory, she headed to Marian's room with a smile. Today she'd help Marian change for the Sunday morning Father's Day breakfast and the celebration ahead. Glancing into the young woman's open room and finding it empty, she turned toward laughter coming from the senior Bournes' master suite. Curious, she crept close and planted her back against the wall to listen.

"I'm sorry that Arthur and Alfred couldn't join us, Daddy. But since they're on their European tour, I couldn't quite ask them to return." May sounded apologetic but happy.

"George tried to get away, but he couldn't. You know how he is." Howard chuckled.

Devyn peeked into the room, careful to remain unseen. But she stifled a surprised giggle when she witnessed all of them still in their nightclothes. Howard sat in a chair pulled up close to his father's bed, while his sisters, all three of them, were plunked casually on their mother's. Mr. and Mrs. Bourne sat with their husband trays over their laps, their breakfasts barely touched.

Marian waved two letters at her mother. "But they sent telegrams!"

Mrs. Bourne grinned as she received them, handing one to her husband. "Read yours first, dear."

Mr. Bourne opened the envelope and scanned it. "It's from Arthur and Alfred. "Happy Father's Day, Daddy. Stop. Wish we all could be there. Stop. Home in August. Stop. Enjoy every moment! Stop. Love, Arthur, Ethel, Alfred, and Hattie." He held the telegram to his chest and closed his eyes. "They're here in spirit, and that's all that matters." He glanced at his wife. "Read yours, darling."

"It's from George." She cleared her throat. "Happy Daddy's Day. Stop. Wish I were there. Stop. Business crazy. Stop. See you at Indian Neck soon. Stop. Love, George." By the end, Mrs. Bourne's voice cracked.

Howard leaned forward and handed his father a package. "This is from Florence. She, too, sends her regrets but had this delivered by courier."

Mr. Bourne opened the package. A beautiful gilded frame glinted in the sunshine.

Marian reached for it. "May I?" She took it and showed her siblings. "This was taken last Christmas. How the photographer got all these people in one photograph amazes me, but what a grand time we had with all of us together!"

"Not all." Mr. Bourne sounded like he might cry, but then he recovered. "Thank you, my precious family. Daughters, you are the jewels of my eye … a ruby, an emerald, and an opal." He bobbed his head at each of the girls. "And you, Howard, are the gold encrusting them all. How I love each one of you! Thank you for this special day."

At the endearing words, Devyn must've made a noise, for Marian turned her way. "Do you need something?"

Devyn stepped into the doorway, swallowed the lump in her throat, and shook her head. "I … I was just checking to see if you needed anything, miss." Her voice quivered.

Marian tilted her head, smiling. "I'm fine. We'll ring if we need anything. Thank you."

Devyn curtsied and hurried away, tears spilling down her cheeks. Not only had she eavesdropped on a private family affair, but in doing so, she'd witnessed more family love than she'd ever seen.

Ever.

Never had her family had one moment—not one—such as she'd seen with the Bournes. A swirl of jealousy, admiration, and pain spun her emotions round and round as she tried furiously to gather them to tuck them away. Finally, she got ahold of them and built her wall up again, brick by brick. How else she could survive the onslaught of painful emotions she couldn't control?

She hurried to the servants' hall, pasting on a shaky smile. It was a lie, but what else could she do?

Reagan shot her a questioning glance. "Good morning! Where have you been?"

"I went to check on Marian, but she was with her parents."

Brice chuckled. "They all are. Howard and Marjorie actually delivered the breakfast trays themselves, and then all four shooed me out of the room. Said it was family time." As usual, admiration shone from his face.

"Scandalous. Why such fine people act like commoners, I'll never understand. Next, they'll dress themselves, and we'll be out of a job." Sofia's words dripped with condescension.

Brice nearly growled his reply. "It's the twentieth century, for heaven's sake, and they're a thoroughly modern family. Slide into the new world, Sofia, and stop making everyone miserable."

Sofia scowled, rose in a huff, and stomped out of the room, leaving her dishes still on the table. Reagan and Nellie giggled quietly. Devyn wanted to cheer Brice's rebuke. Even Cook smirked. Only Brice could say such a thing to Sofia and get away with it.

Nellie redirected the conversation. "We served breakfast to the children at the crack of dawn. My, do they have an exciting day planned!"

Reagan put down her fork. "They breakfasted in their bedclothes?"

Nellie giggled, nodding, and shrugging her shoulders. "It was delightful to see their joy, like little children on Christmas morning."

Brice answered with a grin. "I know they'll have boat races and go swimming, but last night Mr. Bourne mentioned he had a surprise."

Devyn looked at him and then at Reagan. "I can't imagine what it could be."

Brice winked at her. In public. "If I knew, it wouldn't be a surprise, now would it?"

She shrugged and picked up her teacup and sipped. How bold he was getting! She loved the attention but feared it might bring scandal ... or worse.

For the rest of the breakfast, each of them tried to guess what the surprise might be, but then the call buttons began to ring, and they dispersed to answer the summons.

Devyn helped Marian into a soft pink dress and fixed her hair in a casual, upswept style. When ready, they all met in the piazza, dressed in their finest summery day wear.

Howard seemed to be in charge of the affair. "First, we'll have boat races. But we're not going to use the speedboats or steamers or yachts, Daddy." He grinned mischievously. "We youngsters are going to paddle the canoes and the electric gondola is for you and Mother."

Mr. Bourne laughed. "What a fine idea! I haven't used the gondola all summer. To the boathouse, then."

With that, they were off, Devyn following Brice and Reagan with plenty of towels in hand. Sofia was nowhere in sight, and no one asked why.

As they made their way to the boats, Devyn had a more diverting question. "What's an electric gondola?"

Brice answered. "Have you seen pictures of the boats used in Venice, Italy? They're similar to a canoe, only narrower, but in Venice, they use poles instead of oars to push off the shallow lagoon bottom. Here, of course, the river's channel is too deep and the current is strong, so the boat has an electric motor. She's a beauty." He bent close, nearly touching her ear, and whispered, "Like you."

Devyn shivered at the ticklish breath of words, and her emotions stirred, warming her aplenty. As they rounded the corner, she understood what he meant. A shiny black-lacquered vessel sat waiting for them. Either end was tipped up into a decorative point, and in the middle was a tent-like covering, presumably to keep Mr.

and Mrs. Bourne out of the sun.

Mr. Bourne helped his wife climb into the boat. "Secure your life jacket, my dear." Then he turned to his children. "And all of you. Wear your life jackets, please."

Howard playfully rolled his eyes. First, he helped his sisters put on the bulky cork contraptions, and then he donned his own. When everyone was in the boats, Howard spoke. "For the race, we'll start at the dock, go west around the island, and return." He motioned as if drawing a large oval. "First boat back wins. Mac, you can be our ref."

Brice nodded as the skiffs and then the gondola maneuvered out of the boathouse and into the river. A gentle breeze cooled the warm, sunny day, and Canada geese swam nearby as if waiting to watch the race.

Devyn and Reagan followed Brice to the dock's edge. He took out a white handkerchief, ready to start the race. Howard and May leaned forward, clutching their paddles in one canoe. Marjorie and Marian cast them playful, narrowed glances as they waited in the other.

Marjorie called out to Howard. "You two are 'Team Bookends' … the youngest and the oldest." She smirked at her siblings. "We're Team Beauties, right, Marian?" Everyone laughed. "And watch out, Howard. You may be a boy, but we Beauties aim to win." She winked at her brother.

Mrs. Bourne called out from the gondola, "I believe your father and I have a distinct advantage, children."

Brice smiled. "All right. Is everyone ready? On your mark. Get set. Go!"

Off the three boats went, the rowers straining at the paddles, shouting commands, laughing, and seeming to have a grand time. Devyn and the others followed along the shore as she strained to see Mr. and Mrs. Bourne. The gondola was farther out in the current-ridden channel, but they kept up with the canoes, almost hovering near them.

"The gondola can go faster than the canoes, can't it?"

Brice nodded. "Oh yes. But this race is just for fun."

Reagan clapped her hands. "Wouldn't it be grand to ride in it?"

Devyn looked up to the sky, a few wispy clouds dancing on the breeze. "I'm not so sure about that."

About halfway around the island, Devyn, Reagan, and Brice cut across to the other side. By then, they could control their excitement no longer. They began to cheer, clap, and prod the racers on. All three vessels were neck and neck, and Devyn supposed they weren't really racing.

As they rounded the eastern side of the island and neared the dock, Howard pushed into high gear, but so did Marjorie, fighting the current. The gondola stayed next to them, and even over the grunting, splashing, and honking of the geese, Devyn could hear Mr. and Mrs. Bourne laughing gaily. As the three vessels neared the finish line, the rowers in the canoes raised their paddles to allow the gondola to chug past.

Brice waved his handkerchief and shouted, "And the winners of the Father's Day championship boat race are … Commodore Frederick G. Bourne and his lovely wife!"

Everyone clapped, cheered, whistled, and hurrahed as the boats came to dock. The children got out of the canoes. Mrs. Bourne exited the gondola, but Mr. Bourne stayed put. "And now for a surprise. Reagan and Devyn, while my children change into their bathing costumes, please join me for a trip around the island in this fine boat. Mac, you can come too."

Devyn stood aghast. She looked at Mr. Bourne and then at Reagan, who promptly squealed and threw her arms around Devyn's neck, whispering in her ear. "Smile, enjoy it, and stop worrying!"

Devyn squared her shoulders and gave a timid smile as she climbed into the gondola with Mr. Bourne's assistance.

After helping her and Reagan with their life vests, Brice sat next to Devyn, leaning close and whispering near her ear. "You're safe, my fawn. Trust me."

Devyn glanced at Reagan, who giggled with delight. Why should she be afraid? No. She was done with that! Sniffing back her fear, she closed her eyes and prayed for safety. Upon finding a measure of peace, she leaned over to Brice and whispered, "Why did you call him *commodore?*"

Brice grinned, his eyes twinkling in the sunshine. He glanced at Mr. Bourne, who was busy checking the boat, and kept his voice low. "Aye, well, he owns many boats, large and small, and is a member of several yacht clubs, including the prestigious New York Yacht Club, so he was named their commodore from '03 to '05. He's also a member of the Jekyll Island Club and the Chippewa and Thousand Islands Yacht Clubs."

Reagan nodded. "Mr. Bourne is an avid sportsman who enjoys hunting, fishing, and even boxing. But boating is his favorite."

"I heard that. Boating is the best. Are you ready?" Mr. Bourne interrupted their discussion, donned his captain's cap, and waved at those on shore. "Off we go!" He put the gondola into gear, and the boat glided into the river.

The ride was steady, so Devyn admired the lovely view of Dark Island as they made their way around it.

Once, a large ship passed by them, dwarfing their tiny craft and creating quite a wake. But Mr. Bourne turned their vessel gently into the waves, and they barely noticed a bump.

"He's skilled at boating, that's for sure." Devyn relaxed more by the minute.

Brice nodded. "You have no idea. You're in good hands."

Devyn gazed up at The Towers. It was truly magnificent. It had become a part of her and she of it. Unlike when Falan had first brought her here, the castle was her home, if only for the summer. She'd experienced so many things, most memorably what a family should look like, what it *could* look like if love and acceptance and affirmation were the threads that held it together.

And God. Truly, He was the firm foundation upon which this family grew and was held together—through the loss of four children, Mr. Bourne's climb to success, the constraints of society, and more. Devyn vowed that if the Lord ever blessed her with a family, it would be patterned after the Bournes—and not her own.

Brice tapped her shoulder, shaking her from her thoughts. "There's the swimming beach. Remember?" He smiled even as a shadow crossed his handsome face.

"Yes." Devyn scanned the beach. By now, they were on the northern, Canadian-facing side of the island, where she surveyed the evidence of an ongoing construction project. The boathouse roof was still being tiled, and equipment littered the area, but no workers were around. No Falan. None of his nasty friends. She shivered at the memory of their taunts and heaved a deep sigh.

"Are you cold?" Reagan put an arm around her.

"No." Devyn smiled at Reagan and then glanced at Brice, who stared at her until she became self-conscious.

Mr. Bourne pointed to another, smaller boathouse built into the side of the island. "Say, Mac, I've been thinking that I should like to add a pulley system and drop-down floor to this small skiff house one day."

"What a grand idea, sir. You never fail to amaze me." Brice's respect for the man fairly oozed out of him.

Mr. Bourne merely smiled. "Are you enjoying the ride? Reagan? Florence?"

Devyn gulped, but thankfully, Mr. Bourne quickly corrected himself. "Dear me. I'm sorry. Guess I miss my girl so much that you filled her shoes for the moment."

Devyn smiled. "I'm honored, sir."

Mr. Bourne shrugged. "Yes, well. Let's try again. Do you like the ride?"

Devyn and Reagan answered in unison. "Oh yes! Thank you, sir."

They giggled at their simultaneous reply.

~ ~ ~

Brice loved watching Devyn's transformation. Her entire demeanor had changed from fearful to free. Due partly to his encouragement? If so, he'd reassure her again and again … for the rest of their lives.

Really? He'd have to mull that over later.

After the gondola ride, Mr. Bourne returned to the castle while Devyn, Reagan, and Brice went to attend the others. Long before they reached the beach, Brice could hear Howard, Marjorie, May, and Marian laughing, teasing, and splashing. He turned to Devyn and Reagan. "Aye, but they're having a grand time."

"And I don't want to miss a moment of it." Reagan grinned and hurried on ahead.

Brice touched Devyn's arm, bidding her to pause. "How are you faring this crackin' day?"

A perplexed look crossed her features as her brows furrowed, and she bit her lip. He touched her bottom lip, running his finger gently along it. "Careful, or you'll draw blood." He smiled as she relaxed.

"I really enjoyed the boat ride. For the first time ever."

"Aye. Give life a chance, and it'll often surprise you."

Devyn scanned the sky a moment. "I think I'm learning how to tame my fears, and it feels rather freeing. I determined that I wouldn't be afraid, and I wasn't."

"I'm proud of you, Devyn. Just look at all you've accomplished in the short time you've been here. Seems there's nothing you can't do."

"Oh, but there is." She hugged herself tightly, her brow creased.

He touched the small of her back and gently pressed her forward. "We'd better get to the beach."

Devyn nodded and hurried ahead, making it to the beach before him.

When he arrived, Howard shot him a grin and splashed water in his direction. "Want to join us?"

"Afraid not. Your father said to remind you dinner is at one, and then you'll all go fishing. You know that's his favorite."

May giggled. "Everything's his favorite around the water. Boating. Fishing. Watching the ships pass."

Marjorie splashed May as they climbed out of the river and onto the sandy beach. "They're my favorite too."

Devyn handed the girls their towels, and Brice gave Howard his. After the four dried off a bit, they all walked back to the castle.

Brice lagged behind, quietly gesturing for Devyn to join him.

She fell into step beside him, a wistful smile softening her features. "I've come to admire the Bournes so much. They're so loving. So caring. So happy together. I want to have a family just like them one day."

Brice's blood pulsed in his veins. He could feel it in his neck. "So do I."

He swallowed the rest of his thoughts. Those must wait until another time.

CHAPTER 14

"I wish we didn't have to leave so soon, but we simply must get back to Long Island." Marian shrugged. "Miss Preston's birthday party is on Friday, and we can't miss it. Melinda is a darling."

Devyn finished pinning Marian's hair in a perfect updo. "You'll be sadly missed around here." She fixed one last curl. "How's that, miss?"

Marian studied herself in the mirror, touching her hair gently. "In such a short time, you've become quite adept. Well done." She rose and scanned her empty closet, mumbling to herself. "Time to go."

Devyn put the final few things into Marian's train case and followed her with it to the Great Hall. Soon the family ventured down to the boathouse, and Devyn, Brice, Reagan, and Sofia followed.

She marveled as hugs and tears were passed around the family, and loving, tender farewells were made. Devyn's own mother had barely said goodbye when she'd left, and even her younger siblings hadn't seemed to care. The ache pricked her heart and the back of her eyes.

Marian, May, and Howard climbed into the boat as the boatman readied their departure. Mr. Bourne waved. "Farewell, my beloved family. I will miss you day and night."

Mrs. Bourne blew kisses off her hand. "I love you, dear ones."

Marjorie blew one big, two-handed kiss. "Be sure to tell Miss Preston happy birthday and say hello to all our friends back home. We'll see you soon. Be good."

Howard waved back. "You be good, Marjorie, and beat the boys in the boat races."

When the launch was far in the distance, the remaining family sauntered up the bridle path while the staff hurried to the back entrance. Mrs. VanLeer met them at the door. "This morning, we're to strip the beds and give the bedrooms a thorough cleaning." The girls curtsied and left to do their work, but the missus took hold of Devyn's arm. "Let's talk, shall we?"

Devyn nodded. "Of course, missus." She nervously followed her superior into her office, and Mrs. VanLeer bid her to sit. Had she done something wrong?

The missus paused before speaking. "This has been quite a busy few weeks for you, but you've kept up with the double duties quite commendably. I've heard reports from several of the family about you, and they've all been positive." Mrs. VanLeer grinned, placing her hands on the back of her chair before pulling it out and sitting.

Devyn's cheeks warmed at the praise. "Thank you. I wasn't sure I could slip into the lady's maid duties, but Reagan is a good teacher, and I enjoyed it all."

"And you are a quick learner. Well, enough. After you finish the bedrooms and have lunch, I need you to clean out the cobwebs throughout the passageways. I can't imagine how those spiders can multiply as they do, but there must have been a hatch overnight. This morning, I detected more than normal as I passed through."

"Yes, ma'am."

Mrs. VanLeer tilted her head. "You're not afraid of them, are you? Sofia and Reagan are repulsed by them, and besides, you're still the housemaid."

Devyn grinned, pretending to swing a broom. "I've overcome my fear. I'll exterminate them."

"Good. Now off with you." Mrs. VanLeer stood and shooed her. "And thank you."

Devyn curtsied and returned to her duties. As she cleaned Marian's room and then Howard's, she thought more about the Bourne family bond and her family's lack of it. The two families couldn't be more different. By the time she finished and went down to lunch, bitterness and anger boiled and threatened to bubble over.

As she entered the servants' hall, everyone was already at the table, chatting happily.

"This fish is delicious, Devyn. Come and join us." Reagan, who loved every kind of fish, gestured her over.

Devyn grinned despite her mood. "Be right there. I *am* hungry." She wasn't so fond of fish, but she took a small piece and loaded a generous helping of potatoes and carrots onto her plate.

Sofia cast a narrow-eyed smirk at her. "Are you done with your rooms?"

Devyn nodded. "Yes." She quickly took a bite of carrots to keep from saying more.

Sofia huffed. "Well, I need you to do the master bedroom as well. I have other things to attend to."

Devyn chewed as she thought about Sofia's demand. She wasn't her superior. Mrs. VanLeer gave her the assignments. She shook her head. "I have other things to attend to too."

Sofia slapped her hands on the table, hard. "I am your superior, miss, and don't you forget it!"

Everyone stopped. Reagan made a choking sound and clutched her throat, her eyes wide and confused. Brice held his fork midair, his brow furrowed and his face turning an uncomely shade of red. Devyn's blood boiled, but she held back a sharp comment with tightly pursed lips.

For a long time, no one said anything. Finally, Devyn spoke.

"Mrs. VanLeer gives me my tasks. Not you. She's already assigned me my afternoon job, and I will follow her instructions. Not yours."

Sofia's expression grew menacing as she glared at Devyn. A long, strange groan came from deep inside her as she stood and pushed back her chair. "Such cheek. You've crossed me one too many times, young lady. I shall report you—and your indiscretions—and you will undoubtedly receive the consequences of your folly."

The nerve! Devyn stared at Sofia's back as she stomped out of the room, even as dread tried to mix with the anger and bitterness of the morning.

Reagan leaned close. "Don't listen to her. She's an old bat!"

Brice laughed. "True enough. Forget her."

Devyn nodded, but it was hard to ignore the interchange. Despite the fact that for the rest of the meal, the three of them discussed the highlights of the past several weeks and predicted what the next few might look like, Devyn was in no mood for lighthearted chatter. Oh, she pretended to be happy, but Sofia's threats combined with her own previous misgivings added to her simmering emotional stew. She had to think it all through and get it under control before she went crazy.

She needed to be alone, so she didn't tell Brice and Reagan what she'd be doing that afternoon. Instead, she rose, washed her dishes, and waved a casual farewell. "See you at dinner." Scurrying out of the room before anyone would question her afternoon activities, she gathered the broom and cleaning cloths. Then she slipped into the passageway and began her battle with the spiders.

She'd take her angst out on them!

Starting in the wine vault passageway, she found only a few strays, tiny and nearly imperceptible. A few webs were scattered here and there, but not many. Why was the missus so concerned about them?

Grateful she had time to think, she batted Sofia around in her head, swatting another cobweb from its place and squishing the web spinner under her boot. "Take that, Sofia! How dare you treat me with such disdain?"

She climbed the stairs to the next level and found many more invaders. "Where are you all coming from? I'll find your parents, and soon." She smacked, crushed, and pulverized the baby spiders with no remorse. She'd do her job well and show Sofia. She would.

But she couldn't show her mother or her brother or the rest of her family. Would they even care that she tried so hard, worked so hard, and accomplished so much? Not likely. Her father would have, but he ...

She shook off the thought as she climbed yet another flight of stairs, ending up between the dining room and the drawing-living room. Then she climbed one more flight of stairs, where she peeked into the dining room through the grate and, seeing it empty, journeyed around the mezzanine and through two iron gates. There she began to find larger groups of itty-bitty spiders, almost translucent. They scurried to and fro, and she followed them. Like tiny troops of soldiers, they marched away from her and toward … the Round Room dungeon!

Devyn peeked through the bars and groaned. Several large webs held hundreds of babies. She steeled herself for battle, gripping the broom with white-knuckled determination. "So this is your nursery, is it? Well, as you can see, I'm much bigger and, might I add, stronger than you. You may outnumber me, but I shall do battle, and I shall be victorious!"

With that, she let out a screech and went to work tearing down the stronghold of the enemy. First, she swept away the webs around the two narrow windows and opened them, sucking in the fresh river air. Then she turned to the other encampments.

To her surprise, she found the job quite satisfying, especially with the mood she was in. So she kept the onslaught going until she became quite winded and sweaty. She stopped and leaned on her broom, wiping her brow with the sleeve of her dress.

As if out of nowhere, one big, black spider slid down a tiny thread in front of her and seemed to challenge her to a duel. *He must be the commander or at least the father of one of these broods.* With only a gentle breeze, he could swing into her hair. Devyn shuddered, stepped back, and banged into the dungeon door, slamming it shut with a loud clash of metal. Then she lost her balance and fell hard on the cement floor.

The spider troops skittered toward her, so she jumped up, rubbing her backside. She picked up the broom and swept furiously at the dangling web spinner, sending him to his demise with a thorough crushing under her shoe.

Then she remembered the door.

Devyn turned and tried to open it, just for her own peace of mind, but it was shut tight. Stuck! She pulled and pulled, but it wouldn't open.

She was locked in the dungeon!

"Help! Is anyone there?" The secret passageway was quiet, so she went to the window to see if she could call for help from there. No one was around. She returned to the door and banged on it with her broom but found that, too, was fruitless.

"Someone will come through soon enough," she said to herself. Then she turned back to the spiders. "You! You caused this."

Soon she had pulverized or scattered every web spinner she could find. Exhausted, she sat on the cool floor with her back to the far end of the wall, just in case any spiders returned and, more importantly, so she could see if anyone came through the passageway.

"I guess I deserve this. After all, I am ... I'm a murderer." With her stark admission, her wall came tumbling down, and she burst into tears. "I can't hold it back anymore. I'm so tired of fighting, tired of hiding, tired of building this wall."

At that moment, her emotional stew was ready for consumption— the guilt and regret she had penned up for the past decade, the fear of failure, all the criticism, ostracism, condemnation, and rebukes, whether self-inflicted or at the hand of others—others who should have cared for her, loved her, protected her. She'd endured them all for over a decade, and now Sofia seemed to have assumed the role of judge and jury too. Why? What reason did she have?

She pulled her knees up to her chin and flopped her head onto them. "Help me, God. I can't—"

Footsteps sounded. Far in the distance at first. "Hello! I need help, please!" She stood as the footsteps grew closer and closer, so she kept on yelling, "Help me, please!" Her heart raced as the footsteps came faster.

"I'm coming!"

"Brice? Oh, thank God!" Devyn quickly adjusted her uniform and swiped the sweat from her face and the hair from her eyes.

When Brice came around the corner, he stopped short, stared at her for a long moment, and then chuckled. "I knew that was your voice." He paused and scrunched up his face. "But what in heaven have you gotten yourself into?"

"It's a long story, but"—she rattled the dungeon bars—"get me out of here. Please!"

~ ~ ~

Brice showed her the little device under the lockbox that opened the door without a key. He fiddled with it until it finally gave way. "This needs oiling. I'll make sure it gets done, and soon." He walked into the dungeon and took her hand, motioning for her to sit beside him. "A long story, eh? I like stories. Do tell."

After she'd related how she'd come to be locked in the dungeon, he gave her his special, lopsided grin. She had told him how she liked his smile two—no, three—times already.

He winked. "I'm glad I was here for you, though I almost went up the grand staircase. The Bournes have gone out for a boat ride, so all the servants are using the stairs and not the passageways. You might have been locked up and rotting for days."

Fear flashed in her eyes, and her face turned pale. "Why would you say such a thing?"

"I'm sorry. Bad joke." He took her hand and glanced around the dungeon. "I must say, you did a fine job in here. I heard there was a hatch. One of the maids nearly lost her breakfast when she reported it this morning."

Devyn's eyes grew large. "I had no idea there could be so many."

"Aye, there can be more than a thousand, there can."

"I think I killed nearly as many." A pink tinge colored her cheeks, and she tilted her chin up.

He tweaked her nose. "You are quite the little soldier."

Devyn blushed, her smile popping the adorable dimple into place. He gently touched her cheek. He had to. "You're the most beautiful soldier I've ever met." He glanced at her full, parted lips, so soft, so luscious, so …

Clearing his throat, he scooted back against the cold stone wall. He gazed up at the ceiling and sighed. "… and so tempting. Devyn, you can set my heart to racing better than a fast ride in one of Mr. Bourne's speedboats. You fill my mind with dreams and hopes and thoughts I never thought I'd have. I … you …"

He turned to look at her, but tears dripped down her cheeks. "What's wrong?"

"I am. *I* am wrong. I'm not who you think I am, Brice." She furiously shook her head, hugging herself and rocking like a lunatic. "I'm not beautiful or lovely or any of those nice things you say about me, although I take every word in like the air I breathe. I'm not worthy of your admiration." She swiped her tears and struggled to get up, but he grabbed her hand, keeping her from leaving.

"Wait." He stood and took both of her hands, swallowing his nervousness and confusion. "I'll wait. Wait until you're free. Whatever it is that's holding you back. I want you to be free as the gulls that fly over this island. I want you to soar with wings like the eagles that nest on the shore."

"I'll never be free of this." She turned away from him. "Never."

"I don't believe there is anything that God cannot free you from. Nothing. But until then, I want you to lean into our friendship." He waited for Devyn to compose herself and look at him. It seemed like several minutes. "There's an Irish saying, 'May the hinges of our friendship never grow rusty.' I want that for us. Always."

She looked at him and then at the dungeon door. Then an odd expression crossed her face. He tried to guess what she was thinking but could not, so he stood in perplexed silence as her face finally relaxed and spread into a wide smile. She glanced at the iron door again, then back to him. Then she began to giggle, and her giggles got faster and louder until she was laughing boisterously.

"That's funny." She slapped her thigh.

"Funny? I meant for it to be poignant. Romantic even." Women! He'd never understand the fairer sex.

Devyn shrugged, her cheeks turning rosy red. "Sorry. I guess it's all the emotions of the day. Or the week. Or my life."

He wanted her to be free from her own self, or at least from the memories she had apparently battled in that dungeon. "Let's get out of here. Shall we?" He tucked the dustpan and cleaning cloths into the bucket and grabbed it and the broom with one hand, took her hand with the other, and led her away from there. And hopefully, away from the war she fought.

CHAPTER 15

A week later, Devyn rushed to Marjorie's room and knocked gently.

She discerned a cheery voice from inside. "Come in."

After entering, she curtsied to Marjorie, then faced Reagan, trying to stay calm. "Pardon the interruption, but Mrs. VanLeer sent me to fetch you. She says it's urgent and wants you to meet her in her office right away."

Marjorie nodded to Reagan in the mirror. "Go on, then. She can finish my hair." She cast a quick glance at Devyn.

Devyn avoided looking into Reagan's eyes, afraid she'd show the fear she had seen on Mrs. VanLeer's face. But she tried to reassure her friend with a gentle touch before she left the room.

Biting her bottom lip, Devyn picked up the hairbrush and began running it through Marjorie's long tresses.

Speaking to Devyn's reflection in the mirror, Marjorie raised a brow. "Do you know what this is all about?"

Devyn shook her head. "No, but the missus appeared mightily concerned over something."

"Dear me, I hope it's not serious." Marjorie put her hand to her chest.

In less than ten minutes, Reagan returned, eyes red and swollen. "It's my family. A telegram came from my aunt. There's been a terrible accident. My father. My mother. My sister. All are seriously hurt." With that, she whimpered like a tiny child.

Marjorie jumped up and hugged her tightly.

Reagan pulled away, terror scrunching her face into a frightful frown. "I must return home to help with their care as soon as possible."

Marjorie nodded. "Go. Immediately!" She reached into a vanity drawer and pulled out her reticule. Opening it, she retrieved a roll of bills and thrust them into Reagan's hand. "This will cover the train fare and more, and I will instruct Mrs. VanLeer to give you your pay today. Go, and God be with you."

Reagan looked at the roll of bills and then up at her mistress, barely whispering a shaky "Thank you, Miss Marjorie." Then she turned to Devyn, her brows furrowed.

The pained expression on her face nearly made Devyn cry. After they hugged, Reagan drew in a deep breath and squared her shoulders. She swiped away her tears and swallowed. Turning to Marjorie, she pasted on a quivering smile.

"May I be so bold as to suggest that Devyn take my place as your lady's maid? She's learned quickly and is a clever young woman. I'd stake my reputation on it." Reagan nearly begged Marjorie with her eyes.

Marjorie smiled. "What a fine idea!" She studied Devyn. "My sister said you were surprisingly adept in the position for not having any formal training."

Devyn drew in a deep breath and smiled at Reagan. "She's a good teacher. I must credit her for what I've learned."

"Well, then, you're hired." Marjorie pulled out another few bills. "And this is for training her so well."

Reagan stared at the two handfuls of money. "I can't take all this. It's too much."

Marjorie chuckled, folding Reagan's fingers over the bills. "I insist. It would cost five times this much to have the girl formally trained. Take it and go, with my prayers holding you fast." She gave Reagan another hug and gently pushed her toward the door. "And Devyn, you go with her and help pack her things. Then escort her to the train. She needn't be alone at such a time. I will alert the missus of our plan."

Devyn curtsied. "Yes, miss. Thank you."

Reagan curtsied as well. "Thank you, Miss Marjorie. I … I will miss you."

Marjorie nodded. "I will miss you too. Now go."

Devyn and Reagan went to their room and packed Reagan's things. Then they hurried down to the servants' hall, where they found Mrs. VanLeer waiting. She handed Reagan an envelope. "Here is your pay and a bonus, I might add, for your fine work with us. I envision that it will help as your family recovers from their trauma."

Reagan took the envelope and curtsied. "I am grateful ... for everything. Truly."

The missus handed her a basket. "I asked Cook to prepare enough food to get you through to Brooklyn. The train food is far too expensive and not as good as Cook's." She paused and patted Reagan's hand. "I'm so sorry to hear of your plight, dear girl. You and your family will be in my prayers."

After another expression of thanks, Reagan began crying again.

"Miss Marjorie came to set things in motion, but I had already sent ahead to prepare your way. Brice is waiting in the boathouse to escort the two of you to the train."

As she led Reagan along with a hand at her elbow, Devyn's trepidation grew with each step. Go with her in the boat to the bay and then to Hammond? She hadn't crossed the channel or been to her hometown since her first day on the island. And she didn't want to!

But she would do it. For her friend.

As they drew near the south boathouse, Brice and the boatman, Mr. Labrese, were waiting for them on the dock. Brice ran to meet them and took the bags, motioning the girls to follow him quickly. "I'm sorry to hear of your family's accident, Reagan, but we must be on our way if you're to catch the train in Hammond."

Soon the four were in the steamer launch, crossing the channel with ease and swiftness. Devyn marveled at the difference between the jolting, rocking skiff trip she had taken with her brother and the smooth, steady trip in this fine launch. Brice sat next to Mr. Labrese as if to give the girls time together. She smiled at his kindness.

Devyn held Reagan's hand and rubbed it with her other hand. "Will you be all right, traveling so far alone?"

Reagan nodded. "I've been on many trains, although not

unaccompanied. But I shall endure."

"I've never been on a train, and I think I should faint with the fear of it if I had to do what you are doing." Devyn shivered. "How brave you are."

Reagan looked at her through teary eyes. "I don't fear the travel. I fear what I shall find at the end of it."

Devyn patted her hand all the more, speaking as calmly as she could. "What else did the telegram say? Do you know what the accident was or how it happened?"

Reagan shook her head and sniffed. "No, and that's what's so terrifying. I know only what my aunt relayed in her brief message."

"Then we shall trust the Lord to guide you through whatever waters may lie ahead." Devyn hugged Reagan, who promptly laid her head on her shoulder and sighed.

A sudden wave bounced the launch and knocked their heads together. "Ouch!" Devyn rubbed the side of her head.

"Sorry, ladies. That ship created quite a wake." Mr. Labrese pointed to a rusty red vessel.

Devyn looked up to see a huge cargo ship passing them. She'd been so consumed with Reagan's heartache that she hadn't even noticed it approaching. They both smiled, diffusing the tension.

Soon they pulled up to the Chippewa Bay docks, unloaded Reagan's bags, and hailed a nearby wagon to take them to the Hammond train station less than four miles inland. Devyn was grateful the missus had summoned Brice as an escort, for the farmer who drove the wagon was a rather crotchety fellow, spitting tobacco juice several times during their journey over the rough road. Could she have found the courage to hail such a ride had Brice not been there?

"Whoa, Buck!" The farmer pulled the wagon up to the station, and Brice helped Devyn and Reagan out.

"We shouldn't be long, sir," Brice said, handing him a coin.

The farmer nodded, slipped his hat over his eyes, and planted his feet on the railing. Brice and Devyn escorted Reagan to the waiting room, where Devyn made sure she had her ticket, and Brice checked that the train would be there within the hour.

Reagan stood and hugged Devyn, whispering in her ear, "Thank you for being my friend. I shall miss you." Then, still holding onto Devyn, she turned to Brice. "You two go ahead. The driver is waiting, and I'll be fine. Besides, I need time to pray."

Devyn squeezed her in response. "Thank you, and I shall miss you immensely."

Brice stuck his hands in his pockets, tilting his head. "You and your family will be in all our prayers, Reagan. Godspeed."

After the round of hugs and goodbyes, Devyn and Brice climbed into the wagon to return to Chippewa Bay, leaving Reagan in the waiting room.

Brice glanced back at the station and shook his head. "Poor girl. You never know what twists and turns may come in life. I suspect we should be ready for any eventuality and trust God with each moment."

Devyn nodded but said nothing. Trust God with every moment? What about those times when He seemed so far away? *Like the time He let …*

"Miss Marjorie will sorely miss her." Brice interrupted Devyn's musings just in time.

"I am to fill her role." Devyn barely spoke above a whisper as the reality began to dawn on her. She had been promoted!

Brice grinned, his blue eyes the color of the sky above him. "Really? That's quite an honor. I'm proud of you."

She smiled. "I hope I can fill the position well. I've had so little training and have so much to learn."

Brice waved off her worries. "Aye, but you're a clever girl and learn fast. I've seen it myself. Besides, Marjorie is a kind, independent woman."

"But what will I do without Reagan's patient tutelage? I certainly can't depend on Sofia to instruct me."

Brice chuckled. "No, but Marjorie, too, is patient and will surely guide you well."

"I don't deserve such an honor."

Concern weighed upon her heart as the wagon pulled up to the dock.

~ ~ ~

Brice helped Devyn out of the wagon and paid the farmer, grateful he had been there to escort the two women on such a sad journey.

"Miss Reagan's on her way, I 'spect?" Mr. Labrese quirked a questioning brow. "It's a mighty shame, her situation."

Brice nodded. "It is, but the train should be there any minute to take her to her family." He took Devyn's hand to steady her as she climbed into the launch. Then he plunked down next to her.

Mr. Labrese put the launch in gear, and off they went, silent with their own thoughts.

Brice sighed. What a sad day for Reagan but such a life-changing one for Devyn! She'd been promoted nearly to the status of himself in the twinkling of an eye.

He turned to her. "I suppose you'll have to fill both the housemaid and lady's maid roles until they find a replacement for the housemaid job."

Devyn blinked as if she hadn't realized that fact. "I guess so, but I've done both before, and I'm happy to stay busy, especially after losing my friend."

"You haven't lost her. She'll be your friend still. And when her family gets better, perhaps she can return to service with us."

"Perhaps, but until then I shall sorely miss her." Devyn's watery eyes looked so sad, so fearful. One tear spilled onto her cheek, so he reached up and gently swiped it away.

"I'm here. You are not alone."

Her eyes flashed with uncertainty. Or was it misgiving?

"Fear not, my wee fawn. All will be well in due time."

Devyn's brows furrowed, and her eyes narrowed. She looked at him with what appeared to be suspicion. But why?

She shook her head. "No. It will never be well. It's all wrong!"

She'd said the last word with such force that Mr. Labrese turned his head to glance at her. He said nothing, but concern crossed his weathered face.

After the boatman turned back to maneuvering the launch through the choppy channel, Brice patted her hand. "What? What's wrong? You've just been promoted, for heaven's sake. Tell me what's really troubling you. Please."

She bit her bottom lip and furiously shook her head. Then she scooted away from him and folded her arms over her chest in a protective hug.

The wall.

Her infernal emotional wall went up again! If only he had a sledgehammer, he'd smash the thing to bits. He'd burst that dam of … whatever it was. What was it that forced her to protect herself whenever anyone started to get close? What deep, dark secret was she trying to hide?

Deciding not to push her for answers, he watched the castle grow bigger and bigger. Once they pulled up to the dock, Devyn refused his hand, climbed out of the launch, and, without so much as a thank you, hurried toward the castle alone.

~ ~ ~

Devyn couldn't give her heart, her trust, her love to someone again. She'd only just begun to let Reagan in, and now her friend had been taken from her. Like everyone she cared about.

No! She wouldn't care for Brice. She couldn't.

She wanted to. She wished she could.

But she was damaged goods. Guilty of the worst crime of all.

She didn't deserve his friendship, let alone anything more. She'd never be worthy of such a man.

For his sake, she had to keep him safe. From her!

She wouldn't care for another person as long as she lived. It hurt too badly.

She hurried to the servants' hall, to the comfort and distraction of her work. Before she opened the door, she smoothed her uniform and squared her shoulders. She was a lady's maid now even though she didn't deserve that either.

When she entered the hall, Mrs. VanLeer was sitting at the table, sipping tea. She looked up and patted the chair beside her. "Come. Sit." The missus smiled at her. "And get yourself a cup of tea. Tea often soothes the day's troubles like little else can."

Devyn poured a cup of tea and sat. The missus didn't speak for a long time. She only sipped her steaming brew and cast a gentle smile Devyn's way.

"Miss Marjorie told me she hired you to be her lady's maid. Congratulations!" The missus grinned, her dark eyes twinkling playfully.

"Thank you. Reagan suggested it." She tucked her chin, turning her cup in her hands.

"It's quite an honor ... and a place of responsibility. Are you prepared to take on such an important role?"

"I think I am, missus." Her heart raced. "I will do my best."

"And can you also do the housemaid duties? I'll find a replacement, but it may take a while."

"Yes, ma'am. I did both before and enjoyed the busyness." Devyn bit her lip, hoping she was right.

Mrs. VanLeer reached over and touched her forearm. "Well then, that's settled, and your pay will reflect your hard work and willingness to serve."

Devyn allowed the corners of her mouth to turn up. "Thank you, missus. I am honored."

The housekeeper grinned. "Off with you, then. Miss Marjorie has gone fishing with her father, so after you attend to her room and her things, check that the living room and piazza are shipshape. Then you have a rest until your mistress returns. She'll likely want a hot bath following her fishing excursion."

Devyn curtsied. "Yes, ma'am."

She went up to Miss Marjorie's room and put everything in order. Then she descended the stairs and headed for the living room, nearly bumping into Sofia as she rounded the corner. Sofia's tray teetered a tiny bit, but she puckered up her face as if Devyn had committed some terrible offense.

"Pardon me, Sofia. I didn't see you," Devyn said in her most apologetic voice. She would try to be nice to the woman and stay on her good side—if she had one. After all, Papa had always encouraged her to be kind to friend ... and foe.

"Watch where you're going, miss!" Sofia huffed. "Some lady's maid you are, plowing through the castle like a wild animal." She repositioned her tray and scowled down her long nose.

"I *am* sorry. The missus assigned me to clean the living room, and I was just going there." She glanced into the room, wishing she could slam the door in Sofia's face.

"Well, watch your ways, miss, or you'll regret you ever came to serve here." Sofia snapped her chin up and turned on her heel, tapping her shoes in a retreating rhythm of scornful rebuke.

Devyn shook her head as she entered the living room. It barely needed attention. A bit of dust here. A tiny cobweb there. A few small adjustments to a knickknack or a book. She straightened a crooked chair and a crooked pleat in one the drapes and went to the piazza, finding it in pristine condition as well. But she would make sure everything was perfect. Whether as a housemaid or a lady's maid, she'd do her utmost.

Sofia would not get the best of her.

Once Devyn finished tidying the rooms, she decided she'd take a little rest until Marjorie returned, just as the missus had suggested. Before lying down, she went to retrieve her most treasured possession, the royal blue ribbon her papa had so lovingly given her. Just holding it always helped.

She looked under her pillow, but it wasn't there. She looked for it in her drawer, but it wasn't there either. She shuffled her scant things around once again just to make sure she hadn't missed it, but still, no sign of the ribbon.

But then something metallic shimmered through her belongings.

She pulled a fine, gold locket out of her drawer and turned it over. A fancy "B" was scrolled on it. Opening it, she viewed two tiny pictures of little children. It had to be Mrs. Bourne's locket. But why was it here instead of her ribbon?

Devyn's heart sank as her mind produced the answer. She pressed her lips together rather than say it aloud.

Sofia!

CHAPTER 16

Before breakfast, Devyn gently pinned Marjorie's hair in place.
"Why don't you join us for a boat ride today?" Marjorie implored Devyn with her eyes in the dressing table mirror.

Devyn shook her head. "Thank you, but I don't care much for the river, or boats, for that matter."

Three tiny lines formed between Marjorie's nicely plucked eyebrows. "Why ever not? How can you not love the river and boating?"

Devyn swallowed and bit her bottom lip, trying to hold back the dam. Why must she be transported to that terrible day again and again? She blinked back tears as memories flooded her mind, her heart pounding harder and harder with each passing second.

"Are you all right? You're white as my talcum powder." Marjorie stood and grabbed Devyn's shoulders, bidding her to take her own chair at the dressing table. "What's the matter? Come. You can tell me. Are we not friends?"

Devyn glanced at Marjorie's face, so caring, so kind. Friends? She'd never had a friend who expressed such concern for her. Never had a confidant to share her burdens or ease her pain. Could she trust her?

"I … I killed him."

"You what? Killed whom? Devyn, dear, what are you talking about?"

There. She had said it. Finally said it. Said what she'd held deep inside for half her life. For more than a decade. Guilt that prodded her with painful memories. Shame that tortured her with nightmares. Fear that haunted her day and night. She'd built a dam high and sturdy to hold it all back, to keep anyone from knowing the truth.

Now Miss Marjorie knew.

And with that, the dam burst, and Devyn heaved a ragged cry, spewing forth the pain she could no longer contain. She threw her hands up to her face, covering her shame as best she could, but the sound of her lament, her torture, refused to subside. She tried to hold it back. Tried to keep it in. But it overpowered her. Possessed her with an overwhelming strength all its own.

Marjorie thrust a lacy handkerchief into her hands and proceeded to rub her back. "There, there. I'm sure you didn't actually kill anyone. Let it all out. The tale can't be as bad as all that."

"But it can. I killed him. I deserve to be thrown in your dungeon and left there to rot."

Marjorie patted her back. "That dungeon is there for Father's and Flagg's amusement. Nothing more. I don't know what you're talking about, but a gentle soul like you could never have killed anyone. What haunts you so, Devyn? I will keep your secret safe, whatever it is."

Devyn shook her head violently. "No! It is a mortal sin that I alone must bear."

Marjorie continued to pat her back, faster and faster, forming wide circles as her papa had done when he'd put her to sleep at night. Then Marjorie spoke, and her voice was tender. "No one should bear such pain alone. No one. Tell me now, or I shall have to fetch Daddy and have him drag it out of you."

With the threat of Mr. Bourne knowing her shame, Devyn lurched back like a doe caught in a hunter's trap. "No! Please!" She wiped her tears and blew her nose. Then she took in a deep, shuddering breath, trying to gather the strength to confess her sin.

"I killed my father."

Marjorie's dark brows furrowed into a deep crevice. She pulled up a footstool and turned Devyn to face her, sitting with her knees touching hers. The woman took both of her hands in her own and just sat there, gazing deeply into her eyes as if she were studying her very soul. Marjorie swallowed hard, rubbing the back of Devyn's hands with her thumbs. Waiting.

Devyn hadn't lowered her walls to anyone since that day. Not her mother and certainly not Falan. She had shut herself off from all of her playmates, schoolmates, neighbors. Anyone who might get close to her and expose her. But now here was Marjorie, her employer, the daughter of a famous and wealthy man, touching her. Caring.

Devyn dropped her gaze to the ground. How could she tell Marjorie the truth? How could she admit the deed that had cursed her life?

Soft as a hummingbird's flutter, Marjorie reached up and swiped a falling tear from Devyn's face. "Tell me."

She shook her head and studied the flowers on the rug under her feet. "I cannot."

Marjorie tipped Devyn's chin up and nodded. "Yes. You must. You must break free from whatever chains bind you."

Her heart raced with apprehension. Fear. How could she build up that dam again, build up the walls and push back the waters that had already burst forth? How could she run from the ruins of her life? She no longer could.

"I didn't mean to. I was just ten. I wanted to be with my father. He was the one who did all the hugging. Not Mama. Mama was mean. She didn't mean to be, but she was." Devyn knew she sounded like a child, but she couldn't help it. "Papa was kind and fun and made me laugh. He wanted to be with me. He loved me."

Marjorie smiled—just a little. "He sounds wonderful."

"He is. Was. And he loved to fish. He loved the river." When she said the word *river*, her voice cracked, spilling out more tears from the shattered dam. She wheezed out her sorrow and continued. "It didn't matter if it was summer or winter, Papa loved to fish. Falan usually got to go with him, but I begged Papa to let me have a turn. I was big enough, even though I was a girl, I said. Papa agreed, but Mama said no, as usual." Devyn stopped, gnashing her teeth at the memory. She shook it off.

"Papa overruled her for once. Usually, Mama got the last word, but not this time. I had won. I was going fishing with Papa!" She'd been so excited as she'd put on her boots and coat, her hat and mittens. She'd even snuck her younger brother's knickers and put them on under her skirt. She wanted to be warm and cozy for such a special trip.

"It was December, and the ice had formed on the bay. The boys at school told of their ice-fishing exploits, and I wanted to experience such fun. None of the other girls my age had gotten do such a grown-up thing. I was special. Alone with Papa. What a magical day it would be!" An apple-sized lump threatened to choke her, and it took a long while to swallow it whole. Finally, with the help of Marjorie's kind eyes prodding her on, she gathered her courage to continue.

"When we got to the river, we noticed one other fisherman on the far end of the bay. His hole was already cut, and he gave us a cordial wave. The sun shone brightly and glittered off the ice like sparkling jewels. I could see our breath, but it didn't feel cold to me." Devyn paused and glanced at the ceiling. She didn't want to tell the rest of the sordid details but knew she must. It was too late to turn back now.

"Papa made me stay on the shore while he cut the hole. I watched as he gingerly walked on ice, and I thought about Peter walking on the water to Jesus. It made me giggle, and I told Papa about Peter. He said, 'The good Lord will have you walking on water one day, my dear girl. Never stop following Him. Never, ever. Promise?'"

Marjorie nodded.

Devyn drew a quavering breath. "I promised him, and he smiled. 'That's my darling Devyn, a child of God, who will do marvels in you one day.'" At this, she couldn't help but whimper. Some child of God she was, murdering her father and pretending to be something she wasn't.

Marjorie just sat there waiting. Rubbing Devyn's hands and waiting. Patient. Kind. Caring. Devyn had to continue. "Papa worked on the ice hole for what seemed like a long time, whistling as he worked, as he always did. I asked three or four times if I could join him, but he kept telling me to wait until he'd dug the hole, just to be safe. I took off my mittens to hike up the blasted knickers I had put on. By that time, I was regretting that I had added them. Then I heard a loud crack. I looked up and saw Papa falling through the ice!"

Devyn groaned, the weight of the memory threatening to smother her, drown her in the dread she had known a million times since that day. She swallowed the bile rising in her throat and willed herself to continue.

"He went under and then popped up and shouted, 'Stay there!' I couldn't have moved if I wanted to. I was frozen to the ground. He went under again and came back up, grasping the side of the ice. He said, 'Get help! Hurry!'"

At the memory, Devyn shifted in her seat, wanting to get up and run.

But Marjorie continued to hold her hands firmly in her own. Then she reached up and gently brushed a strand of hair that had fallen into Devyn's eyes. Marjorie nodded and almost smiled. "Go on, dearest Devyn."

Could she go on? Could she reveal her failure? Her folly?

Again Marjorie prodded her. "Get it out. You need to let it out."

Tears spilled over her cheeks, and her nose ran. She turned and wiped them on her shirtsleeve as best she could.

"Let me help." Marjorie grabbed another lace hankie from a dressing table drawer and gently wiped her face. "Blow." She held the hankie to Devyn's nose, and Devyn complied, embarrassed and humbled but also amazed that this woman of status would serve a nothing like her.

"Continue," Marjorie said simply and then waited for Devyn to compose herself enough to finish her tale.

"I watched as Papa went under the ice again, but I was still frozen in shock. I looked at the other fisherman, but he was too far away to see what had happened, and besides, his back was to us by then. I tried to yell, but nothing came out. I felt like a rock clogged my throat, choking me, keeping me from yelling for help. It felt like something was holding me, and I couldn't move. For the longest time, I just stood there, waiting for Papa to come up again and tell me what to do. But he never came up."

Devyn choked on her pain, and the floodgates opened. She sounded like the old Irish women who had keened at Papa's wake. She lamented so loudly that she yanked her hands from Marjorie's grasp and tried to cover her mouth to muffle the horrid sound she couldn't control.

Marjorie gently pulled her hands away and took her in her arms, hugging her and patting her back. "There. There. Let it all out. You've held it all in for far too long."

For the longest time, for what seemed like an eternity, Devyn cried, wetting the shoulder of her mistress' beautiful dress. But she could do nothing else. Marjorie held her tight as Devyn released ten years of torture.

Finally, when she had spent all her tears, Devyn pulled back and looked into Marjorie's placid face. Devyn studied her, searching for hate or blame or the accusations she knew would soon come. But she could find none.

Marjorie nodded. "Go on. What happened next?"

"My feet finally let go of the earth, and I ran, ran as fast as I could to the other fisherman. When I got to him, I couldn't speak, so I pulled him toward our fishing hole, and he apparently gathered what had happened. He rushed ahead, but by the time he got there, he wouldn't go onto the ice. He simply shook his head and said, 'It's too late, lass. Go home.'"

Marjorie gave a murmur of deep sympathy.

"Go home? How could I go home and tell Mama I had killed my papa?" Devyn knew Marjorie had no answer for the question, but she had to ask it anyway.

"You didn't kill your papa." The words came from a man's voice behind her. She swung around to find Mr. Bourne entering the room, advancing toward her.

Devyn stood and curtsied out of habit, furiously wringing her hands. "I did! Falan said it was all my fault, and I agree! I never should've begged him to go fishing that day. And when he fell into the freezing water? I should've screamed or run for help. I didn't."

Mr. Bourne pulled her into his arms. He held her close as he stroked her hair. "That was Providence's doing, not yours. You didn't cause the ice to crack, and you didn't choose to lose your voice or your footing. It happened. Things happen, Devyn. Terrible things. When I lost my little Freddie and Helen, and when young Kenneth and my darling Louisa died, I blamed myself too. But God chose for all four of my children to be with Him early on and not grow to adulthood, and He chose your papa to be with Him too. All of our loved ones are in God's hands—a much better place than where we are, I think. Don't you agree?"

Devyn swiped the tears that had wet Mr. Bourne's coat, shirt, and tie. She had lost her papa; the Bournes had lost four little children. How narrow her grief seemed at that moment. "I am so, so sorry."

Mr. Bourne chuckled as he touched his shirt. "Don't be. It was ready for a cleaning anyhow. But back to your father, Devyn. You must hear me now and believe what I say. You *did not* kill your father! You have been believing a lie."

Devyn's eyes darted from Marjorie to Mr. Bourne. Marjorie nodded and smiled. Then she stepped forward and patted Devyn's arm. "He's right, you know. Let it go and be free."

"Mother blames me. Falan too." Devyn looked at the floor as she weighed the Bournes' words. Was it a lie? Was she truly not to blame? Could she ever forgive herself and let it go? Could others? It seemed too miraculous to comprehend.

Mr. Bourne tipped her chin to force her to look at him, just as his daughter had done, just as her father used to do when he wanted her full attention. "You cannot change the opinions of others, but you can choose to forgive yourself and believe the truth. As God's word says, 'Ye shall know the truth, and the truth shall set you free.'"

Devyn gazed at both of the Bournes and prayed they were right. "Thank you for your words. I shall think on them as I try to get free from my guilt."

Mr. Bourne cleared his throat, and Devyn detected tears in his eyes. "I shall pray for you, my dear girl. I shall pray that you will more than consider them. I pray you will choose to believe."

CHAPTER 17

Entering the servants' hall, Devyn stopped short. There sat a former schoolmate quietly eating alone at the table. Her sandy brown hair was pulled up in her mobcap, her housemaid uniform not unlike Devyn's.

Hurrying to greet her, Devyn gave her a warm hug. "Hannah? What in heaven's name are you doing here?"

The young woman's cheerful, gray eyes sparkled. "I've been hired as a housemaid, and I am to take your place. I just arrived an hour ago."

"I'm so glad." Devyn clapped her hands before grabbing a bowl and filling it with stew. As delighted as she felt, the girl was pixie-like, thin as a rail and petite as a schoolgirl. How would she ever manage? However, she kept her concerns to herself. "I'm sure you'll find your work rewarding. The Bournes are ever so nice, and I have grown to like it here."

Hannah smiled as Devyn sat beside her. "Mrs. VanLeer seems nice enough. She said I am to share a room with you and a couple of others. I've put my things away but didn't know you were my roommate until a few minutes ago."

Devyn swallowed and grinned. "I'm glad you're here. Reagan, the girl I replaced, had to leave, and I miss her. But God brought you!"

"Thank you. It's nice to know someone. I thought I'd be the stranger in the camp."

Just then, Sofia entered the room, casting them a steely-eyed glare. She said nothing but spooned stew into her bowl and plunked down across from them.

Forcing a friendly expression, Devyn indicated Sofia. "This is our roommate, Sofia." She touched Hannah on the shoulder. "This is Hannah, our new housemaid."

"I've already been informed, thank you very much. A babe just off the breast, I see."

Hannah shot a wide-eyed glance Devyn's way. Her brows furrowed, and as she took a bite of her stew, the spoon in her hand trembled.

Devyn gave Sofia a dart-riddled stare and bit her bottom lip. The nerve of that bitter old maid. "At least she doesn't take other people's things." She'd taken care of the situation this time, but what about the next?

Before anyone could respond, Devyn turned toward Hannah and continued. "You've grown into such a lovely young lady, Hannah. So tall and becoming. You're eighteen, right?"

"Yes. I'll be nineteen next month." Hannah's voice quivered as she glanced at Sofia.

"Rather skinny and frail looking. I hope you can do the work sufficiently, or they'll can you for sure." Sofia didn't look up, but her face pinched into an ugly smirk.

Brice entered from behind Sofia. "Well, hello. I'm Brice." He smiled at Hannah. "And who do we have here?" His kind tone sweetened the sour atmosphere as he held out his hand.

Devyn slid to the end of the table and introduced the two. Sofia acted as if she hadn't seen Brice, but then she snapped a cold glance his way and returned her attention to her bowl. Hannah scooted away from her as Brice took a seat at their end of the table. Sufficiently shunned, Sofia picked up her bowl and left.

Devyn huffed a sigh. "Good riddance. Watch your back around her, Hannah. She's a wily one and likes to cause trouble."

Brice winked. "Let's be charitable, shall we?"

Although she wondered if he'd be so gracious if he knew about the locket, Devyn nodded. Hannah agreed, and the three engaged in a lighthearted conversation about life on Dark Island.

Just as they rose to wash their bowls, Mrs. VanLeer came into the servants' hall and shot a glance at Devyn. The missus' furrowed brow and stern tone meant only one thing. Trouble. "I'd like to see you in my office. Now."

"Yes, ma'am." Perplexed, Devyn excused herself and followed her into the small office.

There Sofia greeted her with a narrow-eyed look of victory, arms folded across her chest, chin held high and haughty.

Mrs. VanLeer picked up a locket from her desk and displayed it in the palm of her hand. "Do you recognize this?"

Devyn's heart raced, and she swallowed hard. Mrs. Bourne's brooch. "Yes, I found it yesterday and left it on Mrs. Bourne's dresser."

"Fiddlesticks! You stole it." Sofia's accusation shocked her. Infuriated her. Scared her.

Deyvn shook her head furiously, nearly shouting at Sofia as she wrung her hands. "That's not true!" Then she turned to plead with the missus. "It was in my drawer, but I don't know how it got there. So I returned it. I would never steal. Ever!"

Mrs. VanLeer set the locket on her desk, took Devyn's hand, and led her to a chair. "Sit." Then she motioned for Sofia to sit as well. She cast Sofia a warning look and focused on Devyn. "Why didn't you report this?"

Devyn's blood surged in her veins. "I ... I don't know." She glanced at Sofia and back to the missus, shaking her head. "I figured someone must have put it in my drawer, but I didn't want to make false accusations."

Mrs. VanLeer stepped between Devyn and Sofia and angled toward Devyn. "In the future, you must report such mishaps, but since it's been returned, I shall give you the benefit of the doubt. This time. But beware. If you or anyone"—she arched a brow in Sofia's direction—"were to steal even a sugar cube, that person would receive dire consequences. Is that understood?"

Tears stung her eyes, but Devyn held her emotions at bay. Still, her voice quivered. "Yes, ma'am."

The missus turned to Sofia. "And any falsehoods will receive such consequences as well." She paused and stepped back to her desk. "Back to work, then, Sofia. Devyn, please remain behind for a moment."

Mrs. VanLeer waited for Sofia to leave before she spoke. "For the record, I don't believe you took the locket, but since Sofia is Mrs. Bourne's maid, well ..."

Relief flooded Devyn as the housekeeper cleared her throat and changed the subject. "This afternoon, I'd like you to show Hannah the ropes, then stitch up the torn cushions on the Pullman seats in the living room. Mr. Lipton will be here for the Fourth of July celebration tomorrow, and we can't have the cushions in disrepair."

Devyn lowered her eyes, afraid to look at the missus. She curtsied. "Yes, ma'am."

Mrs. VanLeer patted her hand. "Let's leave this conversation here, shall we?"

She curtsied again. "Of course, ma'am."

"All right, then. When you're done with the cushions, send Hannah back to me. Off with you." Mrs. VanLeer smiled and shooed her out the door as if she hadn't just presented her with potential grounds with which to be fired.

Why did being Mrs. Bourne's maid give Sofia power over the others? Apparently, even over Mrs. VanLeer. Devyn couldn't reconcile it.

When she returned to the servants' hall, Hannah got up and hurried to her. "What happened?"

Devyn shrugged. "Nothing that need concern you. She wants me to work with you this afternoon."

"I'm glad. I wasn't sure what to do next. This is quite a daunting place." Hannah's smoky gray eyes darted to and fro. Her reticence reminded Devyn of herself when she'd first come here.

"I felt the same way, but you'll get used to things quite soon." Devyn took Hannah's slender hand and pulled her toward the cleaning closet. "We have some repairs to do. You can sew, right?"

"Oh yes." Hannah smiled, relaxing her shoulders.

"Good." Devyn picked up the wicker sewing box and headed to the secret passageway. "Follow me." On the way upstairs, she prattled on about the passageways and the protocols, proud to be the senior professional and not the outsider for once. "It takes time to learn this castle's ways, but once you do, you'll grow to like The Towers, I'm sure."

Upon entering the living room, Devyn stopped and pointed to the animal heads. "This room gave me quite a fright when I first came here. That moose head, the animal skins, and that portrait of King Charles I—they gave me bad dreams. The men call it the Trophy Room."

Hannah tilted her head to one side. "Why is the portrait creepy? He appears to be a fine king."

Devyn laughed. "Oh, that's because you can open it from the back and spy on people." After Devyn explained the details of the Watch and the passages, Hannah shuddered. Devyn gave her a quick hug. "Don't worry. It's all in fun and only meant to be helpful, not menacing."

Devyn turned their attention to the three alcoves that held pew-like benches sitting face to face with small tables between them. In each alcove, a large, multi-paned window provided bright sunlight and a lovely view of the south channel, where several boats passed by the island. She ventured a long glance. "I've also grown to enjoy the views here."

Hannah nodded, looking over Devyn's shoulder at the view. "It is magnificent, to be sure. But what's this room for?"

"I've seen the family play games and read books here. But I suppose the men talk business here too. Mr. Bourne's office is just over there." She pointed toward a doorway on the far side of the room. "The men often retire here after dinner while the women go to the piazza."

"And we're to sew up the cushions of these unusual benches?"

"Yes. They're Pullman seats from the railroad cars." Devyn inspected the soft-green bench cushions and found three of them in need of repair. She pointed them out to Hannah. One had a ripped seam on the back cushion. One had piping that had disconnected from the cushion and hung loose, and the last had an opening on the seat cushion. "This should be simple enough." She handed Hannah a needle and thread and set her to fix the seat back cushion. "You work on this while I tackle the others."

While they worked, the two chatted about Chippewa Bay and their school days.

Hannah glanced up and smiled. "I spotted your mother at church a few weeks back."

Devyn's shoulders tensed. "Is she well?"

"I didn't speak to her, but she seemed well enough. She always seems irritated, though."

"She is. Always. Sometimes I don't know why she even bothers to go to church; it never helps. At least, ever since ..." Devyn took in a deep breath, bit her lip, and shrugged away the tension her mother's memory brought.

~ ~ ~

Brice knew that look well by now, and he could take no more of the strained expression on Devyn's face. Shaking off the guilt that accompanied his eavesdropping, he sauntered through the door and stopped in front of Devyn. "Are these cushions finally getting the attention they deserve?"

Devyn giggled. "Yes. Simple repairs, really. What do you have there?"

Brice waved a handful of postcards. "These? You've got to see them. They're just dandy. A set of souvenir postcards created for the 1893 World's Columbian Exposition. They celebrate the Singer sewing machine's worldwide success."

Devyn and Hannah stopped sewing and rose as Brice showed them the lithographed pictures of people using Singer sewing machines all around the world.

He flipped through a handful and then went back to the beginning of the pile, turning the first one over. "Each one describes the nation it represents—see here, Tunis—and tells about the location, religion, commerce, and clothing, which, of course, is sewn by machine. Like tiny encyclopedias for us to enjoy. I hear the details are completely accurate."

Devyn put her hand out. "May I?" He handed the postcard to her, and she read the back of the Tunis card. "'One of the Barbary

States in North Africa' …" Hannah peeked over her shoulder, and the two read silently for a moment until Devyn finished reading it aloud. "'Our picture represents a Tunisian woman in her peculiar dress, resting her hand upon the woman's faithful friend the world over, our "Singer," which has its place in multitudes of Tunisian homes.'" She glanced at Brice and smiled. "How clever to promote the Singer sewing machines on postcards with interesting educational facts."

Brice grinned, pride swelling in his chest. "Aye, Mr. Bourne's business brilliance far exceeds some of the more cunning industry titans of our time. While some simply seek fame and fortune, Mr. Bourne aims to fill an important need and make the world a better place. I commend him for that."

Devyn reached for the pile. "May we see them all?"

"Certainly. I don't think the missus would mind as long as you get your work done before dinner." Brice escorted the girls to the middle alcove, where they sat gazing at pictures of lands he knew and ones he'd only dreamed of. Familiar places like Italy and Spain as well as unfamiliar places like Burma, Bosnia, and Romania. The girls read the backs of each one while he touted Mr. Bourne's achievements. "Mr. Bourne helped to expand the Singer Manufacturing Company all around the world until the machines became a common household item. As an outsider to the company, he innovated marketing, research and development, and so much more."

Hannah looked up from the cards. "We have a Singer, although it's a pedal machine and not one of those new-fangled electric ones." Her face shone with pride.

Brice nodded. "Both work well, and the company has continued to be successful even after Mr. Bourne retired in 1905. Do you know that when he retired, the company had more than ninety thousand employees all around the world? He's still one of the company directors, and I hear they still make about three million machines every year."

Hannah gasped. "What an achievement. Is he shrewd and stern? I have yet to meet him."

Devyn shook her head, her blue eyes glistening. "No, he is ever so nice and so are his lovely wife and daughter, Marjorie, to whom I serve as lady's maid. Actually, all the Bournes I've met are fine people, and I respect them even more"—she turned to Brice—"now that you've filled in all these extraordinary details, sir."

He winked at her and picked up the cards, not wanting to embarrass her with more flirtation, so he stood and bowed dramatically. "I'd best be on my way and not keep you fine ladies from your work. The missus would be vexed."

But him? He shot a glance at the chess game on the table in the next alcove. Too bad he couldn't find a way to stay and teach her the game.

~ ~ ~

Devyn followed Brice with her eyes. He smiled at her before he closed the door.

She knew the Bournes were wealthy, successful people, but she hadn't realized the worldwide mark Mr. Bourne had made. No wonder Brice was proud of his employer. At that moment she was too.

As she passed Hannah on her way back to the Pullman benches, the girl let out a sigh. "Now I'm more nervous than ever to meet such people of status. I didn't sleep a wink last night, contemplating what this castle life might be like."

Devyn checked her work on the piping and moved to the ripped seam before commenting. "Don't worry your pretty head, Hannah. These are God-fearing, kind folk who have boatloads of patience for ones such as us." She told her friend about the gondola ride and a few other times she'd experienced their goodness. But she purposely left out her confession, the incident with the locket, and her likeness to Louisa.

Devyn finished sewing the rip at the same time Hannah finished repairing the back cushion. "There. All done." She snipped the thread but dropped her needle on the floor. Reaching down to retrieve it, she glimpsed a fine gold pocket watch tucked far under the bench. She squatted, scooped it up, and stood, nearly bumping into Hannah.

"Where'd that come from?" Hannah leaned in close to look.

"It was under the seat." Devyn turned the watch over to inspect its solid gold case. Flowers and leaves intricately scrolled around the engraved initials *HBD*. "This must be Howard's. The *D* must be for his middle name." She popped it open and read the word *Elgin* on the clock face, which consisted of blue, spade-shaped hands and Roman numerals, while a smaller clock at six o'clock ticked out the seconds.

Hannah touched it gently. "Daddy has an Elgin pocket watch. Says it's the best there is. He inherited it from his rich uncle, Samuel, and keeps it safely hidden away. I've only seen it a few times, and Mama says it's the only thing we have of real value."

Devyn smiled and read the inscription inside the case aloud. "'Happy birthday, son. Love, Daddy and Mother.'" Under the inscription, she read, "'Warranted Standard U.S. Assay.'" She turned to her friend. "What could that mean?"

Hannah tapped it with her finger. "I know! Papa says it means it's solid gold. Like Uncle's."

Sofia appeared at the door, froze for a moment, and then sailed across the floor. She snatched the watch from Devyn's hand, nearly cutting her as she tugged the gold chain through her fingers. "Where did you get that?"

Devyn put her hands on her hips and glared at Sofia. "It was on the floor, under the bench, if you must know. Howard must've dropped it when he was here."

"That's 'Mr. Howard' to you, miss, and I'll have none of your cheek. I'm still your superior, and I deem that you've snatched it. Perhaps you want to weasel your little friend here into your mischief?" She cast Hannah a narrow-eyed scowl. "What other contraband have you hidden away to take off the island for your own gain? The Bournes will hear of this." With that, she turned on her heel and stomped out the door.

Devyn's hands grew cold, and her head got hot. "You have to be my witness that I found it and didn't take it. Sofia is out to get me fired, and that can't happen."

Hannah nodded furiously. "I'll vouch for your character. We've been neighbors since we were in pigtails, and I have only ever known you to be an honest person. Why would she be so vindictive?"

"I have no idea, but we'd better see Mrs. VanLeer at once!"

CHAPTER 18

Brice popped his head into the servants' hall and right back out after announcing, "He's here! It'll be a crackin' good day. Let the Fourth of July celebrations begin!"

Devyn giggled. He sounded like a little boy announcing that Santa had just landed on the island on Christmas Day. She fixed a questioning expression on Mrs. VanLeer. "Why is Brice so excited about Mr. Lipton being here? Does he know him?"

The missus chuckled, her eyes dancing as she set down her teacup. "Know him? He's like a father to him, and he's the reason Brice works for the Bournes. But enough for now. Best get ready for the day." She turned to Hannah and nodded. "And thank you, Hannah, for vouching for the integrity of Miss Devyn."

Hannah stood and curtsied, picking up her dishes to take them to the sink. "Yes, ma'am. Glad I was there when Devyn found the pocket watch." She snapped a glance at Devyn.

Devyn returned an appreciative smile. "Yes, thank you." What if Hannah hadn't been there as a witness? She might be on her way back to her mother.

The missus shooed Hannah to her duties. "Off with you, then. Devyn, stay here so we can go over plans for the *al fresco* luncheon in the tea garden today. Nellie will join us soon."

Devyn finished drying the dishes until Nellie joined them. Putting her wiping rag aside, she hooked her hand on Nellie's elbow and walked with her to the table. "I'm so pleased to be working with you today. What a glorious day, warm and pleasant, with only a gentle breeze. It shall be a delight, don't you think?"

Nellie smiled softly. "I believe so."

Once the two sat, Mrs. VanLeer picked up her list. She turned to Nellie. "Since Mahlon is ill, you'll have to be the lead today. Devyn, this is your chance to learn the ways of table service, and especially of a luncheon tea. Brice will assist as well."

Devyn grinned. Working with Brice? How exciting. But could she do it? "Yes, ma'am. I'm pleased to assist."

The missus talked them through the process, then sent them to the tea garden to prepare.

Devyn followed Nellie down the Indian Path. About halfway to the swimming beach, several stone steps led to a nicely shaded grassy area encircled by a three-foot stone wall. Four chairs surrounded a large wooden table already covered with a fine linen tablecloth.

Nellie clicked her tongue. "Don't the kitchen maids know that the bugs will spoil this?" She pulled off the tablecloth in a huff and bid Devyn to help her fold it. "We won't serve until noon."

Devyn grinned at the efficient, no-nonsense girl before her. Though they were roommates, their diverse interests and duties meant that they seldom got to spend time together. Nellie didn't read, rarely talked, and whenever Devyn noticed her not working, she was sketching.

"I've seen that you like to draw. How did you learn such art?"

Nellie fiddled with the table and chairs, adjusting them with precision. "Mama said I was born an artist, but we never had money for me to learn, so I work to buy the supplies. I can't help it; I feel I must draw or die. It brings me such joy."

Devyn chewed on Nellie's words. Draw or die? Was there anything she cared about as much as that?

Nellie interrupted Devyn's musings. "I was going to the shore to sketch when your brother ..."

The memory of Falan forcing himself on Nellie flashed through Devyn's mind. "Accosted you. I still wish you had reported him."

Nellie's chocolate eyes seemed to melt into dark pools of grief, but then they turned hard. Angry. "He ... he threatened to say I seduced him, and he said that I'd be fired. I can't lose my job. People always believe men over women. Even the Bournes."

Devyn shook her head. "I doubt that's true. They are good, fair people. Besides, my brother is a viper. Always has been." She swallowed more words she wanted to say about Falan. Words that ought not to cross the lips of a Christian woman, sister or not. "He's a bully. Stay clear of him at all costs."

One of the kitchen maids, Dorothy, headed their way with a large and obviously heavy basket. When she reached the tea garden, she set the basket on the table, rubbing her hands together. "The missus says you should set the table and cover it with this sheet." She pinched the corner of an old sheet that covered the basket and promptly left them to do the work.

Nellie laughed. "That girl is one of few words." She looked toward the castle. "The kitchen staff always keeps to themselves."

Devyn nodded, refraining from remarking on Nellie's own reserved personality. "Likely, Cook insists on it."

Nellie shooed a fly off the table and unfolded the tablecloth. They set the table with fine china and silverware, and Dorothy returned with another basket of crystal goblets, pretty teacups, and more. Once everything was in place, Devyn helped Nellie cover the table with the sheet.

Before long, a parade of Bournes and their guest sauntered down the path, followed by kitchen maids carrying a variety of food and drink. Brice pulled up the rear.

How handsome he looked as the sunshine danced on his sandy hair, highlighting the blond strands that reminded Devyn of fine gold. He cast her a wink and smiled. But today, his eyes held a special delight. Was it Lipton's visit that pleased him so or something else?

"Devyn, pour the water, please." Nellie spoke with a commanding tone that caused her to jump into action.

Throughout the meal, she studied Mr. Lipton. The man was likely around sixty, the same age as Mr. Bourne. Smile lines and creases outlined his warm, friendly eyes, and his mustache and triangular goatee danced when he spoke. Everything about him seemed to shout that he was a content and happy man.

Devyn stayed surprisingly busy during the entire meal. She kept the water glasses full, but most of the time, she whisked back and forth from the castle, returning dirty dishes or retrieving fresh pots of tea and food.

Now and then, Lipton cast a friendly comment to Brice, who answered him but kept to his role as servant. By the end of the meal, Devyn was even more confused about the relationship of the two men. Still, she was happy to have watched them and enjoyed the fresh air and sunshine on this lovely summer day.

Upon returning to the tea garden for the final time, Devyn smiled at a great peal of laughter from the lot of them. Mr. Bourne bowed low toward his guest, feigning subservience. "Ah, your grace, shall we retreat to prepare for a friendly boat race?"

Mr. Lipton guffawed. "Stuff and nonsense. You and I both know I'm little more than an Irish-Scot street urchin, so I'll have none of that pomp and circumstance from you, my friend."

Mr. Bourne slapped him on the back. "In that case, prepare to be soundly beaten."

Mr. Lipton shook his head. "You know I hold the America's Cup—for the 'best of all losers,' that is. Perhaps today I shall break my fine record with you, old chap, even without my *Shamrock*." Mr. Lipton let out another loud guffaw as the party proceeded back to the castle, leaving Brice, Devyn, and Nellie to clean up.

As soon as they departed, Nellie held her stomach, leaned over the wall, and vomited.

Devyn hurried to her and rubbed her back. "Oh, Nellie. Are you all right?"

"I held it in as long as I could. I fear I might have a touch of whatever Mahlon has."

Devyn shook her head. "And you're white as that sheet. Go and lie down. We'll finish up here." She glanced at Brice, who nodded in agreement.

Left alone, the two tidied up the tea, Devyn seeking answers to the mystery of Lipton. "Tell me about this Mr. Lipton. How do you know him?"

Brice grinned and turned his eyes to the large steamer passing by the island. "He saved my life. Truly. My parents both died when I was just a wee laddie, so I spent nearly two years on the streets of

Belfast until I made my way to Glasgow, and that was where I met him. Mr. Lipton's ma was Irish too. He was born in a tenement and knew my plight, so he gave me a job as an errand boy when I was but twelve. Aye, but what a kind man he is."

His faraway stare filled Devyn with emotion.

Brice continued. "By then, he was a wealthy man with three hundred stores and a thriving Lipton tea brand. Did you know that he chose to cater to the poor working class so they could enjoy tea like the royals?"

"That is admirable indeed." She touched his arm, and he looked down at her with sky-blue eyes that glistened in the sun.

"Aye. Mr. Lipton must've seen something in me, for by the time I was fourteen, he hired me onto the *Shamrock*, his grand yacht. And that's how I met Mr. Bourne."

Devyn swallowed her confusion. "How did that happen? You were in Scotland."

Brice chuckled. "It was 1903, and I was eighteen by then. Mr. Lipton had challenged the America's Cup holders to a race against his yacht. But Lipton never won. That's what he was referring to by winning the 'best of all losers' cup. 'Tis true, indeed. The America's Cup folks actually gave him a cup and widely publicized it, which made Lipton tea famous in the process."

She still didn't understand. "But how does Bourne come into the story?"

He rolled his eyes and shrugged. "Sorry. I digress. Once the two men met through the yachting competition, they became fast friends. Mr. Lipton knew of my desire to emigrate to America, so somehow, he talked Mr. Bourne into hiring me onto his yacht. When Mr. Bourne's elderly valet, Clancy, retired two years later, he gave me the position."

Devyn shook her head. "It's all rather irregular, hiring a boatman to be a valet and a housemaid to become a lady's maid, isn't it?"

He nodded decisively. "It is, but these men aren't ones who lord power over others or force people to stay in their stations. They both came from humble beginnings and worked their way to the top. When they see someone who wants to do the same, they aid in their success. I am blessed beyond measure to have such benefactors."

"We are, indeed." She ran her hand along the tea garden wall, stunned by a spark of inspiration. "Say, remember the sign on the tunnel wall that said 'In the tea garden' and the key and clue in the wine vault that said 'Fourth rock on the right'? Do you suppose the two are connected?"

Brice slapped the side of his head. "Of course! Why hadn't I thought of that? Let's see what we can find."

Devyn's excitement tumbled in her belly. They hurried to the outside of the wall and counted out four rocks, examining them but finding them secure and unmoving.

She questioned, "Perhaps the inner wall?" They repeated the process but found nothing. "But from the inside here, the fourth on the right would be over there, wouldn't it?" She pointed to the opposite wall.

"You're a clever girl, Detective Devyn."

They scurried over, and Brice touched a rock that was separated from the rest of the wall, dirt seeping from its edges. "There!" He pulled off his serving coat and proceeded to wiggle the stone. Finally, he shimmied it out and pulled out a rusty metal box nearly twice the size of a sheet of paper and more than a hand width deep.

Devyn clapped her hands like a little girl. "We found it! We found it! What's inside?"

Brice tried to open it, but it was locked. He looked at her, his brows knitted together until his face filled with excitement. "The vault. The key!"

"Of course!" Devyn giggled. "You're a sight, sir. Better tidy you up first." She grabbed a napkin from the pile of linens and wiped his brow, then swept the dirt from his hands and even from his shirtsleeves. "There. Much better."

She looked up at his face to find him grinning sheepishly. His gaze darted to and fro before he bent down and planted a firm kiss on her cheek. She melted into his arms but quickly retreated. "Someone might see!"

"Not a chance." He glanced around again and gifted her with

another quick kiss—this time on her lips. "Happy Fourth of July, darling Devyn."

She blinked, touching her lips with her slim, white fingers.

~ ~ ~

Brice shocked himself with his boldness, but Devyn's soft, full lips so close to his were simply too tempting to resist. Something about Devyn's innocent kindness melted his resolve to stay professional and keep his wits about him.

"What do you say we finish this adventure?" He stepped back, still holding the metal box. "Let's see if the key will open this before we're called to other duties."

"Yes. Let's." A huge smile lightened her eyes and beautified her already pretty face.

Brice grabbed the heaviest basket of dishes while Devyn gathered the soiled linens. Once they returned to the castle, he left the basket with the kitchen maid as Devyn disappeared down the hallway, headed for the laundry.

He went to the wine vault and waited for her, anticipation growing by the moment. Hopefully, she wouldn't get waylaid by the missus or sent to assist Miss Marjorie before they could finish their detective work. Sure enough, a few minutes later, Devyn appeared in the doorway, eyes dancing a jig of excitement.

Brice grinned. "I'm keen to try it now. Ready?"

"Yes, oh yes! I'm simply aching to know if it's the treasure key." Devyn chewed on a finger, shifting from foot to foot.

He turned to remove the note and key. He placed the message on the shelf above the one where he'd put the box, then held the key out to her. "Looks like it might fit, eh?"

Devyn studied the key and the lock and nodded. Glancing into the Great Hall, she closed the door. "Let's keep this to ourselves for now."

Brice ceremoniously slipped the key into the lock and wiggled it. He wiggled it again. And again. "It's not working." He pulled it out and blew into the lock, reinserted the key, and resumed jiggling it until the tumblers finally gave way.

Devyn scooted closer. She touched his shoulder, sending a shiver down his spine. "What's in there?"

Her obvious delight made him laugh. "You open it." Brice held the box out to her and steadied it as she slowly, reverently, opened the squeaky metal lid and peeked inside.

Brice nearly touched his head to hers as they examined the contents. Indian artifacts. Old coins. Native American arrowheads, small spearheads, and flints. He carefully picked up each one to examine it. "I wonder where these came from."

Devyn shrugged as she lifted out a coin. "1812? This must be from the War of 1812." She pulled out a handmade pewter spoon. "And this too."

He nodded. "This is quite a find! I shall have to present it to Mr. Bourne immediately."

She grabbed his forearm and squeezed. "We did it!"

Brice patted her hand. "Yes. We did it. Together."

~ ~ ~

Excitement about the treasure spread through the castle like wildfire, and suddenly Devyn felt like a famous archeologist. Miss Marjorie applauded her. Mr. and Mrs. Bourne hugged her. Thanked her. And Sir Lipton—she was told he was a baron and thus to be called 'sir'—laughed heartily as he slapped Brice on the shoulder and winked at her.

So that's where Brice learned the habit!

By evening, the entire castle had evacuated to the dock, where they were to watch the Chippewa Bay fireworks display. The family and their esteemed guest sat in Adirondack chairs, sipping fine wine. Devyn and Brice stood within earshot of the Bournes and Sir Lipton, just in case something was needed. Sofia hovered on the far side of the group, eyeing Devyn with her usual pursed expression of disdain.

No matter. Not even Sofia could spoil such a lovely night.

Brice looked up to the stars and spoke softly. "Tell me about your father. Please."

Devyn glanced at him, and he gave her a look of tender compassion—or was it love?—before returning his gaze to the heavens. Had Mr. Bourne told him about her confession to Miss Marjorie, or did he just innocently want to know?

Somehow the night, the moment, lent to baring her soul, and she quietly, reverently, told him the entire tale.

No tears. No pain. No guilt. Where had they gone?

When she finished her story, Brice stood silent for several moments. "My father died in a shipwreck when I was ten. There's an Irish saying that goes, 'May you never forget what is worth remembering, nor ever remember what is best forgotten.' It reminds me to forget the pain and remember the man."

"Mac, ol' lad. Come over here and introduce me to the lovely lass you're jabbering with."

Devyn swallowed hard, shaken by Brice's confession or Sir Lipton's call, she couldn't say.

When Brice officially presented her to Sir Lipton, the baron took her hand and kissed it as if she were a fine lady. A blush burned her cheeks at the honor.

Just then, fireworks lit up the night sky, bursting into sparkling enchantment. Devyn curtsied and stepped back as Lipton's attention turned to the celebration. Relieved that she didn't have to carry on a conversation with him, she returned to her place of safety. As she did, the fireworks drew her eye upward to the tower, illuminating two figures looking out the window. She shot a glance to where Sofia had stood. Empty. She looked up again to study the tower intruders.

Sofia … and Falan.

CHAPTER 19

Devyn stood near the pergola, a brick-paved, covered pavilion with spectacular easterly views of the St. Lawrence, where she could catch a glimpse of Sir Lipton departing Dark Island. She held tight to her broom with one hand and shielded her eyes from the bright sunshine with a hand over her brow. *Such a nice man. It's sad to see him go so soon.*

The St. Lawrence sparkled in the sun, waves dancing with the breeze. The river was growing on her, and that made her happy.

With a sigh, she stepped into a small stand of trees and wiped her brow, catching a bit of the river breeze before returning to the pergola to finish sweeping it as Miss Marjorie had instructed.

Falan stepped out from behind a tree. "What did you do with it, Devyn?" He grabbed her arm and squeezed it, his eyes filled with anger. Or was it hate?

"Ouch!" Devyn squealed in pain, trying to shake herself loose, her heart racing, her mind filling with dread. "Let me go. I don't know what you're talking about." She scanned the area and found no one around to help. "Let me go."

"Not on our dead father's grave. Where's the treasure box? I've bin lookin' fer it fer near five years now. What do ya know? Tell me. It's mine, and I'll have it if ya know what's good for ya." Falan pressed his dirty fingers into her arm, bruising it, she was sure.

"Mr. Bourne has it. Let me go." Fear stole the rest of her words, her throat filling with bile. How wicked could he be?

Falan loosened his grip on her arm but still encircled it with his claw-like fingers. His eyes narrowed, and a smirk rose on his thin lips. He slowly turned his head from side to side, cracking the vertebrae. "I saw the gap in the tea garden wall last night and figured you and that Mick had somethin' ta do with it. Figured my treasure box had been hid there. But now Bourne has it?"

Devyn stiffened. "Of course, he has it. It's his island, isn't it?"

"Well, I need ya ta find it and fetch it fer me. The treasure's mine, whether he owns the land or not. My old pal, Oscar, and me found all them arrowheads and coins and spoons when we were buildin' this castle. But the fool went and hid 'em fer safe keepin', and then he done gone and kicked the bucket afore he told me where he stashed the box. I been lookin' fer it ever since. How long'll it take ya, girl?"

Devyn shook her head. "I cannot steal from the Bournes! Those artifacts are rightly theirs, found on their island, no matter who originally found them. Surely, you see that, Falan."

"I see no such thing. I've labored on and off this island fer a pittance and deserve what's rightly mine."

Just then, Marjorie giggled on her way to the pergola, her lemon-yellow gown flashing through the trees.

Falan let go of Devyn but hissed out a threat. "Say a word, and you'll regret the day you were born." He slipped silently behind the nearby bushes.

Devyn swallowed a whimper and took a deep breath. Then she pasted on a pleasant smile and a professional demeanor, stepped into the open, and met Miss Marjorie on the path. "Sorry I haven't gotten the pergola swept yet, miss. I was unavoidably detained, but I'll get to it right away."

"Hurry on, then, and I'll enjoy a stroll in the rose garden while you work." Miss Marjorie handed her a book and an icy glass of tea. "Take these with you, please." She hesitated, searching her face. "Are you all right?"

Devyn darted her gaze to the ground and curtsied. "Yes, ma'am. I'll be quick."

Marjorie cast her a doubtful smile but sauntered toward the rose garden, while Devyn scurried under the pergola. Wicker lounge chairs and a picnic table made it a perfect place to relax on such a day. At least, for someone whose brother had not threatened her again.

Devyn pulled a cloth from her pocket and brushed off the furniture, casting a glance here and there to make sure Falan didn't reappear. She prayed for protection and for wisdom to know what to do about her brother and his threats.

She willed herself to remember the tender side of him when he was young. The protective older brother who was a mischievous boy but one who stuck up for her when she needed him most. When their neighbor Timmy had chased her with a spider and locked her in the outhouse. Before they'd lost their father and their ma had grown more bitter than she already was. Before the ice-fishing accident.

That's what she'd call it, for that's what it was. Mr. Bourne and Miss Marjorie had set her straight on that. Finally. Why had she believed the lie for half her life? She tossed a prayer of gratitude to the heavens for the Bournes, for the truth, and for the freedom she now experienced.

Letting her fear go, she pulled dozens of dead leaves from the creeping vines that created a pretty decoration on the brick columns upholding the pergola roof. Tiny white flowers seemed to dance on the vines, and she picked off those that were fading. She took in a fragrant whiff of their scent before she swept the leaves, grass, and twigs from the brick floor.

"Don't you just love this spot on the island?" Marjorie's return made Devyn whirl around. "Smell this. It's scrumptious." She extended the pink rose she held for Devyn to whiff. "Only God could create such a heavenly scent, don't you think? Perfumers cannot recreate it, no matter how hard they try."

Devyn closed her eyes and took in the fragrance. "It's heavenly, all right." When she opened them, she noticed several cocoons in the corner of the pergola roof. "Look!" She pointed as Miss Marjorie took a seat on one of the chaise lounges and followed Devyn's finger with her gaze.

Marjorie planted a finger on her chin. "They are monarchs, I believe, since the chrysalis is that bright green. Last month, I noticed dozens of caterpillars around here but thought little of it." She paused and stared up for a few moments. "Do you know that the pupa sheds its skin and hangs upside down, changing from an ugly caterpillar to a beautiful butterfly in less than a month? Then they fly free before migrating to their southern home. Some say all the way to Mexico!"

Devyn looked up from picking a few fading blossoms off the vine. "Really? Can tiny creatures truly fly that far?"

Marjorie nodded. "Scientists are still studying them, but yes, that's what I've read. I suppose they ride on the breeze a good bit of their trip, stopping to eat lots of nectar along the way."

Devyn stepped closer to the cocoons and counted them. "Six. I hope to see them hatch one day. They are magnificent creatures, to be sure."

Marjorie stared at Devyn until she grew uncomfortable. Then Miss Marjorie smiled. "I think you're rather like that pupa, ready to emerge as a beautiful butterfly." She paused before continuing. "You've lived a caterpillar's life, crawling on your belly as it were and appearing to be something to be crushed rather than who you truly are. You've lived in the shadows—in a cocoon—for far too long. And now you can go through the metamorphosis of becoming a beautiful butterfly who can catch the wind and bring beauty to the world."

Devyn's eyes stung, and her throat grew thick with emotion. She tried to blink the wetness away, but tears slid down her cheeks. Turning her back, she swiped them away.

Marjorie rose and stepped close, taking her free hand. "I don't say this to hurt you. I want to encourage you. I admire the courage it took to confess what you did a few days ago and believe it was a big step toward your transformation. I await to see you emerge into the beautiful butterfly I'm sure you'll become."

Devyn sniffed, swallowing the sweet-tasting words. She curtsied. "Thank you, Miss Marjorie. Truly, you are a benefactress of kindness."

Marjorie dropped Devyn's hand and waved off the compliment. "Stuff and nonsense. I only speak the truth. And when we're alone, you needn't call me 'miss.' We are the same age and friends, are we not?"

Devyn blinked. Friends? With her mistress? With a wealthy woman to whom she was a mere servant girl? "I … I thank you. I'm not sure I can adjust to such a request. But I'll try."

At that, Marjorie chuckled. "Don't fret. Whether you use the term or not is nothing to worry about. Now, I think I shall read awhile, so if you'd like to see if Mrs. VanLeer is in need of your services, go ahead."

Devyn curtsied. "Thank you, Miss … ah, eh … Marjorie." She giggled with the discomfort of the unusual familiarity.

~ ~ ~

From the library window, Brice caught a glimpse of Devyn returning to the castle. The smile on her face revealed a peace he had never before seen on her features. A pall of sadness had always marred what would otherwise be the face of an angel. Would it return like it always did? And why?

Brice excused himself from Mr. Bourne's presence and hurried out the door, catching Devyn just before she went into the laundry. "Top of the morning to you, miss!" He jumped, clicking his heels together, just to make her laugh. She gifted him with an amused giggle, one that revealed her dimple.

"Aren't you a little large to be a leprechaun? And where's your green suit?" She winked at him, just as he'd done to her a dozen times. This was a first for her.

Mr. Bourne stuck his head out the door, interrupting their banter. "Say, Brice! Why don't you see if Hooley will take the four of us on a boating excursion? She's still at the pergola, is she not?" He glanced at Devyn.

Devyn curtsied. "Yes, sir, she is reading."

Mr. Bourne rolled his eyes. "Always has her nose in a book, that girl. Tell her to power up the *Moike*, and let's go enjoy this splendid day! Everyone else is busy, but you two can come and help with the picnic. I'll meet you at the dock at noon."

Within the hour, Brice joined Devyn, Marjorie, and Mr. Bourne in the boat. Marjorie drove while Devyn turned a sorry shade of green and held on for dear life.

Mr. Bourne turned to her. "Say, Miss Devyn, you needn't be afraid of my daughter's boatmanship. She's as seasoned as any man her age. I gave her this speedboat for her sixteenth birthday, and she enjoys every time she can show off her skills. You're in good hands with her."

Marjorie picked up speed, a wide, determined grin on her face. She wove between several boats and then ran alongside a huge ship heading toward Lake Ontario. Once she caught up to the ship's bow, she cast a quick, mischievous glance at her father, cut in front of the vessel, and headed for a cluster of small islands.

Devyn turned as white as the snow, so Brice slid along the bench to sit beside her. "Are you okay? You appear to be a bit green around the gills."

With huge blue eyes, Devyn glanced his way and promptly turned to vomit over the side of the boat. Brice held her shoulders while she expelled her breakfast.

Mr. Bourne tried to hide his amusement, but his dancing eyes told Brice the truth. "Say, Hooley! Hold up a minute, will you? Seems we have a predicament back here."

Marjorie turned and noticed Devyn's troubles, so she backed off the throttle and put it into neutral. "Dear me, Devyn, I'm so sorry. I get a little carried away when I'm behind this wheel."

Brice handed Devyn a handkerchief, and she wiped her mouth, but not before turning a bright shade of red. "Forgive me. I fear I'm not used to being on the water. And this boat is … well, rather fast."

Poor girl. Brice's heart hurt for her embarrassment. Here she was trying to be brave in front of her mistress and Mr. Bourne, but her stomach rebelled.

Mr. Bourne waved. "See here. Don't be ashamed. Why, I've lost my breakfast, lunch, and dinner during various boat rides. Consider it an initiation into the world of boating, my dear."

Marjorie shook her head. "Daddy!" She turned to Devyn, her hands still on the wheel as they floated on the waves, the motor in idle. "I'm sorry, dear girl. I must confess that I like to go fast and too often get carried away with my own foolishness. And though I've beat several former Gold Cup winners in boat races, I needn't race with you in the vessel. I promise I'll take it easy and mosey around the islands from now on."

Mr. Bourne chuckled, and Brice covered a grin. Marjorie "mosey"? That was like asking a cheetah to stroll. Brice handed Devyn a canteen of water, and she took a sip.

Before long, the ship caught up to them and presented them with a large wake, dangerously rocking the *Moike*. "We need to move on. Are you all right?" Marjorie glanced at Devyn, who simply nodded, her eyes downcast.

Marjorie put the boat into gear but kept it moving at a snail's pace. But when Devyn's complexion returned to its usual pretty pink and she smiled again, she made the now-boring boat ride most rewarding.

Brice realized his hands were still planted on Devyn's shoulders—a little too familiar in the presence of the Bournes. He pulled back and set them on his lap, sliding a few inches away from Devyn. Would Mr. Bourne notice such closeness and reprimand him?

Thankfully, the master sat looking out at the passing shoreline and smiling contentedly. But then he cast Brice a sideways glance, followed by a knowing grin, which made Brice's face grow hotter than a fish fresh out of the frying pan.

Mr. Bourne shouted over the engine noise. "Shall we stop here and fish, Hooley, dear?"

Marjorie nodded and pointed the vessel toward the nearby island. "Did you know, Devyn, that when they first started selling the islands, Andrew Cornwall and his partner, Mr. Walton—the two men who owned the Thousand Islands—restricted the sales so every other island would be virgin land and never purchased? Quite the forethought, don't you think?"

Devyn nodded at Marjorie and then glanced at Brice. She tried to hand his handkerchief back to him. "Thank you."

But he folded it back into her palm. "Keep it," he said, and then he shot her a reassuring smile. "All better?"

She bit her bottom lip, glancing back at Mr. Bourne and up at Marjorie. "Yes, but a little embarrassed."

Brice untied his shoes and took them off. Then he removed his socks. "Don't be. Mr. Bourne is right. We've all lost our lunch."

Marjorie eased the boat up onto a sandy beach and turned off the motor. Brice rolled up his pant legs, jumped out into ankle-deep water, and tugged the boat to safety. Marjorie removed her hose and shoes, as did Mr. Bourne. Devyn followed their example while trying to keep the hem of her dress down.

Brice wiggled his finger for her to come close. She pressed her palms to her skirts, hesitating to take his hand. When she did, he patted the side of the boat. "It's okay. It's the St. Lawrence way. We're all just barefoot woebegones." His easygoing chuckle did the trick, eliciting a responding chuckle from her as she stepped out of the boat.

"Ahhh, this feels so good." Devyn wiggled her toes in the sand before stepping out of the water.

Once Brice assisted everyone to shore and retrieved the fishing poles, tackle, and finally the picnic basket, it was time for him to bait the hooks.

Devyn eased up to his side. "I don't know how to fish, Brice. What shall I do?"

He shrugged her cares away. "Set up the picnic, and after we eat, I'll help you. Mr. Bourne and Marjorie need little help. They're seasoned fishermen … well, fisherman and woman."

After a half an hour of fishing, Devyn had the picnic ready, so they stopped for their meal. Once they'd enjoyed a simple fare of bread, cheese, and carrots—and Cook's tangy lemonade—the party was ready to resume their angling.

Brice sidled up to Mr. Bourne. "Mind if I tend to Miss Devyn? She's never fished."

The twinkle in Mr. Bourne's eye told him that he knew Brice had feelings for Devyn. Knew there was more to their relationship than Brice had let on. Knew he was falling in love with her.

Where did that thought come from? Brice drew in a quivering breath and glanced at Devyn. *Do I? Love her?* He shook off the thought and pasted on a casual, professional demeanor.

Brice walked up to where the two women were talking.

Devyn's tone spoke of respect and admiration. "You've been driving that boat since you were sixteen? How incredible!"

Marjorie laughed. "It's Daddy's fault entirely. He gave me the bug. Didn't you?" She feigned offense as she scolded her father.

Brice joined in the laughter as Mr. Bourne slapped a hand across his belly and bowed. "I beg your pardon, miss. How careless of me." Then he cast in his line and challenged her. "Who'll catch the first fish?"

"I will!" Marjorie plunked her line into the river, her face fiercely determined.

"They're always competing." Brice laughed, turning to Devyn. "There's an Irish saying. 'Making a new beginning is one-third of the work.' Shall we make a new beginning and initiate you into the world of fishing?" He pulled a worm from the jar they had brought and began weaving it onto the hook.

"I always wanted to fish with my father but never had the chance. I'm glad I'm learning with you." Devyn stepped near him to speak, tickling his senses.

He nodded and smiled, wishing they were alone on this island. Alone to tell her how he really felt.

CHAPTER 20

Devyn opened her eyes to the bright morning sun shining in the windows. She'd overslept! She jumped out of bed, dressed, and hurried to the servants' hall, where she found her roommates eating breakfast.

She plopped two pancakes on her plate and poured a cup of tea, placing them on the table before plunking down next to Hannah. "Why didn't you wake me? I'm late."

Hannah blinked. "I did wake you. You said you needed a minute."

Devyn groaned. "I don't even remember that. Sorry."

"No one's said anything, so you're all right." Hannah touched her arm.

Mrs. VanLeer swept into the room carrying a newspaper folded into a perfect rectangle. She cleared her throat and stood at the head of the table. "As I'm sure you've heard, Mr. Morgan will be visiting the Bournes today. Devyn, you will have to serve the shore dinner since the kitchen maids must prepare for the formal dinner tonight, and besides, you've already had practice with the recent fishing excursion picnic. You and Brice can accomplish that, correct?"

Devyn nodded. "Yes, ma'am. Although I know nothing about shore dinners."

The missus waved off her concern. "It's simply setting up and preparing a luncheon on shore while the party fishes, and then you serve them when they return to the island. Brice has served shore dinners several times."

"Oh, I can do that." It sounded a lot like the picnic they'd served a few days ago on the outing with Mr. Bourne and Marjorie, but was hot food involved? Was the presentation more elegant? Devyn waited for further instructions but received none. Her confident reply must have reassured the missus.

"Good, then. Hannah, walk with me, and I shall give you your day's duties." Mrs. VanLeer hurried toward the door, Hannah following her like a duckling after its mother.

Brice nearly collided with them in the doorway but respectfully stepped aside. "Sorry, missus. Top of the morning to you!"

His cheery greeting set butterflies fluttering in Devyn's empty belly. She hopped up and piled four of the biggest pancakes on a plate and handed it to him. "Good morning, Brice."

"Thank you. It isn't often that I get served." Brice winked, making her knees go weak. How often he could turn her into a sentimental schoolgirl these days.

Once she resumed her seat, she sought his advice. "I'm to serve the shore dinner with your help. I didn't want to bother Mrs. VanLeer, but I could do with a few more details. Maybe you could start by telling me more about this Mr. Morgan."

Brice raised one of his eyebrows. "Surely, you've heard of J.P. Morgan, the famous banker and investor? He's one of the richest men in America." Syrup dripped off a piece of his pancake as he held it midway between his mouth and plate.

Devyn's cheeks burned. "Oh yes! I didn't realize he was the Morgan we were talking about. He's coming here?"

"Beg pardon. I guess you wouldn't have known." He paused and ate a bite of his sticky breakfast. "J.P. Morgan is on his way to Montreal for a finance meeting. The Bournes have been friends with the Morgans for years, but this is the first time he's visited here."

Devyn nodded, bidding her embarrassment to quell. Such a naive ninny she was. She sipped her tea and considered how the likes of her could be in the presence of the likes of J.P. Morgan.

"So give me a picture of what a shore party is like." Devyn took a bite and chewed.

"Traditionally, it's a big fishing party. Several skiffs rally at one island, disperse to fish until noon, partake of a shore dinner, and then fish again until late afternoon. Since we'll have a small party, we'll take the steam yacht. They'll drop us off to prepare the meal while they fish." Brice paused, his eyes lighting up. "I'm glad you'll assist me. I was dreading the day; now I relish it!"

Hannah returned and joined them for the remainder of the meal. "*The* Mr. J.P. Morgan is coming? My heart's all aflutter at the thought."

Devyn giggled, Brice chuckled, and both nodded.

"And we are to serve him." She glanced at Brice and shrugged.

Brice shook his head. "Stop fretting. He's just a man."

Silenced by the truth, Devyn took another sip of tea. Just a man. She recalled what her schoolteacher, Mr. Beyer, had said about the titans, as he called them. Her teacher had seemed enamored by men like J.P. Morgan, Andrew Carnegie, Rockefeller, and Vanderbilt. Mr. Beyer had spent many hours touting their fame, fortune, and accomplishments. Perhaps that's why she anticipated Morgan's arrival with such trepidation.

Devyn remembered that Rockefeller had gotten rich with oil and Carnegie with steel, but there was something special that Morgan had done for the country. What was it, again?

"Brice, didn't J.P. Morgan save the government somehow? I cannot recall the details."

He swallowed before speaking. "Aye. He bailed out the government to the tune of sixty-something million to restore the Federal Treasury surplus of a hundred million when it nearly ran out of gold during the Panic of 1893. After that, he put forth a plan for the government to buy gold and back the people's savings, but President Cleveland wouldn't abide it."

Hannah nodded. "I remember that from Mr. Beyer's civic lessons. He was quite keen on the idea."

Devyn shrugged her shoulders. "Guess I've been away from the classroom too long."

Mrs. VanLeer returned, scattering the three of them to their duties. "Our guest shall be here within the hour, so you two need to ready the dinner." She cast a worried gaze on Devyn and Brice.

Devyn followed him into the kitchen, where Cook had already

prepared baskets of food. After carrying the supplies to the boathouse and setting them in the boat, Brice helped the boatman, Labrese, haul a wooden folding table and chairs into the vessel and then move the yacht out to the dock. Just as they finished, a steamer pulled up, delivering Mr. J.P. Morgan to the island.

Brice wiped his hands and hurried to greet their guest, while Devyn stood back in silent nervousness. Brice welcomed him and bid him to join the Bournes in the castle, but halfway down the bridle path, Mr. and Mrs. Bourne and Marjorie met him.

"John, old friend, welcome to Dark Island." Mr. Bourne reached out to shake his hand and clap his shoulder as he reached him.

All three Bournes wore delighted expressions. Would Mrs. Bourne join them for the excursion too? Devyn thought not since the missus was dressed in a soft-yellow day dress.

Mrs. Bourne received a kiss on her hand from Mr. Morgan, a kiss from her husband, and a hug from Marjorie before retreating to the castle. The rest of the party headed toward the dock.

Mr. Bourne led the way, waving his hand back toward the castle. "I'll show you around The Towers when we get back. I hear a storm might develop later, so we want to enjoy fishing early."

J.P. Morgan nodded. "Fine with me." He didn't smile. Didn't seem enthusiastic. He seemed ... tired.

Devyn curtsied to the men and greeted Marjorie, and they all boarded the yacht.

Marjorie bid Devyn to sit by her. "Mother isn't feeling well, else she'd accompany us. I'm glad you're here." She patted Devyn's hand and smiled.

Devyn whispered, "I'm glad *you're* here." She'd be far less nervous with another woman around than being alone with such a famous man.

Soon Labrese put the yacht in gear and eased out into the channel. As they rounded the island, she caught sight of Sofia and her brother talking on the shore. Sofia had her hands on her hips and Falan his arms crossed over his chest in his usual defiant stance. What were they up to?

Devyn mulled the scene over while the yacht moved beyond

sight and across the water. After the speedboat incident, relief flooded her at the calm and secure pace.

"You okay?" Brice approached from the cabin and sat next to her.

She nodded, smiled, and tried to relax. No need to stir trouble on what was supposed to be a pleasant outing. But the memory of her brother and Sofia on the shore still niggled at her.

Oblivious to Devyn's real struggle, Marjorie smothered a smirk. "I know. This is a little different than the ride I gave you. Sorry." She grinned, shrugging her shoulders.

"It's all right. I just wasn't used to it." Devyn tried to give her a reassuring smile.

Mr. Morgan slapped Mr. Bourne's shoulder. "Say, would you like to join us for a meeting on Jekyll Island? I'm trying to make plans for the first Federal Reserve System and finally regulate the fool financial system. We must avoid another treasury panic like we had in '93."

Mr. Bourne sat silent for a moment. "I agree. Let me know the dates of the meeting, and I'll see what I can do."

"Jolly good. We need fellows like you to set President Taft and his cabinet on the right track." Morgan sat back and surveyed his surroundings. "This is a mighty beautiful spot in the world, I must admit."

"It is. That's why I enjoy summering here. There's probably an island or two left if you want to retire."

Mr. Morgan fairly growled a guffaw. "Me, retire? Are you mad? I shall drop in the saddle on my way to more production, more innovation, more profit. That's the Morgan mantra."

Mr. Bourne laughed. "I suppose you're right, but don't miss all the beauty along the way."

Morgan's admiration of the river proved short-lived. He harrumphed and popped open a gold pocket watch to check the time. "Beauty is in the eye of the beholder. For me, beauty is the color green. On bank notes."

Marjorie swept her hand toward an island they approached. "We have plenty of green here."

Labrese pulled the yacht up to a sandy beach down shore from a massive rock outcropping. He turned and spoke over his shoulder. "We won't be long here. Mac and I'll have the dinner fixin's unloaded in a jiffy."

Devyn glanced at Brice and then at Marjorie, who gave her a hand to stand. "Here's where you disembark to ready the shore dinner. We'll bring back some perch, smallmouth bass, or bluegills—maybe all three—to accompany the meal."

Once off the yacht, Devyn waited for the supplies to be deposited by rowboat on the beach. Then the yacht departed as Marjorie waved. "See you at noon."

She waved back. What an interesting young lady. Fishing alone with her father and his friend. She'd never met such an accomplished, diverse, and independent woman who was so comfortable with both finery and fishing. ·

"Let's set this up, shall we?" Brice pulled Devyn from her admiration, and before long, they had the table and chairs set up under a stand of trees, a roaring campfire blazing in a sandy pit on the beach, and the rest of the cooking supplies laid out on the table.

Brice fried salt pork and onions in a large iron skillet while Devyn cut already scrubbed potatoes into pieces. Once the meat was done, Brice removed it and added the potatoes, browning them while she worked on a salad.

"You can make a fire *and* cook? You're a man of many talents, Brice." She admired him as a grin spread across his handsome features.

"One does what one can." He winked. "Labrese taught me, and now I teach you. It's what makes our world of service go round."

Devyn smiled, but as she thought about the world of service, her heart sank. Could she spend her life as a maid—like Sofia? Surely not. And what were Sofia and her brother doing together, anyway? She let out an angry huff, dropping the knife she'd been using.

"A penny for your thoughts?"

Devyn snapped a glance at him. "Why do you ask?"

He'd grown serious. "Now that we have this time alone—away from the likes of Sofia and other ears—why don't you tell me what's really been bothering you these past few weeks—and now? You try and hide your worries with a cheery disposition, but I can see them in your eyes. Something's amiss."

~ ~ ~

The shadow of sorrow—or was it fear?—had darkened Devyn's face far too long. For weeks, he'd sensed she wasn't ready to talk, sensed he should wait, but Brice could wait no longer.

Devyn stopped preparing the salad, a strange expression crossing her features. "I saw them together in the tower during the Fourth of July celebration, and I saw them together again today. Up to some mischief, I suppose."

"Who? What are you talking about?"

She bit her lip, her eyes filling with moisture. "Falan and Sofia. Just now on the shore and weeks ago during the fireworks."

Confused, Brice removed the iron skillet from the fire and hurried to her, pushing a campstool toward her. "Sit. Tell me everything."

Devyn sat and watched gulls fly overhead. He followed her gaze and stood, waving his arms to shoo them away. "Fool birds. Think you can get our dinner? Shoo! You'll not get a morsel from us today."

That yielded a tiny laugh from her. Her shoulders relaxed, and she finally spoke. "They're up to something. I just know it. And that day with the racing boat? Falan intercepted me on the way to the pergola. Threatened me."

Brice detected fear in her eyes. "Threatened you? Whatever for? Why didn't you tell me before now?"

She swallowed hard and shrugged. "I don't know. I guess I'm used to holding in secrets and afraid to trust others. He said the treasure box we found in the tea garden was rightly his, that he'd found the arrowheads and such. When I told him Mr. Bourne had it, he instructed me to steal it. Said that if I told anyone, I'd regret it. Oh, Brice. I'm so scared. Scared of my own brother!"

Brice grabbed her hands, but that wasn't enough. He took her in his arms and held her while she burst into tears. "Let it out. Let it all out, dear one." He stroked her hair, patted her back, tried to console her. He'd throttle the monster she called her brother—he would—if Falan ever laid his filthy paws on her again.

Keeping his intemperate thoughts to himself, he tried to calm her cares. "He's all bombast and blather. He'll not hurt you if he values his life."

With the handkerchief he handed her, she wiped her eyes, then blew her nose. "But his eyes hold such hate. Ever since Papa … since the ice-fishing accident. And Sofia? I don't trust her as far as I can skip a stone on the water. What could they be up to, do you think?"

Brice didn't doubt the two could be scheming, but he wouldn't throw fuel on the fire of her fears. "I don't know, but God does. There's an Irish saying, 'Count your joys instead of your woes; count your friends instead of your foes.' I think that pertains here. Count on your friends—the Bournes and yours truly—to keep you safe. Your foes will not bring you woe, not as long as I have breath in my body. Leave it in my hands, dear one."

She sniffled. "Thank you, Brice. Truly."

He pulled out his pocket watch. "Goodness. They'll be back within the half hour. I'm sorry, but we need to finish this meal." Before returning to their work, Brice gave her a hug and a kiss on the top of her head. He glanced at her lips, wanting to taste their sweetness.

"Of course." Devyn hopped up from her seat, smoothing her apron, adjusting her mobcap, and pasting on a professional demeanor, which made Brice laugh. She crushed some eggshells and dropped them into the enamel coffee pot to remove the bitterness and keep the grounds on the bottom. Then she finished preparing the coffee.

"You're the most charming woman I've ever met, Devyn. I'll grant you that. Covering your cares with such professionalism. I couldn't be prouder to know such a fine lady."

Devyn pursed her lips and tilted her head, her brow in a deep furrow. "'A little flattery will support a man—or woman—through great fatigue.' James Madison said that. Your words refresh me. Thank you, kind sir."

With that, they returned to their duties in comfortable silence. As he fried the potatoes, his anger over Falan's wickedness began to sizzle too. How could he get that evil fellow off the island for good? He'd have to find a way.

Before long, the yacht returned, and Labrese rowed the passengers to shore. Brice helped Marjorie out, and the men followed, Labrese with a stringer of several freshly caught fish— bass and perch but no bluegills. Brice and Labrese made quick work of filleting the fish while Devyn served the fatback and onion sandwiches and a salad with Thousand Islands Dressing, of course, and crumbles of fatback.

Brice shook the filets in a paper bag already prepared with flour, salt, and pepper, and Labrese fried the fish, turning them only once. Devyn prepared plates of fish and potatoes, serving them with a gentle smile.

Mr. Bourne expressed his thanks before turning to his guest. "Sorry we didn't catch any bluegills, Morgan. Perhaps we'll hook some this afternoon."

Marjorie looked to the sky. "But, Daddy, it appears the storm may come sooner than we'd anticipated. Perhaps we should return to the island after our meal?"

Bourne and Morgan studied the building cloud bank as it grew darker and the wind picked up.

"You're right, Hooley. We'd better cut this fishing excursion a bit short." Mr. Bourne turned to Labrese. "Do we have time for coffee and dessert, old chap?"

Labrese nodded. "I 'spect so. Mac here is frying up the French toast now, and Miss Devyn already has the coffee in hand. Care for some now, sir?"

Mr. Bourne downed his lemonade. "Please. And did you add some extra whiskey to the batter, Mac?"

"Already have, sir. It's the Thousand Islands way, is it not?" Brice chuckled.

Mr. Morgan guffawed. "Whiskey in French toast batter? Now

that's a fine idea."

Mr. Bourne shook his head. "Only a tad for flavor."

Brice flipped the last piece of French toast and pulled the heavy skillet off the fire, but dark clouds released a few raindrops here and there, and within minutes, it began raining in earnest. He could see the lightning approach. "We'd better head back, sir!"

Labrese nodded, already dousing the campfire, while Devyn gathered the dishes and cooking utensils as fast as she could. Brice hurried to collapse the chairs and table and encouraged Marjorie, Morgan, and Bourne to head for the safety of the yacht.

A loud thunderclap shook the ground, and Devyn squealed, jumping back and tripping over a tree root, falling on her backside.

"Head for the rowboat, miss. Mac and I'll finish up," Labrese commanded.

Within moments, Brice and Labrese had loaded the table and chairs and collected the remaining items, and they too rowed for the safety of the yacht. Devyn handed the men towels, but they were soaked to the skin. She clicked her tongue. "Good thing it's a warm rain, else you'd catch your death!"

Labrese rubbed his wet head with the towel. "Been in far worse, my dear." He turned to Mr. Bourne. "Better hold up while the lightning passes, sir. Would you like your dessert now?"

Mr. Bourne patted his stomach. "Yes, thank you. How about it, John?" Morgan nodded. "Mac, why don't you entertain the ladies with your tin whistle while John and I have our dessert and talk in private?"

"Aye, sir. Be keen to."

As Brice played songs from his Irish homeland, Labrese served the men their dessert, and Devyn tended to Miss Marjorie. He played a sorrowful ballad that made Devyn's pretty lips frown and then a jig that caused her to smile and move her feet. What would it be like to play for her, alone, long into the evening on a cold winter's night?

CHAPTER 21

Devyn pinned Miss Marjorie's hair into a perfect chignon, then helped her finish dressing for her outing. She'd grown to like her work as a lady's maid. Perhaps she could find such a position after the summer was over if she'd be able to receive a good reference from the Bournes.

Marjorie surveyed herself in the mirror. "You truly are skilled at this, Devyn." She nodded a thank you before retrieving her reticule. "We shall be gone until dark, I expect. The Frontenac Hotel is simply buzzing with business this time of year, and with the band playing on this fine day, it'll be even busier than usual. I hope we shall see some of our river chums."

"I hope you shall." Devyn nodded. "I hear it's a fine place, though I've not been there."

She wasn't fishing for a chance to join them. She was just being polite. Truth was, she expected to have a day to relax and enjoy a bit of peaceful solitude after J.P. Morgan's visit. After all, they'd been hopping to meet his every need for five full days. On top of the tension and worries about her brother—and Sofia.

"Perhaps you can accompany us next time." Marjorie tilted her head and tossed her a kind smile. "Enjoy your day of rest. You deserve it."

Devyn curtsied. "Thank you. I think I shall."

After seeing the Bournes off, Devyn decided to take a stroll around the island before snuggling up with a good book, though her nerves became taut at the possibility that her brother might try to find her. Somehow, Falan always seemed to know when she was alone and helpless. Vulnerable to his venomous attacks. And then there was Sofia and her cruelty. Devyn still couldn't understand what Falan and Sofia were up to, but finally sharing it with Brice had helped. Just knowing someone cared.

But even taking a walk made her anxious. Was there anyone who could come to her aid now if she needed it? Hannah was busy doing whatever housemaid chores Mrs. VanLeer had assigned her for the day, and Brice was nowhere to be found. Fear tried to grip her, but she kept it at bay, whispering a prayer for protection as she squared her shoulders and headed along the southeastern shore of Dark Island, careful to avoid the north boathouse.

Along the way, she stopped to admire fish jumping, boats passing, birds soaring on the breeze. She took in full lungs of fresh air as she listened to seagulls screeching and ducks quacking. "You're not so bad as I once thought. In fact, I've come to rather enjoy you, mighty old river." She laughed at her own silliness, but she didn't care. Somehow, the St. Lawrence had weaseled its way into a special pocket of her heart, and she'd keep it there.

Suddenly, sounds of water splashing in the distance caught her attention. Could it be a muskrat? A flock of gulls resting along the river's edge? No. It sounded more ... human. Devyn shuddered as a picture of Falan and his gang flashed through her mind. She listened. No. It sounded like a solitary swimmer. But it could still be one of them.

She made her way carefully along the shore while hiding behind bushes and trees like a coyote stalking a rabbit. She jumped when she stepped on a brittle twig which snapped like a gunshot. She darted a glance around to make sure she was the prowler and not the prey and nearly giggled out loud at the ridiculousness of it all.

Devyn shook her head. "What's the matter with me? It's probably just a boater taking a dip." She stepped out from behind the bushes and headed toward the swimming beach. She'd catch that trespasser and send him on his way. Cresting a small knoll, she spotted a man swimming parallel to the beach. Sure enough, some vagabond intruding on the Dark Island solitude.

"You there! You shall not trespass on the Bourne estate, sir. Off with you now, or I shall fetch someone to deal with you." She'd used her most commanding voice, hoping fear didn't underscore her words.

The swimmer stopped but didn't turn around. Then he dove below the surface and didn't come up. Devyn scanned the area, growing more alarmed by the second. Just as panic had begun to set in, he popped out of the waist-level water and laughed.

"Brice? You scoundrel. You gave me a fright." She planted her hands on her hips and prepared to give him a proper scolding. But she stopped short when she took in his form-fitting, navy-blue tank suit. Though it covered him from elbows to knees, it also featured his physique in an altogether alluring way. She yanked her eyes from him and turned toward the trees. "Forgive my intrusion. I thought you a trespasser."

She bit her lip as the sand crunched beneath Brice's feet, and he laughed. "Aye, I get that a lot. And what were you going to do? Cuff me and throw me into the dungeon?"

Devyn touched her burning cheeks, patting them into submission. "I didn't know you'd be here, swimming alone."

"Devyn. Darling. Come here and let's talk." Brice sounded closer now.

She turned and let out a breath she didn't realize she'd been holding. Thankfully, a cotton robe covered him from head to toe. He held out his hand, waiting for her to join him a dozen feet away. When she did, Brice bid her to sit on a large, flat rock near the shore.

"I often come for a dip. Sometimes before the crack of dawn. Other times, it's after Mr. Bourne has retired for the night. Today I couldn't resist a refreshing swim. I don't suppose you swim?"

Devyn shook her head. "Not a whit. Nor do I want to." She wrinkled her nose in disdain.

Brice patted her hand. "Aye, maybe one day you shall. What have you planned on this fine day?"

She shrugged her shoulders. "Reading, I suppose. It's nice to not have a plan now and then."

"Share some of the day with me, will you?" Brice's eyes pleaded with sky-blue desire.

She nodded. "I'll stay a while." A comfortable silence ensued, but she needed his opinion. "I could use your advice about Sofia and Falan. Mr. Morgan's visit offered a distraction for a while, but I could tell you were concerned when I told you about Falan's threat. Now I find myself afraid day and night, worried what might be around the next corner. Fearful of the next false accusation or confrontation. Whatever shall I do, Brice?"

~ ~ ~

Brice pondered her situation for several moments before answering. How could he ease her worry without trivializing it? For it wasn't trivial. Somehow, Sofia had the ear of Mrs. Bourne and appeared to enjoy her respect, even admiration. How and why, he couldn't imagine. Sofia's connection to Falan made her even more a force to be reckoned with. His fair fawn would have to tread lightly, but he couldn't stop his own fears from surfacing in his response.

"It's true that Falan needs to be dealt with, but not at the expense of you losing your job here. That wouldn't do. Not at all." He couldn't bear to never see her again. Resolve firmed his voice. "I will keep an eye on the two of them, and I promise to protect you. You must tell me immediately if anything else happens. No more secrets. Agreed?"

"Agreed." She nodded, plucking a blade of sea grass. "It helps to know that you're watching out for me, but I can't seem to keep the threats and the cruel things they say out of my head. Who's to help me with *that*?"

He glanced at a flock of sparrows that had just landed to rest while crossing the channel. "You mustn't take what they say to heart, Devyn. Surely such threats are just bluster."

She heaved a ragged sigh. "But Mother and Falan, and now Sofia, as well as so many others along the way, have blamed and shamed me, falsely accused me, and threatened me. They have pained me, every one of them. Every word goes straight to my soul, and I am sick of being hurt."

Brice pointed to the flock of birds. "See those sparrows? The

Good Book says, 'Are not five sparrows sold for two farthings, and not one of them is forgotten before God?' Even the very hairs on your pretty head are numbered, Devyn. He knows them all. He does not forget you. He hears every hurtful word that comes your way."

Devyn fiddled with a blade of grass, not looking at him, but he could tell she was listening.

"When I became an orphan, I felt so alone. People pushed me, shoved me, even hit me. Called me names and said I was nothing. Rubbish. One man said that the likes of me should die and make room for others. But then, Mr. Lipton took a liking to me. Said I was a fine boy. Said I was clever. And gave me a job. Gave me a cot in the storage room of his shop. And told me God loved me. God saw me. And He sees you, too, dearest one."

Devyn sniffed and, casting aside the remains of the grass, swiped her eyes with her apron but still didn't look at him. So he took her hand and continued. "You must choose to pay no mind to what others say or do. You're so much more valuable than little birds. Like me, you must find your identity in who God says you are. Not in what other people say."

She nodded. "You're right, of course. I've heard that. Read it. But I don't know how to accomplish such a feat. Even as a wee one, whenever someone called me a name, accused me, blamed me, berated me, I took it to heart and accepted what they said. They were always bigger. Wiser. Especially Mama."

Brice stifled a sound that sounded too much like a growl. He swallowed his anger. "Older is not always wiser. There are some very foolish, even wicked, people in this world. Mr. Lipton taught me to consider the source before accepting something someone says about me, whether it be a compliment, rebuke, or even a promise."

Devyn let out a tiny "hmmm …" and chewed on her lower lip for what seemed an eternity.

Brice let her ponder what he'd said and stood up with a stretch to give her time and space. He picked up a handful of flat, smooth stones and began skipping them along the top of the water.

"How do you do that?" Devyn rose and drew near, curiosity

filling her features with an adorable little-girl look that made him want to scoop her up and dunk her. He cleared his throat along with his foolish desire.

Instead, he picked up another smooth stone and threw it into the river, skipping it several times. "It takes a little practice, but I can teach you."

"Yes. Please. I've always wanted to learn."

Brice grinned wide and searched along the shore, selecting two flat, smooth stones about the size of his palm.

He led her closer to the water's edge and moved around behind her, almost mimicking her shadow. "Watch." He held one rock in his hand and placed one in hers, adjusting her fingers so she could spin the stone. He showed her again how he held it just so, and then he pulled his hand back and, with a thrust, he let the rock go, skipping it off the tranquil water.

"One. Two. Three. Four. Not bad. Now you try." He tapped her arm gently.

Devyn gazed into his eyes with uncertainty, but she adjusted the stone he had placed in her hand. "Like this?"

He nodded as she held the edge of it between her thumb and fingers, but when she let it go, it plopped like an anchor and sank straight into the water.

"You'll get it. Let me show you again." He smiled and patted her shoulder. Then he came closer and wrapped his arms around her. He placed another rock in her hand, adjusting it and her fingers. He took in a whiff of the fresh soap in her hair and on her skin. She smelled so …

"Now what?" Devyn's words yanked him from the distraction, and he chuckled.

"You pull back your arm, then with a sharp toss, let go of the rock. On three." Relishing the closeness, he pulled back her arm. "One. Two. Three." With a whip of her arm, she complied and let the stone soar low through the air and across the surface of the water.

She squealed and counted. "One! Two! Three! Four! Five! I did it!" Her eyes darted to his, and she shrugged. "*We* did it. Thank you, Brice." She scrambled to pick up a few more flat, smooth stones and tried it herself. Each time she skipped them three or more times. She clapped and jumped and did a little jig, all the while smiling and giggling.

Brice watched her celebration, casting an eye on her happy dimple, her sparkling eyes, her joyful spirit. "Just as a stone can skip off the top of the water, so you must let negative words skip off your soul, sweet Devyn."

Her face turned serious, and her eyes brimmed with tears. "I see." She gazed down at the sandy beach and then back up to him. "I shall try."

Brice couldn't help it. He took her in his arms and held her tightly, stroking her hair and kissing the top of her head. She snuggled into his arms, not even complaining that he was still a little damp from his swim or smelled like the river.

A sharp voice spoke above them. "You, Miss McKenna, are nothing but a hussy. A common tramp." Sofia stood on the bank, arms folded across her chest, glowering. "The Bournes shall hear of this indiscretion, and we'll be done with you. You shall never have a place in decent society. Never should have." She shook her head before turning and stomping back toward the castle.

~ ~ ~

With a troubled glance at the empty bank, Devyn chewed her lip and swallowed.

Brice patted her arm before stepping back. "Now is a great time to practice letting her words roll off you. She's just a bitter old maid, and the Bournes won't believe such prattle. Trust God, and trust the truth. You are not what she says. Never could be."

Devyn took a deep breath and rolled her shoulders. "I'll do my best." She smoothed her dress before taking a step toward the castle, then smiled and waved her hand for him to join her. "Shall we?"

By the time they swept into the servants' hall, Devyn had cast her worries aside. Her time with Brice was all that mattered, and his words had buoyed her spirits like nothing ever had.

From the kitchen, Mrs. VanLeer approached her quickly, her brows knit, her eyes foreboding. "Mrs. Bourne would like to see you. Immediately." Her terse tone made Devyn's heart race. "She's in the library."

Devyn curtsied, then trembled her way through the Great Hall. Had she been remiss in tossing aside the concerns about Sofia? Probably. Likely. Surely.

With her hand lifted to the heavy, closed door, she stifled a groan, then whispered a prayer.

Upon Devyn's knock, Mrs. Bourne said, "Come in." Once she entered, the missus added, "And shut it behind you, please."

Devyn did as she was bid.

Mrs. Bourne sat by the fireplace with a book on her lap. She looked none too happy. "Sit, Devyn. We need to talk."

Devyn curtsied and sat on the edge of her chair. She folded her hands in her lap to keep them from trembling. Mrs. Bourne gazed at the crackling fire and snapped her gaze toward Devyn, then back at the fire. The silence screamed in Devyn's ears as she waited for the missus to speak.

Mrs. Bourne flipped her book closed. "What did you do today, Devyn, while we were away?"

Sofia. She had to spread her poison, her lies, her innuendos.

"I … I took a walk around the island and enjoyed the river." That was the truth. Well, most of it.

"And did you meet anyone while on your walk?"

Devyn bit the inside of her cheek to keep from crying. "I … I ran into Brice while on my walk. He was swimming, and we talked."

"Talked? Is that all?"

"Yes. No … I don't know." Devyn's heart surged, and her throat choked her with emotion. How could she defend herself? How could she let Sofia's negative words skip off her heart when she didn't even know what they were? She'd already been judged by the missus, and her interrogation cut deeply.

Mrs. Bourne waited for her to expound. But what should she say?

"He ... he showed me how to skip stones on the water. We talked. He ... he's a good friend, missus."

Mrs. Bourne shook her head. "Just a good friend? I think not. I have it from a reliable source that there is much, much more to your friendship."

Devyn blinked back tears and swallowed the accusation. She could let Sofia's words skip into oblivion. But Mrs. Bourne's? They hurt. "I do care for Brice. And I think he cares for me too. But ... well ... he has never been inappropriate. Ever."

"And you? Have you been inappropriate?"

What had that nasty old maid told the missus? Devyn shook herself from her anger and glanced at Mrs. Bourne. Her face held a sadness that broke her. A whimper escaped Devyn's lips, and the dam burst. She threw her hands up to her face. Hidden in the darkness of her wet hands, she tried, and failed, to collect herself.

"Devyn. Look at me, please." Mrs. Bourne's voice sounded softer than before. Motherly.

She swiped away the moisture from her face and looked up at the missus. Her eyes still held sadness, but a layer of compassion buffered it. Clearly, Mrs. Bourne was disappointed in her.

"Truly, I ... we ... did ... have done nothing inappropriate."

Mrs. Bourne shook her head. "Sofia has informed me otherwise. You embraced? In public? Devyn, that is inappropriate. And so, it is with much sadness that Mr. Bourne and I forbid you and Brice to be together, alone, at any time. If you do, you will both be dismissed. Is that understood?"

Devyn croaked out a shaky "yes, ma'am" as her heart sank to her feet. She was sad that she couldn't be with Brice. But even more, she was mortified that Mr. and Mrs. Bourne had found her wanting.

CHAPTER 22

Devyn set down her fork and took a sip of tea. The pancakes tasted like paste. The air grew suffocating, its humidity stifling. Gray clouds blew in from the north, threatening to make the day even drearier and more depressing than the previous night's restrictions had.

Sofia sat across from her, gloating, smirking, casting triumphant glances from her to Brice—who completely ignored Devyn. Not a "good morning" or a smile. Nothing. It was as if she didn't exist.

Tension filled the air until Hannah looked at each one of them and said, "What's wrong?"

Devyn quickly took a mouthful of pancake and let the pasty goo sit on her tongue. She couldn't answer her. Brice shoveled food into his mouth as if his life depended on it. He wouldn't answer her either.

But Sofia did. "Oh, some staff discipline for inappropriate behavior between certain individuals. I'd say that some of us may be teetering on dismissal."

Hannah gasped as if she'd been told of some great crime. Thankfully, she asked no more questions. She just hurriedly finished her breakfast and excused herself without another word. Brice followed and left Devyn alone with Sofia.

"Watch your ways, miss." Sofia glared at Devyn, who wanted to slap the smirk off the woman's face.

But Devyn didn't respond or even excuse herself. She picked up her dishes, washed and dried them, and hurried out of the hall as fast as she could, a tear slipping down her cheek. "Help me, Lord. Please!"

She hurried to Miss Marjorie's room to prepare her mistress for the day. But soon the wind picked up, and it started to rain. Marjorie harrumphed. "Oh, bother, and I was going to take the *Moike* up to Alex Bay. I guess it's a day of reading and writing. But no arithmetic." She laughed at herself. "Do you like arithmetic?"

Devyn shook her head. "Never cared for it. But teacher said I was quite good at it."

Marjorie laughed. "My tutors said the same. Well, perhaps I shall paint today. Let's go to the library, shall we? I hate to be alone on such a gloomy day."

Devyn glanced around. The bed was still unmade, and the room needed tidying. "Shall I finish here before I join you?" She hoped so, for she needed time alone.

Marjorie's kindness came through her voice. "Take your time." She glanced out the window, rain pummeling the glass. "Looks like we'll be inside for the entire day."

"Thank you, miss." Devyn curtsied and caught herself. "Ah, Marjorie."

"I think it's a lost cause, getting you to switch to my name rather than 'miss.' But don't fret, for I care not, either way." Marjorie laughed as she waved a goodbye and exited the room.

Devyn blew out a breath, trying to release the tension building in her chest. She made the bed and tidied the room. She'd become quite adept at her daily tasks, almost enjoyed the routine. None of it seemed difficult, not even daunting. It was comfortable. Safe.

Safe? Would her life ever feel safe? She tried to remember a time, even as a young child, when someone wasn't picking on her. When someone didn't tease or accuse her. Even when she'd been a wee one, Falan's presence had loomed like a slithering snake, ready to strike at any moment. A little push here. Blame there. She shuddered at the memory of Falan telling Papa that he'd witnessed her stealing a penny from his dresser. She'd been just five and had gotten a switch for it. But she'd known, just known, he was the real thief, especially when she'd found a new comic book in the barn.

An apple would disappear, and she'd be blamed. A glass of spilled milk became her fault, even if it was out of her reach. Somehow,

Mama always believed her big brother. Always thought she was the culprit. Then, after the ice-fishing accident …

And now? The Bournes think I'm a hussy. Dear God. How ever shall I face them?

She shook herself free from her sadness before it could cause her to shirk her duties as Marjorie's lady's maid. At least Marjorie thought her capable and competent. She scanned the room to make sure she hadn't missed anything, to make sure she'd done her best before leaving to attend Miss Marjorie's needs.

Upon entering the library, the memory of the encounter with Mrs. Bourne came flooding back. The look of disappointment. The condemnation. The ultimatum. Her throat constricted, and she bit her lip to keep from whimpering. It was so unfair!

"Pick out a puzzle, will you?" Marjorie pointed to a shelf where several boxes were stacked.

Devyn nodded. "Any one in particular?"

"No. I've done them all at one time or another. You choose."

Devyn surveyed the stack and pulled out the third box. She shook it gently, but it didn't sound like puzzle pieces. She took the box to Marjorie. "This doesn't sound right. Perhaps a box within a box?"

Marjorie questioned with her eyes but said nothing. When she lifted the top, a journal sat inside. "Why, what in the world is Florence's diary doing in here? And where's the puzzle?" She pulled out the journal, her eyes twinkling. "What juicy gossip might be in here?" She laughed, and a mischievous expression danced on her face. "This is better than a puzzle any day." She pulled her legs up under her skirts and snuggled on the sofa, opening the diary with tittering pleasure.

"If you don't mind, I'll just do some dusting while you enjoy that." Devyn smiled at her. "I never had a sister, but I believe I'd be as curious as you are."

"Yes, well, we Bourne girls are all curious creatures. Proceed, then." Marjorie pulled the book up to her face, hiding her naughtiness.

Devyn went to the cleaning closet, retrieved a dusting cloth, and returned to the library. She dusted the already clean shelves, books, and mantel, but she was happy to be lost in a mindless duty. Alone with her thoughts.

How could she vindicate herself? The Bournes had begun to feel like family, and she'd hoped to find a permanent position—somehow—in their employ. But now? The look on Mrs. Bourne's face told it all—she was a condemned woman. She had lost the trust of these special people. Why?

Because a wicked, bitter old woman is trying to advance herself by smearing others.

She turned to the beautiful, mahogany-colored, wooden folding desk engraved with "F. G. B." Mr. Bourne's special traveling desk. Before dusting it, she touched the soft, red fabric that lined the interior. She ran a finger over the little pocket marked "stamps" and another marked "memorandum." There was a place for stationery, envelopes, pens, pencils, scissors, and more. A large blotter took up half the desk, and a tiny calendar barely the size of her hand showed the month of July 1910.

She began to dust the desk, but suddenly it started to slide off its stand. "Oh my!" She dropped her cloth and grabbed the desk before it hit the floor, but its contents scattered everywhere. "No. This can't be happening. Not today." Her voice quivered as she spoke to no one in particular.

Marjorie hurried to her side. "It's okay, Devyn. I've toppled Daddy's desk a dozen times, even broke a hinge once. That stand is far too tipsy." Marjorie bent down and helped Devyn retrieve a few of the items.

She bid her mistress to return to her reading while she put the stationery items back into their proper places in the desk. "Thank you. I can finish."

Marjorie returned to her reading just as Mrs. VanLeer came into the room, looking aghast at Devyn on her hands and knees, picking up papers and envelopes still strewn about. "What's the meaning of this mess?"

Marjorie answered before Devyn could. "The desk toppled is all. It needs a stronger stand."

The missus blinked, apparently not having seen Marjorie. She nodded. "Yes, well, may I please borrow Devyn for a little while? I need her to run an errand."

"Surely. I have some interesting reading to do." Marjorie winked at Devyn. "Off with you, then."

Devyn gathered the remaining stationery and set it on the desk. "I'll tidy this when I get back."

Marjorie shook her head. "No need. I shall finish it presently. None will be the wiser, right, missus?" She cast a glance at Mrs. VanLeer and smirked.

Devyn curtsied, giving Marjorie a grateful smile. "Thank you, Miss Marjorie."

On the way to the servants' hall, Mrs. VanLeer enlightened Devyn to the nature of her assignment. "I need you to take the chicken soup to the Reid crew. Two—yes, two—of the kitchen maids are unwell today."

She stopped short. "May I please have Hannah join me?" She couldn't go near the north boathouse and into her brother's lair alone.

The missus furrowed her brow. "Whatever for? You'll have a cart to haul everything."

"Oh, please, missus. My brother …"

Mrs. VanLeer scowled. "What about your brother?"

"I … well … we don't exactly get along, and I don't want to meet him alone."

The missus shook her head, sighing her frustration. "All right, then. You may fetch her. But no dawdling."

~ ~ ~

Devyn found Hannah straightening the linen closet. "The missus said you can accompany me on an errand. Can you come now?"

Hannah smiled. "Surely. What are we to do?"

Devyn filled her in on the way to the kitchen. "We have to deliver lunch to the Reid crew in the north boathouse."

Hannah shivered. "Through the tunnel? I still get a fright going underground."

Devyn patted her hand as they descended the stairs. "I used to as well, and I still don't like it. But it's the best way to stay out of the rain."

When the girls entered the kitchen, the kitchen maid had the large pot of soup and two loaves of bread sitting on a metal rolling cart. Devyn thanked her and began pushing it. "I'll drive it, but you make sure the cart doesn't get away from us, okay?"

Hannah nodded, her eyes shouting uncertainty, maybe even fear. "I've not been to the north boathouse yet, and on such a stormy day."

"Don't worry. We'll manage." As Devyn pushed the metal contraption through the tunnel, the rattling and clanging reverberated off the walls. Then a wheel stuck, bringing the cart to a jolting stop. "This fool thing is useless. Do you think we can carry this heavy pot and the bread?"

She took one of the towels covering the still-warm bread and wrapped it around the cast iron handle. "This pot is heavy. I think it'll take both of us to carry it."

After some adjusting, they found a way to carry it between them and hold a loaf of bread each with their free hand. Though they had to stop and rest several times, they were soon in the boathouse and delivered the lunch to the boathouse kitchen staff.

Hannah wiped her brow. "Glad that's done! Can we look around a bit?"

A chill climbed up Devyn's spine. "I'd rather not. Let's get back."

"But why? Such a curious place needs exploration." Hannah took her hand. "Come on. Just a little?"

"Oh, all right. Just a little."

Devyn followed Hannah around, surprised how interested the girl seemed. When they got to the engine room, Hannah peeked in, *ooh*ing and *aah*ing. The workers grunted and complained about something, but when Devyn stepped in behind Hannah to see what they were doing, she stopped and immediately stepped back into the shadows.

Falan was one of the workers banging on a pipe.

Hannah stood in the doorway, eyes wide as she leaned in to observe the noisy machinery. She innocently addressed the men. "Hello. I was just taking a look around the boathouse. It's quite an interesting place." She curtsied, her eyes alight with adventure.

Devyn, on the other hand, held her breath and tried to make herself as small as possible.

"Well, well, if it isn't little Hannah Banana," Falan teased the girl. "What are you doing on the island? Do you remember me?"

Falan's voice drew near as Hannah stepped back, her sweet face reflecting the moment her excitement turned to horror. Falan followed her and grabbed her hand, planting a kiss on it. Then he turned and noticed Devyn. "You! What are *you* doing here, father killer? Didn't I tell you to stay off my turf?"

Devyn pasted herself to the wall, shocked by his hateful accusation. But then she remembered Mr. Bourne's words. "How dare you call me such a vile thing, Falan?"

"If the shoe fits." Falan seemed to notice Hannah's shock and dropped her hand. As if he were a rattlesnake about to strike, he slithered up to Devyn and stood within inches of her face, his foul breath choking her. "You, dear sister, are the vile thing. Where's the …" He glanced Hannah's way, stopped himself, and turned sickeningly sweet. His thin lips lifted in an evil, disingenuous grin, and he whispered inches from Devyn's ear, his proximity bringing bile to her mouth. "You forgot to bring me the box I asked for. Where is it?" He grabbed her arm, pretending to be affectionate, but squeezed it hard.

"You're hurting me. I don't know what you're talking about. Let me go!" She allowed her voice to rise in an attempt to draw the men out of the engine room, but the noise must've muffled her pleas. She glanced at Hannah for help, but the girl stood wide-eyed and unmoving.

So with all her strength, Devyn shook herself free and scooted under his arm, hurrying to Hannah's side. She grabbed her friend's hand and pulled her away. "Come. We must get back to work. The missus said we mustn't dawdle."

Devyn had to nearly drag the girl from the boat slip, out of the boathouse, and into the tunnel. Only then did they stop to catch their breath. But Devyn kept a wary eye on the boathouse door in case her brother might follow them. Thankfully, he did not.

Hannah whimpered, chewing her fingernails. What would she say to the girl who'd witnessed her brother's wickedness? Would Hannah tell the missus? If she reported the incident and Falan ran his mouth, both Devyn and her brother would likely be dismissed, and then where would Mama get money to feed the young ones? No. She'd have to risk gaining the girl's confidence. She'd tell Brice when she could, but only him.

It took several minutes to calm Hannah down, but once she did, she put her plan into action, trying to keep her voice lighthearted and casual. "Do you remember my older brother from public school?"

Hannah nodded. "Only a bit. I was only a wee thing, but I remember that he was always with those two other big boys who kept getting into trouble. They scared me then. He scares me now. I didn't know he was here on the island. Are the other boys here too?" The girl's eyes darted back toward the boathouse, and her fear was palpable.

"No. Just Falan's here. He's a beastly brother, but he's mostly all hot air."

"But he hurt you. I heard you cry out in pain."

"Oh, that. I'm sure he didn't mean to hurt me. He's just too strong for his own good." A prick of conscience told her she was on the wrong path with that lie. But she wanted to stay on the island. Wanted to stay in the Bournes' employ. At least until she showed them she was trustworthy.

Trustworthy … and lying? She shook her head in shame.

"Devyn. Are you all right?" Hannah looked at her with a furrowed brow, her lips pinched tight.

"I'm fine. Let's get back to the castle, shall we? And let's leave Falan's teasing in the boathouse, okay?"

Hannah shook her head. "The missus should know you were treated poorly, Devyn. Even if he is your brother, he should not treat a woman so. And he harrassed me too."

Devyn's stomach churned. She thought she might lose her breakfast. She swallowed hard, trying to think of what to say, how to defend a person who should never be defended. If she had her way, Falan would be in the dungeon and the key tossed into the deepest part of the St. Lawrence River. But her way couldn't be the way, could it?

How could she report him without Falan incriminating her too? He was so skilled at turning the truth. Always had been. He could fool their parents, the teacher, even the preacher. And likely, he'd fool the Bournes as well.

"I know, Hannah. His teasing is unkind. But we're both fine, are we not? Let's leave the matter in the hands of the Lord and not give it another thought. After all, in the end, He is the one who will judge between the just and the unjust, is that not true?"

Hannah nodded, but it was several long moments before she finally, mercifully, relaxed her shoulders. "Very well. We'll leave it there."

Devyn blew out a breath she hadn't realized she'd been holding. "Yes. We'll leave it in the Lord's hands."

Question was, could she trust Him to bring justice, or would He leave her on her own?

CHAPTER 23

"The Mr. Vanderbilt is coming?" Devyn surveyed Marjorie's smiling face in the mirror as she buttoned the back of Marjorie's morning dress.

Serving the likes of J.P. Morgan had been nerve-racking enough, and now Mr. Vanderbilt, the famous railroad tycoon? As far as her teacher had been concerned, Vanderbilt was at the top of the "famous" list. What would Mr. Beyer think of her meeting this powerful man?

Marjorie shook her head as Devyn finished with the tiny pearl buttons. "No, not the elder Vanderbilt. Neily, one of the sons." She paused, shrugging her shoulders. "I mean, Captain Cornelius Neily Vanderbilt III. He's a captain in the New York National Guard and was a childhood friend of my eldest brother, Arthur. He has quite a creative turn of mind, so that's why Daddy asked that I give him my room for his stay."

"Do you want all your things moved downstairs?" Devyn glanced around.

"Just my everyday things and one or two gowns. He'll only be here a few days." Once Devyn finished the buttons, Marjorie rose and twirled. "I just love this dress, don't you?"

Devyn nodded. "That soft, pale yellow looks lovely on you."

"Thank you. Now, I'll leave you to it. You know what I like, so I'll let you decide what to move to the room downstairs." Checking herself in the mirror one last time, Marjorie pinched her cheeks, then smiled. "Toodle-oo."

Devyn surveyed the room again and huffed. It'd take a dozen or more trips up and down the narrow stairs to move Marjorie's things. Why Neily Vanderbilt needed this room, she'd never know. "Oh, well. Best get busy." She rolled her eyes at hearing her own words. She'd been speaking her mind out loud far too often these days. A habit she needed to break before she got herself into trouble.

Indeed, it took more than a dozen trips up and down the stairway before Marjorie's things were finally relocated. She'd left a half-dozen gowns in the back of the closet, but the man would have plenty of room to hang his things. Would he bring a valet? If so, where would the man stay?

Once Devyn finished the task, she needed to prepare the room for this Neily chap. She grabbed the cleaning bucket and stopped by the linen closet to fetch fresh linens, finding Hannah there too.

Now that the bulk of the moving was done, Devyn's concern turned into an anticipation she wanted to share with her friend. "Can you believe we'll meet one of the famous Vanderbilts? This one can't be old since Marjorie said he was a friend of her brother."

Hannah bit a nail. "I pray I don't meet him. Mr. Morgan was enough for me."

Devyn riffled through the linens to find the finest sheets. Pulling them out of the pile, she dropped the pillowcase. She bent to pick it up but screeched instead. "Eeeek! A snakeskin."

Hannah jumped back. "No! I hate snakes. If there's a skin, that means there's a snake."

Both girls scurried out of the closet. Devyn's heart pounded. "I hate them too. I do. But we have to prepare for the man's arrival. He's to be here before dinner." Gingerly, she darted into the closet, grabbed the linens, and scurried out. "What do you need, Hannah?"

Hannah bit her fingernail again, her eyes wide with fear. She pointed toward the closet. "Towels."

By now, Devyn had gotten control of her fear and retrieved a stack of linens for the girl. "If the snake were in there, he'd likely have shown himself by now." She handed Hannah the towels. "But we mustn't fear. There are no poisonous snakes on the islands. Only garters and water snakes. Brice told me so."

Hannah swallowed. "Good to know, but I still don't like the slithering creatures, poisonous or not."

Devyn giggled. "Nor do I, but we'd better get back to work. See you later."

Devyn went her way and Hannah hers, and by midafternoon, everything was ready for their guest. Marjorie busied herself writing her part of a round-robin letter, so Devyn helped Nellie and Mahlon set a beautifully formal dinner table as Mrs. VanLeer had requested.

Once their task was complete, the staff enjoyed an early meal in the servants' hall. Devyn stayed close to Hannah and avoided Sofia. Halfway through her chicken and dumplings, Brice appeared, a huge grin on his face.

"He's here, and without a valet. Guess I'm going to do double duty." Brice scooped up a plate of food and sat far from Devyn. He glanced at her, but she couldn't read any emotions on his face.

As Sofia scrutinized her, Devyn took a bite and ignored him. No. She wouldn't give the woman an ounce of anything that she might use as a weapon. She turned to Hannah. "I'm to be the Watch over dinner tonight. What'll you be doing?"

Hannah shrugged. "I'll help in the kitchen. Since we have the majority of the cleaning well in hand, the missus is expanding my experience. When she learned that I've always dreamed of having a bakery, she gave me this opportunity."

"Oh, stuff and nonsense." Sofia cast Hannah a condescending glare. "You'll never own a business. Dreams are for the rich, the famous, and the mad."

Devyn whispered in Hannah's ear. "Don't listen to the old bat. You can do anything you put your mind to."

Sofia turned her guns on Devyn. "Rude. Improper. Unacceptable. Imagine! Whispering at the dinner table. You condemn yourself at every pass, miss."

Brice finally spoke up. "Let them alone, will you? And let us eat in peace for once." After scolding Sofia into silence, he addressed the lot of them. "Captain Vanderbilt is talking with Mr. Bourne in his office and shan't be disturbed at present. But dinner will be served promptly at seven, according to Mahlon."

Hannah spoke up, curiosity filling her words as it had in the boathouse. "What's he like, this famous captain?"

"He's a fine fellow. Mid-thirties, amiable, regal, serious." Brice paused. "I've met him before when he had his family with him."

Devyn wanted to know more but feared addressing him. She poked Hannah, prodding her to ask more.

The girl seemed eager to comply. "Tell us about them. Please?"

Brice nodded. "A nice wife. The daughter of a New York banker. Wilson, I believe." He took a sip of his milk. "Two adorable children. A girl, Grace, who is about ten or so, and the oldest boy, Cornelius IV, who is a few years older."

Hannah giggled. "Four Corneliuses? How ever can they tell them apart?"

Brice shrugged. "I don't know, but I'd better go and dress the third." With that, he took one last bite, excused himself, and left the hall.

Devyn fought back tears. *With Mr. Vanderbilt here, when will I get time alone with Brice to keep my promise about Falan?* More importantly, after the censure they'd received from the Bournes, did he even still want her to?

After she tended to Marjorie's evening dress, she took her place behind the grate. Though she was excited to get a glimpse of the guest, her feelings about seeing the Bournes were bittersweet. How she'd grown to love them, but now, with her reputation cast in a poor light, she swallowed the lump in her throat and attempted to dispel the memory of Mrs. Bourne's sad eyes. Why did the woman believe Sofia so blindly, completely? Anyone close to her could see, should see, the old maid's devious nature.

Just then, the sound of feet shuffling prompted her to peer through the grate. Brice and Nellie took their places in the dining room as Mahlon opened the door for the dinner party. Captain Vanderbilt entered first with Marjorie on his arm, chatting gaily, and behind them, Mr. and Mrs. Bourne. Such a grand entrance for such a small party.

Once they were all seated, the beautiful dance of formal dining began. Devyn marveled at the elegant way the servers swept in with food and drink at just the right moment and swept back out without bringing attention to themselves.

Mr. Bourne gave Captain Vanderbilt a nod. "Tell the ladies about this underground railroad. I think it's a fine idea."

Devyn was glad he sat facing the grate so she could observe him closely. The handsome man was tall and thin, with a well-trimmed, thick mustache and beard matching his coffee-brown hair. Dark eyes scanned the women before he spoke.

Captain Vanderbilt smiled at Mrs. Bourne. "I'll spare you much of the technicalities, but after seeing the subway systems in London and Paris, I partnered with August Belmont Jr. to draw up plans for such an efficient expansion of our own New York City line. We call the partnership the Interborough Rapid Transit Company, and I've brought the blueprints for the Brooklyn Rapid Transit expansion with me for Mr. Bourne's perusal. We're seeking investors and thought your husband might like to be a part of this fine venture."

Mr. Bourne turned to the women. "This man has quite the mind. He's improved locomotives and freight cars, and his patents are many—a corrugated firebox, a cylindrical tank car for hauling oil by railroad. And now this? A subway under New York City that will transport thousands each day to and from Manhattan to Brooklyn and out to the other boroughs? Just think what it would do to alleviate the crowded streets above."

Devyn had never been to New York City, but Mr. Beyer had shown the class pictures of how crowded it was. She'd imagined the smell, the noise, the fear of such a throng of people, horses, wagons, buggies, and even the new-fangled motorcars. She wasn't sure she'd be interested in visiting such a place, but to descend under the ground to ride a train in the dark? Oh my!

When Devyn again focused on the conversation, the captain was speaking, and the topic had changed. "… my dear Grace is well, and so are the children."

Mrs. Bourne spoke, her voice kind. "And how is your mother? It's been over a decade since your father passed, but I'm sure one never gets over such a loss."

A strange shadow passed over Captain Vanderbilt's face. His brows furrowed, and he shook his head. "It's been eleven years, and I still haven't seen her, but my brother, Alfred, tells me she's faring well."

"Please forgive me. I forgot of your troubles." Mrs. Bourne turned to her husband. "Did you seek an update on the Yacht Club, dear?"

What a strange turn of the conversation. What troubles? Devyn listened even more closely.

Mr. Bourne nodded. "The New York Yacht Club remains in good hands ever since I turned the commodore position over to this man."

Captain Vanderbilt chuckled, his voice deep and warm. "I aim to skipper the *Aurora* and win the King Edward VII Cup in Newport, Rhode Island, this fall."

"How long is that sloop, old chap?" Mr. Bourne leaned in.

"It's a sixty-five-footer, and she's a beauty." Vanderbilt grinned, apparently quite proud of his vessel.

Marjorie turned to the man. "If you bring it up to the islands, I'll race my *Moike* against you, and I'll likely win."

The entire table laughed at her challenge, and Marjorie's napkin slid off her lap and onto the floor. Devyn hurried downstairs to alert the staff, sneaking into the doorway and trying to catch the gaze of someone. Thankfully, Nellie noticed her and hurried over.

Devyn whispered. "Miss Marjorie's napkin is on the floor."

Nellie patted her hand. "Thank you. I hadn't noticed."

Devyn nodded and returned to her post, pleased she had been able to help, even a little. Back in her spot behind the grate, she watched as Brice poured wine into the men's glasses. How she missed talking to her friend, a man who seemed to know her heart, care about her, and to provide the wisdom she needed. Now she was forbidden to glean such help from him.

Mrs. Bourne was asking their guest about his subway expansion. "What of the National Guard? Will they participate?"

The captain shook his head. "The New York National Guard is a fine and growing organization, but as aide to the division commander, I'm quite certain he won't call up the guard for this."

Mr. Bourne slapped the table. "Well, I shall invest in your venture. I'll send you back to New York with a satchel of capital."

Captain Vanderbilt reached out and shook his hand. "Thanks,

my friend. You won't regret it."

Dinner done, the women retreated to the piazza while the men stayed in the dining room to discuss further business over glasses of brandy. Devyn wasn't sure whether to stay or go, but just as she rose to leave, Mr. Bourne spoke. "I'm so sorry your parents never approved of your lovely Grace. It pains me to hear you're still disenfranchised from your mother. I know Alice to be such a gentle soul."

"Thank you, sir. It pains me as well, and I pray we'll reconcile soon." The captain hung his head, his shoulders sagging.

Mrs. VanLeer appeared and glanced through the grate. "Devyn, you're needed with the women. Leave the men to their business." She shooed her down the steps.

Devyn curtsied and hurried to the piazza, where Sofia served the women tea. Marjorie bid her to come near. When she did, Mrs. Bourne gave her a tentative smile. "You cast shadows of Louisa nearly every time I look at you."

Devyn stared at the flowers on the rug beneath her feet. "I'm sorry, missus. I don't mean to sadden you."

The missus shook her head. "Oh, you don't. You just remind me of her, and though bittersweet, it touches a mother's heart."

Marjorie cleared her throat. "The men are still talking in the dining room, are they not?"

Devyn nodded. "Yes, miss. I just left the Watch."

"Would you fetch me my book? I left it in the side table drawer, and you didn't bring it downstairs with my other things." Marjorie glanced at her mother. "I didn't think I'd need it tonight, but I'm not a whit tired and would like to read for a while. And bring my shawl too. There's a chill in the air."

Devyn curtsied. "Yes, miss. I'll fetch them promptly."

She hurried up the three flights of stairs to the Rapunzel Room. She still liked the name Marjorie had given it. After knocking, though, she entered timidly, uncomfortable to be in what was now Captain Vanderbilt's abode.

She glanced around before gathering the book and shawl. On the dresser sat an apothecary jar half filled with white powder, a leather-covered journal, and a small painting signed "Remington."

Though Remington was a summer resident of the area, Devyn had only ever known that he painted and sculpted scenes of the Wild West. This painting was different. A canoe paddled by eight native Indians glided on lily-padded, tranquil waters. It looked like it could be a local pond, but a white man stood in the middle of the canoe. An explorer, maybe? She'd learned the explorers had sometimes hired the native Indians.

Devyn pulled her attention from the painting and gathered Marjorie's book and shawl. She hurried to return them but bumped into Brice as she was rounding the first landing of the stairs. "Oh. Sorry."

Brice glanced up toward Marjorie's room. "What were you doing up there? Miss Marjorie's down here." He pointed toward her temporary lodgings.

"She asked me to get her book and shawl is all." Devyn stepped back, clamping her lips together.

"Carry on, then." Brice's tone was formal, but when she turned to leave, he touched her arm gently. "Chin up."

Devyn blinked and nodded. "I … I need to speak with you soon. About Falan."

Brice's neck turned red. "What's he done now? Are you all right?"

"Yes, but he warned me to get the treasure box to him and harassed Hannah. I thought you should know." She swallowed hard, biting her lip.

"Thank you for telling me." He gave her a half smile.

Could she still trust him to watch out for her? Devyn nodded before hurrying to the piazza and back to Marjorie's side.

~ ~ ~

The following day, Marjorie and Mrs. Bourne took tea in the tea garden. A soft breeze kept the bugs at bay, and wispy clouds held the heat of the sun behind them. Devyn assisted Sofia as she served a lovely afternoon tea on white china and sparkling crystal.

"I wonder how Daddy and the captain are faring on their fishing excursion. I wish I could have gone." Marjorie gazed at the river and sighed.

Mrs. Bourne patted her hand. "Now, now. They needed time to talk business, and besides, you should be about more womanly things. I've always given you girls the freedom to explore all that life has to offer, but there is a time and a place for all of it."

"I know, Mother. But I can only do so much reading and painting and needlepoint. I just love to be out on the water, to catch a hearty muskellunge, to feel the wind in my hair. I can only attend so many parties before I think I'll go mad!"

Mrs. Bourne chuckled. "I know. You're not one to relish frivolity and finery. But do try to find peace in this place, dear one."

Marjorie nodded. "Oh, I do. I love Dark Island and this beautiful St. Lawrence River. If only the end of summer would never come."

"Well, it will, and we'll return to Long Island and our life there. But for now, rest easy, my sweet." Mrs. Bourne reached over and touched her daughter's cheek so tenderly that Devyn felt a wee bit jealous. She couldn't remember a moment when her own mother had shown her such affection, and it tore at her heart.

"How much is Daddy investing in Captain Vanderbilt's rapid transit project? I think it's a fine scheme." Marjorie smiled as she glanced up at the treetops above her.

Mrs. Bourne shook her head. "Never you mind about that. Sometimes I think you ponder things a woman should not contemplate."

Devyn turned away, attempting to give mother and daughter a bit of intimacy. But when her eyes landed on Sofia, a scheming scowl and condemning eyes replaced the view of the tranquil scene, and a chill ran down her spine despite the warm day.

CHAPTER 24

Two days later, Devyn pondered Sofia's growing antagonism as she sat down for breakfast. The more she thought about it, the more it worried her. She couldn't look at Sofia without apprehension and fear, for the woman continued to scowl, smirk, and cast her piercing looks of disdain every time Devyn encountered the woman. Devyn had even begun sitting next to Sofia just so she could avoid looking at her, but hatred hung over Sofia like an approaching thundercloud. Why? Why was Sofia so set on persecuting her?

Devyn finished her bowl of oatmeal and turned to Hannah. "What's on your agenda today?"

Hannah patted her mouth with her napkin before answering. "I have a day of mending to do, but I don't mind. I love to sew. You?"

"I must move Marjorie's things back into the Rapunzel Room."

"That's *Miss* Marjorie to you," Sofia huffed. "You will never learn, will you?"

Devyn swallowed any response and rose to leave. "I'm done here." She smiled at Hannah. "Have a good day, my friend."

Hannah waved before Devyn slipped into the secret passageway. When she got to the wine vault door, the raised, anxious voices of the captain and the Bournes came from the Great Hall. Devyn hid behind the door and listened.

"The money satchel was in my room when I came down to breakfast, and now it's gone!" Captain Vanderbilt's accusation came out in one hurried breath.

Devyn bit back her shock. Someone had stolen Mr. Bourne's money?

Mr. Bourne nearly shouted, calling for Brice. "Mac? Come

down here at once."

From far above her, Devyn detected Brice's voice. "Yes, sir." His footsteps descended the staircase and hurried to the group. "Yes?"

Mr. Bourne sounded angrier than she'd ever imagined he could be. "The investment capital is missing! Who, besides you and the captain, has been in his room?"

Brice cleared his throat. "I've seen no one. Except …"

"Except who?" Mr. Bourne's curt tone sent a shiver down her spine.

"Devyn retrieved a few items for Miss Marjorie last night."

Mrs. Bourne spoke. "It's true. Marjorie needed her book and shawl and sent her to fetch them."

Mr. Bourne shouted. "Devyn? Where are you?"

Devyn slunk back into the passageway.

Mrs. Bourne spoke. "Don't shout, dearest. Brice, go and fetch the girl. Immediately."

More feet shuffling. Brice was coming to find her. Devyn closed the door and stepped into the passageway, her hands shaking as if she had the palsy. What would she do? How could she show them she wasn't the thief? She paced the passageway, trying to make sense of it, trying to make a plan. Then she heard Brice call her.

"Devyn? Are you there?"

Devyn shot up a prayer for help. "Yes, I'm here."

Brice appeared and grabbed her hand. "Hurry. We've a crisis on our hands. Mr. Bourne's investment funds are missing."

Devyn pulled him to a stop, her eyes filling with tears. "They think I took it? You think I stole it?"

Brice shook his head. "No. Never. But they want to question you. Come. They are waiting." Again, he pulled, and she resisted.

"But they think I took it?" Devyn whimpered like a sick puppy, her head throbbing, blood rushing until she thought she'd faint. She leaned against the wall.

"Are you all right? You're white as a corpse." Brice took her arm, but she closed her eyes.

"I may as well be dead. The ones I love think I'm a common thief."

Brice tilted her chin up. "Look at me."

She refused, squeezing her eyes tight.

"Devyn. Look. At. Me!"

At his command, she complied.

"No one thinks you stole anything. They just want to talk to you. Come on. They're waiting." He wiped the moisture from her cheeks with his thumbs and kissed her forehead. "Come."

Buoyed by his words but still sniffing back tears, Devyn followed until they were at the wine vault door. Brice opened it and gave a gentle push. "You go first. I'll follow you."

Devyn gulped a fortifying breath and stepped into the vault. The party talked quietly at the far end of the Great Hall.

Then she spotted Sofia.

~ ~ ~

"Go on, then." Brice prodded Devyn, but when he noticed there were four people huddled together, he stopped. "Sofia."

She was up to no good. Again. He would fix this once and for all. He would fight for the virtue of the woman he loved. He didn't care if the Bournes forbade them to be together. He was done with pretending. Blast it!

Brice drew their attention away from the vile woman. "We're here." He took Devyn's hand, would continue to hold her hand. She needed him.

She had him.

Devyn glanced at his hand on hers and then at his face, eyes wide. She seemed to be thanking him. Or was she warning him? He gave her hand a tender squeeze.

Both Mr. and Mrs. Bourne glanced down at their entwined hands. He didn't let go, even as Devyn wriggled her hand to dislodge his grip. He held it tighter.

"May I speak, please?" Brice addressed Mr. Bourne, who nodded for him to continue. "This woman is innocent. I know her to be a person of integrity."

"You'd defend her, for you're likely in cahoots with the woman."

Sofia's smug scowl accompanied eyes so evil Brice wanted to drag her to the dungeon and lock her up himself. She turned to the Bournes. "Search her things and see. She's been sneaking around the castle since she got here, and her improper conduct is evidence of the kind of person she is."

Mrs. Bourne shot up a palm. "Quiet. Enough!"

The missus turned to Devyn. "We've had our moments, but I don't believe you to be a thief. Do you know anything about this matter, miss?"

Devyn shook her head. "Nothing whatsoever, ma'am."

Sofia scoffed.

"Stop, or you'll be dismissed at once, Sofia!" Mrs. Bourne's voice rose with her anger.

Mr. Bourne put up both palms to silence the lot of them. "All right. Let's settle down. We men will check the dormitory, though I'm sure we'll find nothing." He glanced at the women. "Ladies, please retire to the library and wait for us there."

Mrs. Bourne bid Devyn and Sofia to go ahead of her, and Brice gave Devyn's hand a squeeze before letting it go. He watched the three women disappear into the library before following the men up the stairs.

Mr. Bourne shook his head as they entered the women's room. "Where do we begin?"

Captain Vanderbilt glanced around. "Let's divide and conquer, though I don't relish the idea of going through ladies' things."

Mr. Bourne agreed. "Nor do I, but it must be done. Mac, check the water closet and these two closets and beds." He pointed to those nearest him. "Captain, you take the south side, and I'll take the north."

Brice agreed. "Yes, sir." Quickly, he checked the water closet, clothes closets, drawers. Then he checked the bed—in, on, and under.

"Here!" The captain fairly hollered. "Money. Large bills. Under the ... well ... underthings."

Brice and Mr. Bourne ran to his side. Sure enough. A small pile of large bills held together by a rubber band. Just weeks ago, Brice had recounted and banded that very pile.

"Whose drawer is this?" Mr. Bourne nearly pushed the captain aside and began riffling through the things. At the bottom, he found an envelope. He pulled it out and showed them the name on it: Devyn McKenna, Chippewa Bay, New York.

Mr. Bourne's face turned red. He crumpled up the envelope, grabbed the pile of money, and growled. "Come. Let's deal with this."

The captain glanced at Brice, his face showing the same disbelief and the confusion Brice felt. Not Devyn. Not his Devyn. It couldn't be! He tried to make sense of it all as he followed the men down the stairs and into the library.

Mr. Bourne was already waving the banded pile of bills at Devyn. Sofia stood in the shadows, her grin triumphant.

"It was in your drawer, miss!" Mr. Bourne stood just inches from poor Devyn, who looked as if she might faint dead away. "Isn't that right, Captain?"

Captain Vanderbilt nodded, his eyes a mixture of pain and confusion. "Afraid so. Found it myself."

"But I didn't put it there, sirs." Devyn lamely tried to defend herself. "I'd never steal, not a toothpick."

Sofia grunted. "No indeed. Your sneaky ways are ones of a professional thief."

Mrs. Bourne shot an angry glance at her. "Another word, and you'll be dismissed. Do you hear me?" She pointed a warning finger at Sofia. "Silence!" The missus turned to Devyn, a pained expression sending wrinkles to her face. "How did it get there then, Devyn?"

Devyn looked up, her face pasty grey. She put her hand over her mouth and heaved, vomit spewing all over the rug.

Brice hurried to her side, pulling out a handkerchief. "Are you all right?"

Devyn shot a look of disbelief at him. Of course, she wasn't all right. Suddenly, Brice realized what was happening. He turned to Mr. Bourne. "Excuse me, sir. I may have an answer."

Falan.

Without waiting for permission, Brice broke into a run. He ran out the front door and headed to the north boathouse.

He searched the building for Devyn's brother, but he seemed nowhere to be found. Asking worker after worker, he finally got an answer. The older man pointed to an island in the distance. "I saw him in the skiff, heading to Corn Island a while ago. Probably fetching some vegetables."

Brice nodded a thank you and ran to the south boathouse. He had to get there, and fast.

The *Moike*.

As Brice entered the boathouse, Labrese was busy shining the gondola. "Labrese! Fire up the *Moike*. We have an emergency."

The man stared at him as if he hadn't heard him.

"Hurry, sir. There's no time to lose."

Labrese didn't even ask for details.

Brice jumped into the *Moike* and tried to figure out how to catch the villain unawares. How could they sneak up on the island? Surely, if Falan noticed Brice, he'd run for his life. At least, he should!

Within minutes, Labrese had the *Moike* out on the river and heading toward Corn Island, making a wide arc to avoid being seen. When Brice filled the boatman in on their mission, Labrese whistled low and long. "So old Oscar did write on the wall, and in the tunnel, of all places. The key and note were useless without the clue to where the box was hidden."

"What?" Brice turned to him, brows raised. "You knew of this?"

The older man gave a somber nod. "So happens I spoke to Oscar just before he passed. He's been caretaker for that famous artist, Frederic Remington, ever since he helped to build The Towers, you know." Labrese pointed over his shoulder toward Remington's summer house in the distance. "A month or so ago, he fell ill suddenly, and by the time he tried to share his secret, he was delirious with fever. He told me of finding the treasure with Falan and how Falan had insisted on keeping it. That sat less and less well with Oscar as time went on. He wanted to die with his conscience clear, but he kept mumbling about 'the writing on the wall' so he'd remember the 'rocks in the garden.' I thought he was out of his head until he gave me the key and note and begged me to hide it from Falan."

Brice's mouth hung open. "So you are the one who put the key in the wine cellar."

"Yes. For safekeeping. I'd intended to find the treasure and present it to the Bournes, but I've had little time to search. And I don't have much excuse to walk about the castle or grounds hunting for treasures, now, do I?"

"This answers a lot of questions. Let's catch this villain and be done with it!"

Slowing the boat, Labrese grinned over his shoulder. "I'll agree to that. Falan has always rubbed me the wrong way."

As they neared the island, Brice lay low. "Take me around to the back, and I'll slip out of the boat. Then have the boat ready for when I catch him. And pray!"

Brice prayed as well. He begged for mercy, for success in finding the thief and the satchel of Mr. Bourne's money. It had to be Falan, but how had he gotten into the castle and out again without getting caught?

"Do you want this?" Labrese extended a pistol.

Brice blinked. "No. I'm not skilled with weapons." Instead, he held up a rope. "This should do."

He removed his shoes, socks, coat, and vest and steadied himself for the altercation. Soon Labrese had pulled the boat around, and Brice slipped into the river and swam as quietly as he could to shore. A shiver ran down his spine as he crouched among the taller plants, surveying the tiny island for Devyn's brother. Birds flew overhead, and three swooped down and hovered over an area about twenty feet from him before continuing on their way.

Brice headed in that direction. He stopped, straining to decipher a strange sound. Snoring?

His heart began thumping wildly, his hands began to sweat, his breath releasing in little puffs. He crouched lower, crept closer until he spotted him.

Falan. Asleep between two rows of corn, with his head on Mr. Bourne's satchel!

Brice could see the boat from where he hid, so he stood and silently waved for Labrese to join him, then considered how to best capture the criminal.

As Labrese made a stealthy approach, Brice readied the rope, keeping a careful watch over Falan.

Just then, a large moth alighted on Falan's nose. Brice froze. Falan swatted at it and mumbled. "Sofia? You were supposed to wait till it was dark to join me."

Just as he thought. Sofia was in on it too!

Falan rolled over and returned to sleep. Brice almost laughed at the ridiculousness of it. Some criminal.

Although Falan must have known the tunnel well, Sofia must have let him into the castle and planted the money in Devyn's drawer. When he got his hands on the woman, she'd regret the day she was born! Both of them would.

The sound of a dead cornstalk crunching under his feet pulled Brice from his thoughts. Too loud! Falan began to stir. Within seconds, he opened his eyes and bolted upright. The slithering, slimy smirk spreading across his face became a look of surprise that quickly turned to fear.

"You're not Sofia." He jumped up and drew his hands into fists. He looked at the satchel and then at Brice and back at the satchel again.

But Brice was closer. He stepped up, hovering over the loot. "Oh no, you don't. Thief!"

Falan took a step back and tripped over a broken cornstalk. He crashed into a row of corn, crushing several as he landed on the sharp edges of the broken stalks. "Ugh..." He groaned and rolled over, attempting to rise again, but Labrese was at his side with the gun pointed at him.

"Steady, lad. Stay right where you are," Labrese ordered. Then he addressed Brice. "Tie up his hands."

Brice complied, pulling the rope a bit tighter than needed until Falan moaned. "You'll get more than a rope burn, villain, if I have anything to do with it." Brice jerked him to a standing position and roughly led him toward the boat.

Before putting Falan in the vessel, Labrese tossed Brice another piece of rope. "Tie his feet up too. We wouldn't want him going for a swim." He gave a mocking chuckle.

As Brice knelt, Falan spat at him. Brice rewarded him with a good, hard cuff to his jaw, drawing blood.

Labrese took Falan by the neck and squeezed. "Try that again, and you'll be begging for your life. I've had training in overcoming pirates, rum runners, and other villains, and you're not much more than a cockroach, in my estimation."

Brice let out a chuckle, and Falan let out a growl. "You can't prove it. Can't prove anything." He licked the blood from his lips and sat up straight. "I found the satchel when I came to pick the corn."

Labrese and Brice howled with laughter as they heaved him into the boat and set him down hard on the hull. Labrese handed Brice his gun and pointed to Falan. "Shut that trap of yours, or I'll put my dirty sock in it." He started the engine and turned to Brice. "If he so much as moves a muscle, put a bullet in him."

Brice saluted him. "Be glad to, sir."

Once they returned to the castle, they deposited Falan in the dungeon, still tied up tight. Labrese locked the door and handed Brice the key. "I'd like to throw this in the river, but I expect Mr. Bourne will want to use it when the sheriff gets here. I'll go fetch him now."

Brice nodded as Labrese left, then faced Falan. "There's an Irish saying, 'Tell the truth and shame the devil.' I'd advise you to think on that while I'm gone."

Falan spit in his direction, but he was too far away to find his mark.

Brice shook his head without so much as a glance at him. "You're a sorry little man, Falan."

~ ~ ~

When Brice entered the library, the atmosphere felt like a wake. Not only were the Bournes, Captain Vanderbilt, Devyn, and Sofia there, but Mrs. VanLeer, Mahlon, and Cook had joined them, sitting silently. They all seemed so deep in thought that when he entered, no one even noticed him.

Brice cleared his throat. "Mystery solved." He held out the satchel and grinned.

Captain Vanderbilt bolted to his side and took the leather bag. "Where?" His startled gaze swept over Brice from head to toe, where water still dripped from the hem of his pants onto the rug. "In the river? But it's not wet."

Brice shook his head. "May I have the floor, sir?"

Mr. Bourne nodded.

Devyn slumped in the corner of the window seat, more like a little rag doll than the courageous woman he'd come to admire. He waited for her to look up, but she didn't, so he addressed the group. "Devyn is innocent, just as I thought. Labrese and I caught Falan on Corn Island with the satchel under his head." The small crowd murmured and groaned as one, surprise filling their faces. "But he had an accomplice, one who let him into the castle and was to meet him on the island to share in the spoils." More murmurs. More groans.

Brice turned his entire body toward Sofia, who was sitting to his left. "Would you like to enlighten us as to whom Falan's accomplice might be?"

Mrs. Bourne stood and let out a cry. "Sofia? You?"

Sofia shook her head violently. She stood, her gaze darting toward the door. She stepped toward it, but Brice stood in her way. "Get out of my way. You have no proof!" She pushed him, but he held firm, grabbing her arm.

"No?" He grinned and turned to the captain. "Sir, would you be so kind as to open the satchel?"

Captain Vanderbilt complied and pulled out a paper package. "It says 'Sofia's take.'" He showed the group. More *oohs* and *ahhs*, and a few titters of disbelief.

Sofia tried to wriggle out of Brice's hold, but her efforts proved fruitless. He addressed the room. "Labrese is fetching the sheriff. Falan is currently locked in the dungeon, and if you'll excuse me, this one should join her co-conspirator, don't you think?"

The group clapped and agreed, but Brice held his hand up to bid silence. "But first, there is someone here who was unfairly blamed, a fine young woman who never deserved our suspicions, especially coming from the likes of this one." He gave Sofia a good shake and smiled in satisfaction.

Mr. Bourne cleared his throat. "You're right, Mac. Miss Devyn deserves an apology from us all."

CHAPTER 25

Devyn trembled at the morning's events, and even though she'd received apologies and comfort from the lot of them, it was still so rattling. Sitting in the quiet of the library helped. A little.

Mrs. Bourne insisted that Devyn remain there with her while Mrs. VanLeer, Mahlon, and Cook returned to their duties. She held Devyn's hand and patted it with her other hand while the men talked in the far corner of the room. The woman said nothing, but her comforting touch and the warmth of her maternal instincts meant the world to Devyn just then.

Suddenly, Marjorie burst into the library. "Labrese said the sheriff arrested Sofia and Devyn's brother. What happened?" She shot a glance at Devyn. "Are you all right?"

"Yes, thank you." Devyn cast a quivering smile at her mistress.

Mr. Bourne held up a hand to Marjorie. "Steady, girl. We'll update you soon enough, but first, we need to get Captain Vanderbilt to the train."

The Captain didn't seem to be in a hurry. He chuckled, his arms crossed over his chest, a glint of pleasure in his eyes. "I wouldn't have missed this unusual morning for anything. But know, sir, that my knowledge shall be left here on your island. I shan't speak a word of it."

Mr. Bourne slapped him on the back. "Thank you, sir, but I fear that somehow the story will leak, and the papers will likely find such intrigue irresistible. I'm just glad we got the money back, and everyone is safe and sound."

Vanderbilt patted the satchel that sat securely on his lap. "I must admit that the entire matter was rather surprising and disconcerting."

"I agree." Mrs. Bourne's pale complexion revealed her distress. Devyn ached with the betrayal the missus must be feeling at her maid's wickedness. After all, Sofia had been in a place of trust for a long time, and she'd broken that trust.

Brice had entered the room while she was deep in her thoughts. "It isn't surprising to Devyn or me. We've been trying to put the puzzle pieces together for some time now." He paused to toss Devyn a smile before turning to Mr. Bourne. "It's all in order, sir. Sofia and Falan are firmly in the hands of the law. The sheriff will return tomorrow to take our depositions, but he asked that you, Captain Vanderbilt, please stop by the jail and deliver yours before you leave the Thousand Islands region."

Marjorie sighed. "I take a little trip across the channel to have a leisurely tea with Fanny Post, and chaos comes to the island. I missed all the excitement." She cocked her head. "Come to think of it, Sofia has been needling me to join her intrigue for weeks. Hindsight is always clearer. A while back, she left me a note that said something like, 'I must speak with you immediately. I have scandalous news to share.' She addressed it to *M* and signed it only with an *S*. I knew her handwriting but chose to ignore it."

Devyn tossed Brice a knowing grin. So that's who *M* had been.

Mr. Bourne shook his head. "Such conspiring should never have taken place. But we'll sort that out later. Now ..." He turned to the captain. "Shall we deliver that deposition and get you to the station?"

Captain Vanderbilt stood, a firm grasp on the satchel. "I hate to miss hearing the whole story, but yes, I should go if I'm to catch the evening train."

"Mac, old boy, why don't you accompany us to the mainland and fill us in on the details?" Mr. Bourne handed the treasure box to Brice. "The sheriff might need these artifacts for evidence, but I want them back to show to my grandchildren one day." He waved his hand toward the door. "Shall we?"

"I'd be honored, sir." Brice glanced at Devyn. "Are you all right?"

She nodded. "I'll be fine. Thank you." She tried to give him a reassuring smile, but her lips quivered.

Captain Vanderbilt walked over to the women and bowed regally. "Mrs. Bourne. Miss Marjorie. Miss. Thank you for your hospitality. I bid you farewell." He kissed Mrs. Bourne's and Marjorie's hands and gave Devyn a nod. "Chin up. The law will deal with them in due time."

Devyn stood and curtsied, surprised that such a man would give her the time of day. "Thank you, kind sir."

With that, the men excused themselves, leaving the three women alone.

Devyn couldn't just sit there and mope, so she turned to Mrs. Bourne and Marjorie and smiled, hoping they'd return to some form of normalcy. "Shall I bring you some tea?"

Mrs. Bourne nodded. "That would be lovely, dear."

Devyn curtsied and hurried to the kitchen, where all eyes turned to her as she entered the room.

"Are you all right, miss?" Cook's sympathetic frown surprised her.

"All is well, Cook, thank you. The missus and Miss Marjorie would like tea, please."

"Of course." Cook scurried to make it herself, obviously shaken by the day's events. She clicked her tongue as she filled the teapot and placed scones on a plate. "I had a premonition Sofia was up to no good. Now who'll tend to the missus?"

Devyn shrugged as Mrs. VanLeer entered the room and answered the question. "I'll tend to her for now. It's little more than a week until we return to Long Island. We'll hire a new maid there."

The reality that the Bournes—and Brice—would be leaving so soon brought Devyn a deep sadness. She'd be saying goodbye to a family she'd grown to care for, a place she'd learned to enjoy, a man she knew she loved. Tears filled her eyes, and she blinked them back. She simply couldn't return to her mother's home. She didn't belong there, and besides, what would her mother say about Falan? Surely, Mother would blame her for his incarceration. Mother always did. But where would she go?

"Are you all right, miss?" Mrs. VanLeer touched her arm, shaking her from her worries. "Fear not. You're safe now."

"But I'm not." Devyn's throat constricted with emotion.

"Yes, dear, you are. Those scoundrels are gone, the money is safe, and so are you." Mrs. VanLeer patted her back.

Devyn shook her head and picked up the tea tray. "Excuse me, but I must get the tea service to the missus."

Mrs. VanLeer nodded. "Proceed then. We'll talk later."

Devyn carried the tea service to the library and set it down on a side table. "Cook sent you some lovely scones and clotted cream as well."

Marjorie rubbed her hands together. "Marvelous. Cook's scones are the best I've ever tasted. Have you tried them?"

Devyn shook her head, poured the tea, and served the women. When she was done, she debated whether she should exit and leave mother and daughter alone, but Mrs. Bourne surprised her. "Come, miss. Have some tea with us and try a scone."

Join them for tea? How unusual. But Devyn decided this was no ordinary day. "Thank you, missus. I'd be honored."

Devyn retrieved a teacup from the kitchen and returned to the library, excited and quite perplexed that she'd been asked to join them. After pouring her cup, choosing a scone, and sitting nearby, silence reigned for several moments until the missus spoke.

"I am quite ashamed, Miss Devyn, and must ask your forgiveness." Her sad eyes sought Devyn's pardon. "I believed Sofia and her scandalous lies and innuendos without considering the source or of whom those lies were told." She glanced around the room. "We must judge a book by its content, not just its cover."

Marjorie set her teacup down. "But, Mother, you didn't know. Sofia seemed to be quite trustworthy."

Mrs. Bourne shook her head. "I knew, deep down, the woman had a wagging tongue. The Good Book says, 'Judge not, that ye be not judged.' Sofia was always looking at other people's faults instead of her own. She had a habit of putting others down and always trying to imply that someone was up to no good, but I chose to ignore that flaw, to all our detriment."

Marjorie shrugged. "We all did."

Her mother dismissed the pardon. "That may be true, but we

also ignored the character of this sweet young thing." Mrs. Bourne turned to Devyn. "Since you began working here, I've only known you to be a kind, gentle soul, willing to do whatever was asked of you. Your actions spoke louder than the words Sofia spoke about you."

Devyn tried to swallow the bite of scone but found it hard to do so. Before she could think of what to say, the missus continued.

"I think it's the book of James that says we mustn't slander one another. But I think we mustn't even allow slander to be voiced in our presence. If we do, then we are accomplices to it, are we not? Who is Sofia to judge you? Who am I to accept her judgment? Only God judges rightly." Mrs. Bourne took Devyn's hand. "Forgive me, dear girl. Please?"

She nodded, patting the missus' hand that was still atop her own. "Of course, Mrs. Bourne."

"Thank you. I appreciate your absolution." She paused and looked at Devyn's plate. "Now then, how do you like the scone?"

Devyn smiled. "Miss Marjorie is correct; it's the best. Cook truly is a skilled woman."

Mrs. Bourne and Marjorie laughed, lightening the atmosphere. But soon it grew serious once again.

"And regarding the ban we placed on you and Brice, I will talk with Mr. Bourne, but I'm sure he'll agree that there is no need for that now." Mrs. Bourne smiled as she removed her hand from Devyn's and turned to her tea.

Marjorie's brows furrowed. "What ban?"

Devyn swallowed those pesky crumbs stuck in her throat as Mrs. Bourne answered her daughter. "Sofia suggested the two have a rather inappropriate relationship, but when I consider the source of those suggestions and look at the character of Brice and Devyn, I feel I was in error to impose such a restriction."

Marjorie grinned. "Brice is a fine chap and a good match for you, miss."

What could she say in response to that? Agreeing with Marjorie was one thing; admitting she agreed in front of Mrs. Bourne was altogether another affair entirely.

Thankfully, a knock on the library door interrupted the rather uncomfortable conversation, and Mrs. VanLeer entered. Her eyes rounded at the sight of Devyn sitting at tea with the two women. "Excuse me, missus, but if you don't need Devyn for a while, I could use her to help with a few things."

Mrs. Bourne smiled. "Certainly. And thank you, Miss Devyn."

Mrs. VanLeer quirked a questioning brow as she waited for Devyn to join her. Once they were in the Great Hall, the housekeeper wanted answers. "I'm confused. What were you doing having tea with the two of them?"

Devyn curtsied. "I'm sorry, but the missus asked me to join them. She … well … she wanted to make things right about Sofia."

Mrs. VanLeer shrugged her shoulders. "It's a topsy-turvy world these days, but as long as everything has settled right, I shall speak of it no more." She paused at the grand staircase. "Hannah is clearing out Sofia's things as we speak, so I'd like you to make sure Marjorie's room is ready for her and the guest room is put back in order. I should think being about your work might soothe the frazzled edges of today's strange circumstances."

Devyn nodded. "I think it shall. Thank you, missus." She turned to climb the staircase, but Mrs. VanLeer stopped her.

"And, Devyn, forgive me for thinking poorly of you on account of Sofia's unfounded accusations. I should not have doubted you."

Devyn curtsied, emotion brimming over her lashes in the form of hot tears. "Thank you, missus. That means a lot."

Mrs. VanLeer cleared her throat and returned to her professional demeanor. "Well then, off with you. But when you're finished, unless Miss Marjorie needs you, have a rest until dinnertime."

Devyn nodded and ascended the stairs, surprised at the turn of events. Though it'd take a little while to not feel the sting of accusations and innuendos, the day was one she'd never forget.

Before attending to Marjorie's room, she stopped by the dormitory to use the water closet but found Hannah with her head under Sofia's bed. She knelt near her friend. "What are you doing, Hannah?"

Hannah bumped her head on the side rail. "Ouch. You surprised me." She rubbed her crown and sat on her haunches, her eyes wide. "You won't believe this. Well, maybe you will." She paused and moved to sit on the bed.

"What, Hannah? Do tell." Devyn looked around the room. Hannah had stripped Sofia's bed and had begun packing the woman's things in an old portmanteau and carpetbag.

"Jewelry. Money. And a gold pocket watch! Sofia was going to steal all of them. I found them among her things. But she also had my journal and my mother's brooch." Hannah frowned, looking as if she'd cry any moment.

"There, there. You still have them. That's what matters now. And Sofia will get her justice soon enough." Oh, but she might find her own possessions among the thief's contraband. "Did you find a blue ribbon in Sofia's things?"

Hannah nodded. "Yes. A royal blue ribbon. I already packed it away, but I'll fetch it for you."

Devyn jumped up and put her hand to her chest. "Oh, please do. It was the last thing my papa ever gave me before he … before he went to heaven. It's been missing for weeks. That foul, horrid thief!" Anger surged through her blood, her face growing hot, hatred filling her thoughts. Unforgiveness filling her heart.

Just then, the Lord's Prayer came to mind. Devyn excused herself to visit the water closet. She needed to be alone.

After closing the door, Devyn whispered the prayer she had prayed every night before going to sleep. "'Our Father which art in heaven, Hallowed be thy name. Thy kingdom come, Thy will be done in earth, as it is in heaven. Give us this day our daily bread. And forgive us our debts, as we forgive our debtors.'"

Forgive us as we forgive others? Even Sofia?

Especially Sofia … and Falan.

No. Her brother didn't deserve forgiveness. He was a scoundrel. They both were!

"'And lead us not into temptation, but deliver us from evil.'" Wasn't it evil to refuse to forgive?

Forgive them both.

Hannah knocked on the door, interrupting her prayer. "I found it! Your ribbon is on your bed."

"Thank you! I'll be out in a minute." Devyn swiped a tear.

"Take your time. I'm still packing up Sofia's things."

For several minutes, Devyn waged war within herself. How could she forget all the nasty things Sofia had said and done? How could she let go of the lifetime of hatefulness she'd endured under her brother?

She finally succumbed to the understanding that she had to forgive them both, so she whispered a simple "I forgive them." But why didn't she feel the same freedom she had seen in Mrs. Bourne's eyes when she forgave her?

When she returned to the room, Hannah picked up the ribbon and handed it to her. Devyn hugged her and said, "You'd better fetch the missus. The sheriff might need all this for evidence."

Hannah took a step back and raised her hand to her mouth, biting a nail. "Oh my. I hadn't thought about that. I will go right now."

The girl scurried from the room, and Devyn returned to her duties. She made more than a dozen trips back and forth between Marjorie's room and the guest room, praying and wondering about what was to come in the days and weeks ahead.

Leaving Dark Island, The Towers, and the Bournes gnawed at her. She would surely miss Marjorie, but she'd miss Marjorie's parents even more. The kindness Mrs. Bourne showed her, the motherly love that always warmed her heart. And the missus' apology? She'd never received even one simple "sorry" from her own mother, even though Devyn deserved dozens of them for all the cruel, heartless things her mother had said and done over the years. Yet here was Mrs. Bourne, a woman of stature and fame, humbling herself to ask forgiveness from a simple servant girl such as herself.

She climbed the narrow stairway to Marjorie's room for the final time, careful to keep the gowns she carried from touching the stairs. She picked up her pace at the thought she was nearly finished with the move.

And what about herself? Like Mrs. Bourne, she'd chosen to

forgive, but was it real? It didn't feel real. When she thought about Sofia and Falan and all they'd done, anger threatened to rise up. She pushed it down.

"I forgive." She sensed only a tiny change, but it was a start.

Devyn decided to say the two-word phrase every time she noticed even a twinge of anger, indignation, bitterness, resentment—any of it. She would not let them take root in her now, or ever!

Had her mother let unforgiveness poison her heart? She considered the idea as she entered Marjorie's room and hung the last of her gowns in the closet.

She closed the closet door and went to the window to watch the gulls flying free on the breeze. They swooped here and there, seemingly without a care in the world, and she remembered Brice's comment about God caring for her even more than the birds.

She didn't want to be like her mother. She had never wanted to be like her, but until now, she hadn't understood what had made her mother so mean. Bitterness had filled her heart. Unforgiveness had consumed her and made her the mean-spirited woman she had become. Could it be that her mother blamed God more than her for her father's death?

The revelation shocked her. Saddened her. But it also encouraged her. She would not become like her mother. She'd forgive them all, even her mother. If she had to do it a dozen times a day for the rest of her life, she'd forgive.

CHAPTER 26

The next morning, Devyn left the library feeling as if she'd endured a boat race in a thunderstorm. "I'm afraid it's your turn, Miss Marjorie." She gave her mistress a quick curtsy. "At least the sheriff is a kind man."

Devyn trudged across the Great Hall and plunked down beside Brice, who was also waiting to give his deposition. "That was harder than I thought it'd be. Falan may be a wayward soul, but he's still my brother. And telling a stranger the sordid details of my family life was simply mortifying."

Brice took her hand and squeezed it gently. Though they'd been freed from the restriction placed on them being together, she didn't want to endanger that freedom, so she pulled back and wrapped her arms around her waist. "I'm sorry it was so hard, but truly, I'm glad it happened."

"Glad? Whatever do you mean, Brice?" Devyn's tone held a touch of irritation, but she didn't care.

Brice glanced at her and sighed, his eyes melancholy. "That didn't sound right. What I mean is that, well, their sins have found them out. Doesn't the Good Book say, 'Out of the abundance of the heart the mouth speaketh'? I think that also includes a person's actions. Sofia's and Falan's words and deeds have shown what's in their hearts, and now they can be reckoned with. Perhaps being caught was the only way they could learn from their mistakes. Hopefully, they will both see the error of their ways and change."

Devyn nodded. "I pray they do."

Soon Marjorie came out of the library, and it was Brice's turn to talk to the sheriff. He gave Devyn a wink and a shrug. "Here goes."

Labrese knocked on the doorframe as Brice disappeared into the library. "Mailbag's here." He handed the leather pouch to Marjorie and gave her a quick head bow before retreating.

Marjorie grabbed the mailbag key and opened the pouch. She riffled through several letters until she stopped at one. "It's from Reagan." She set down the rest of the correspondence and sat in the chair Brice had occupied. "Let's see how she and her family are faring."

"Shall I fetch a letter opener?" Devyn knew Marjorie liked to keep her letters neat and tidy.

Marjorie shook her head. "I can't wait. It's the first correspondence we've received from her." A flash of fear crossed her face. "I hope it's not bad news."

Devyn gave her a reassuring smile. "I'm sure it's good. After all, we've all been praying for her and her family."

Careful to keep the envelope intact, Marjorie opened the letter. She unfolded the paper and began to read. Devyn leaned in to see the beautifully scripted writing, but Marjorie's hands shook so that she couldn't decipher the words.

"What does it say?"

Marjorie grinned. "It's good news, Devyn. Her family is healing well, and she can return to service come September. I must write her straightaway." Without another word, Marjorie hurried into the hall, up the stairway, and out of sight.

Devyn swallowed the lump in her throat. Though she was happy for Reagan, she'd be out of work and forced to return to her childhood home. She'd forgiven her mother—or at least was trying to—but could she go back to that hateful environment? Could she endure the constant criticism, the blaming, even the slaps and smacks her mother imparted on a daily basis? She feared that living there would negate the good things she'd learned throughout the summer.

Devyn's bowed head snapped up when Mrs. VanLeer swept into the room. "Ah, you're done here, miss? Would you help Hannah carry the laundry upstairs?" She waved her arm.

Devyn stood and hurried to follow Mrs. VanLeer to the laundry.

There Hannah handed a huge stack of clean clothes to Devyn. "Can you carry all that? It's quite a load."

She nodded. "Certainly. I'm glad to help. How are you today, Hannah?"

The younger maid responded as they made their way through the secret passageways. "I'm fine now. But my time with the sheriff was quite taxing. I never dreamed I'd be involved in a crime so scandalous as this one."

Devyn choked back embarrassment. "I know what you mean. And a crime my own flesh and blood committed."

Hannah nodded. "Chippewa Bay and the entire region will be gossiping about this for months and months." Despite the dismay she'd expressed over the ordeal, her voice carried a tinge of excitement. "Can you imagine what the newspapers are going to say? I expect the story will be told in all the surrounding papers, maybe even the *Watertown Times*. And maybe the *New York Times* will pick up the story and serialize it since the scandal had to do with such famous men as Colonel Vanderbilt and Mr. Bourne." Hannah stopped in her tracks and glanced at Devyn, her face turning bright red. "Oh dear! I should not have prattled on so."

How dare she? As they reached the master bedroom, Devyn couldn't respond, or she'd surely cry. Or snap. Her family scandalized? Wasn't it enough that she'd borne the shame of her father's death, her mother's bitterness, her brother's wickedness? She'd done nothing wrong, yet now this was her "family scandal"? She swallowed the lump in her throat and set the laundry on Mrs. Bourne's dresser. "Excuse me. I have other things to attend to."

She rushed out the door and stayed inside the passageway for a long time, hidden from the others, processing the details of the past few days, hoping no one would use this same tunnel. She sat on the cold, hard floor and let her tears flow. She'd held them in for far too long, trying to be professional, attempting to be strong. But it was too much. Too much to bear the reality that she, too, would be scandalized forever by choices that other people had made. How could she live under such a shadow? Maybe she could get a good reference from the Bournes and head out West where no one knew of the scandal or cared about the family she came from. Surely, there would be need for a lady's maid there.

"Devyn? Are you here?" Brice's voice stirred her from imagining her life in the Wild West. She swiped away her tears with the hem of her apron and cleared her throat.

"I'm here. Just a moment." Devyn rose and headed toward his voice that came from the direction of the wine vault. Once she got there, she found a grinning man.

"I've good news." Brice grabbed her hand and pulled her out of the passageway and into the vault. "The sheriff's gone, and the Bournes have given us the afternoon off. Miss Marjorie said she was catching up on some correspondence, and Mr. Bourne suggested I teach you how to fish."

Devyn's mind spun in confusion. "Go fishing? Today?"

Brice chuckled. "Why not? It's a beautiful summer's day, and we've had far too much seriousness and worry in the past twenty-four hours, don't you think? Besides, I'd be honored to be the first to help you learn the sport since your father didn't get the chance to do so."

At the memory of her father and the ice-fishing accident, Devyn's eyes brimmed with tears. She shook her head. "Today may not be a good day. I'm rather spent already. Perhaps I should hide away and gather my wits."

Brice swiped away a tear with his pinky finger. "We don't have to fish, darling Devyn, but I'll not have you be alone after all you've been through. Let's go and get some fresh river air, shall we?"

She nodded reluctantly and followed him out the front door. On the landing sat some fishing equipment. Brice handed her the basket. "In case we get hungry." He gathered the fishing poles and tackle box. "And in case we decide to fish." He shrugged his shoulders and winked. "But no pressure."

What a thoughtful man. "Thank you, Brice." Devyn gazed up at the bright blue sky. "This might be a good idea after all."

They walked in silence toward the swimming beach but turned north. "My favorite fishing spot is just a bit farther."

Devyn nodded, following Brice along a well-worn path. She'd

been there before but didn't know it was his special place. How many times had he been there and she'd missed him?

He stopped and held his palm out. "Shhhh ... something's here!" His whisper was accompanied by an index finger over his lips. He stepped closer to the shore slowly, carefully, and bid her to follow with a wave of his hand.

Devyn crept along behind him, her heart thumping in her chest. What could it be? A trespasser? A muskrat? It sounded big. A loud croaking sound made her jump and squeal. She slapped a hand over her mouth, but Brice tugged it away.

"Look! A great blue heron." He pulled her into the clearing to see a beautiful, statuesque bird with a huge fish in its mouth. The creature, nearly as tall as herself, shook its prey and worked its strong jaw muscles until it maneuvered the fish around and then swallowed it whole. The heron's s-shaped neck wiggled until the lump disappeared down toward its stomach.

Then the huge bird cautiously, gracefully, took two long strides. Devyn absorbed the moment as the heron turned their way as if to say goodbye. Unfurling its gigantic wings, it took flight, beating the air so hard she could hear the *whoosh* even from where she stood.

Brice threw up his arms. "Take all our cares and worries with you, majestic one!"

Devyn mimicked him and tossed her cares up and away as well. "Yes! Take them away."

Brice's head snapped her direction. He gifted her with a tender smile before turning back to watch the heron soar on the wind.

~ ~ ~

Brice's heart flooded with such love, such joy, such compassion for his Devyn that he thought it might explode.

"What a beauty! I've never seen a great blue heron before." Devyn leaned into him, drawing him from his thoughts.

"They are rather solitary creatures, so I think his visit was providential, don't you?"

Devyn nodded but pulled away with a glance behind them. Still afraid someone would reprimand them for showing affection? Or still afraid to receive it? She edged over to a nearby boulder and took a seat. "I'll watch while you get set up."

There was so much more Brice wanted to talk with her about, but he'd learned not to push her, to wait on the right timing. So he grabbed a fishing pole and worm and cast his line out into the water. While he fished, he prayed. Prayed for revelation. Prayed for peace.

"Look what I found!" Devyn's voice sounded like a little girl's as she hurried up to him. Her excitement was palpable. "A four-leaf clover. Right there at my feet." She thrust it toward him.

Brice set down his pole and chuckled as he took the green leaf. "There's an Irish saying, 'A best friend is like a four-leaf clover; hard to find and lucky to have.'"

Without hesitation, Devyn threw herself into his arms and squeezed his middle. "You're the best friend I've ever had. Thank you for your words of wisdom."

He tossed back his head and laughed. "And you're rather mighty for such a wee thing. You'll break my ribs if you squeeze any harder. Not that I'm complaining."

Devyn relaxed her grip and giggled. "Sorry. I'm a bit overcome with my emotions. They've been tossed hither and yon, batted around by truth and lies, yanked around like—Brice! Your fishing pole is moving."

Indeed, the rod jerked and slithered toward the river. He hurried to retrieve it, grabbing it—and whatever was trying to steal it. He heaved and pulled and reeled it in, hoping the creature wouldn't break his line. "Grab the net, Devyn, and hurry. It's a big one. Maybe even a muskie."

She did as he asked. "A muskellunge? They're a prize-winning fish, aren't they?"

"Aye." He heaved in the line. If only … "But seldom are they caught from land. Maybe it's just a large bass." He continued to reel until he identified the long, pencil-like fish. "It's a muskellunge, all right. By crackie, hand me that net."

Brice scooped up the large, light-silver and green fish with dark, vertical stripes on the flank of its body and pulled it to shore. "It's nearly three feet long. Well, what do you know about that?"

Devyn's eyes danced as if she'd seen an angel instead of a predatory fish. "I want to try to catch something. Please?"

Brice grinned, pleased she'd caught the fishing bug. "Of course, but let's release this big mama."

"It's a girl?"

He laughed as he disconnected the hook to let the creature slide out of his net and back into freedom. "Aye, lass. She was probably looking for a place to hide her eggs, so we want to let her go so her young 'uns can populate these waters." Brice stretched his back. "That old girl must've weighed thirty pounds." Handing Devyn a rod, he touched her arm. "Now let's see what you can catch, shall we?"

Devyn nodded, holding the pole gingerly. "I need lots of help, sir."

Brice wrapped an arm around her shoulders. "Aye. Since the pole already has the hook and bobber, we'll make that a lesson for another day. Normally, you tie your line to the tippet at the top of the pole and to the swivel at the bottom of the line. Then you add a snelled hook and weight." He pointed out each part of the pole and line as he spoke. "Then you rig a bobber so you can see when you get a bite."

Devyn rolled her eyes and shot him a mischievous grin. "That's a lot to learn."

Brice chuckled. "Aye, well, now you have to bait the line with this." He picked a wiggling worm out of the jar in his tackle box and handed it to her. She wrinkled her nose and puffed out a breath.

"Show me?"

He shook his head but complied, weaving the worm onto the hook.

"Ewww ... disgusting."

He tweaked her nose with a clean finger. "You'll be doing it from now on, or else you can't be called a genuine fisherwoman. But now, you're ready to cast your rigged line."

He came around the back of her and put his hand over the one of hers which held the pole. "Hold your rod upright, and swing the line like a pendulum until it reaches the spot where you want it to be. Then lower the tip and let your line sink into the water." He did the motion with her, her body close to his, enticingly so. He took a whiff of her hair. He wanted more but cleared his throat. "Now you watch the bobber. When it wobbles or jerks, you have a fish."

He stayed there, holding her for a few minutes, enjoying every moment, wishing it'd never end.

"It's wobbling, Brice! Help me." Devyn wiggled in his arms, her excitement both alluring and charming. He wrapped his hand around hers and squeezed.

"Wait a second, and then pull up hard to set the hook." He showed her how, and when the tip began to bend, the line became taut. "Now you have a fight on your hands, lovely lass." He let go of her hand and stepped back.

Devyn glanced at him, her eyes sparkling, her smile wide. A few minutes later, she pulled in a small sunfish. She giggled with glee as she held the line, her small catch wiggling in the air.

"Aye, now you're an experienced fisherwoman, for sure."

"Thanks to you." As he helped her stow the fish in their basket, she looked up at him, their faces inches apart. "So many of the good things in my life now are thanks to you, Brice."

She was ready to talk about the deep things. Brice straightened, took her hand, and looked deep into her eyes, into her heart. "Earlier, did you truly let go of the mountain of cares you've carried?" He'd prayed for weeks, even in the midst of their painful separation, for her to find forgiveness and peace.

Devyn chewed on her bottom lip as she seemed to think his question over. "Yes, I believe so. Although I keep finding that anger and unforgiveness try to weasel their way back into my thoughts. I've chosen to forgive, but how can I truly forget?"

Brice took her in his arms and held her tight. "I understand your dilemma. You know from my past that I've faced the same challenge." He paused and whispered a prayer for wisdom. "Forgiving is a decision of the will. You have to choose it, but your memories and feelings will fight like the dickens to take away the peace and freedom that comes with forgiving others. We can't forget all the wrongs we've experienced, but we can give them to God and take every unforgiving and angry thought captive and put it back in its prison where it belongs."

Devyn sniffed and looked up at him. Then she gently pushed away. She hugged herself and swallowed hard before speaking. "But my mother. After I leave here, I have nowhere else to go, and she'll not take kindly to my being there or putting her precious son in jail."

Brice shook his head. "Changing hearts is God's business, but I think that unless she has a changed heart toward you, you cannot go back there."

"But doesn't staying away mean I don't forgive?" Devyn's face scrunched up.

"You can still forgive yet not trust someone. And caution doesn't mean we haven't forgiven. It means we're wise."

CHAPTER 27

The mid-morning sun peeked through the window as Devyn pinned the last curl atop Marjorie's head. She stole another glance at her face. The young lady's silence meant she was deep in her own thoughts. Was she up to some mischief? Worried about something? Nervous?

"Are you all right, miss?" Devyn prodded.

Marjorie pasted on a casual air. "Right as rain. Just mulling something over in my head, but it's nothing for you to worry about." Marjorie got up and walked to the door, not even looking back. "Thanks for your good work. I'll see you later."

The brush-off niggled at Devyn. Was Marjorie trying to distance herself since the Bournes and their permanent staff would be moving back to Long Island just four days hence—without her? Sadness swirled inside Devyn, as it had for the past several weeks.

No more Bournes. No more Brice.

She made Marjorie's bed, hung her clothes, and tidied the room, several times swiping at the tears she'd tried to hold back. Where would she go? What would she do? And how could she even think about saying goodbye to the man she loved? She'd prayed and dreamed and even hinted at wanting to be hired on permanently, but no offer from the Bournes had come. And no offer for a future with Brice had come either. Now what?

She tied back the curtains, looking out the window, the river alive with activity. A grand new ship heading east toward the ocean. Several small skiffs plodding west and east and south toward the mainland. Fishermen, boatmen, and average people enjoying a lovely summer's day on the magnificent St. Lawrence River. All of them engaged in the beauty of God's creation. She drank in the view.

Just like them, Devyn had learned to love the river.

She shook her head as she surveyed the world outside the Rapunzel Room window. She'd come to Dark Island kicking and fighting, resentful and reticent. She'd despised the idea of being a lowly housemaid in a castle on an island surrounded by the river that took her father's life. She rolled her eyes at the memory of her old self.

She was a different person now.

Devyn squared her shoulders, shaking off the melancholy, and gave a determined snap of her chin. She'd finish strong, put on a happy face, and show everyone that, no matter what, she was a professional lady's maid now. Her ticket out of Chippewa Bay and out from under her mother's mean thumb would be an excellent reference from the Bournes.

Yes, she'd go out West and make a new life for herself. Maybe all the way to Colorado.

She left Marjorie's room and strolled through the secret passageways, chuckling at the memory of how she'd feared these corridors when she'd first come to the castle. Running her hand along the cool, stone walls, she whispered to them. "So many memories. Hold them close and don't forget me. In a hundred years, remember I was here."

In the servants' hall, Devyn found Hannah already eating lunch. She nodded to the younger girl and turned to scoop some chicken salad onto a plate. Swallowing her memories along with the emotions that came with them, Devyn took her meal and sat across from her friend. "Good day. Where is everyone?"

Hannah glanced around the room and shrugged. She flashed a mischievous grin. "Strange, isn't it?"

Devyn quirked a brow. "And Marjorie is in a mysterious state too. Have you seen Brice today?"

Her eyes holding a trace of mystery, Hannah took a sip of lemonade. "He ate and ran off to do something or other."

Devyn joined her in enjoying the tangy drink. "So what will you do when you're done here? Will you go back home?"

Her friend shook her head. "My mother's sister lives in Watertown and just had twins. I'm going to winter with her and help with them."

"Twins? How lovely."

Hannah smiled. "Yes, well, I do love babies, and the family is quite well off. Maybe I'll meet a handsome young man while in the city."

Devyn's heart dropped to her knees. She'd already met the handsome young man of her dreams, but soon he'd be yanked from her life for good.

"Are you unwell? You look like you lost your best friend." Hannah's brows knit into one, concern filling her face.

"It's just that ... well ..." Dare she voice it? "I have nothing to look forward to."

Hannah reached across the table and patted her hand. "But you do! You'll have a fine reference to take wherever you want to go."

Devyn nodded. "Yes. I should have that."

The two ate in silence for a few minutes until Mrs. VanLeer came into the room. "Devyn, when you're done here, Miss Marjorie asked that you retrieve her book from the pergola. She doesn't want it spoiled with the wind dancing about so."

"Yes, ma'am. I'll get it right away." Devyn attempted to rise, but Mrs. VanLeer motioned for her to sit.

"Finish your meal. That chicken salad is too good to waste." The missus winked and flashed an indiscernible smile at Hannah.

Devyn turned to see Hannah return the smile. After Mrs. VanLeer retreated, she asked, "What was that all about?"

The girl shook her head, a guilty smile crossing her face. She said nothing, but Devyn didn't have the energy to press her. She scooped one last bite into her mouth and chewed. "She's right about this being good. Cook's quite a miracle worker."

Hannah laughed. "I'll miss her cooking, to be sure."

Devyn stood. "Have a nice afternoon. I'd best be off and gather that book." She washed and dried her dishes and fled from the hall before the lump in her throat stopped her from further conversation. Even young Hannah had something to look forward to.

Devyn trudged toward the pergola, sweeping her gaze across the river as she walked. So beautiful. So peaceful. She paused, sucked in the river's scent, and turned her face toward the warm sunshine. Just four more days and it'd all be a distant memory.

Her bottom lip quivered, and she bit it back into submission. For heaven's sake, she'd not start blubbering over that which could not be. She hurried to the pergola to complete her task, but when she got there, she stopped short.

On top of the book was a bouquet of pink and red roses. A white satin ribbon held them together with a note tucked under the bow.

"What's this?" She glanced around, but she was alone. Had some secret admirer left Marjorie a love note? Maybe snuck onto the island unawares to declare his undying love for her? That'd be a fun ending to the summer on Dark Island.

Curious and excited to discover the identity of the mysterious gift giver, she drew close and slid the note out from under the bow. *To Devyn McKenna.*

Devyn blinked. She'd seen the white ribbon in Marjorie's room just yesterday. Perhaps this was her special way of offering a kind reference. But as she gazed at the script, she realized it wasn't Marjorie's handwriting. It looked more masculine. Maybe Mr. Bourne?

Carefully, she opened the letter and read it.

Dearest Devyn,

This has been a summer to remember. Meeting you has altered my world forever. There's an Irish saying ...

Devyn squeaked out a tiny cry and darted her gaze to the bottom of the page. Brice? She returned to read the letter.

'May the most you wish for be the least you get.' What do you wish for? I wish for a lifetime with you by my side. With warm affections and hope for the future, Your Brice

Devyn spun around, searching for the author of this letter, the man who might change her world, be the answer to her prayers, the miracle she'd been waiting for? But still, she was alone.

Perplexed, she gazed down at the letter and reread it. Was she dreaming?

She whirled at a rustle in the nearby bushes. Brice stepped onto the pergola, dressed in his formal livery, eyes twinkling with merriment. Wearing a grin so wide it must have hurt. Devyn had never seen him looking so handsome, so hopeful, so happy.

"Brice? What is … this?" She shook the letter still in her hand as he rushed over to her and took her other hand. He kissed it and knelt on one knee.

"Marry me, my darling Devyn, and make me the happiest man on earth." Brice smiled, but his eyes now held a twinge of fear. Or was it uncertainty?

Was he simply asking her because she had nowhere else to go? Was he trying to rescue her from going back to her mother, or did he truly want her hand for no other reason but true love? And would he lose his job with the Bournes if he did marry? She'd heard that could happen.

"But you'll be going back to Long Island, and I? I … must stay here. At least for now. I haven't received an invitation to be part of the Bourne's permanent staff, and I dare not endanger your position." Her voice shook despite her desire to sound convincing. "I'll not have you give up everything you hold dear for me."

"I hold you dearest of all, Devyn. Marry me?" Brice implored her with his crystal-blue eyes that appeared almost frantic. "Please?"

Devyn pulled her hand away and turned her back on the man she loved, on the castle that had changed her life. He rose, took hold of her shoulders, and spun her around to face him again. She stared at the brick pergola floor.

"What's wrong? Look at me." With a gentle touch to tilt her chin, he frowned when she couldn't hold back her tears. He waved a hand at The Towers as if bidding someone there to come.

Whatever he thought he was doing, how ever he thought to convince her, he had to hear her out. "I'll not endanger your fine job with these marvelous people, Brice. You cannot marry and retain your position. Everyone knows that. I've decided to go West and find work there." She paused as his jaw dropped, then forced out the rest. "I love you too much to see you give up this life for me."

As she gave in and sobbed over her loss, he grabbed her and held her tightly. But she must hold firm. He deserved a happy life. She'd find hers. Somehow.

Gently, Brice drew her away from his chest, plucked a handkerchief from his pocket, and wiped her face. "What do you wish for, dearest one? Truly wish for? Tell me."

Devyn searched his face, his expression urging her to answer. She had to be honest with him. Honest with her heart, just this once. "You."

~ ~ ~

Brice let out the deep sigh that he'd been holding back. She did want him.

This wasn't at all the way he'd imagined things would go. He'd thought she'd read the note, smell the roses, and fall into his arms, shouting *yes! Yes! YES!* They'd kiss and make their plans for a long life together.

But she'd already decided to go out West? To that wild, uncouth, beer-brawling, gun-toting, uncivilized part of the world that would surely swallow her whole? No!

Brice pulled Devyn close and held her tight, stroking her hair. "It's all right. Everything will work out."

She tried to wriggle out of his arms, but he held her close to his chest. *Not yet, dear one. Not yet.* He glanced over her shoulder at their salvation approaching.

She stopped struggling and turned her face up to his. "But it won't be all right. It'll never be all right."

Brice nodded for Mr. Bourne to speak. "You're wrong. The love you two share can make life right for Mac and for you." Mr. Bourne's grin mirrored his wife's and his daughter's. And Brice's.

Upon hearing her employer's voice, Devyn glowed the prettiest pink Brice had ever seen, her wide eyes matching the fawn's startled look of so long ago. Her gaze darted to the right and to the left as she tried to get out of his arms, but he held her tight. Just for fun.

Finally, he released her, allowing her to wipe her tears before she spun around to face the three Bournes, all smiling and waiting for her to speak.

True to her professionalism, Devyn curtsied low and plastered on a humble smile. "Sir. Missus. Miss." Her head bobbed at each one. The poor girl must've been perplexed and embarrassed to the utmost.

Marjorie saved the moment. "Oh, Devyn. It's been such fun to be co-conspirators in Mac's little plan. I could hardly hide my excitement from you this morning, and I didn't sleep a wink the night before. Did you say yes? Surely, you said yes."

Devyn shook her head. "I cannot endanger his position with all of you."

Mrs. Bourne laughed. "My dear girl, this is the twentieth century, and you could never endanger his life with us. He loves you. We love you."

Devyn's whimpers shook her entire body, and she turned back to Brice.

"Just listen to them." He slid his hand down her arm.

Mrs. Bourne stepped close and took Devyn into her arms. "My little Louisa girl. There, there. It'll be all right." The missus patted Devyn's back until she calmed. "Don't you know that you've become a part of our world too? We love you like a daughter, especially after the integrity you showed with the debacle involving Sofia and your brother. We want you to come back to Long Island with us. With Brice."

Devyn pulled back from Mrs. Bourne's matronly hold and wiped her eyes again. She looked over the missus' left shoulder at Mr. Bourne and her right shoulder at Marjorie, who both nodded agreement. Finally, Devyn spoke. "But Reagan is returning to serve Miss Marjorie. I shan't be needed and don't want to be in the way of Brice's career."

Mrs. Bourne chuckled. "Oh, dear girl, I have decided that you shall be *my* lady's maid!"

Devyn blinked and gasped so loudly Brice chuckled. "Me?"

Mr. Bourne nodded. "Yes, you. That way, when we go on our European tour this fall, you can accompany us as Mrs. Brice McBride, and the two of you can have your own little wedding tour, of sorts. Will that suit you?"

Devyn glanced at Brice, her eyes wide. Then she turned and looked at the three Bournes with a mixture of joy, gratitude, and awe. It took her a full, eternal minute before she answered Mr. Bourne and, in doing so, answered Brice.

"Yes, sir. That would suit me just fine."

Brice stepped up to her, turned her to face him, and took her hand. "Let's try this again, shall we?" He again knelt on one knee and kissed her hand, blotting out the Bourne audience and focusing on the most precious person in the world.

He cleared the lump that tried to stick in his throat. "My darling Devyn. When I look into your eyes, I see us, two trees planted side by side, our roots growing together deeper and deeper as the years go by, and our children sprouting like seedlings around us. I love you with all my heart and would be honored if you'd be my wife. Again I ask, will you?"

Devyn smiled, nodding her head furiously. "Yes, yes, of course. Yes!"

Brice laughed. "Whew! That's better."

Mr. Bourne clapped his hands, and the Bourne women shouted, "Rah, rah!"

As Brice stood, Mrs. Bourne took Devyn's hand. "You deserve the very best, someone who will cherish you without limits, let you grow without borders, and love you without end. Brice, dear girl, is that man. Congratulations!" She patted Devyn's cheek and dropped her hand. "Husband. Daughter. Let's leave these two young people to talk things through."

Marjorie gave Devyn a hug. Mr. Bourne patted her shoulder, and the three returned to the castle, leaving Brice and Devyn alone.

He picked up the bouquet of roses and laid it in Devyn's arms. She inhaled a deep whiff and closed her eyes. "Thank you, Brice.

These are lovely." Then she glanced around the pergola. "This all was so very magical. I cannot take it in."

Brice took her in his arms to kiss her, wanting to seal their love. Needing to seal it. But a sudden movement took his gaze away from her.

CHAPTER 28

She'd be Brice's wife, Mrs. Bourne's lady's maid! She'd belong with them forever.

Devyn's wonder and joy were just about to culminate in the kiss she craved from Brice when his attention flickered to the top corner of the pergola.

"Look, Devyn." He gently turned her and pointed out several cocoons wiggling in the still summer air. "They're hatching."

Devyn threw her hands up to her mouth. "I've always, always wanted to see the monarchs hatch."

The first butterfly struggled to free itself from the cocoon it had woven. Tiny. Tight. Until now, hadn't that been the story of her life as well? She'd been an ugly caterpillar crawling around aimlessly when she first came to the island. Then, somewhere between her trials and her struggles, she'd become a pupa, beginning a painful transformation, wishing for hope, waiting for a new beginning. Her friendship with Brice and Reagan and even Miss Marjorie had cocooned her in the beginnings of love, healing, and hope. The winds had tossed her to and fro, the great storm with Sofia and Falan threatening to destroy her cocoon.

"It's emerging." Brice interrupted her thoughts. "I've never seen the like of it. And look there." He pointed to the right. "A second monarch is beginning to hatch too."

Devyn squeezed his hand and smiled. "I'll never forget this moment as long as I live."

Brice kissed her palm, sending a lightning bolt of love up her arm that made her heart skip wildly. "Nor will I, my betrothed."

She giggled, overcome by joy she never knew existed. Just

then, the first monarch squeezed out of its cocoon and wriggled, stretching and flapping its wings until they completely unfolded. "She's free!"

Brice nodded. "So are you, sweet Devyn. So are you."

Yes, she was free. Free from the past and free to embrace the future. No more Sofia or Falan or Mama. No more living in fear or making plans to settle in the Wild West. No more guilt of killing her father, and that was the sweetest of all. Or was it?

Devyn searched her heart as she watched the second butterfly emerge. She shook her head. No, although freedom from the guilt was healing and helpful, the freedom she found in forgiving those who had hurt her was the sweetest by far.

She turned to look at her future husband. "I love you, Brice."

He was lost in the miracle of metamorphosis, and it took a moment for him to look at her. A gentle smile turned the corners of his lips upward, and his eyes danced with delight. "Oh how I love you, my darling Devyn."

She laid her head on his chest, listening to his heart beat steady and slow. He inhaled and exhaled, her head rising and falling with the motion. If only this moment would never end.

But it would end, and there were bound to be so many, even better moments ahead. Since the day of her father's passing, she'd never looked forward to the future. Never dreamed of a future. Now she held the future in her arms.

Brice kissed the top of her head as butterfly number two stretched out its wings and finally flew to the other monarch. They appeared to be caressing each other, so Devyn turned her head up toward Brice, hoping that he would follow their lead. She wanted him. Wanted to feel his warmth. Wanted his promise of their future to be sealed with a kiss.

~ ~ ~

Brice tore his eyes from the dancing monarchs and beheld unmistakable desire in his Devyn's eyes. Felt it in her arms that held him tight. Heard it in her almost indiscernible sigh. Her lovely face held his gaze, imploring him to kiss her. Her lips quivered as they parted, a tender smile drawing her dimple out. Brice touched it at last, and his heart filled with abandon.

Love.

Blissful love.

He breathed a whispered "my darling Devyn" and touched his lips to hers, gently at first, seeking her approval, waiting for her desire to grow.

It did. He sensed it. Knew it, so he deepened his kiss, pressing his mouth to hers as she relaxed in his arms and returned the kiss. She sought his lips, sought his love.

Then he stopped, opening his eyes to the angel in his arms, the woman of his dreams, responding to him.

"I love you, Brice." Tears trickled down her cheeks even though her eyes were closed, her lips seeking another kiss.

At her passion, her desire for him, his heart began to dance a jig until the thumping distracted him. He gifted her with a quick peck and chuckled as he caressed her neck with his lips, trying to catch his breath, to calm his racing heart.

Brice met her questioning eyes, so full of passion and love as she smiled at him. He planted a gentle kiss on the tip of her nose. "I need to steady myself, woman, else you might have to bury me before you marry me."

Diffusing the tension, she nodded and clutched her chest. "You're right, of course." She glanced up at the castle. "And we don't want to create a scandal for the Bournes, do we?"

Brice threw back his head and laughed heartily. "That's true enough, my dear."

~ ~ ~

Devyn grinned at the man who would one day be her husband. "So now what? I've been making plans to say goodbye, and now my life has suddenly become as charming as a fairy story."

Brice shrugged and licked his lips. "Aye, well, in fairy stories the prince and princess marry and live happily ever after, right? I say we take that path."

She recalled the taste of his kisses and smiled. "Well, yes. I agree. But how do we go about doing that? I don't want to go back to Mama's until we marry."

He shook his head. "You'll not have to. I'll borrow a skiff today, and we shall go and tell her together. And say goodbye. Then you can live here, in peace, until our wedding day."

Devyn rolled her eyes at his jest. "But when and where will that be?"

"What is the most you wish for, Devyn? If I can make that happen, it will be the least you get." Brice grinned that little-boy grin she so adored.

"My wish? I would like to be married here, on the island where we met. With the people I love." She shrugged her shoulders, a little reticent to admit such a dream.

"Hah! I knew it. I just knew it and have already sought the Bournes' permission to get married. Here. Tomorrow!" Brice beamed, raising his arms as if he'd won the Olympics.

"Tomorrow?" Devyn swallowed, tasting the sweet excitement, the delicious promise of a new life. Tomorrow.

"We can call on the preacher when we go to see your family. Will that suit you?"

"Yes, yes, a thousand times yes!"

Brice nodded. "Do you know that you've said 'yes' more today than I've ever heard from you?"

Devyn grinned. "And I suspect I'll say it much more from now on."

~ ~ ~

Brice steadied Devyn as she climbed out of the skiff. "Lead the way, my dear. We'll visit your family and then see to the preacher."

She twisted a piece of her dress, fear in her eyes. He gave her a quick hug and slipped her hand in the crook of his arm, holding it firmly and securely. "Not to worry. I'm here. No one will hurt you now."

Devyn led him down Heron Road until they came to a small clapboard house that had seen better days. Paint peeled off the outer walls. An unkempt yard begged to be cleaned, mowed, and tended. A tiny garden, half dead, cried for water and attention.

Brice gave her a quick kiss. "I'll take the lead if you want me to."

Devyn shook her head, squared her shoulders, and raised her chin. "No. I'm not the same person I was when I left this place."

"I agree." He nodded as she stepped with greater confidence up the uneven stone walk to the front door and knocked. He followed close behind her as a woman yelled from deep inside.

"One of you rascals git the door, and if it's some peddler, make 'em skedaddle, ya hear?"

When the door opened, a trio of dirty boys stood staring at their sister and him. They appeared to be just a few years apart, the youngest barely past a decade, but all three had a hardness that couldn't be denied.

Three pairs of eyes darted from Devyn to him, their faces bewildered. As if in unison, they appeared to comprehend what they were seeing, and all three of their jaws dropped.

Devyn smiled. "Hello, boys. I have someone for you to meet."

The tallest boy ran to the back of the house and hollered. "It's the girl, Mama. Come and see what the cat dragged in!"

Devyn rolled her eyes as she pulled Brice into the house. He scanned the room, struggling to keep his disgust from showing on his face. Clothes, old newspapers, dirty dishes, and what looked to be a whittling project littered the small room. Something rotting made him want to hold his breath. Brice's gaze darted to the floor. Mouse droppings everywhere.

A heavyset woman entered the room, her straggly hair tied up in a bandana, a dirty apron over a tight, threadbare housedress. Her feet bare. "Well, if it isn't the girl. I was wondering when you'd be back to help with all this mess." She swept her arm in a wide arc, wafting body odor from a full six feet away. "'Bout time."

"It's good to see you, too, Mama." Devyn appeared to make every attempt to turn her grimace into a smile.

Her mother thrust out her hand. "Did you bring my money?"

Devyn pulled out an envelope and handed it to her, then retreated rapidly to his side. "Mama, this is Mr. Brice McBride, Mr. Bourne's valet." She turned to him. "Brice, this is my mother, Mrs. Iverna Mckenna."

The woman's eyes narrowed to tiny slits of disapproval. "Hmmm. You can leave her here and go. You've done your duty, sir."

Devyn shook her head and spoke up before Brice had the chance to offer his greeting. "No, Mama. You don't understand. I ... well ... we ..." She suddenly seemed to become tongue-tied and turned to him for help.

Brice complied. "Nice to meet you, missus. Aye, well, I have come for another reason."

The missus folded her arms over her ample chest and scowled at Devyn. "Well, what has she done now? I'll not pay a penny for that girl's folly. She's a no-good problem child, and I wash my hands of her." She swiped a dirty hand along her skirt, then promptly plunked both of them on her hips. "She's been nothing but trouble from the start, she has, so don't expect me to bail her out of anything."

Brice's blood boiled as he understood, firsthand, why Devyn didn't want to come home. "Ma'am, you're mistaken. She's done nothing wrong. In fact, she's done everything right." Brice took Devyn's hand and slipped it into the crook of his arm, patting it gently. "She's to be my wife not twenty-four hours hence. I've come to ask your blessing on our marriage."

Devyn's mother shot a pointed finger at her, face aghast. "Her? You want to marry *her*? What's wrong with you, boy?"

What was wrong with this *woman*? This bitter, mean, wicked woman. "Yes. I want to marry her. I love your daughter and so do the Bournes. We are going to marry tomorrow and leave for Long Island on Friday."

The boys guffawed, slapping each other on their backs and pointing at their sister. The shortest one smacked his thigh. "Gettin' hitched, are ya?" Then he pointed at Brice. "Better keep a strap ready for that girl like Mama always did."

Devyn shot a scolding glare at her brothers. "Hush up, all of you. Now!" Then she faced her mother. "I shan't be returning, Mama. I'm done here. I pray you'll find peace someday."

Mrs. McKenna shook her head. "You took my peace when you killed my man, girl."

Devyn sliced her free hand through the air. "No. I'll not accept blame for that anymore. Accidents happen, Mama. I did not kill my father." She glanced at her brothers and snapped her chin up. "Your father." She glared at her mother. "Your husband. Moreover, I have forgiven you for all the …"

The woman's eyes turned wild, and she rose up like a bear ready to attack. "Get out of my house. Now!"

Brice grabbed Devyn's hand and pulled her toward the door. "We shall pray for you, ma'am. You and Devyn's brothers."

They were out on the road now, but the missus shouted, shooing them away. "Save your breath, boy, and don't come back."

After the door slammed, they'd scarcely made it to the edge of the yard before Devyn's steps faltered. Brice tugged her into his arms. She trembled—he could only assume with sad memories— and he with indignation and the desire to protect her. But that door to her past was closed, and nothing would stop him from holding her up from now on.

~ ~ ~

Devyn stood in front of Marjorie's mirror, wearing the prettiest baby-blue gown she'd ever seen. The stylish linen dress was richly embellished with raised embroidered roses, fancy cutwork, and delicate crocheted lace. The skirt skimmed her hips perfectly, then widened dramatically toward the beautifully draped hem. "Are you sure it's all right for me to borrow this, Marjorie? It's too elegant."

Marjorie shook her head. "No. It's not all right to borrow it. You shall keep it and give it to your firstborn daughter, whom you will name Marjorie after me."

Devyn giggled, turning to hug her mistress. "It's a deal, and I'd be honored. Thank you."

Hannah, who'd been helping her dress and fixing her hair,

placed some extra bits of baby's breath on Devyn's wide-brimmed straw hat. Hannah picked up the hat and took a whiff of the rosebuds encircling the crown, the white ribbon that had tied Devyn's bouquet just yesterday now woven among the flowers and her father's royal blue ribbon adorning the back. "I thought you'd like your special ribbons to accompany you down the aisle. Not only will you look beautiful, Miss Devyn, but you'll also carry a memento of your loved ones with you." Hannah placed the hat on Devyn's head, adjusting the ribbons and tweaking a flower.

Devyn choked up at the thoughtfulness of her friend. "Thank you both. This day is more than a dream come true."

Marjorie nodded. "For us too. I've known Mac for more than five years, was even a bit smitten over him when I was a silly schoolgirl. But you two are perfect for each other."

Devyn's face grew warm as she startled at Marjorie's admission.

Marjorie turned to Hannah. "And you'll please move a few of my things downstairs? I'll show you what I'll need. This room shall be the honeymoon suite tonight." She shot a warning finger at Devyn. "I insist."

Devyn's eyes filled with tears. "Oh, Miss Marjorie. I hadn't even thought that far ahead, but you did. Thank you ever so much. Are you sure?"

Her mistress nodded. "I'm more than sure." She winked, pulling another blush to Devyn's cheeks.

A knock drew her attention away from thoughts of the wedding night. It was Mr. Bourne. He stepped into the room and looked around. "Ah, this is such a nice room, and what a view." He glanced out the window before turning to Marjorie and touching her arm. "You and the maid may head downstairs, and I shall escort the bride to her groom."

Marjorie kissed her father's cheek. "A marvelous plan, Daddy." She patted Devyn's shoulder before exiting the room with Hannah on her heels.

Devyn swallowed her surprise and chewed on her lip. Mr. Bourne would escort her? Her little-girl dream of her own daddy walking her down the aisle one day had been buried in Chippewa

Bay on that cold winter day. "Thank you, sir. That means more than I can say."

Mr. Bourne nodded. "Mrs. Bourne and I have grown to love you, dear girl, and not because you remind us of our dearest Louisa, but because you are you. And we love our Mac—Brice—as well." He paused and cleared his throat. "I think it was the prophet Jeremiah who wrote, 'For I know the thoughts that I think toward you, saith the Lord, thoughts of peace, and not of evil, to give you an expected end.'"

Devyn wasn't sure why he was quoting such a Scripture, so she stayed silent.

"What I mean to say is that God has had a plan for you all along, Devyn. Through all the pain and heartache that you've endured, He planned to give you hope and a good, good future. And you shall find that in the arms of our Mac."

Devyn wrapped her arms around her waist. "I know, sir. And I know that I am blessed beyond measure on this day and for all the days ahead."

Mr. Bourne pulled out his pocket watch and checked it. "Shall we go, then? I know a certain young man who is anxious to see the most beautiful woman on this island." He took her hand and slipped it into the crook of his elbow, leading her forth with a chuckle. "And don't tell the missus or my daughter I said that."

"I won't, sir." She gave him a conspiratorial smile.

He paused on the first landing of the stairway. "By the way, you'll have the latest Singer sewing machine delivered to you as our wedding gift. As our dear Irish Brice would say, 'May you always walk in sunshine. May you never want for more. May angels rest their gentle wings, right beside your door.'" Mr. Bourne leaned over and gave her a fatherly peck on the cheek.

"Thank you."

Devyn's heart felt as if it would jump right out of her chest as she walked with Mr. Bourne toward the pergola where the wedding was to take place. She couldn't imagine being any happier than she was at this moment.

And then she saw Brice.

EPILOGUE: A YEAR LATER

Devyn held baby Marjorie in her arms as she adjusted herself on the speedboat's seat. "This is your first ride in a boat, the first time on Dark Island, and the first time at The Towers." She looked down at the cooing, curly-top cherub and adjusted her bonnet. "You'll love it here, wee one, just like your papa and I do." She planted a kiss on her chubby cheek.

Brice reached over, took the baby from Devyn's arms, and settled her on his lap. "How's the *Moike* doing, Miss Marjorie?"

"She's in tip-top shape, thanks to Labrese. Shall I give it a go?" Marjorie glanced at Devyn for agreement.

Devyn nodded and turned to Brice. "Hold on tight to Captain Marjorie's namesake. She doesn't need a bath right now."

"Will do, my darling." He blew her a kiss.

Marjorie grinned, opening the throttle and letting her boat speed toward The Towers, smacking over the waves and wakes of other boats. "My *Moike*'s a joy to drive. Do you want to try, Devyn?"

Devyn blinked. "Me? No, thank you. I'd rather just be a passenger and stay safe in my seat."

Marjorie shook her head and laughed. "Maybe another time, then."

When they got to the island, Mr. and Mrs. Bourne sat waiting for them on the dock bench. Marjorie, Brice, Devyn, and the baby disembarked, received hugs, and headed up the bridle path toward the castle.

"How was your trip over the channel?" Mr. Bourne raised an eyebrow at Devyn.

She shifted baby Marjorie in her arms and patted her stomach.

"It was fine, sir. Not even a touch of the jitters."

Mrs. Bourne reached for the baby, wiggling her fingers and clicking her tongue as the wee one held out her chubby arms for the matron of the castle. "I've missed you, sweet thing." She planted a kiss on the baby's cheek and turned to Devyn. "Is she three months by now?"

"Almost." Devyn touched her daughter's arm. "And look at all the hair!" She untied the bonnet to reveal a mass of tight brown curls.

Mrs. Bourne laughed. "Just like my Marjorie had at that age. I wonder if she'll like speed like this one." She jerked her chin and cast Miss Marjorie a playful grin.

"Oh, Mother. That's not all I like." Marjorie slipped her arm into the crook of her mother's elbow and gave her a squeeze.

Mr. Bourne broke up the womanly banter. "So how is Sir Lipton?"

Brice glanced at Devyn. "He's quite the businessman, I'll give him that. Reminds me of you, actually. Efficient. Organized. Dedicated." He stepped onto the front entrance stoop and opened the door. "Ah, how I miss this place." He waved an arm for them to enter, putting on his valet demeanor but with a playful grin.

"I miss this place too." Devyn smiled at Brice as she passed him in the doorway. She waited for him to close the door and slipped her hand onto his forearm.

"We'll have tea in the library." Mrs. Bourne motioned them into the room. "I know it's your favorite place in the castle, Devyn."

"It was"—Devyn corrected her—"until we got married in the pergola."

Mrs. Bourne laughed. "Yes, well, I thought it a bit too windy for wee Miss Marjorie. We'll enjoy the pergola another day." Still holding the baby, she smacked another kiss on the child's cheek and received a hearty giggle.

"She laughs like you, Devyn." Mrs. Bourne handed the baby back to her and sat in her favorite chair. The others joined her and, once they got settled, a maid brought in the tea service.

Mr. Bourne folded his arms over his chest. "I miss you, Mac, and often wonder if it was wise for you to take the position with Sir Thomas. What are you doing, actually?"

Brice took a sip of tea and set the cup on its saucer. "Have you heard of tea bags, sir?"

Mr. Bourne shook his head, but Mrs. Bourne nodded. "Several of the ladies on Long Island were talking about them. Seems that several years ago, someone made tiny, hand-sewn fabric bags to put tea samples in."

Brice nodded. "Exactly. But the tea importer, Mr. Thomas Sullivan, meant for the customer to take the tea out of the bag before brewing it. Instead, the customers found it easier to brew the tea in the bag, and *voila*! The tea bag was born."

Mrs. Bourne quirked a brow. "Are they in the stores yet?"

Devyn joined the conversation, shaking her head. "That's what my husband is going to change. Sir Lipton has been itching to implement this new innovation, so he made Brice the new vice president over the tea bag division of the Thomas J. Lipton Tea Packaging Company."

Mrs. Bourne leaned over and patted her leg. "It's nice to hear the pride in your voice, dear girl."

"Oh, I am so proud of him." Devyn tilted her head and smiled at Brice. "He'd always dreamed of becoming a businessman just like you, Mr. Bourne. It was one of the first things he'd ever shared with me. He respects you greatly, sir."

Brice nodded. "That I do. Why, if it wasn't for you ..." His voice cracked, and he swallowed.

Mr. Bourne flicked away the compliment with a wave of his hand. "Thank you, but I always knew you were born for something great, Mac. Vice president—that's an impressive title, and creating a new division will be quite a challenge. But tell me more about Sir Thomas' plans for expansion."

"They are hiring as we speak—scores of seamstresses to sew the bags, packaging and shipping staff, and others. Once we have a full house, we'll begin production. That's why we took the time away now—we'll be full steam ahead within the month." Brice smiled at Devyn. "I'll oversee the sewing department, packaging wing, and shipping line, all the while keeping the price of tea bags affordable to the everyday family. Oh, and I'm tasked to add instructions on the packaging, as no one else has ever done. Perhaps you can help me with that, sir?"

Mr. Bourne nodded. "Be glad to help."

Brice grinned as he stirred his tea with a tiny silver spoon, mischief dancing in his baby blues. Devyn knew that look well. He tilted his head. "Is this Lipton tea?"

Marjorie laughed. "I can see we'll have to adjust our tea tastes to fit our new family connection with Lipton. Won't Cook have a fit?"

Everyone laughed, and Devyn nodded. "She will at that. Cook has two tins of tea on her shelf. One for the family and one for the staff. I remember one time last summer Reagan picked up the wrong tin, and Cook slapped her hand, aghast at the girl's mistake."

Another round of laughs startled wee Marjorie, and she began to cry. Miss Marjorie stood and reached out to take the baby. "Give her to me. I'll walk her a bit and let you four talk." She cast a worried glance at her mother that Devyn noted but failed to comprehend.

She stood and handed her daughter to Marjorie. "Thank you." She kissed her little hand and addressed her. "Be a good girl."

Miss Marjorie kissed the top of the baby's head and cooed. "You can call me Auntie Hooley, dear girl. Let's go for a walk and get to know one another, shall we?"

Devyn's heart swelled with joy. Here she was a guest in the castle instead of a housemaid. Or lady's maid. Maybe even more than a guest.

Marjorie closed the door, and Mrs. Bourne turned to Devyn. "How do you like living in Hoboken, New Jersey? That's where the company is located, am I right?"

Devyn nodded. "Yes, and it's just fine. We have a lovely brownstone just a few blocks from the plant, and the home came furnished with several lovely pieces. I even have a housekeeper. Imagine that!"

Mrs. Bourne grinned. "Imagine that, indeed. That's what this twentieth century has brought. Class divisions are falling like soldiers on the battlefield, and I say good riddance."

Mr. Bourne raised his teacup. "To the McBrides' success."

His wife raised her cup too. "Hear, hear!"

Mrs. Bourne set down her cup and rose, walking over to the fireplace and retrieving an envelope that sat on the mantel. She handed it to Devyn. "This came in the mailbag when we first arrived this summer. Knowing you'd be coming to visit, we held onto it instead of redirecting it. I was afraid it might get lost."

Devyn took the envelope and read it aloud. "Devyn McKenna, The Towers, Dark Island, New York." She gasped. "This is Mama's handwriting." She bit her lip, her hands shaking as she tore open the envelope. Had something terrible happened? Why else would her mother bother to write?

She glanced at Brice and unfolded the letter as the room grew still. The only sound was the ticking of the clock. She scanned the letter and sighed. "She's all right, thank heavens."

Mrs. Bourne smiled. "Good. I was afraid something bad might have happened, given the ... family circumstances. Do you want to be alone with your husband and talk it over?"

Devyn shrugged. "No. It's good, actually." She gazed at Brice and waved the letter in his direction. "Would you read it to us, please? I cannot."

Brice took the paper and scanned it. The corners of his lips turned up. "Hmm ... listen." He cleared his throat before beginning. "'Devyn, I assume this letter finds you well. Though we parted on bad terms, I want you to know that I am returning to my old self after all these years. After you told me that you forgave me, it took a long while for me to realize that you had good reason to fear me and need to forgive me. I hurt you. I now realize Falan has many faults. My boy is faring well but has not changed his ways, and I see now why the two of you never got on.'"

Devyn shifted in her seat and clasped her hands in front of her chest. "Thank you, Lord." She turned to her husband. "Miracles do happen."

Brice whistled his amazement. "Aye. After meeting her, I didn't think this possible." He glanced at Devyn, and she shook her head, tears filling in her eyes. She bit her bottom lip to hold back her raw emotions.

He continued. "'I also want you to know that I met a man. We married and are moving out West to a place called Cripple Creek, Colorado. He's a miner and plans to make it big with your brothers and him working in the mines out there. I suppose I shan't see you again in this life, so I wish you well. Mother.'"

Silence filled the room as Brice folded the letter and slipped it back into the envelope. "She didn't even give us her married name. How could we ever reply to her?"

Mrs. Bourne released a soft sigh. "Perhaps she doesn't want you to reconnect. Some things are better left where they lay, dear boy. I recently read a work from George Eliot, one of the famous Victorian novelists. As I recall, he said something such as, 'What greater thing is there for human souls than to feel that they are joined for life—to be with each other in silent unspeakable memories.' We have such memories, dear ones."

Mr. Bourne nodded. "Well said, my dear." He glanced at Brice and then turned to Devyn, leaning forward and smiling. "Family isn't always just blood. It's those who want you in their life and accept you for who you are. Family is a group of people who love you no matter what."

Just then, Marjorie brought her sleeping namesake to Devyn and laid the wee one in her arms. Devyn glanced around the room and smiled, her heart overflowing with love, peace, and joy. Yes, she did have family after all.

THE END

AUTHOR'S NOTES

In 1905, the *New York Times* labeled The Towers "The Castle of Mysteries." The Towers is over a hundred years old and now called Singer Castle. It's a fully furnished tourist attraction, and you can even stay in the royal suite for the night. This Gilded Age summer home remains much as it was then, so I encourage you to add it to your "bucket list" of places to visit. Check it out at https://www.singercastle.com, and follow them on Facebook at: https://www.facebook.com/SingerCastleDarkIsland.

While writing this story, I enjoyed two private tours of the twenty-eight-room castle as well as the outbuildings and island with Judy Keeler. Her wealth of knowledge, along with the more than three hundred photos taken by my husband, Dale, provided a treasure trove of information. So did Robert and Patty Mondore's two nonfiction books, *Singer Castle* and *Singer Castle Revisited*. Philip Selvaggio's biography, *Frederick Gilbert Bourne: Forgotten Titan of the Gilded Age*, gave me further insight into the man and the Bourne family. With all this, I had plenty of "scope for the imagination," as Anne Shirley put it.

Devyn, Brice, and the other servant characters are fictional. I had fun creating them, many of them from friends and family I love so dearly (but not Falan, of course).

The Bournes, however, are real. They were one of the wealthiest families in America, very well-connected in the early twentieth century. They were also godly, humble, and kind, and I tried to portray this in the story. I also include a lot of accurate, fascinating, historical information about J.P. Morgan, Thomas Lipton, and Neily Vanderbilt, as well as accurate details about the castle and the

Thousand Islands in 1910. I hope you enjoyed learning about this Gilded Age family, castle, and island.

Made in the USA
Middletown, DE
12 April 2020